PENGUIN  CLASSICS

A CELTIC MISCELLANY

ADVISORY EDITOR: BETTY RADICE

PROFESSOR KENNETH JACKSON was born in 1909 and educated at Whitgift School and St John's College, Cambridge, where he read classics and archaeology and anthropology. He was a Fellow of St John's College and a lecturer at Cambridge University from 1934 to 1939. He was Professor of Celtic Languages and Literatures at Harvard University, and from 1950 until 1979 was Professor of Celtic Languages, Literatures, History and Antiquities at Edinburgh University. His most notable books include *Language and History in Early Britain*, *The International Popular Tale and Early Welsh Tradition*, *The Oldest Irish Tradition*, *A Historical Phonology of Breton*, *The Gododdin* and *The Gaelic Notes in the Book of Deer*. He was elected Fellow of the British Academy in 1957 and appointed CBE in 1985.

Kenneth Jackson died in 1991; in his obituary *The Times* declared him 'a master of all four of the major Celtic languages ... and a world authority on most, if not all, of the subjects his Edinburgh chair called upon him to profess'.

A CELTIC
MISCELLANY

Translations from the Celtic Literatures

KENNETH HURLSTONE
JACKSON

PENGUIN BOOKS

PENGUIN BOOKS

Published by the Penguin Group
Penguin Books Ltd, 27 Wrights Lane, London W8 5TZ, England
Penguin Books USA Inc., 375 Hudson Street, New York, New York 10014, USA
Penguin Books Australia Ltd, Ringwood, Victoria, Australia
Penguin Books Canada Ltd, 10 Alcorn Avenue, Toronto, Ontario, Canada M4V 3B2
Penguin Books (NZ) Ltd, 182-190 Wairau Road, Auckland 10, New Zealand

Penguin Books Ltd, Registered Offices: Harmondsworth, Middlesex, England

First published by Routledge & Kegan Paul 1951
Revised edition published in Penguin Books 1971
17 19 20 18 16

Printed in England by Clays Ltd, St Ives plc
Set in Monotype Baskerville

TO

JANET, STEPHANIE

AND ALASTAR

CONTENTS

7

LOVE

8

'CELTIC MAGIC'

CONTENTS

BARDIC POETRY

PREFACE

There have been a number of anthologies of translations from Celtic literature[1] published since Charlotte Brooke's *Reliques of Irish Poetry* (1789), though hardly any are now still in print. They have mostly been limited each to selections from some one of the Celtic languages alone, and the great majority of them have been taken from poetry only.

The purpose of this book is to provide in the first place fresh translations, not to reprint those of others. Then, to give selections not only from poetry but also from prose: mostly short, occasionally longer passages, chosen to illustrate the prose literature of the Celtic peoples; for a verse anthology is necessarily only one-sided. And third, to include material from all six Celtic literatures and from all periods from the beginning to the nineteenth century. I had intended firmly to exclude all those pieces which turn up constantly in Celtic anthologies and to give only such as would be new to the majority of readers; but in the case of some old favourites I weakened and admitted them, because one could really hardly leave them out in a representative collection. Those who miss some works with which they have long been familiar will understand why they are not here.

A word must be said on the method of translation. Eighteenth- and nineteenth-century taste would accept – indeed preferred – renderings which were nothing but the wildest paraphrases, at least if they were made from languages which the readers did not themselves know. The later nineteenth century favoured an artificial semi-Biblical English which might degenerate into pure Wardour Street. Traces of these are still with us. We still sometimes meet the outrageous paraphrase, particularly in translations into English verse, where it is excused on the ground that it 'renders the spirit' rather than the word; but is used

1. Throughout this book *Celtic literature* is used as a convenient abbreviation for 'the literatures composed in the Celtic languages'.

15

primarily of course because it makes it possible to rhyme and scan in English. On the whole, however, a much higher standard of accuracy is usually expected, because the reader naturally wishes to feel that he is really getting as near as possible to the original, unhampered by the translator's notions of style or his struggles with a rhyming dictionary. The intention in this book is, above all, normally to keep as close as is possible to the actual wording of the original, so far as this is consistent with rendering it into ordinary grammatical English prose; to give an exact and accurate, though not slavish, translation which should stop (I hope) this side of unnatural English. Occasionally there are small departures;[1] for instance the order of a couple of adjectives may be transposed if failure to do so would give an excruciating consonant clash or impossible rhythm in the English; and in the poetry, especially in the Welsh *cywyddau*, where a highly inverted and interlocking order of words and phrases is found, this had to be disentangled – indeed in the *cywyddau* the constant short clauses in apposition necessarily must be rearranged, with conjunctions and the like, to make sense to the reader. In some instances there are mild archaisms, not inconsistent with the date of the material, such as the use in medieval poetry of 'Marry' when the Celtic has the actual phrase meaning 'by Mary'; it would seem pedantic to object to such things when they express the original much better than any modern periphrase could do. Granting all this, I think the reader may take it that in so far as I was able I have tried to render the original with exactness into as plain and fitting an English as I can.

Of necessity this meant that poetry had to be turned as prose; since, no matter what the defenders of verse translation may say, it is not feasible to give anything like a close equivalent in English verse, or at least to sustain it throughout a whole book. Therefore, to distinguish clearly between those passages which are in prose in the sources and those

1. Here and there an emendation has been made silently in the texts where the need for one, and its form, is obvious to Celticists; a few rather less obvious ones are mentioned in the Notes.

which are in verse, the initial word of the latter is printed with a very large capital letter, except in the case of those where the stanzaic arrangement makes it obvious they are verse (of course stanzas separate in the original are separate here). I had planned to print each verse line as a single line in English, in the manner of Arthur Waley and Kuno Meyer, but although this worked well in some cases, in others the entangled style of the original made it out of the question; so that it seemed best to print them all simply as continuous prose. There are a few exceptions to this, the chief being nos. 184 and 185, the two selections from Merriman's *Midnight Court*, and nos. 68 and 186. With the pieces from Merriman the tremendous swing of the Irish verse absolutely imposed a rhythmical swing, amounting to metre, on the English; and to avoid giving an impression similar to 'prose-poems' or poetry printed as prose, these two passages are given with the verse lines of the original as separate lines of print. No. 68, *Fhir a' Bhàta*, is sung to such a well-known tune that again the verse rhythm, and consequently the line arrangement, was unavoidable. No. 186 had to be treated similarly because of its form of dialogue and refrain. This does not involve any serious misrepresentations.

At the end of each piece in the book the language of the original is stated, together with the author's name if this is known, and the approximate date – occasionally the precise date can be given. It will be noticed that a number of selections are described as 'Scottish-Irish'. This clumsy term was coined to describe those compositions of the fifteenth to seventeenth centuries which were written in Scotland by Scottish authors but in the language of literature which, though common to the poets of Ireland and Scotland at the time, is regularly regarded as Irish. They are certainly not in Scottish Gaelic, and could not be so described, and to call them Irish would conceal their Scottish origin. As to the dates, the early tales of the Celtic people were constantly being re-told, and manuscript versions would be re-copied, with a greater or lesser degree of modernization, from century to century. When a tale found in a later manuscript is more or less entirely, or at any rate obviously, in the language of, for instance, the ninth century, with some few modernizations, it is described here simply as *ninth century*;[1] but when it is very much modernized, and only some clues here and there, linguistic or otherwise, show the probable date of its older source, the words *ninth-century original*[1] are used instead. Omissions are indicated by dots; and passages which are extracts from longer sources are similarly marked at the beginning or end or both, as may be appropriate. At the end is a pronouncing glossary of the Celtic names. In the text the usual English equivalent of Irish names is regularly used when this is some well-known one; for instance it would be rather absurd, for the kind of reader for whom this book is intended, to print *Sinann* instead of *Shannon*. In such cases no pronunciation is given. When the actual Celtic form is used, however, mostly of rather obscure names, or such as have no English equivalent, or occur in early sources, a phonetic rendering is given in the glossary. No doubt I have not been entirely consistent in deciding which form to use, but this is perhaps unavoidable.

One of the purposes of this book is to try to give the reader some material from which to judge what the Celtic literatures are really like. Generalizations are of course dangerous, since six languages are involved, covering a stretch of as much as thirteen centuries in the case of Irish and Welsh. Some remarks are given at the beginning of each section into which the book is divided. As a mere note, it may be said here that Celtic literature began in early times, and continued in the Middle Ages, as the entertainment of an aristocratic social system, composed by a professional class of literary men who were supported by the aristocracy; that later, as that system broke down (in Ireland in the seventeenth, in Scotland in the eighteenth century, in Wales, with reservations, finally in the sixteenth), it was replaced by a more popular, often a semi-folk kind of composition; and that in recent times a modern literature,

1. Without prejudice as to what still older hypothetical sources may lie behind.

on a footing comparable to those of the other countries of
Europe, has been in process of formation, with the writing
of novels, plays, and so on. The great mass of Celtic
literature is in Irish and Welsh, with Scottish Gaelic third;
that of Manx is extremely small and all comparatively
recent, and that of Cornish (the language died out in the
eighteenth century) and Breton not great, except in modern
times in the case of Breton. In this book, however, recent
literature is excluded, precisely because it is so largely a
modern European one and no longer so characteristic of
traditional Celtic thought. Hence the amount of Manx,
Cornish, and Breton here is very small indeed.

The explanatory note at the beginning of the individual
sections below will tell the reader something of what Celtic
literature is. Here it is necessary only to take up the question
of what it is not. Since the time when Macpherson exploited
Celtic sources to provide a public eager for Romantic
material with what they wanted, it has been the fashion to
think of the Celtic mind as something mysterious, magical,
filled with dark broodings over a mighty past; and the
Irish, Welsh, and the rest as a people who by right of birth
alone were in some strange way in direct contact with a
mystical supernatural twilight world which they would
rarely reveal to the outsider. The so-called 'Celtic Revival'
of the end of last century did much to foster this prepos-
terous idea. A group of writers, approaching the Celtic
literatures (about which they usually knew very little, since
most of them could not read the languages at all) with a
variety of the above prejudice conditioned by the pre-
Raphaelite and Aesthetic movements and their own
individual turns of mind, were responsible for the still
widely held belief that they are full of mournful, languishing, mysterious melancholy, of the dim 'Celtic Twilight'
(Yeats's term), or else of an intolerable whimsicality and
sentimentality. Although scholars have long known,[1] and all

1. Compare the opinion of Whitley Stokes quoted in his obituary in
1909 in the *Celtic Review*, VI, 72, that Irish literature is 'strong, manly, pur-
poseful, sharply defined in outline, frankly realistic, and pitiless in logic'.

educated people really acquainted with the Celtic literatures now know, that this is a gross misrepresentation, the opinion is still widely held; and for instance a Welshman can hardly publish a book of the most realistic and cynical short stories without some reviewer tracing in them the evidences of 'Celtic mysticism' or the like. In fact, the Celtic literatures are about as little given to mysticism or sentimentality as it is possible to be; their most outstanding characteristic is rather their astonishing power of imagination. The selections given below will, I hope, bear witness to this.

This book was first published in 1951 by Messrs Routledge and Kegan Paul. The selection of passages in this, the Penguin, edition is exactly the same, and their general appearance seems at first sight little altered. There are, however, considerable changes in detail, chiefly minor but not entirely so. One of the main reasons for this is that when I first wrote, in 1949–50, the tremendous work on Celtic lexicography now in process of being published had hardly begun, with the result that in the absence of adequate collections of dated examples the meanings of many words were ill-documented and obscure. Again, many of the originals have since been much better edited than they were then, and in some cases the discovery of better MSS., or other great textual improvements or emendations, have changed the appearance of some of the extracts a good deal. Such, for instance, is the case with nos. 176 and 221. This applies especially to the section on Nature (nos. 12ff.), particularly nos. 12, 14, 16, 17, 18 and 24. However, I have not always felt able to follow the rather drastic emendations of some editors, notably in nos. 12, 16 and 18.

A further reason for many of the differences between this edition and that of 1951 is the fact that in the course of twenty years I have often changed my mind, both about the exact shade of meaning, in their context, of words or phrases in the original, and also about what words or phrases would mostly closely express this in English. Finally,

there were some inaccuracies of translation which I have
tried to remove. In these regards I should like to express my
most grateful thanks to my friends Professor Thomas Parry,
Mr Gordon Quin, and the Rev. William Matheson, for
their generous, painstaking, constructive, and most helpful
criticisms and suggestions.

The information about the people and places mentioned
in the translations has been very much increased; see the
Index, Notes, and footnotes, particularly the Index.

K.H.J.

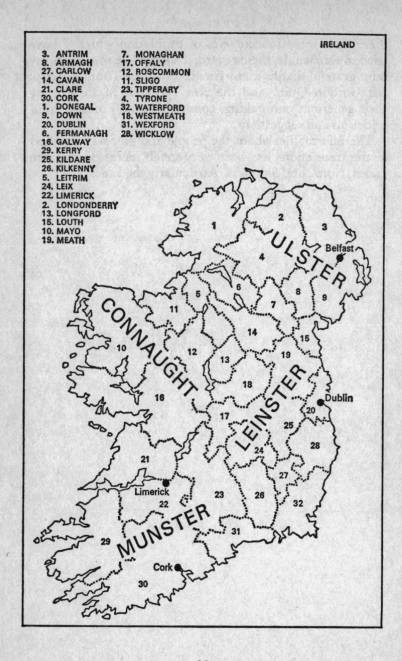

IRELAND

3. ANTRIM
8. ARMAGH
27. CARLOW
14. CAVAN
21. CLARE
30. CORK
1. DONEGAL
9. DOWN
20. DUBLIN
6. FERMANAGH
16. GALWAY
29. KERRY
25. KILDARE
26. KILKENNY
5. LEITRIM
24. LEIX
22. LIMERICK
2. LONDONDERRY
13. LONGFORD
15. LOUTH
10. MAYO
19. MEATH

7. MONAGHAN
17. OFFALY
12. ROSCOMMON
11. SLIGO
23. TIPPERARY
4. TYRONE
32. WATERFORD
18. WESTMEATH
31. WEXFORD
28. WICKLOW

WALES

ANGLESEY

FLINT

Carnarvon

CAERNARVON

DENBIGH

MERIONETH

MONTGOMERY

RADNOR

CARDIGAN

Cardigan

PEMBROKE

CARMARTHEN

BRECKNOCK

MONMOUTH

Swansea

GLAMORGAN

Cardiff

Severn

HERO-TALE AND ADVENTURE

NOTE

Literary historians are familiar with the concept of what is called the Heroic Age. The theory is that early in the evolution of society a stage is reached when, in a materially and socially simple context, an aristocratic warrior caste dominates the scene; and its interests – fighting and adventure on the part of the chiefs (for the common people are counted as of no importance) – are expressed in the form of straightforward, often extremely effective stories composed and handed on by a class of professional poets and reciters. Usually the picture is that of some paramount chief surrounded by a number of lesser chiefs, each with his band of faithful followers. For these people war and freebooting are the natural mode of life; glory for heroic deeds is desired above all things, and death is welcome if it is followed by deathless fame. The supreme chief is regarded as a middle-aged man, of glorious reputation. Among his supporters there is typically a handsome young warrior whose deeds of bravery are unrivalled; an older, wise, cautious hero; and so on. The Homeric poems are the standard example, together with the early Teutonic epic literature of which *Beowulf* is the best known case; that is, the ancient unsophisticated epic, as distinct from literary epics like the *Aeneid* and *Paradise Lost*.

In early Ireland we have a considerable body of stories which represent the literature of another heroic age; the only important difference is that they are prose tales, not epic verse, and the reason is that all Celtic narrative is characteristically in prose, since verse is reserved for the expression of emotion. Conchobhar, the great king of Ulster, is the Irish Agamemnon; Cú Chulainn, the glorious but short-lived hero, is the Achilles; their enemies, the men of Connaught, are led by their king and queen Ailill and Medhbh.

There is little doubt that the state of affairs and the

general social pattern described in these tales actually existed in Ireland at some time, though probably none of the individuals are historical. When it existed, and how old the tales really are, is the question. As they stand, their language and other evidence shows that very few can have been written down before the eighth century, and probably none before the seventh; but a considerable period of oral transmission before this is likely on several counts. All that can be said is that the background of these stories is fairly certainly older than the coming of Christianity to Ireland in the fifth century, and belongs to a semi-barbarous stage such as was noted among the Continental Celts by Greek and Roman writers in the first century B.C.; how much older than the fifth century we have no reliable means of knowing, though the native opinion in the Middle Ages (itself of no independent historical value) assigned it to the time of the birth of Christ.

Of the selections given here, the first five are from the two older versions of the chief tale, the Iliad of Irish story, the *Cattle Raid of Cooley*. All of them belong to the Ulster group of tales except no. 10, which comes from a body of stories about legendary kings, and no. 11. No. 6 is an extract from the tale of the death of Cú Chulainn, and is an episode in the tragic and dramatic account of how he was first daunted and bewildered by magic, deceived and apparently betrayed by those who loved him, and lured out alone to his destruction with the foreknowledge that he was doomed. No. 11 is from the Middle Irish version of the *Odyssey*, and so is not an example of Irish hero-tale at all; it is included here for the sake of contrast, and especially as an illustration of the way in which the Irish mind could take over extraneous material and transform it into something typically Irish. The wonderful colours of the dog Argus are quite characteristic of Irish hero-tale, in which the tendency to exaggeration which is inherent in the literature as a whole is given full play. Compare the story of Ceithern, no. 5. This is a matter in which the Irish tales do differ from the early epics of other peoples; they are inclined to desert the natural and possible for the impossible and supernatural, chiefly in the form of fantastic exaggeration. One should not misunderstand this, however; it was not done in all seriousness, but for its own sake, for the fun of the thing. Besides, Homer also has his impossible and supernatural aspects – only with him they are expressed as the gods, for whom all things are natural and possible.

HERO-TALE AND ADVENTURE

1. How Cú Chulainn Got His Name

. . . Culann the smith lived in the land of Ulster. He prepared a feast for Conchobhar, and went to Emhain to invite him. He told him that he should come with few companions, unless he brought genuine guests, for it was not lands and demesnes that he had, but his hammers and his anvils and his fists and his tongs.[1] Conchobhar said he would come to him with only a few. Culann went away to his stronghold to furnish and prepare food and drink.

Conchobhar sat in Emhain until it was time to break up, when the day came to an end. The king put on his light travelling clothes, and went to say farewell to the boys. Conchobhar went out on the green, and he saw something at which he marvelled – three times fifty boys at one end of the green and one boy at the other end of it, and the one boy was defeating the three times fifty youths at the goal and in driving the ball. When they were playing the hole-game (for the hole-game used to be practised on the green at Emhain), and when it was their turn to hurl and his to keep goal, he would catch the three times fifty balls outside the hole, and none would get past him into the hole. When it was their turn to keep goal and his to hurl, he would put the three times fifty balls into the hole without missing. When they were playing at pulling off each other's clothes, he would rip their three times fifty garments from them, and all of them were unable even to tear his brooch out of his cloak. When they were wrestling, he would throw the same three fifties to the ground under him, and enough to hold him could not all get round him.

Conchobhar began watching the little boy: 'Ah, my warriors,' said Conchobhar, 'lucky is the land that the little

1. i.e. he was not rich enough to entertain many guests; see Notes.

boy whom you see came from, if only his deeds as a man were to be as his boy deeds are.' 'It is not right to speak so,' said Ferghus; 'as the little boy grows, his deeds of manhood will grow with him. Let the little boy be called to us, to go with us to enjoy the feast to which we are going.' The little boy was called to Conchobhar. 'Well, little boy,' said Conchobhar, 'come with us to enjoy the feast to which we are going.' 'I will not go, though,' said the little boy. 'Why is this?' said Conchobhar. 'Because the boys have not had their fill of feats of play and sport, and I will not leave them until they have had their fill of play.' 'That is too long for us to be waiting for you, little boy, and we will not at all.' 'Go on before me,' said the little boy, 'and I will go after you.' 'You are not familiar with the way at all, little boy,' said Conchobhar. 'I shall follow the tracks of the host and the horses and the chariots.' And Conchobhar came after that to the house of Culann the smith.

The king was waited on, and they were honourably welcomed according to their rank and accomplishments and rights and nobility and breeding. Reeds and fresh rushes were spread under them, and they began to drink and make merry. Culann asked Conchobhar, 'Well now, O king, have you made an appointment for anyone to come after you to this stronghold tonight?' 'Indeed, I have not so appointed,' said Conchobhar, for he did not remember the little boy whom he had appointed to come after him. 'Why is this?' said Conchobhar. 'I have a good bloodhound; when his dog-chain is loosed from him, no traveller or wayfarer would dare to approach the same canton as him; and he recognizes no one but me myself. As for strength, he can do the work of a hundred.' Then Conchobhar said, 'Let the bloodhound be loosed for us, so that he may protect the canton.' His dog-chain was loosed from the bloodhound, and he made a swift circuit of the canton; and he came to the terrace where he was accustomed to be guarding the rampart, and stayed there with his head on his paws; and wild, savage, fierce, rude, surly, and pugnacious was he who was there.

As for the boys, they remained at Emhain until it was time for them to break up. Each one of them went to the house of his father and his mother or his foster-mother and his foster-father, but the little boy went on the tracks of the company until he arrived at the house of Culann the smith. He took to shortening the way before him with his playthings. When he reached the green at the stronghold where Culann and Conchobhar were, he threw all his toys ahead except only his ball. The bloodhound observed the little boy, and bayed at him, so that the baying of the bloodhound was heard throughout all the tribal lands; and what he wanted was not to bite him up to eat, but to swallow him down at one gulp past the trunk of his ribs and the width of his throat and the midriff of his chest. And the boy had no means of defence; but he threw a cast of the ball so that it went down the gaping gullet of the bloodhound's throat, and brought all the internal guts in him out through the back way; and he seized him by the two legs and dashed him against a standing stone, so that he fell in scattered pieces on the ground.

Conchobhar heard the bloodhound's bay. 'Alas, my warriors,' said Conchobhar, 'we have done ill in coming to take part in this feast!' 'Why is this?' said everyone. 'The little lad who arranged to follow me, my sister's son, Sédanta son of Sualtamh, has been killed by the hound.' All the far-famed Ulstermen leaped up together; though the gateway of the rampart was wide open, each went out straight forward, over the palisade of the stronghold. Quick though they all were to reach him, Ferghus got there soonest, and took up the little boy from the ground on to the support of his shoulder; and he was brought into the presence of Conchobhar. And Culann came out and saw his bloodhound in scattered pieces, and it made his heart beat against his ribs. He came across into the stronghold afterwards. 'Your arrival is welcome, little boy,' said Culann, 'for the sake of your mother and father, but it is not welcome for your own sake.' 'Why are you angry with the boy?' said Conchobhar. 'You did ill to come to me to taste my drink and eat my food, for my goods are perished goods now, and my livelihood a lost livelihood. It was a good retainer that you have taken from me, who guarded my flocks and herds and cattle for me.' 'Do not be angry at all, father Culann,' said the little boy, 'for I will give a just judgement concerning this.' 'What judgement on it could you give, boy?' said Conchobhar. 'If there is a puppy of that hound's breeding in Ireland, it shall be brought up by me until it is fit for service like its father. During that time, I myself will be the hound to protect his herds and his cattle and his land.' 'A good judgement you have given, little boy,' said Conchobhar. 'Indeed, I could not have given a better,' said Cathbhadh; 'why should not *Cú Chulainn*[1] be your name because of this?' 'Not so,' said the little boy, 'I prefer my own name, Sédanta son of Sualtamh.' 'Do not say that, little boy,' said Cathbhadh, 'for the men of Ireland and Scotland shall hear of that name, and the mouths of the men of Ireland and Scotland shall be full of that name.' 'I am content then, if I shall be so called,' said the little boy. So that it was in this way that the glorious name *Cú Chulainn* stuck to him, since he killed the hound which belonged to Culann the smith . . .

Irish; author unknown; early twelfth century.

2. *Cú Chulainn and the Charioteer*

. . . They came thence on the next day across Ard, and Cú Chulainn let them go on before him. At Tamhlachtae Órláimh a little to the north of Dísert Lóchaid he came upon the charioteer of Órlámh, son of Ailill and Medhbh, cutting wood there (or according to another source it was Cú Chulainn's chariot shaft that had broken, and he had gone to cut a shaft when he met Órlámh's charioteer). 'The Ulstermen are behaving disgracefully, if it is they who are over there,' said Cú Chulainn, 'while the army is at their heels.' He went to the charioteer to stop him, for he thought

1. i.e. 'The Hound of Culann'.

he was one of the Ulstermen. He saw the man cutting wood for a chariot shaft. 'What are you doing here?' said Cú Chulainn. 'Cutting a chariot shaft,' said the charioteer; 'we have broken our chariots in hunting that wild doe Cú Chulainn. Help me,' said the charioteer, 'but consider whether you will collect the poles or trim them.' 'I shall trim them, indeed,' said Cú Chulainn. Then he trimmed the holly poles between his fingers as the other watched, so that he stripped them smooth of bark and knots. 'This cannot be your proper work that I gave you,' said the charioteer; he was terrified. 'Who are you?' said Cú Chulainn. 'I am the charioteer of Órlámh son of Ailill and Medhbh. And you?' said the charioteer. 'Cú Chulainn is my name,' said he. 'Woe is me, then!' said the charioteer. 'Do not be afraid,' said Cú Chulainn; 'where is your master?' 'He is on the mound over there,' said the charioteer. 'Come along with me then,' said Cú Chulainn, 'for I never kill charioteers.' Cú Chulainn went to Órlámh, and killed him, and cut off his head and brandished the head before the army. Then he put the head on the charioteer's back, and said, 'Take that with you,' said Cú Chulainn, 'and go to the camp so.' . . .

Irish; author unknown; ninth century.

3. The Killing of Edarcomhol

. . . Then Ferghus went on that mission. Edarcomhol, son of Idh and Léthrenn, foster son of Ailill and Medhbh, followed him. 'I do not wish you to go,' said Ferghus, 'and not out of dislike for you. Only, I am unwilling that you should encounter Cú Chulainn, because of your haughtiness and arrogance, and the fierceness and savagery, the recklessness and violence and fury of the other, Cú Chulainn. No good will come of your encounter.' 'Can you not protect me against him?' said Edarcomhol. 'I can so,' said Ferghus, 'but only you must not treat what he says with contempt.' They went away in two chariots to Delgu.

Cú Chulainn was playing draughts with Loegh at that time, and the back of his head was towards them, and Loegh's face. 'I see two chariots coming here,' said Loegh; 'there is a big brown-haired man in the leading chariot, with bushy brown hair on him, a crimson cloak around him with a golden brooch in it, and a hooded tunic with red embroidery on him. A convex shield with a rim of ornamented white bronze on it; a broad spear in his hand, with bands from head to butt; a sword as long as the rudder of a boat across his thighs.' 'That big rudder that father Ferghus brings is hollow,' said Cú Chulainn, 'for there is no sword in its scabbard but a sword of wood. For I have been told,' said Cú Chulainn, 'that Ailill caught them unawares when they were asleep, he and Medhbh, and took away his sword from Ferghus and gave it to his charioteer to keep, and a wooden sword was put in his scabbard.'

Ferghus arrived at that point. 'Welcome, father Ferghus,' said Cú Chulainn; 'if a fish swims into the rivers, you shall have a salmon and a half; if a flock of birds comes to the plain, you shall have a wild goose and a half; a handful of water-cress or dulse, a handful of brook-lime, and a drink from the sand. If it happens to be your watch, you shall have someone to go to the ford to meet all comers, so that you may go to sleep.' 'I believe it well,' said Ferghus, 'it is not for your food that we have come; I know your house-keeping here.' Then Cú Chulainn received the message from Ferghus.

Ferghus went away then. Edarcomhol remained, staring at Cú Chulainn. 'What are you staring at?' said Cú Chulainn. 'You,' said Edarcomhol. 'The eye quickly takes that in,' said Cú Chulainn. 'So I see,' said Edarcomhol, 'I do not know why anyone should be afraid of you. I see no horror nor terror nor overpowering of odds in you. You are a pretty boy only, with weapons of wood and with impressive tricks.' 'Even though you abuse me,' said Cú Chulainn, 'I shall not kill you, for the sake of Ferghus. But if it were not for his protection of you, your stretched entrails and your scattered quarters would reach from here to the camp, after your chariot.' 'Do not threaten me so,' said Edarcomhol; 'that famous treaty that you have ratified, namely to fight single combats, it is I who shall fight against you the first of the men of Ireland tomorrow.'

He went away then. He turned back from Méithe and Ceithe, saying to his charioteer, 'I have boasted,' said he, 'in the presence of Ferghus, to fight with Cú Chulainn tomorrow; but I cannot wait for it. Turn the horses back again from the hill.' Loegh saw this, and said to Cú Chulainn, 'Here is the chariot back again, and it has turned its left side towards us.'[1] 'That is not a debt to be denied,' said Cú Chulainn; 'down with us to the ford to meet him, to find out,' said Cú Chulainn. 'I do not want what you are asking of me,' said Cú Chulainn. 'You have got to,' said Edarcomhol. Cú Chulainn cut the sod which was under his feet, so that he fell on his back with the sod on his belly. 'Go away,' said Cú Chulainn, 'I cannot bear to wipe my hands on you. I should have cut you into many bits just now, if it had not been for Ferghus.' 'We shall not part in this way,' said Edarcomhol, 'until I take your head or until I leave my head with you.' '*That* is what will happen,' said Cú Chulainn. Cú Chulainn struck him with his sword above his armpits, so that his clothes fell off him, but he did not wound his skin. 'Go now,' said Cú Chulainn. 'No,' said Edarcomhol. Then Cú Chulainn passed the edge of the sword over him so that it cut his hair off as if he had been shaved with a razor, but he did not make even a scratch on his skin. But since the oaf continued to be troublesome and importunate, he struck him on the top of his head so that he split him to the navel.

Ferghus saw the chariot go past him with the one man in it. He turned back to expostulate with Cú Chulainn. 'It was wrong of you, you little devil,' he said, 'to violate my protection. You think my club is short!' 'Do not be angry with me, father Ferghus,' said Cú Chulainn. He threw himself prostrate, and Ferghus's chariot drove over him

1. An insult.

three times. 'Ask his charioteer whether I began it.' 'Not you, indeed,' said his charioteer. 'He said,' said Cú Chulainn, 'that he would not go until he took my head or else left his head with me. Which would you prefer, father Ferghus?' said Cú Chulainn. 'Truly, I prefer what has been done,' said Ferghus, 'for it was he who was insolent.'

Then Ferghus thrust a spancel withe through Edarcomhol's heels and drew him after his own chariot to the camp. When they were going across rocks, the one half came apart from the other; when over smooth ground, they came together again. Medhbh saw him. 'That is not the affectionate play of a tender puppy, Ferghus,' said Medhbh. 'Well, the boorish cur should not picked a fight with the great Hound whom he could not match,' said Ferghus. His grave was dug then, his gravestone was set up, his epitaph written in *ogham* letters,[1] and his wake was held . . .

Irish; author unknown; ninth century.

4. Cú Chulainn's Meeting with Findabhair

. . . 'I know,' said Medhbh, 'what is good now. Let us send someone to him to get a truce of the sword for the host from him, and he shall have half the cows that are here.' This message was brought him. 'I will do that,' said Cú Chulainn, 'provided that you do not break the compact.'

'Let a message be sent him,' said Ailill, 'offering Findabhair to him, if he will keep away from the hosts.' Maine Athramhail went to him; he went to Loegh first. 'Whose man are you?' he said, but Loegh did not answer him. Maine spoke to him like that three times. 'Cú Chulainn's man,' he said, 'and do not pester me, in case I happen to cut your head off.' 'This man is angry,' said Maine as he turned away from him. After that he went to speak to Cú Chulainn. Cú Chulainn had taken off his shirt, and the snow was all round him up to his waist as he sat, and the snow had melted for a cubit around him because of the intensity

1. An early Irish alphabet, something like runes, used for inscriptions.

of the warrior's heat. Now Maine asked him in the same way three times, whose man he was. 'Conchobhar's man! and do not pester me; but if you pester me any longer I shall cut your head off as one takes off a blackbird's head.' 'It is not easy to talk with these two,' said Maine. Then Maine went away from them and told his tale to Ailill and Medhbh.

'Let Lughaidh go to him,' said Ailill, 'and offer him the girl.' Lughaidh went thereupon, and told Cú Chulainn this. 'Father Lughaidh,' said Cú Chulainn, 'this is a cheat.' 'It is the word of a king that has spoken it,' said Lughaidh, 'there will be no cheat in it.' 'Let it be done so,' said Cú Chulainn. At that, Lughaidh went from him and told Ailill and Medhbh this answer. 'Let the buffoon go in my guise,' said Ailill, 'with a king's crown on his head, and let him stop at some distance from Cú Chulainn so that he may not recognize him; and let the girl go there with him, and let him betroth her to him; and let them come away quickly so. It is likely that a fraud could be imposed on him in this way so that he will not hold you up, until the time when he comes with the Ulstermen to battle.'

Then the buffoon went to him, and the girl with him, and he spoke to Cú Chulainn from a distance. Cú Chulainn went to meet them, and it chanced that he recognized by the man's way of speaking that he was a buffoon. He hurled at him a sling-stone which was in his hand, so that it burst into his head and brought his brains out. He came up to the girl; he cut off her two plaits and thrust a stone through her cloak and through her tunic; and thrust a stone stake through the middle of the buffoon. Their two standing stones are still there, the standing stone of Findabhair and the standing stone of the buffoon. Cú Chulainn left them in that plight. Ailill and Medhbh sent to seek their people, for they thought they had been a long time. They were seen fixed in that way; and all this was heard throughout the encampment. There was no truce for them with Cú Chulainn after that . . .

Irish; author unknown; ninth-century original.

5. Ceithern's Blood-transfusion and Death

... Then the men of Ireland told Mac Roth, the chief courier, to go to Sliabh Fuaid to keep watch and ward for them, so that the Ulstermen should not come against them without warning or notice. Mac Roth went on as far as Sliabh Fuaid. Mac Roth had not been there long, when he saw a single chariot-warrior on Sliabh Fuaid coming towards him from the north by the straightest route. There was a man in the chariot making for him, stark naked, without any weapon and without any accoutrements at all except for an iron spit in his hand. He was goading on his charioteer and his horses alike, and it seemed as if he thought he could not reach the armies alive at all. And Mac Roth came with the tale of this news to the place where Ailill and Medhbh and Ferghus were, with the nobles of the men of Ireland. Ailill asked news of him when he arrived. 'Well now, Mac Roth,' said Ailill, 'did you see any of the Ulstermen on the trail of this army today?' 'I do not know, indeed,' said Mac Roth, 'but I saw something – a single chariot-warrior coming across Sliabh Fuaid by the straightest route, and a man in the chariot, stark naked, without any weapon and without any accoutrements at all except for an iron spit in his hand. He was goading on his charioteer and his horses alike; and it seemed as if he thought he could not reach this army alive at all.'

'Who should you think that is, Ferghus?' said Ailill. 'Truly, I think that it would be Ceithern son of Fintan who came there.' Ferghus was right about that, that it was Ceithern son of Fintan who came there. And so Ceithern son of Fintan came up to them, and the camp and laager were thrown back on themselves, and he was wounding everyone around him, in all directions and on all sides, but he himself was wounded from all directions and all sides; and he came from them after that with his entrails and his intestines hanging out, to the place where Cú Chulainn was, to be healed and cured. And he demanded a doctor of Cú Chulainn, to heal and cure him. 'Well now, father

39

Loegh,' said Cú Chulainn, 'take yourself off to the camp and laager of the men of Ireland, and tell the doctors to come away to cure Ceithern son of Fintan. I give my word, if they do not come, even though they are under the earth or locked up in a house, I shall bring death and demise and violent decease upon them before this time tomorrow, unless they come.'

Loegh went forward to the camp and laager of the men of Ireland, and told the doctors of the men of Ireland to come away to cure Ceithern son of Fintan. The doctors of the men of Ireland thought this hard, to go to cure their foes and their enemies and their alien rivals, but they feared Cú Chulainn would play death and demise and violent decease upon them if they did not go. So they came. As each one of them arrived, Ceithern son of Fintan showed him his wounds and his gashes, his lacerations and his bleeding cuts. Every one of them who said he would not live and was not curable, Ceithern son of Fintan struck him a blow with his right fist on the flat of his forehead, so that he brought his brains out for him through the openings of his ears and the sutures of his head. Now Ceithern son of Fintan killed up to fifteen doctors of the men of Ireland; the fifteenth doctor, however, he got him with only a glancing blow, but he fell lifeless and utterly stunned among the bodies of the other doctors, for a long time and a great while. Íthall, doctor of Ailill and Medhbh, that was his name.

Then Ceithern son of Fintan demanded another doctor of Cú Chulainn, to heal and cure him. 'Well now, father Loegh,' said Cú Chulainn, 'go for me to Fínghin the prophetic physician, Conchobhar's doctor, to Ferta Fínghin at Leca on Sliabh Fuaid. Let him come away to cure Ceithern son of Fintan.' Loegh went forward to Fínghin the prophetic physician, Conchobhar's doctor, to Ferta Fínghin at Leca on Sliabh Fuaid, and he told him to come to cure Ceithern son of Fintan. Fínghin the prophetic physician came, and when he arrived Ceithern son of Fintan showed him his wounds and his gashes, his lacerations and his bleeding cuts. . . . 'Now, Fínghin, prophetic physician,' said Ceithern son of Fintan, 'what prognosis and what advice do you give me at this time?' 'What I tell you, truly,' said Fínghin the prophetic physician, 'is that you should not exchange your grown cows for calves this year,[1] because if you do so it is not you who will have the use of them, and they will bring you no profit.' 'That is the prognosis and advice that the other doctors gave me, and certainly it brought them no advantage nor increment, for they fell at my hands; and no more will it bring you advantage nor increment, and you too shall fall at my hands.' And he gave him a mighty and violent kick with his foot, so that he fell between the two wheels of the chariot. . . .

Nevertheless, Fínghin the prophetic physician gave Ceithern son of Fintan his choice, either to lie sick for a long time, and to get help and remedy afterwards; or else a bloody course of treatment for three days and three nights, so that he could himself ply his strength on his enemies. What Ceithern son of Fintan chose was the bloody course of treatment for three days and three nights, so that he could himself ply his strength on his enemies; for this is what he said, that he would not leave anyone after him whom he would rather have vindicate and avenge him, than himself. Then Fínghin the prophetic physician asked Cú Chulainn for a tub of marrow to heal and cure Ceithern son of Fintan. Cú Chulainn went forward to the camp and laager of the men of Ireland, and all the cattle and herds and stock that he found there he brought away with him; and he made a tub-full of marrow from them, meat and bones and hides, and Ceithern son of Fintan was set in the tub of marrow until the end of three days and three nights. And he began to soak in the tub-full of marrow, and the tub-full of marrow went into him, through his wounds and his gashes, in his lacerations and his many cuts. Then he arose out of the tub of marrow at the end of three days and three nights, and he got up with the board of his chariot to his belly, so that his entrails and intestines might not fall out.

1. Apparently a proverb.

That is the time when his wife, Finda daughter of Eochu, came from the north from Dún dá Bhenn with his sword for him. Ceithern son of Fintan went against the men of Ireland. But this must be said, they brought warning of him from Íthall the doctor of Ailill and Medhbh, who had lain lifeless and utterly stunned among the bodies of the other doctors for a long time and a great while. 'Well now, men of Ireland,' said the doctor, 'Ceithern son of Fintan will come to seek you, having been healed and cured by Fínghin the prophetic physician; and do you make ready for him.' Then the men of Ireland set Ailill's clothes and his golden crown on the standing stone in the country of Ros, so that Ceithern son of Fintan should exercise his fury on this at first, when he arrived. Ceithern son of Fintan saw that, Ailill's clothes and his golden crown on the standing stone in the country of Ros, and, for want of knowledge and information, he thought that it was Ailill himself who was there; and he made for it and thrust the sword through the standing stone till it went in up to the hilt. 'Here is a trick,' said Ceithern son of Fintan, 'and on me this trick has been played. And I give my word, until someone is found among you who will take those royal robes about him, and the golden crown, I will not withhold my hand from them, hacking and smiting them!' Maine Andoe, son of Ailill and Medhbh, heard that, and he took the royal robes about him and the golden crown, and came forward through the midst of the men of Ireland. Ceithern son of Fintan pursued him hotly, and hurled a cast of his shield at him, so that the ornamented rim of the shield severed him in three to the ground, himself and his chariot and charioteer and horses. Then the hosts buffeted him all round on both sides, so that he fell at their hands in the straits in which he was . . .

Irish; author unknown; early twelfth century.

6. Cú Chulainn in the Valley of the Deaf

. . . On that day the guarding of Cú Chulainn was assigned to the daughters of kings and chiefs of Ulster and to his own dear mistress, Niamh daughter of Celtchar son of Uithe-char; and the women consulted together that day, how they should guard Cú Chulainn, and the conclusion that they came to was to take Cú Chulainn with them to the Valley of the Deaf, for that dark valley was a secure place, difficult to explore. And the women-folk came to entice him away with them out of the town, so that he should not be listening to the vexations of the witches or the outcries of the sorceresses, as they bewitched him and provoked him to meet his enemies. And Niamh daughter of Celtchar came to him and said to him, 'Dear lad, it is we that the Ulster-men and Conchobhar have set to guard you today; and come with me and the women-folk, and let us go to my stronghold to drink and amuse ourselves, for I have a liquor that is a protective charm for you to drink.' And he came out of the bower with her, and they took him with them to the Valley of the Deaf; and when he saw that, he knew it was the Valley of the Deaf that he saw. 'Alas,' said Cú Chulainn, 'this is the Valley of the Deaf, and I will never go there'; and he did not stay long so.

At the same time the Children of Cailidín[1] conjured up huge battalions around the Valley; and he saw a vision of the whole land as overrun with raiding bands, and as a meeting-place of general visitation, and as filled with all one shout of clamour and of war-cries; so that the warrior was weakened and bewildered by that mighty combat. 'Alas for my trip and my expedition with the women, which has delayed and endangered me, without my weapons and my horses and my armour; so that the chance to hold back the raids and the conflicts among the armies and to protect the province has escaped me!'

He went forward to Emhain. 'Let my horses be caught for me and my chariot harnessed, so that I may go against the men of Ireland!' 'You gave me your word,' said Niamh, 'that you would not go against the men of Ireland until I gave you leave.' 'If I did, I will not go,' said he. And they went forward out of the town; and the eldest of the sons of

1. Six witches and wizards, deadly enemies of Cú Chulainn.

Cailidín came and stood before the bower. Cú Chulainn arose and made to tackle him, but Niamh clasped her two arms round him and made him sit down. 'Stay with me,' said Niamh, 'and keep your oath.' Cú Chulainn sat down dejectedly; and the Children of Cailidín went away when they saw that Cú Chulainn had been stayed, and they came to the encampment of the men of Ireland. 'Have you brought us Cú Chulainn with you?' 'We have not,' they said, 'if we do not bring you him tomorrow, take these six heads off us!' They lay there that night.

As for Conchobhar, Cathbhadh and Genann of the Bright Cheeks and all the druids were brought to him the next morning, and Conchobhar asked what guard they would set over Cú Chulainn that day. 'We do not know,' they all said. 'I know,' said Conchobhar, 'take him with you to the Valley of the Deaf today, for this is why it is called the Valley of the Deaf – if all the men of Ireland were around it, and were raising cries of battle on high, no one who was in the valley would hear them; and if those same cries were being raised inside the valley, no one who was outside the valley would hear them. That is why it is right for you to take Cú Chulainn with you into that valley; and guard him today wisely and very cunningly, until the augury and the omen become valid and until Conall comes from the wide regions of the Picts to help him.' 'Great king,' said Niamh, 'he refused to go to that valley for me and all the women-folk, though we begged him the whole day long.' 'Let Cathbhadh and Genann of the Bright Cheeks and all the poets, and the women-folk along with Eimher,[1] go to him, and take him to the valley; and make carousal and amusements and skilful entertainments, so that he shall not hear the incitements of the hosts trying to perplex him.' 'I will not go with them,' said Eimher, 'to the valley, but let Niamh go with him, with my blessing, for it is she he finds it most difficult to refuse.' And that was the conclusion on which they settled.

The women and youths and poets and sages of the whole

1. Cú Chulainn's wife.

province came to him, with Cobhthach of the Sweet Tune, the harper, to play music to him, and Fercheirtne the poet with them, watching over him. And Cathbhadh came before him and began to entreat him, and went on to the couch beside him, and gave him three kisses earnestly and eagerly; and 'Dear son,' said Cathbhadh, 'come with me today to drink at my feast, and all the women and the poets shall come with us; and it is tabu[1] for you to refuse or shun a feast.' 'Alas,' said Cú Chulainn, 'it is not a good time for me for drinking and amusement now, when the four great provinces of Ireland are burning and swiftly plundering this province, and the Ulster warriors are in the sickness of labour,[2] and Conall is in foreign parts; and the men of Ireland are reproaching and shaming me, and saying that I am skulking away from them. And yet if it were not for you and Conchobhar and Genann and the poets, I would go, and I would bring a sudden scattering of enemies on them, so that their dead would be more numerous than their living.' And Eimher and all the women began to entreat him, and this is what they said to him: 'Dear Cú,' said she, 'you have never broken off a trip or expedition which you made, until the present time. O my first love, my beloved only choice among wooers of the men of the world, and only darling of the women-folk and poets of the world and of all Ireland, for my sake go with Cathbhadh and Genann and Niamh daughter of Celtchar, to drink at the feast which Cathbhadh has ready for you.' And Niamh faced him and began to plead subtly in her sweet voice; and he went with them very reluctantly, and they came into the valley. 'Alas,' said Cú Chulainn, 'for a long time I have been avoiding this valley, for I never came to a place I disliked more than this; and the men of Ireland say that I have come there to skulk away from them,' said Cú Chulainn. And they went forward into the vast royal hall which had been made ready for him by Cathbhadh, and the Liath Macha and the Dubh Sainghlenn[3] were unharnessed in the valley bottom; and Cú Chulainn sat on the king's seat in the hall, and

1. See Notes.   2. See Notes.   3. Cú Chulainn's horses.

Cathbhadh, Fercheirtne, and the poets sat on the one hand
of Cú Chulainn and Niamh and the women-folk on the
other hand; and their musicians and entertainers sat at the
other bench facing them. And they began to eat and drink,
with music and sport, and set up ample mirth and merri-
ment. Thus far their doings.

The doings of the Children of Cailidín are now made
known. The three skinny-handed daughters of Cailidín
came to the green at Emhain, and went where they had
seen Cú Chulainn the night before, and did not find Cú
Chulainn there. Since they did not find him, they searched
all Emhain, and did not find him, and they marvelled that
Cú Chulainn was not in the company of Eimher or Conchobhar or the other heroes of the province; and they
understood clearly that it was the magic arts of Cathbhadh
that were concealing him from them. And they arose like
birds of the air and explored the entire province, looking for
him, until they came over the Valley of the Deaf, and they
saw the Liath Macha and the Dubh Sainghlenn at ease at
the bottom of the valley, and Laegh son of Rianghabhar in
charge of them beside; and they understood that Cú Chulainn was in the valley, and they heard the noise and the
music of the poets around Cú Chulainn. Then the Children
of Cailidín gathered shaggy sharp downy thistles and light-
topped puff-balls and fluttering withered leaves of the
wood, and made many armoured warriors of them; so that
there was not a peak nor a hill around the valley which was
not filled with hosts and battalions and troops, so that the
hideous quick wild cries that the Children of Cailidín
raised around it were heard even to the clouds of heaven
and the walls of the firmament; so that the entire land was
full of woundings and raids, of burnings and swift lamenta-
tions, and of the bleating of trumpets and· horns, through
those magic arts of the Children of Cailidín. And when the
women-folk heard those continual cries, they themselves set
up other loud cries against them; and yet Cú Chulainn
heard those cries more than anyone else.

'Alas,' said Cú Chulainn, 'great are these cries that I hear from the men of Ireland as they plunder the entire province; and for that, the end of my victorious career has come, and the province has reached the brink of Doom now and of its existence.' 'Let that pass,' said Cathbhadh, 'this is nothing but false, feeble, evanescent hosts which the Children of Cailidín have conjured up against you, and there is nothing in it but deception; and neither heed nor notice them.' And they began to drink and entertain themselves for another while, until they heard the great cries outside which the Children of Cailidín raised again around the valley. And when those who were watching Cú Chulainn heard this, they themselves set up cries and arguments and sports around Cú Chulainn; and the Children of Cailidín grew weary at last, and they perceived that they got no profit in any of their wizardries, against Cathbhadh and the women.

'Stay here and reinforce the armies,' said Badhbh, daughter of Cailidín, to her two sisters, 'while I go to the valley to meet Cú Chulainn, though it may be death that I get for it.' And she went forward deceitfully and shamefully to the hall, and went inside in the shape of one of Niamh's women, and called the queen out to her. And a large party of the women went with the queen, and Badhbh drew them thus a long way from the hall, with magic arts and deceptive wizardry, and set them in a mist of intoxication and bewilderment throughout the valley, and put a magic mist between them and the hall after that; and she herself came away from them, for she knew that Niamh had made Cú Chulainn give his word that he would not go to meet the men of Ireland until she herself gave him leave. And Badhbh put the form of Niamh on herself, and came where Cú Chulainn was, and told him to go to meet the hosts; and 'My soul, hero and warrior, dear Cú,' said she, 'Dún Delgan has been burned, and Magh Muirtheimhne and Machaire Conaill and the whole province have been plundered, and the hosts have reached to Emhain; and it is I that the nobles of the province will reproach for keeping you back and not letting you go to avenge their country and hold up the hosts; and truly I know too that Conall will kill me for not setting you free to protect the province and to meet the rest of the men of Ireland.' 'Alas, Niamh,' said Cú Chulainn, 'hard it will be to put trust in women after this, and I had thought you would not give me this leave for the gold of the world and the wealth of the universe; but since it is you who give me leave to go to a vexed and overwhelming meeting with all the men of Ireland, I will go there,' said Cú Chulainn . . .

Cú Chulainn came out of the hall, and called to Laegh to catch the horses and harness the chariot. And Cathbhadh arose, and Genann of the Bright Cheeks and all the women-folk after him, and all laid their hands upon him, but they could do nothing; and they came out of the valley, and Cú Chulainn began to gaze around him on the province on every side. And Badhbh came away after that; and they raised the great cries loudly and terribly as before. Cú Chulainn heard, and many strange and horrible phantasms appeared to him such as he had never seen till then; and he understood then that all his tabus were broken. Then Cathbhadh began to soothe him with kind words, and said to him, 'Dear son,' he said, 'stay here for my sake if only for today, and do not go to meet the men of Ireland; and I will hold back the magic of the Children of Cailidín from you from now on.' 'Dear foster-father, there is no cause for me to stay now; the end of my life has come, and my tabus are broken, and Niamh has given me leave to go to meet the men of Ireland; and I will go there, since she gave me leave.' Niamh laid hold of Cú Chulainn as they spoke together. 'Alas, dear Cú,' said Niamh, 'I would not give you leave for all the gold on the earth, and it is not I who gave it but Badhbh daughter of Cailidín, who came to you in my shape to beguile you; and do you stay for my own sake, my beloved, my fair sweetheart.' But Cú Chulainn did not believe anything she said; and he ordered Laegh to catch the horses and prepare the chariot . . .

Irish; author unknown; fifteenth century.

7. *The Story of Deirdre*

The men of Ulster were drinking in the house of Feidhlimidh son of Dall, Conchobhar's story-teller. Now Feidhlimidh's wife was waiting on the company, standing before them, and she was pregnant. Drinking-horns and servings of food went round, and they raised a howl of drunkenness. When they were about to go to bed, the woman went to her couch. As she crossed the middle of the house the baby shrieked in her womb, so that it was heard throughout the courtyard. Everyone inside jumped up at each other at that screech, so that they were face to face in the house. Then Senchae son of Ailill proclaimed, 'Do not stir,' said he, 'let the woman be brought to us so that the cause of this noise may be discovered.' The woman was brought to them then . . . Then she ran to Cathbhadh, because he was a seer; . . . and Cathbhadh said:

'Within the cradle of your womb
cries a woman of curling yellow golden hair,
with slow grey-pupilled eyes.
Like the foxglove are her purple cheeks,
to the colour of snow we compare
the spotless treasure of her teeth.
Bright are her lips, of vermilion red.
A woman through whom there will be many slaughters
among the chariot-warriors of Ulster.' . . .

Then Cathbhadh put his hand on the woman's belly, so that the baby stormed[1] under his hand. 'Truly,' said he, 'it is a girl there, and *Deirdriu* shall be her name, and evil will come of her.' The girl was born after that . . .

'Let the girl be killed,' said the warriors. 'Not so,' said Conchobhar, 'the girl shall be taken by me tomorrow,' said Conchobhar, 'and shall be brought up under my own will, and shall be the woman who will be in my company.' And the Ulstermen did not dare correct him in this.

1. *Ro derdrestar.*

It was done, then. She was brought up by Conchobhar until she was the most wonderfully beautiful girl in Ireland. In a court apart she was reared, so that none of the Ulstermen might see her until the time when she should sleep with Conchobhar; and there was no one who might be allowed into that court but her foster-father and her foster-mother, and also Lebhorcham, for she could not be excluded because she was a satirist.[1]

Now once upon a time the girl's foster-father was skinning a stolen calf in the snow outside, in the winter, to cook it for her. She saw a raven drinking the blood on the snow. Then she said to Lebhorcham, 'I should dearly love any man with those three colours, with hair like the raven and cheek like the blood and body like the snow.' 'Honour and good luck be yours,' said Lebhorcham, 'it is not far from you. He is in the house beside you, Noísiu the son of Uisliu.' 'I shall not be well, truly,' said she, 'until I see him.' . . .

Now when he, this same Noísiu, was alone outside, she stole away out to him as if to pass him by, and he did not recognize her. 'Pretty is the heifer which passes by us,' said he. 'The heifers are bound to be well-grown,' said she, 'where there are no bulls.' 'You have the bull of the province, the king of Ulster,' said he. 'I would choose between you two,' said she, 'and I would take a young little bull like you.' 'Not so,' said he, 'because of Cathbhadh's prophecy.' 'Is it to reject me that you say that?' said she. 'It is indeed,' said he. At that she leaped at him and seized his ears on his head. 'Two ears of shame and derision are these,' she said, 'unless you carry me off with you.' 'Away from me, woman,' said he. 'That will happen to you,' she said. At this his roar went up from him. When the Ulstermen beyond heard the roar, every one of them fell upon the other. The sons of Uisliu came out to restrain their brother. 'What is the matter with you?' they said, 'do not let the Ulstermen kill each other because of your fault.' Then he told them what had been done to him. 'Evil will come of it,' said the warriors. 'Though it should, you shall

1. On the power of satire see p. 195.

not be in disgrace as long as we are alive. We will go with
her into another land. There is not a king in Ireland who
will not make us welcome.' This was their conclusion. They
went off that night, with a hundred and fifty warriors of
theirs and a hundred and fifty women and a hundred and
fifty hounds and a hundred and fifty servants, and Deirdriu
along with the others with them.

They were under pledges of safeguard for a long while
all round Ireland (and their destruction was often attempted
through the plots and wiles of Conchobhar), round from
Assaroe southwest to Howth again to the northeast. However the Ulstermen hounded them across to the land of
Scotland, and they settled down in the wilds there. When the
hunting of the mountain failed them they turned to taking
the cattle of the men of Scotland for themselves. These
went to destroy them in a single day, whereupon they went
to the king of Scotland, and he admitted them into his
household, and they took service with him; and they set up
their huts on the green. Because of the girl the huts were
made, so that no one should see her with them, for fear they
would be killed for her sake.

Once upon a time then, the steward went early in the
morning so that he went round their house. He saw the
couple asleep. He went thereupon and woke the king. 'I
have not found a woman worthy of you until today,' said
he; 'there is a woman worthy of the King of the Western
World with Noísiu son of Uisliu. Let Noísiu be killed immediately, and let the woman sleep with you,' said the
steward. 'No,' said the king, 'but do you go to woo her for
me secretly every day.' That was done. But what the
steward used to say to her by day, she would tell her
husband straightway the same night. Since nothing was got
from her, the sons of Uisliu were ordered to go into risks
and fights and difficulties, so that they might be killed.
Nevertheless they were so steadfast in every slaughter that
it was impossible to do anything to them in these attacks.

After taking counsel about it with her, the men of Scotland were mustered to kill them. She told Noísiu. 'Go away,'

said she, 'for if you have not gone away by tonight you will be killed tomorrow.' They went away that night, so that they were on an island of the sea. This was told to the Ulstermen. 'It is sad, Conchobhar,' said the Ulstermen, 'that the sons of Uisliu should fall in a hostile land through the fault of a bad woman. It would be better to escort them and feed them, and not to kill them, and for them to come to their land, rather than to fall before their enemies.' 'Let them come, then,' said Conchobhàr, 'and let sureties go for them.' That was brought to them. 'It is welcome to us,' they said; 'we shall go, and let Ferghus and Dubhthach and Cormac son of Conchobhar come as sureties for us.' These went and escorted them from the sea.

Now, through the counsel of Conchobhar people rivalled each other to invite Ferghus to ale-feasts, for the sons of Uisliu declared that they would not eat food in Ireland except the food of Conchobhar first. Then Fiachu son of Ferghus went with them, and Ferghus and Dubhthach stayed behind, and the sons of Uisliu came until they were on the green at Emhain. Then too Éoghan son of Durthacht, the king of Fernmhagh, came to make peace with Conchobhar, for he had been at war with him for a long time. It was he who was entrusted with killing the sons of Uisliu, with the soldiers of Conchobhar around him so that they might not come at him.

The sons of Uisliu were standing in the middle of the green, and the women were sitting on the rampart of Emhain. Then Éoghan went against them with his troop over the green, but the son of Ferghus came so that he was beside Noísiu. Éoghan welcomed them with a thrusting blow of a great spear into Noísiu, so that his back broke because of it. At that the son of Ferghus threw himself and put his arms round Noísiu and bore him under, so that he cast himself down on him. And this is how Noísiu was killed, right down through the son of Ferghus. They were killed then all over the green, so that none escaped but those who fought their way out by point of spear and edge of sword; and she was brought across to Conchobhar so that she was in his power, and her hands were bound behind her back.

Then this was told to Ferghus and Dubhthach and Cormac. They came and did great deeds straightway; that is to say, Dubhthach killed Maine son of Conchobhar, and Fiachna son of Feidhelm, daughter of Conchobhar, was slain by the same thrust, and Ferghus killed Traighthrén son of Traighlethan and his brother; and this was an outrage to Conchobhar. And a battle was fought between them after that on the same day, so that three hundred Ulstermen fell between them; and Dubhthach killed the girls of Ulster before morning and Ferghus burned Emhain. Then they went to Ailill and Medhbh, because they knew that couple would be able to support them; but it was no lovenest for the Ulstermen. Three thousand was the number of the exiles. Till the end of sixteen years, weeping and trembling never ceased in Ulster at their hands, but there was weeping and trembling at their hands every single night.

She was a year with Conchobhar, and during that time she did not smile, and did not take her fill of food or sleep, and did not raise her head from her knee . . . 'What do you see that you most hate?' said Conchobhar. 'Yourself, surely,' said she, 'and Éoghan son of Durthacht.' 'Then you shall be a year with Éoghan,' said Conchobhar. He put her then at Éoghan's disposal. They went the next day to the assembly of Macha. She was behind Éoghan in a chariot. She had vowed that she would not see her two husbands together on earth. 'Well, Deirdriu,' said Conchobhar, 'it is the eye of a ewe between two rams that you make between me and Éoghan.' There was a great boulder of stone before her. She dashed her head on the stone so that her head was shattered, so that she died.

Irish; author unknown; ninth century.

8. The Death of Conchobhar

The Ulstermen were very drunk, once, in Emhain Macha. Great disputes and contentions arose between them –

Conall, Cú Chulainn, and Loeghaire. 'Bring me,' said
Conall, 'the brain of Meis-Geghra, so that I can talk to the
warriors who are contending.' It was the custom among the
Ulstermen in those days to take out the brains of any
warrior whom they killed in single combat, out of his head,
and to mix them with lime, so that they became hard balls.
And when they used to be disputing or contending, these
would be brought to them so that they had them in their
hands. 'Well now, Conchobhar,' said Conall, 'until the
warriors who are contending do a deed like this one in
single combat, they are not worthy to contend with me.'
'That is true,' said Conchobhar.

The brain was put then on the shelf on which it used
always to be. Everyone went his way on the next day, to
amuse himself. Now Cet son of Madu came on a tour of
adventures in Ulster. This Cet was the most troublesome
monster in Ireland. He came across the green at Emhain
with three heads of Ulster warriors. While the buffoons
were playing with the brain of Meis-Geghra, that is what
one buffoon said to the other.[1] Cet heard that. He snatched
the brain from the hand of one of them and carried it off
with him, for Cet knew that it was foretold that Meis-
Geghra would avenge himself after his death. In every
battle and every fight that the men of Connaught used to
have with the men of Ulster, Cet would carry the brain in
his belt, to see whether he could bring about a famous deed
by killing an Ulsterman with it. One day this Cet came east
and drove a spoil of cattle from Fir Ros. The Ulstermen
pursued and caught up with him, but the men of Connaught
arrived from the other side to rescue him. A battle was
fought between them; Conchobhar himself came into the
battle. Then the women of Connaught begged Conchobhar
to come aside so that they might look at his figure, for there
was not on earth the figure of a man like the figure of
Conchobhar in form and shape and dress, in size and
straightness and symmetry, in eye and hair and whiteness,
in wisdom and good manners and speech, in garments and

1. i.e. that this was Meis-Geghra's brain.

54

splendour and array, in weapons and amplitude and dignity, in habits and feats of arms and lineage. This Conchobhar was indeed not imperfect. Now it was through the prompting of Cet that the women made this appeal to Conchobhar. He went on one side by himself, to be looked at by the women.

Cet came, then, so that he was in the midst of the women. Cet fitted Meis-Geghra's brain into the sling, and slung it so that it struck Conchobhar on the top of his skull, so that two-thirds of it were in his head, and he fell headlong on the ground. The men of Ulster leaped towards him and carried him off from Cet. . . . The fight was kept up till the same hour the next day, after what happened to the king; and then the Ulstermen were routed. Conchobhar's doctor, Fínghin, was brought to him. It was he who used to tell from the smoke that went up from the house how many people were ill inside, and every illness that was there. 'Well,' said Fínghin, 'if the stone is taken out of your head you will die immediately. If it is not taken out, however, I could heal you; but it will be a disfigurement to you.' 'We would rather have the disfigurement than his death,' said the Ulstermen.

His head was healed then, and was sewn up with a golden thread, for the colour of Conchobhar's hair was like the colour of gold. And the doctor told Conchobhar he should take care that anger should not seize him, and that he should not mount on horseback, and should not have to do with a woman, and should not eat food gluttonously, and should not run. So he remained in that dangerous state, as long as he lived, for seven years, and he was not able to be active but to stay in his seat only; until he heard that Christ was crucified by the Jews. A great trembling came on the elements at that time, and heaven and earth shook with the monstrous nature of the deed which was done then – Jesus Christ the Son of the Living God crucified though guiltless. 'What is this?' said Conchobhar to his druid, 'what great evil is being done today?' 'It is true,' said the druid, 'it is a great deed that is done there, Christ the Son of the Living God crucified by the Jews.' 'That is a great deed,' said

Conchobhar. 'That man,' said the druid, 'was born the same night that you were born, that is, on the eighth day before the calends of January, though the year was not the same.'

Then Conchobhar believed; and he was one of the two men in Ireland who believed in God before the coming of the Faith, and the other was Morann. 'Well now,' said Conchobhar, 'a thousand armed men shall fall at my hand in rescuing Christ.' He leaped for his two spears then, and brandished them violently so that they broke in his fist; and he took his sword in his hand next and attacked the forest around him, so that he made an open field of the forest. . . . And he said, 'Thus would I avenge Christ on the Jews and on those who crucified Him, if I could get at them.' With that fury, Meis-Geghra's brain sprang out of his head, so that his own brains came out, and he died of it . . .

Irish; author unknown; ninth century?

9. How Celtchar Killed the ' Brown Mouse'

. . . And this is the second plague next, namely the Brown Mouse; that is, a puppy which a widow's son found in the hollow of a tree-trunk, and the widow reared it until it was big. At last however it turned against the widow's sheep, and killed her cows and her son, and killed her herself; and went after that to the Great Pig's Glen. It would devastate a farmstead in Ulster every night, and lie asleep every day. 'Rid us of it, Celtchar!' said Conchobhar. Celtchar went to the woods and brought away an alder log, and a hole was bored through it as long as his arm, and he boiled it in fragrant herbs and honey and grease, until it was supple and tough. Celtchar went to the cave where the Brown Mouse used to sleep, and entered the cave early before the Brown Mouse should come after its ravages. It came with its snout lifted up to the scent of the trunk, and Celtchar pushed the trunk out through the cave towards it. The hound took it in its jaws and set its teeth in it, and the teeth stuck in the tough wood. Celtchar dragged the trunk towards him and

the hound dragged in the other direction; and Celtchar
thrust his arm along inside the log, until he brought its
heart up through its mouth, so that he had it in his hand.
And he took its head with him . . .

Irish; author unknown; ninth-century original.

10. How Cobhthach Contrived his Brother's Death

Cobhthach the Lean of Bregia, son of Ughaine Mór, was
king of Bregia; but Loeghaire Lorc, son of Ughaine, was
king of Ireland. He too was son of Ughaine Mór. Cobhthach
was jealous of Loeghaire for the kingship of Ireland, so that
a wasting sickness seized him, and his blood and his flesh
withered from him, whence he was called 'the Lean of
Bregia'; but he had not succeeded in killing Loeghaire.
Loeghaire was summoned to him after that, to give him his
blessing before he died . . . 'Come tomorrow,' said Cobhthach, 'to build my tomb and set up my gravestone and
conduct the wake for me, and perform my funeral lament,
for I shall shortly die.' 'Good,' said Loeghaire, 'it shall be
done.' 'Well now,' said Cobhthach to his queen and his
steward, 'say that I am dead, without anyone else knowing,
and let me be put in my chariot with a razor-knife in my
hand. My brother will come hastily to bewail me, and will
throw himself on to me; perhaps he will get something from
me.' That came true. The chariot was brought out; his
brother came to bewail him, and threw himself down on
him. He planted the knife in him at his midriff so that the
point came up out of him at the tip of his heart, and he
killed Loeghaire so . . .

Irish; author unknown; ninth century?

11. The Recognition of Ulysses

. . . 'Good people,' said the queen, 'who are you at all?' 'I
am Ulysses son of Laertes,' said he. 'You are not the Ulysses

whom I knew,' said she. 'I am indeed,' he said, 'and I will describe my credentials'; and then he told of their secrets and their talks together and their hidden thoughts. 'What has happened to your looks, or your men,' said she, 'if you are Ulysses?' 'They are lost,' he said. 'What was the last of your keepsakes that you left with me?' she said. 'A golden brooch,' said he, 'with a silver head; and I took your brooch with me when I went into the ship, and it was then you turned back from me,' said Ulysses. 'That is true,' she said, 'and if you were Ulysses you would ask after your dog.' 'I had not thought it would be alive at all,' he said. 'I made it a broth of long life,' said she, 'because I saw that Ulysses loved it greatly. And what sort of dog at all is that dog?' she said. 'It has white sides and a light crimson back and a jet-black belly and a green tail,' said Ulysses. 'That is the description of the dog,' she said, 'and no one in the place dares give it its food except myself and you and the steward.' 'Bring the dog in,' said he. And four men went to fetch it, and brought it in with them. And when it heard the sound of Ulysses' voice, it gave a tug at its chain so that it laid the four men flat all over the house behind it, and jumped at Ulysses' breast and licked his face. When Ulysses' people saw that, they leaped towards him. Whoever could not get at his skin to kiss him covered his clothes with kisses . . .

Irish; author unknown; thirteenth century?

NATURE

NOTE

The most striking quality about the early medieval Celtic literatures, the more striking when one compares other contemporary literatures of Europe, is their power of vivid imagination and freshness of approach; as if every poet, gifted with a high degree of imaginative insight, rediscovered the world for himself. Where other medieval literatures are conventional and even hackneyed, early Celtic literature is capable of being highly original. This is not true of that genre which was most esteemed by the Celtic peoples themselves, the official 'bardic' poetry described below; though even there the irrepressible vividness of Celtic thought breaks through. Fortunately other kinds of poetry were composed apart from the bardic, and it is there that the qualities referred to are mainly found.

They are seen particularly in the nature poetry of early Ireland, in which the feeling of freshness is very clear. Comparing these poems with the medieval European lyric is like comparing the emotions of an imaginative adolescent who has just grown up to realize the beauty of nature, with those of an old man who has been familiar with it for a lifetime and is no longer able to think of it except in literary terms. Nowhere else in medieval European literature could one find poems like nos. 12, 13, 17, 18 or 19. The truth is that in its earlier period Celtic literature did not belong at all to the common culture of the rest of Europe; nor did it ever become more than partly influenced by it.

Not all the poems given in this section are of this kind. In the poetry of Dafydd ap Gwilym (nos. 25–30) we have something more sophisticated. As noted on p. 91, the French lyric certainly played some part in influencing Welsh poetry at this time and before, but its effect on Dafydd is obscured by the brilliance of his own genius. Dafydd created also his own conventions; the constant woodland setting for his love affairs may well be his expansion of a Provençal idea, but the strings of bold metaphors in which he describes objects like the snow and the stars are almost entirely his own. Also his own is the theme of the disasters which befell him on his way to keep an appointment with his mistress, his obstruction by the mist or the night, which give the opportunity for this scintillating display, and for much good-humoured self-mockery. No. 31 is a forgery by an eighteenth-century poet in the manner of the fourteenth, which does not make it the less charming a poem.

The old Celtic freshness lingered on in spite of the increasing influence of European literature. We still see something of it in no. 33, composed in 1600; and even nos. 37 and 38, characteristic products of the nineteenth-century variety of the Romantic movement, seem to preserve a little. Two other selections given elsewhere (nos. 157, 158) which might have been included in this group have some of the marks of eighteenth-century English poetry, but much of their treatment is still truly Celtic. It is significant that almost no folk poetry of the last few centuries is included here; the notion that folk literature, Celtic or otherwise, teems with superbly original nature poetry is largely a fantasy of those who have read only a few picked specimens in anthologies.

NATURE

12. May-time

May-time, fair season, perfect is its aspect then; blackbirds sing a full song, if there be a scanty beam of day.

The hardy, busy cuckoo calls, welcome noble summer! It calms the bitterness of bad weather, the branching wood is a prickly hedge.

Summer brings low the little stream, the swift herd makes for the water, the long hair of the heather spreads out, the weak white cotton-grass flourishes.

... The smooth sea flows, season when the ocean falls asleep; flowers cover the world.

Bees, whose strength is small, carry with their feet a load reaped from the flowers; the mountain allures the cattle, the ant makes a rich meal.

The harp of the wood plays melody, its music brings perfect peace; colour has settled on every hill, haze on the lake of full water.

The corncrake clacks, a strenuous bard; the high pure waterfall sings a greeting to the warm pool; rustling of rushes has come.

Light swallows dart on high, brisk music encircles the hill, tender rich fruits bud ...

... The hardy cuckoo sings, the speckled fish leaps, mighty is the swift warrior.

The vigour of men flourishes, the glory of great hills is unspoiled; every wood is fair from crest to ground, fair each great goodly field.

Delightful is the season's splendour, winter's rough wind has gone; bright is every fertile wood, a joyful peace is summer.

A flock of birds settles . . .; the green field re-echoes, where there is a brisk bright stream.

A mad ardour upon you to race horses, where the serried host is ranged around; very splendid is the bounty of the cattle-pond, the iris is gold because of it.

A timid persistent frail creature sings at the top of his voice, the lark chants a clear tale – excellent May-time of calm aspect!

Irish; author unknown; ninth–tenth century.

13. The Coming of Winter

I have news for you; the stag bells, winter snows, summer has gone.

Wind high and cold, the sun low, short its course, the sea running high.

Deep red the bracken, its shape is lost; the wild goose has raised its accustomed cry.

Cold has seized the birds' wings; season of ice, this is my news.

Irish; author unknown; ninth century.

14. Winter Cold

Cold, cold, chill tonight is wide Moylurg; the snow is higher than a mountain, the deer cannot get at its food.

Eternal cold! The storm has spread on every side; each sloping furrow is a river and every ford is a full mere.

Each full lake is a great sea and each mere is a full lake; horses cannot get across the ford of Ross, no more can two feet get there.

64

The fishes of Ireland are roving, there is not a strand where the wave does not dash, there is not a town left in the land, not a bell is heard, no crane calls.

The wolves of Cuan Wood do not get repose or sleep in the lair of wolves; the little wren does not find shelter for her nest on the slope of Lon.

Woe to the company of little birds for the keen wind and the cold ice! The blackbird with its dusky back does not find a bank it would like, shelter for its side in the Woods of Cuan.

Snug is our cauldron on its hook, restless the blackbird on Leitir Cró; snow has crushed the wood here, it is difficult to climb up Benn Bó.

The eagle of brown Glen Rye gets affliction from the bitter wind; great is its misery and its suffering, the ice will get into its beak.

It is foolish for you – take heed of it – to rise from quilt and feather bed; there is much ice on every ford; that is why I say 'Cold!'

Irish; author unknown; eleventh century.

15. Winter

Keen is the wind, bare the hill, it is difficult to find shelter; the ford is marred, the lake freezes, a man could stand on a single stalk.

Wave after wave covers the shore; very loud are the outcries before the heights of the hill; scarcely can one stand up outside.

Cold is the bed of the lake before the tumult of winter; the reeds are withered, the stalks are broken, the wind is fierce, the wood is bare.

Cold is the bed of the fish in the shelter of the ice, the stag is thin, the reeds are bearded, short is the evening, the trees are bowed.

Snow falls, white is the surface, warriors do not go on their foray; cold are the lakes, their colour is without warmth.

Snow falls, white is the hoarfrost; idle is the shield on the old man's shoulder; very great the wind, it freezes the grass.

Snow falls on the top of the ice, the wind sweeps the crest of the close trees; fine is the shield on the brave man's shoulder.

Snow falls, it covers the valley; the warriors hasten to battle, I shall not go, a wound does not allow me.

Snow falls on the hillside, the horse is a prisoner, the cattle are lean; it is not like a summer day today . . .

Welsh; author unknown; eleventh century?

16. The Four Seasons

Once upon a time Athairne came on a journey in the autumn to the house of his foster-son Amhairghen, and stayed the night there; and was about to leave the next day. But Amhairghen said, to detain him:

'A good season for staying is autumn; there is work then for everyone before the very short days. Dappled fawns from among the hinds, the red clumps of the bracken shelter them; stags run from knolls at the belling of the deer-herd. Sweet acorns in the wide woods, corn-stalks around cornfields over the expanse of the brown earth. There are thorn-bushes and prickly brambles by the midst of the ruined court; the hard ground is covered with heavy fruit. Hazel-nuts of good crop fall from the huge old trees on dykes.'

Again he made to leave in the winter, but then Amhairghen said:

'In the black season of deep winter a storm of waves is roused along the expanse of the world. Sad are the birds of every meadow plain, except the ravens that feed on crimson blood, at the clamour of harsh winter; rough, black, dark, smoky. Dogs are vicious in cracking bones; the iron pot is put on the fire after the dark black day.'

Again he made to leave in the spring, but then Amhaírghen said:

'Raw and cold is icy spring, cold will arise in the wind; the ducks of the watery pool have raised a cry, passionately wail-ful is the harsh-shrieking crane which the wolves hear in the wilderness at the early rise of morning; birds awaken from meadows, many are the wild creatures from which they flee out of the wood, out of the green grass.'

Again he made to leave in the summer, and Amhairghen said, letting him do so:

'A good season is summer for long journeys; quiet is the tall fine wood, which the whistle of the wind will not stir; green is the plumage of the sheltering wood; eddies swirl in the stream; good is the warmth in the turf.'

Irish; author unknown; eleventh century.

17. A Storm at Sea

A great tempest on the ocean plain, bold across its high borders; the wind has arisen, wild winter has slain us; it comes across the great fierce sea, the spear of the wild winter season has overtaken it.

The deeds of the plain, the full plain of the ocean, have brought alarm upon our enduring host; but for something more momentous than all, no less, what is there more wonderful than this incomparable tremendous story?

When the wind sets from the east the mettle of the wave is roused; it desires to pass over us westwards to the spot where the sun sets, to the wild broad green sea.

When the wind sets from the north the dark stern wave desires to strive against the southern world, against the expanse of the sky; to listen to the swans' song.

When the wind sets from the west across the salt sea of rapid currents, it desires to pass over us eastwards to the Tree of the Sun to seize it, to the wide long distant sea.

When the wind sets from the south across the land of the Saxons of stout shields, the wave strikes the island of Scid, it has reached up to the headland of Caladh Ned with its mantled, grey-green cloak.

The ocean is full, the sea is in flood, lovely is the home of ships; the sandy wind has made eddies around Inbher na dá Ainmhech; the rudder is swift upon the wide sea.

It is not peaceful, a wild troubled sleep, with feverish triumph, with furious strife; the swan's hue covers them, the plain full of sea-beasts and its denizens; the hair of the wife of Manannán[1] is tossed about.

The wave with mighty fury has fallen across each wide dark river-mouth; wind has come, winter's fury has slain us, around Kintyre, around the land of Scotland; the flooded torrent gushes forth, mountainous and raging.

Son of God the Father of vast hosts, protect me from the horror of wild tempests! Righteous Lord of the Feast, only protect me from the mighty blast, from Hell with towering tempest!

Irish; author unknown; eleventh century.

18. The Hermit's Hut

. . . I have a hut in the wood, none knows it but my Lord; an ash tree this side, a hazel on the other, a great tree on a mound encloses it.

1. i.e. the sea; see Index.

Two heathery door-posts for support, and a lintel of honey-suckle; around its close the wood sheds its nuts upon fat swine.

The size of my hut, small yet not small, a place of familiar paths; the she-bird in its dress of blackbird colour sings a melodious strain from its gable.

The stags of Druim Rolach leap out of its stream of trim meadows; from them red Roighne can be seen, noble Mucraimhe and Maenmhagh.

A little hidden lowly hut, which owns the path-filled forest; will you go with me to see it?...

A tree of apples of great bounty, ..., huge; a seemly crop from small-nutted branching green hazels, in clusters like a fist.

Excellent fresh springs – a cup of water, splendid to drink – they gush forth abundantly; yew berries, bird-cherries ...

Tame swine lie down around it, goats, young pigs, wild swine, tall deer, does, a badger's brood.

Peaceful, in crowds, a grave host of the countryside, an assembly at my house; foxes come to the wood before it – it is delightful ...

Fruits of rowan, black sloes of the dark blackthorn; foods of whorts, spare berries ...

A clutch of eggs, honey, produce of heath-peas, God has sent it; sweet apples, red bog-berries, whortleberries.

Beer with herbs, a patch of strawberries, delicious abundance; haws, yew berries, kernels of nuts.

A cup of mead from the goodly hazel-bush, quickly served; brown acorns, manes of briar, with fine blackberries.

In summer with its pleasant, abundant mantle, with good-tasting savour, there are pignuts, wild marjoram, the cresses of the stream – green purity!

The songs of the bright-breasted ring-doves, a beloved movement, the carol of the thrush, pleasant and familiar above my house.

Swarms of bees, beetles, soft music of the world, a gentle humming; wild geese, barnacle geese, shortly before All Hallows, music of the dark torrent.

A nimble singer, the combative brown wren from the hazel bough, woodpeckers with their pied hoods in a vast host.

Fair white birds come, cranes, seagulls, the sea sings to them, no mournful music; brown fowl out of the red heather.

The heifer is noisy in summer, brightest of weather; not bitter or toilsome over the mellow plain, delightful, smooth.

The voice of the wind against the branchy wood, grey with cloud; cascades of the river, the swan's song, lovely music.

A beautiful pine makes music to me, it is not hired; through Christ, I fare no worse at any time than you do.

Though you delight in your own enjoyments, greater than all wealth, for my part I am grateful for what is given me from my dear Christ.

Without an hour of quarrel, without the noise of strife which disturbs you, grateful to the Prince who gives every good to me in my hut . . .

Irish; author unknown; tenth century

19. Arran

Arran of the many stags, the sea reaches to its shoulder; island where companies were fed, ridge where blue spears are reddened.

Wanton deer upon its peaks, mellow blaeberries on its heaths, cold water in its streams, nuts upon its brown oaks.

Hunting-dogs there, and hounds, blackberries and sloes of the dark blackthorn, dense thorn-bushes in its woods, stags astray among its oak-groves.

Gleaning of purple lichen on its rocks, grass without blemish on its slopes, a sheltering cloak over its crags; gambolling of fawns, trout leaping.

Smooth is its lowland, fat its swine, pleasant its fields, a tale you may believe; its nuts on the tips of its hazel-wood, sailing of long galleys past it.

It is delightful for them when fine weather comes, trout under the banks of its rivers, seagulls answer each other round its white cliff; delightful at all times is Arran.

Irish; author unknown; twelfth century.

20. The Hill of Howth

Delightful to be on the Hill of Howth, very sweet to be above its white sea; the perfect fertile hill, home of ships, the vine-grown pleasant warlike peak.

The peak where Finn[1] and the Fianna used to be, the peak where were drinking-horns and cups, the peak where bold Ó Duinn brought Gráinne one day in stress of pursuit.

The peak bright-knolled beyond all hills, with its hill-top round and green and rugged; the hill full of swordsmen, full of wild garlic and trees, the many-coloured peak, full of beasts, wooded.

The peak that is loveliest throughout the land of Ireland, the bright peak above the sea of gulls, it is a hard step for me to leave it, lovely Hill of delightful Howth.

Irish; author unknown; fourteenth century?

1. See Index.

21. Deirdre[1] Remembers a Scottish Glen

Glen of fruit and fish and pools, its peaked hills of loveliest wheat, it is distressful for me to think of it – glen of bees, of long-horned wild oxen.

Glen of cuckoos and thrushes and blackbirds, precious is its cover to every fox; glen of wild garlic and watercress, of woods, of shamrock and flowers, leafy and twisting-crested.

Sweet are the cries of the brown-backed dappled deer under the oak-wood above the bare hill-tops, gentle hinds that are timid lying hidden in the great-treed glen.

Glen of the rowans with scarlet berries, with fruit fit for every flock of birds; a slumbrous paradise for the badgers in their quiet burrows with their young.

Glen of the blue-eyed vigorous hawks, glen abounding in every harvest, glen of the ridged and pointed peaks, glen of blackberries and sloes and apples.

Glen of the sleek brown round-faced otters that are pleasant and active in fishing; many are the white-winged stately swans, and salmon breeding along the rocky brink.

Glen of the tangled branching yews, dewy glen with level lawn of kine; chalk-white starry sunny glen, glen of graceful pearl-like high-bred women.

> Irish; author unknown; fourteenth century?

22. The Ivied Tree-top

My little hut in Tuaim Inbhir, a mansion would not be more delightful, with its stars as ordained, with its sun, with its moon.

1. See no. 4.

It was Gobán[1] that has made it (that its tale may be told you); my darling, God of Heaven, was the thatcher who has thatched it.

A house in which rain does not fall, a place in which spears are not feared, as open as if in a garden without a fence around it.

Irish; author unknown; ninth century.

23. Suibhne the Wild Man in the Forest

Little antlered one, little belling one, melodious little bleater, sweet I think the lowing that you make in the glen.

Home-sickness for my little dwelling has come upon my mind, the calves in the plain, the deer on the moor.

Oak, bushy, leafy, you are high above trees; hazel-bush, little branchy one, coffer of hazel-nuts.

Alder, you are not spiteful, lovely is your colour, you are not prickly where you are in the gap.

Blackthorn, little thorny one, black little sloe-bush; water-cress, little green-topped one, on the brink of the blackbird's well.

Saxifrage of the pathway, you are the sweetest of herbs; cress, very green one; plant where the strawberry grows.

Apple-tree, little apple-tree, violently everyone shakes you; rowan, little berried one, lovely is your bloom.

Bramble, little humped one, you do not grant fair terms; you do not cease tearing me till you are sated with blood.

Yew, little yew, you are conspicuous in graveyards; ivy, little ivy, you are familiar in the dark wood.

Holly, little shelterer, door against the wind; ash-tree, baneful, weapon in the hand of a warrior.

1. The legendary miraculous builder.

Birch, smooth, blessed, proud, melodious, lovely is each entangled branch at the top of your crest.

Aspen as it trembles, from time to time I hear its leaves rustling, and think it is the foray . . .

If on my lonely journey I were to search the mountains of the dark earth, I would rather have the room for a single hut in great Glenn mBolcáin.

Good is its clear blue water, good its clean stern wind, good its cress-green watercress, better its deep brooklime.

Good its pure ivy, good its bright merry willow, good its yewy yew, better its melodious birch . . .

Irish; author unknown; twelfth century.

24. Suibhne Praises the Garbh

The cry of the Garbh, tunefully calling, that calls out where it meets the wave; great lovely schools of fish swimming by its brink.

I delight in my patient stay, watching the flood-tide fill the sandbanks; the mighty torrent of the great Garbh, and the sea-water thrusting it back.

It is pleasant to see how they wrestle, the flood-tide and the cold ebb; alternately they come, up and down every time.

I hear a strain of music in the Garbh, with its wintry clearness; I fall asleep at its loud murmur on a very cold night of ice.

The melodious birds of the shore, musical and sweet are their familiar voices; longing for them has seized me, for their chanting the Hours.

Sweet I think the blackbirds warbling, and to listen to Mass; short I think my stay on the ridge above Duradh Faithlenn.

At their sound I fall asleep on peaks and on tree-tops; the tunes which I hear are music to my soul.

The singing of psalms with psalm-purity at the Point of Ros Bruic which does not endure;[1] the roar of the brown stag belling from the slope of cold Erc.

The very cold sleep of a whole night, listening to the billowy sea, the multitudinous voices of the birds from the wood of Fidh Cuille.

The sighing of the winter wind, the noise of the storm in the oak-tree; the cold sheet of ice groans, breaking up at the cry of the Garbh . . .

Irish; author unknown; twelfth century?

25. To May and January

WELCOME[2], with your lovely greenwood choir, summery month of May for which I long! Like a potent knight, an amorous boon, the green-entangled lord of the wildwood, comrade of love and of the birds, whom lovers remember, and their friend, herald of nine score trysts, fond of exalted colloquies. Marry, it is a momentous thing that the faultless month of May is coming, with its heart set on conquering every green glen, all hot to assert its rank. A thick shade, clothing the highways, has draped every place with its green web; when the battle with the frost is over, and it comes like a close-leaved canopy over the meadow hedges, the paths of May will be green in the place of April, and the birds will celebrate for me their twittering service. There will come on the highest crest of the oak-trees the songs of young birds, and the cuckoo on the heights in every domain, and the warbling bird and the glad long day, and white haze after the wind covering the midst of the valley, and bright sky in the gay afternoon, and lovely trees, and grey gossamer, and many birds in the woods, and green leaves

1. Seems to refer to the fact that the place came soon afterwards to be called Tech Moling.
2. See Preface, p. 16 f.

on the tree branches; and there will be memories, Morfudd, my golden girl, and a manifold awakening of love. How unlike the black wrathful month which rebukes everyone for loving; which brings dismal rain and short days, and wind to strip the trees, and sluggishness and fearful frailty, and long cloaks, and hail showers, and rousing of the tides, and cold, and tawny floods in the brooks and full roaring in the rivers, and days angered and wrathful, and sky gloomy and chill with its darkness hiding the moon. May it get, I freely vow, a double share of harm for its surliness!

Welsh; Dafydd ap Gwilym, *c.* 1325–*c.* 1380.

26. *The Birch-wood Bower*

THE happy birch-wood is a good place to wait for my day-bright girl; a place of quick paths, green tracks of lovely colour, with a veil of shining leaves on the fine boughs; a sheltered place for my gold-clad lady, a lawful place for the thrush on the tree, a lovely place on the hillside, a place of green tree-tops, a place for two in spite of the Cuckold's wrath; a concealing veil for a girl and her lover, full of fame is the greenwood; a place where the slender gentle girl, my love, will come to the leafy house made by God the Father. I have found for the building a kind of warden, the nightingale of glorious song under the greenwood, in his fine tawny dress in the leafy grove; a symbol of woodland delight, a forester always in the copse guarding the tree-tops on the skirt of the slope. I shall make us a new room in the grove, fine and free, with a green top-storey of birches of lovely hue, and a summer-house and a fine bed, a parlour of the bright green trees, a glorious domain on the fringe of the green meadow. An enclosure of birches shall be maintained, with corner-seats in the greenwood; a chapel of the lovely branches would not displease me, of the leaves of the green hazels, the mantles of May. The fine trees shall be a solace, a soot-free house for us today; if my girl will come to my house, I will go to hers. 'Little grey-winged nightingale, you are my love-messenger in early May! Help me, there on the crest of the thicket, arrange a tryst between Morfudd and me.'

Welsh; attributed to Dafydd ap Gwilym, *c.* 1325–*c.* 1380

27. *The Snow*

I CANNOT sleep, I cannot leave the house, I am distressed because of it. There is no world, no ford, no hillside, no open space, no ground today. I won't be tempted out of my house into the fine snow, at the word of a girl. What a plague the thing is, feathers on one's gown that cling like the spume of fighting dragons! My excuse is that my clothes would be all as white as the clothes of a miller. After New Year's Day, it is no lie, everyone dresses in white fur; in the month of January, the first of the series, God makes us into hermits. God has whitewashed the black earth all around; there is no underwood without its white dress, there is no copse without its coverlet. Fine flour is the fur on every bough, flour of the sky like the flowers of April; a bitter cold sheet over the greenwood grove, a load of chalk flattening the wood, a mirage of wheaten flour, a mail coat vesting the level ground. The soil of the plough-land is a cold grit, a thick tallow on the face of the earth, a very thick shower of foam, fleeces bigger than a man's fist; throughout North Wales they made their way, they are white bees from Heaven. Whence can God raise up so great a plague? Where is there room for so many goose-feathers of the saints? Own brother to a heap of chaff, in its ermine shirt, the snow is skilled to leap the heather. The dust has changed to snowdrifts now, where once was bird-song and the narrow lanes. Does anyone know what sort of folk are spitting on the ground in the month of January? White angels it must be, no less, who are sawing wood up in Heaven; see, from the floor of the flour-loft they have raised the plank trap-door. An ephemeral silver dress of ice, quicksilver, coldest in the world, a cold mantle (too sad that it stays), the cement

A CELTIC MISCELLANY

of hill and dale and dyke, a thick steel coat, heavy as a landslide, a pavement greater than the sea's graveyard; a great fall it is upon my land, a pale wall reaching from sea to sea. Who dares cry shame upon it? It is like lead on the cloak! Where is the rain?

Welsh; attributed to Dafydd ap Gwilym, c. 1325–c. 1380.

28. The Mist

I MADE a perfect tryst with my slender lovely girl, we pledged ourselves to steal away – but my journey was all in vain. I went out early to wait for her, but a mist sprang up as night came on; a cloudy mantling made the road dark, as if I were in a cave; all trace of the sky was hidden and the empty mist rose to the heavens. Before I could step one pace on my journey not a spot of the land was to be seen any more; neither the birch-wood slope, nor the shore, the hills, the mountains, nor the sea. Woe to you, you great yellow mist, that you did not ebb for a while once you were made! Like a cassock you are of the grey-black air, a very sheet without an end, the blanket of yonder lowering rain, a black weft from afar, hiding the world; like a vapour from the ovens of Hell, the smoke of the world bred up from far off, the smoke of the ghost-fires of Hades, a thick mantle over this earth, the web of the spiders of the sky that fills every place like the high seas. Thick you are, and clammy, O father of the rain, its homestead and its mother; a loveless crop un-sunned, a pannier of sea-coal between the sun and me, a drizzling hurdle which brings night by day to me, a day like night – are you not graceless? Thick snow that covers the hill above, a land of grey frost, father of high-waymen! Strewn by the brisk snow of January, a bonfire-smoke from the great wide air; crawling, scattering hoarfrost up to the bare hills covered with brushwood and heather; an insubstantial flying sorcerer, wide home of the Fairy Folk, robe of the crag, fleece of the domed sky, cloud of the wandering planets, haze from the waves of the ocean; you are a sea from Hades, very great, ugly of hue and hideous, on the hill before me, a thick dark cloud down below. Stumbling, I turned aside into a wide swamp, a place like Hell, where a hundred grinning goblins were in every gully; I could not find, in that hellish marsh, a space not choked with tangled scrub. I shall not go trysting with my sweetheart again in the wide mist – I am too timid!

> Welsh; attributed to Dafydd ap Gwilym, *c.* 1325–*c.* 1380.

29. *The Stars*

BEFORE God, my lass, I must make my way from the groves of this year's May-time, down the goodly slope through the hillside woods, my fine-haired girl, before I can drink on the hill above and under the birch-trees see our bed. But my love is reckless and loudly boastful, and rashness will lead men astray. I spent a third of the night in great anxiety on a most miserable journey, to get a kiss from my generous sunny-hearted girl, since I had her consent. I crossed the highway, and became night-blind on the bare moor; last night it was, on a long winding pitch-black road, like Trystan looking for his white slender love. Many a damp long-backed ridgy field I travelled, toilsome and wide; I made my way through nine thickets and along beside ancient ruined walls, and thence to the stronghold of the goblins – loathesome mates! From the great green stronghold next I got among the bogs on the brow of the great mountain; the black headland lay dark in front of me, it was perplexing, as if I were locked in a dungeon when utterly betrayed in battle. I crossed myself, with a hoarse shriek, but all too late – it was cold comfort! I have heard (I grew horribly cold) a poem about how that dreadful pair with the scaly hides were covered in a golden cloth and put inside a stone vat.[1] Just so with me, by my ill fortune, stuck in that most deadly bog. I offered bail, vowing to go on a pilgrimage to

---

1. See no. 128, pp. 148–9.

Llanddwyn if I were brought out safe. The Son of Mary the Virgin, pleasant talisman of faith, does not sleep when it is time for high salvation; He saw how great was Ap Gwilym's plight, and God was merciful, He lit for me the rushlights of the Twelve Signs,[1] a thick shower to banish dire affliction. Proud and sudden, the stars came out for me, the cherries of the night; their glow was bright as sparks from the bonfires of seven saints. The flaming plums of the cheerless moon, the full fruits of the frosty moon, the moon's hidden glands, the kernels of fine weather are they, the light of the big nuts of the moon of the hue of our Father's sunny paths; like hailstones of the brilliant sun, the mirrors, the half-pennies of great God, lovely as red gold under the hoarfrost, the saddle-jewels of the hosts of Heaven. The sunshine has hammered shield-rivets into the sky, a cause of deep longing; skilfully they were driven in one by one, a throng in the wide pale sky; the swift wind cannot dislodge these sky-pegs from their peg-holes. Wide is their orbit, the wind does not wash them, they are embers of the mighty heavens; a set of pieces of shining make for diceing and backgammon, on the vast game-board of the sky; head-dress pins of the great firmament, our thoughts are all on them. Until last night, thank Heaven, I was never astray or late, or failed to keep my tryst; but praise to the pure light, like a bright path, the clover-flowers on Heaven's face, that came to my aid, though I was so late, like gilded frost, marigolds of the air. The wax candles of a hundred altars, at their long task in the wide sky, the well-formed rosary-beads of blessed God scattered from off their string, they showed me carefully the valley and the hill, the reward for all my folly, and the roads to Anglesey and my own road – all my desire, may God forgive it! Before I slept a wink, I came at day-break to my true-love's hall. I make no parade of my sufferings, but only say this to my generous girl: 'The keen-edged axe shall not be struck twice against the side of the rock!'

Welsh; attributed to Dafydd ap Gwilym, *c*. 1325–*c*. 1380.

1. Of the Zodiac.

30. *The Burial of the Poet, Dead for Love*

M y bright-shaped girl, with the brow like the lily, under
your web of golden hair, I have loved you with a strong
enduring worthy love – marry, is there any help for me?
I have not requited you for your treatment, for fear of your
family avenging its honour, but make in my distress a
bitter sighing for desire of you. Reckless beauty, white
lovely gem, if you slay me for this you shall be held guilty,
holy-relic of grace – beware, girl, the blood-price for me!
As for me, I shall be buried in a grave among the leaves of
the gay greenwood. Tomorrow I shall have my funeral
rites performed by the green birches, under the ash-tree
boughs; a white cere-cloth shall wrap me round, a bright
shroud of the summer clover; a coffin I'll have of the green
leaves to do me honour, to seek God's grace; the flowers of
the woods shall be the pall, and eight boughs shall make the
bier. A thousand seagulls from the sea shall come to carry
my bier; a host of fine trees, the field-mouse shall swear it,
my jewel of bright aspect, shall be my escort; and my
church the summer glade in the hillside copse, my dearest
girl. The two images, good to pray to, shall be two nightin-
gales among the leaves, and you may choose them; and
there, by the wheatfield, shall be altars of twigs and a
flower-pied floor, and a choir – the door will not be closed
indignantly, for the Cuckold does not know it. Grey-friars
too, who know not how to damn, though they know the
Latin tongue of birds and the best metre of grammar from
leafy books, shall be there in their fine habits; and the goodly
organ of the hayfield, and the continual sound of bells.
There among the birch-trees of Gwynedd the grave is made
ready for me, a fair green place, the climax of life's glory,
in St Nightingale's Church in the woods of song. On the
green trees shall the cuckoo sing, like an organ, Paternosters
and Hours cleverly, and psalms in antiphony, for my soul's
sake. Masses I shall get in the summer months, and sweet

greetings on visits of love. May God come to keep the appointed meeting with his poet in Paradise!

Welsh; attributed to Dafydd ap Gwilym, c. 1325–c. 1380.

31. The Poet's Arbour in the Birch-wood

GLOOMY am I, oppressed and sad; love is not for me while winter lasts, until May comes to make the hedges green with its green veil over every lovely greenwood. There I have got a merry dwelling-place, a green pride of green leaves, a bright joy to the heart, in the glade of dark green thick-grown pathways, well-rounded and trim, a pleasant paling. Odious men do not come there and make their dwellings, nor any but my deft gracious gentle-hearted love. Delightful is its aspect, snug when the leaves come, the green house on the lawn under its pure mantle. It has a fine porch of soft bushes; and on the ground green field clover. There the skilled cuckoo, amorous, entrancing, sings his pure song full of love-longing; and the young thrush in its clear mellow language sings glorious and bright, the gay poet of summer; the merry woodland nightingale plies incessantly in the green leaves its songs of love-making; and with the daybreak the lark's glad singing makes sweet verses in swift outpouring. We shall have every joy of the sweet long day if I can bring you there for a while, my Gwenno.

Welsh; Iolo Morgannwg; 1747–1827.

32. To a Birch-tree Cut Down, and Set Up in Llanidloes for a Maypole

LONG are you exiled from the wooded slope, birch-tree, with your green hair in wretched state; you who were the majestic sceptre of the wood where you were reared, a green veil, are now turned traitress to the grove. Your precinct was lodging for me and my love-messenger in the short nights of May. Manifold once (ah, odious plight!) were the carollings in your pure green crest, and in your bright green house I heard every bird-song make its way; under your spreading boughs grew herbs of every kind among the hazel saplings, when your dwelling-place in the wood was pleasing to my girl last year. But now you think no more of love, your crest above remains dumb; and from the green meadow and the upland, where your high rank was plain to see, you have gone bodily and in spite of the cost to the town where trade is brisk. Though the gift of an honourable place in thronged Llanidloes where many meet is good, not good, my birch, do I think your rape nor your site nor your habitation. No good place is it for you for putting out green leaves, there where you make grimaces. Every town has gardens with leafage green enough; and was it not barbarous, my birch, to make you wither yonder, a bare pole by the pillory? If you had not come, at the time of leaves, to stand in the centre of the dry crossroads, though they say your place is a pleasant one, my tree, the skies of the glen would have been the better. No more will the birds sleep, no more will they sing in their shrill note on your fair gentle crest, sister of the dusky wood, so incessant will be the hubbub of the people around your tent – a cruel maiming! and the green grass will not grow beneath you, for the trampling of the townsmen's feet, any more than it grew on the wind-swift path of Adam and the first woman long ago.[1] You were made, it seems, for huckstering, as you stand there like a market-woman; and in the cheerful babble at the fair all will point their fingers at your suffering, in your one grey shirt and your old fur, amid the petty merchandise. No more will the bracken hide your urgent seedlings, where your sister stays; no more will there be mysteries and secrets shared, and shade, under your dear eaves; you will not conceal the April primroses, with their gaze directed upwards; you will not think now to inquire,

1. i.e. when driven out of Eden into the desert.

fair poet tree, after the birds of the glen. God! Woe to us, a cramped chill is on the land, a subtle dread, since this helplessness has come on you, who bore your head and your fine crest like noble Tegwedd of old. Choose from the two, since it is foolish for you to be a townsman, captive tree: either to go home to the lovely mountain pasture, or to wither yonder in the town.

Welsh; Gruffydd ab Addaf ap Dafydd, fl.*c.* 1340–*c.* 1370.

33. *The Mansion of the Woods*

'A Welsh ballad to the air: *Aboute the Banck of Elicon.*'[1]

They have sent forth their cry, the loquacious lads, yesterday they heard it under the green trees, pure and churchlike, three lifetimes to the gentle laureate poets – the linnet from the brake, the blameless nightingale, solemn and celestial; the pure-toned thrush, sweet rascal; the blackbird, he whose zeal is greater; and the woodlark soaring wantonly, catching the skylark's tune; singing, scattering so much fancy, so gay, so fresh, the accent of true passion.

Not far is the grove, with notes unceasing, the April grove, thick with the primrose, a place of fair song and of daisies; a dell of clover in May-Day vigour, in its green dress with true abundance, filled with joy; the flowers on the hawthorn tips, the slender birch in its green leafage. Fine is the fountain, lovely the place where it wells up under the saplings – the bright water, the limpid water, a place of fair well-being, a place to sleep, a place to learn whole tunes of melody.

I would have all pleasures in my dwelling, I would sing 'The Gentle Girl of Gwynedd' in gay harmonious music, and 'The Irish Girl, Comely Elir', 'The Horned Oxen', 'The Maiden's Laughter',[2] all in the mansion of the bright greenwood; singing loud of the glad fallows, with the birds

1. In English.   2. Apparently names of Welsh airs.

intermingling, singing auspiciously a snatch to the Lord, a golden course of fame and glory; tunings, songs, some modulations, fancies, change of voices, in the countless woodland halls.

Many are the tree-tops of the far-seen woods, many the tree-trunks of deep timber; and many there the bright tunes of praise, in this place of many a full sweet-stringed prelude; they bring many a panegyric to the tenants of the meadows; every fowl is in full voice, every tree in its pale green tunic, every plant with all its virtue, every bird with a laureate poet's mouth. It is not sick, but sprightly, with heavenly notes; not troubled, but treble; and Venus owns the mansion.

It is good for men to be entertained, it is good for girls to be amused, it is good for lads on Sunday.[1] How fair this is, no offence to the aged, fair for the young, no cause of anger, in the greenwood and green meadows. How fair true God the Father made it, his gifts and grace so glorious! How fair each tone, how fair each turn, so it all be guiltless! The earth so fine, early with wheat, and the woodland such sweet land, a place of grace abounding.

Welsh; Edmund Price, Archdeacon of Merioneth; 1544–1623.

34. To the Sun

Greeting to you, sun of the seasons, as you travel the skies on high, with your strong steps on the wing of the heights; you are the happy mother of the stars.

You sink down in the perilous ocean without harm and without hurt, you rise up on the quiet wave like a young queen in flower.

Scottish Gaelic; traditional folk prayer.

1. In this verse the Archdeacon is arguing against the Puritans and Sabbatarians.

35. To the New Moon

Greeting to you, new moon, kindly jewel of guidance! I
bend my knees to you, I offer you my love.

I bend my knees to you, I raise my hands to you, I lift up
my eye to you, new moon of the seasons.

Greeting to you, new moon, darling of my love! Greeting
to you, new moon, darling of graces.

You journey on your course, you steer the flood-tides, you
light up your face for us, new moon of the seasons.

Queen of guidance, queen of good luck, queen of my love,
new moon of the seasons!

Scottish Gaelic; traditional folk prayer.

36. To the Moon

Greeting to you, gem of the night!

Beauty of the skies, gem of the night!

Mother of the stars, gem of the night!

Foster-child of the sun, gem of the night!

Majesty of the stars, gem of the night!

Scottish Gaelic; traditional folk prayer.

37. The Mountain Stream

Mountain stream, clear and limpid, wandering down
towards the valley, whispering songs among the rushes – oh,
that I were as the stream!

Mountain heather all in flower – longing fills me, at the
sight, to stay upon the hills in the wind and the heather.

Small birds of the high mountain that soar up in the healthy wind, flitting from one peak to the other – oh, that I were as the bird!

Son of the mountain am I, far from home making my song; but my heart is in the mountain, with the heather and small birds.

Welsh; John Ceiriog Hughes; 1833–87.

38. Winter and Summer

All the sweetness of nature was buried in black winter's grave, and the wind sings a sad lament with its cold plaintive cry; but oh, the teeming summer will come, bringing life in its arms, and will strew rosy flowers on the face of hill and dale.

In lovely harmony the wood has put on its green mantle, and summer is on its throne, playing its string-music; the willow, whose harp hung silent when it was withered in winter, now gives forth its melody – Hush! Listen! The world is alive.

Welsh; Thomas Telynog Evans; 1840–65.

LOVE

NOTE

It is remarkable that love in itself plays a very small part in early Celtic literature. Almost without exception the theme is used only as the motive of a tale; so in no. 39 Oenghus falls in love with the fairy woman, but the story is concerned merely with the way in which he finally succeeds in winning her. So also with the tale of Trystan and Esyllt, no. 40, or of Deirdriu and Noísiu, no. 7. There is no attempt to dwell on the subject for its own sake, or to enter into the personal, psychological, side of the question. In fact, in the early literatures there is practically no real love *poetry*, but only tales about love affairs. Love poetry as such first appears in any quantity under the influence of foreign romantic movements. We have it foreshadowed in the rare poems to women which belong to the Welsh bardic material of the twelfth to fourteenth centuries, and developed fully in the fourteenth and subsequent centuries in the poems of Dafydd ap Gwilym (cf. nos. 41–3) and his followers. Here the influence of French and Provençal romantic love-poetry, and perhaps of the songs of the Goliards, is clear, probably having reached Wales through the medium of the Normans; though there may well be other, native, factors involved, as some think. It is found next in Ireland in the fourteenth to seventeenth centuries, where in bardic poetry some of the poets, and perhaps more often their noble patrons themselves, composed love poems (e.g. nos. 44–57) whose fundamental inspiration derives from the French love-lyric, as Robin Flower has shown (*The Irish Tradition*, Oxford, 1947). In both Irish and Welsh the medieval Continental lyric appears in strangely transmuted forms, yet the foreign origin is there. It is impossible to render the elegance of these Irish and Scottish-Irish poems, since it depends so much on metre, syntax, and word order, on the carpentry of poetry as well as the content.

With the last group here, nos. 58–69, we are on quite different ground. These are folk songs, or near folk songs, and that is an international art which has its own conventions, of which a simple kind of romantic love is one; and hence these poems are not so much purely Celtic as Celtic expressions of an international literary genre. Certain folk-song conventions well known in other literatures are evident in some of these, for instance the conversation between mother and daughter in no. 69.

LOVE

39. The Dream of Oenghus

Oenghus[1] was asleep one night, when he saw a girl coming
towards him as he lay on his bed. She was the loveliest that
had ever been in Ireland. Oenghus went to take her hand,
to bring her to him in his bed. As he looked, she sprang
suddenly away from him; he could not tell where she had
gone. He stayed there till morning, and he was sick at heart.
He fell ill because of the apparition which he had seen and
had not talked with. No food passed his lips. She was there
again the next night. He saw a lute in her hand, the sweetest
that ever was; she played a tune to him, and he fell asleep
at it. He remained there till morning, and that day he was
unable to eat.

He passed a whole year while she visited him in this way,
so that he fell into a wasting sickness. He spoke of it to no
one. So he fell into wasting sickness, and no one knew what
was wrong with him. The physicians of Ireland were
brought together; they did not know what was wrong with
him in the end. They went to Fínghin, Conchobhar's
physician, and he came to him. He would tell from a man's
face what his illness was, and would tell from the smoke
which came from the house how many people were ill in it.

He spoke to him aside. 'Ah, unhappy plight!' said
Fínghin, 'you have fallen in love in absence.' 'You have
diagnosed my illness,' said Oenghus. 'You have fallen into
a wretched state, and have not dared to tell it to anyone,'
said Fínghin. 'You are right,' said Oenghus; 'a beautiful
girl came to me, of the loveliest figure in Ireland, and of
surpassing aspect. She had a lute in her hand, and played it
to me every night.' 'No matter,' said Fínghin, 'it is fated

1. Son of the Daghdhae (see below).

93

for you to make a match with her. Send someone to Boann,[1] your mother, that she should come to speak with you.'

They went to her, and Boann came then. 'I am attending this man,' said Fínghin, 'a serious illness has fallen upon him.' They told his story to Boann. 'Let his mother take care of him,' said Fínghin; 'a serious illness has fallen on him. Have the whole of Ireland scoured to see if you may find a girl of this figure which your son has seen.'

They spent a year at this. Nothing like her was found. Then Fínghin was called to them again. 'No help has been found in this matter,' said Boann. Said Fínghin, 'Send to the Daghdhae,[2] that he should come to speak with his son.' They went to the Daghdhae, and he came back with them. 'Why have I been summoned?' 'To advise your son,' said Boann; 'it is as well for you to help him, for it is sad that he is perishing. He is wasting away. He has fallen in love in absence, and no help is to be found for him.' 'What is the use of talking to me?' said the Daghdhae, 'I know no more than you do.' 'More indeed,' said Fínghin, 'you are the king of the fairy hills[3] of Ireland. Send someone to Bodhbh, king of the fairy hills of Munster; his knowledge is noised throughout all Ireland.'

They went to him. He welcomed them. 'Welcome to you, men of the Daghdhae,' said Bodhbh. 'That is what we have come for.' 'Have you news?' said Bodhbh. 'We have; Oenghus the son of the Daghdhae has been wasting away for two years.' 'What is the matter with him?' said Bodhbh. 'He has seen a girl in his sleep. We do not know where in Ireland is the girl whom he has seen and loved. The Daghdhae bids you seek throughout Ireland for a girl of that figure and aspect.' 'She shall be sought,' said Bodhbh, 'and let me have a year's delay to find out the facts of the case.'

They came back at the end of the year to Bodhbh's house at the Fairy Hill beyond Feimhen. 'I went round the whole

1. The nymph of the Boyne.
2. 'The Good God', chief of the pagan Irish gods.
3. 'The hollow hills', barrows in which the gods or fairies dwelt.

of Ireland until I found the girl at Loch Bél Dragon, at Crotta Cliach,'[1] said Bodhbh. They went to the Daghdhae, and they were made welcome. 'Have you news?' said the Daghdhae. 'Good news; the girl of that figure which you described has been found. Bodhbh bids you let Oenghus come away with us to him, to know whether he recognizes the girl when he sees her.'

Oenghus was taken in a chariot to the Fairy Hill beyond Feimhen. The king had a great feast ready for them, and he was made welcome. They were three days and three nights at the feast. 'Come away now,' said Bodhbh, 'to know whether you recognize the girl when you see her. Even if you do recognize her, I have no power to give her, and you may only see her.'

They came then to the lake. They saw three times fifty grown girls, and the girl herself among them. The girls did not reach above her shoulder. There was a chain of silver between each couple; and a necklet of silver round her own throat, and a chain of refined gold. Then Bodhbh said, 'Do you recognize that girl?' 'I do indeed,' said Oenghus. 'I can do no more for you,' said Bodhbh. 'That is no matter, then,' said Oenghus, 'since it is she that I saw; I cannot take her this time. Who is this girl, Bodhbh?' said Oenghus. 'I know, truly,' said Bodhbh, 'she is Caer Ibhormheith, daughter of Ethal Anbhuail from the fairy hill of Uamhan in the land of Connaught.'

Then Oenghus and his people set off for their own country. Bodhbh went with him, and talked with the Daghdhae and Boann at Bruigh Maic ind Óaig.[2] They told them their news, and told how she seemed, in figure and aspect, just as they had seen; and they told her name and the name of her father and grandfather. 'We feel it to be discourteous that we cannot content you,' said the Daghdhae. 'What you should do, Daghdhae,' said Bodhbh, 'is to go to Ailill and Medhbh, for they have the girl in their province.'

The Daghdhae went till he reached the lands of Connaught, with three score chariots in his company. The king

1. The Galtee mountains. 2. New Grange mound, on the Boyne.

and queen made them welcome. They spent a full week banqueting round the ale after that. 'What has brought you?' said the king. 'You have a girl in your country,' said the Daghdhae, 'and my son has fallen in love with her, and has become sick. I have come to you to find out whether you may give her to the lad.' 'Who?' said Ailill. 'The daughter of Ethal Anbhuail.' 'We have no power over her,' said Ailill and Medhbh, 'if we had she should be given him.' 'This would be good – let the king of the fairy hill be summoned to you,' said the Daghdhae.

Ailill's steward went to him. 'You have been ordered by Ailill and Medhbh to go to speak with them.' 'I will not go,' said he, 'I will not give my daughter to the son of the Daghdhae.' That is told to Ailill; 'He cannot be made to come, but he knows why he is summoned.' 'No matter,' said Ailill, 'he shall come, and the heads of his warriors shall be brought with him.' At that, Ailill's household troops and the men of the Daghdhae rose up against the fairy hill, and overran the whole hill. They brought out three score heads, and the king, so that he was in captivity at Cruachu.

Then Ailill said to Ethal Anbhuail, 'Give your daughter to the son of the Daghdhae.' 'I cannot,' said he, 'her magic power is greater than mine.' 'What is this great magic power she has?' said Ailill. 'Easily told; she is in the shape of a bird every other year, and in human shape the other years.' 'What year is she in the shape of a bird?' said Ailill. 'It is not for me to betray her,' said her father. 'Off with your head, unless you tell us!' said Ailill. 'I will not hold out any longer,' said he; 'I will tell you,' said he, 'since you are so persistent about her. Next All Hallows she will be at Loch Bél Dragon in the shape of a bird, and wonderful birds will be seen with her there, there will be three times fifty swans around her; and I have made preparations for them.' 'I do not care, then,' said the Daghdhae; 'since you know her nature, do you bring her.'

Then a treaty was made between them, between Ailill and Ethal and the Daghdhae, and Ethal was let go. The Daghdhae bade them farewell and came to his house and told his news to his son. 'Go next All Hallows to Loch Bél Dragon, and call her to you from the lake.' The Mac Óag[1] went to Loch Bél Dragon. He saw three times fifty white birds on the lake with their silver chains, and curls of gold about their heads. Oenghus was in human shape on the brink of the lake. He called the girl to him. 'Come to speak to me, Caer!' 'Who calls me?' said Caer. 'Oenghus calls you.' 'I will go, if you will undertake on your honour that I may come back to the lake again.' 'I pledge your protection,' said he.

She went to him. He cast his arms about her. They fell asleep in the form of two swans, and went round the lake three times, so that his promise might not be broken. They went away in the form of two white birds till they came to Bruigh Maic ind Óaig, and sang a choral song so that it put the people to sleep for three days and three nights. The girl stayed with him after that.

Irish; author unknown; eighth (?) century original.

40. How Trystan Won Esyllt

At that time Trystan ap Trallwch and Esyllt the wife of March ap Meirchion went wandering as outlaws in the wood of Celyddon, with Golwg-Hafddydd as her handmaid, and Y Bach Bychan as his page carrying pasties and wine, together with them; and a bed of leaves was made for them. And March ap Meirchion went to Arthur to complain of Trystan and to entreat him to avenge the insult against him, since he was more nearly related to Arthur than Trystan was; for March ap Meirchion was cousin to Arthur, and Trystan was only a cousin's son. 'I will go, I and my bodyguard,' said Arthur, 'to seek for you either satisfaction or its refusal.' And then they surrounded the wood of Celyddon.

Now it was a magic property in Trystan that whoever drew blood from him died, and whoever he drew blood

1. i.e. Oenghus.

from died. And when Esyllt heard the noise and the talking on all sides of the wood, she trembled in Trystan's arms, and Trystan asked her why she trembled, and she said it was through fear for him ... And then Trystan rose up and took his sword in his hand, and made for the fight as fast as he could, till he met March ap Meirchion, and March ap Meirchion said, 'Even though I kill him, it would cause my own death.' And at that the other men said, 'Shame on us if we bestir ourselves for him.' And then Trystan went through the three armies unharmed ...

Then March ap Meirchion went to Arthur again, and complained to him that he had got neither compensation for his wife nor its refusal. 'I know no counsel for you but this,' said Arthur, 'to send harpers to play to him from far off; and after that to send poets and eulogists to praise him and turn him from his anger and his wrath.' And this they did. And after that Trystan called the minstrels to him and gave them handfuls of gold and silver; and then the chief peacemaker was sent to him, that is, Gwalchmai ap Gwyar ...

And then Trystan and Gwalchmai went to Arthur, ... and there Arthur made peace between him and March ap Meirchion. And Arthur spoke with the two of them in turn, but neither of them was willing to be without Esyllt; and then Arthur awarded her to the one of them while the leaves should be on the trees and to the other while the leaves should not be on the trees, the married man to choose. And he chose when the leaves should not be on the trees, because the nights would be longest at that time, and Arthur told that to Esyllt. And she said, 'Blessed be the judgment and he who gave it;' and Esyllt sang this *englyn*:

> 'There are three trees that are good,
>   holly and ivy and yew;
>   they put forth leaves while they last,
>   And Trystan shall have me as long as he lives.'

And so March ap Meirchion lost Esyllt for good.

Welsh; author unknown; fifteenth–sixteenth century.

41. Secret Love

I HAVE learned the art of carrying on an active love affair,
elegant and daring, in secret; and how best in fine words
to come to tell love stealthily. Such is the pining of a furtive
lover that secret love is best for one while we are among
crowds – I and my girl, a wanton couple – and no one
suspects that we talk together through this our amorous
speech. Once, with our trust in each other, we were able to
carry on our dalliance for a long time; but now our measure
is more restrained, to a mere three words, because of
scandal. Plague on him of the wicked tongue, may he be
fettered with infirmity and be the butt of ill fortune, for
casting words of slander on the two of us, whose names were
unblemished. Very glad was he if he got warning, while we
used to make love undiscovered. I haunted the home of
my golden girl – I adored the leaves – while the green leaves
lasted. It was delightful for us a while, my girl, to pass our
lives under the same birch-grove; to dally in the secluded
wood – the more delightful; together to lie hidden, together
to range the sea-shore, together to linger at the woodland's
edge, together to plant birch-trees (oh happy labour!),
together to entwine the shapely plumage of the boughs,
together with my slender girl to tell of love, together to
look out on the lonely fields. A blameless art it is for my
girl to walk the wood together with her lover, to keep
countenance, to smile together, to laugh together lip to lip,
together to lay us down by the grove, together to shun the
crowd, together to lament our lot, together to pass time
pleasantly, together to drink mead, together to make love,
together to lie, together to maintain our true stealthy
passion – but no more shall be told of this.

Welsh; Dafydd ap Gwilym, *c.* 1325–*c.* 1380.

42. The Jealous Husband

DAILY I am tormented by love of her who will not believe
me. I have given great and enduring love to a girl like

99

Esyllt,[1] the Jealous Husband's treasure. It is not easy, it is endless chagrin, for a poor man to gain the tall fair girl – blessings on her head! I cannot win my lass of the slender brows, her gaoler will not allow her to be won; for if she goes to some public place – fairest creature – the blackguard comes to escort her. Let not the Jealous Husband, however vile, try to keep her for himself. The Jealous Husband, sour fellow, does not love playfulness, and has set his face against sport; he does not love the nightingale nor the cuckoo, nor the linnet any more than he would a fox, nor the trusty darksome wood, nor singing songs, nor the nuts of the hazel. To mark the tune of the small birds of May, and the green leaves, would only distress him. The talk of the thrush and the proud nightingale under the greenwood is what he hates. It is odious to the feeble Jealous Husband to hear the hounds and the harp-string; and well I know it, the Jealous Husband, boorish and livid, is odious to me. Let the fair girl whose brow is as white as dice desert her mate within six months, and *I* shall love her henceforward; I love none but married women. I hope to see the measuring rod, and clay and stones being shovelled over the husband of my fair young lass, and a load of sods for eight hired oxen piled upon the churl; from my own estate I would freely give him his own length of earth. The girl shall be seen to be mine, and Esyllt's husband under his crosses in the hollow grave, in his hempen shroud, with the yellow alder coffin for his horse. My God, if I could get my way he should not live a month with my consent. *She* does not care if he is buried, and if he's buried *I* should not care either.

Welsh; attributed to Dafydd ap Gwilym, *c.* 1325–*c.* 1380.

43. *The Seagull*

FAIR seagull on the seething tide, like snow or the white moon in colour, your beauty is unsullied, like a patch of sunlight, gauntlet of the sea; lightly you skim the ocean

1. cf. no. 40.

wave, swift proud bird whose food is fish. You would ride at anchor over there side by side with me, sea lily, of the hue of glossy paper, like a nun, on the crest of the sea flood. To the maid of chaste reputation (she shall get fame far and wide) go, seagull, to the corner of the castle wall, and look to see her of the colour of Eigr[1] on the bright rampart. Tell her my words according, and let her choose me – go to the girl. If she is alone, make bold to greet her, be tactful with the dainty girl, and you shall have pay; tell her that I, her courtly, polished lad, cannot live unless I win her. I love her, the patron of all my vigour; good sirs, neither hale Merlin with the flattering lips, nor Taliesin,[2] ever loved a fairer than she! She is a Venus for whom men compete, under her copper-coloured hair, of perfect form, most neat and comely. Ah seagull, if you come to see the cheek of her who is loveliest in Christendom, unless I get a gentle answer the girl will be my destruction.

Welsh; Dafydd ap Gwilym, *c.* 1325–*c.* 1380.

44. In Defence of Women

Woe to him who speaks ill of women! it is not right to abuse them. They have not deserved, that I know, all the blame they have always had.

Sweet are their words, exquisite their voice, that sex for which my love is great; woe to him who does not scruple to revile them, woe to him who speaks ill of women!

They do no murder nor treachery, nor any grim or hateful deed, they do no sacrilege to church nor bell; woe to him who speaks ill of women!

Certain it is, there has never been born bishop nor king nor great prophet without fault, but from a woman; woe to him who speaks ill of women!

1. The mother of King Arthur.   2. See Index.

They are thrall to their own hearts, they love a man slender and sound – it would be long before they would dislike *him*. Woe to him who speaks ill of women!

An old fat greybeard, they do not desire a tryst with him – dearer to them is a young lad, though poor. Woe to him who speaks ill of women!

Irish; Earl Gerald Fitzgerald; fourteenth century.

45. *To Her Hair*

Woman with the veil of hair, I see all through your soft-threaded locks that which would put to shame the hair of Absalom son of David.

In your bright-braided tresses there is a flock of cuckoos in the pangs of labour, a bird-flock which does not sing and yet torments all men.[1]

Your long, fair crown of ringlets spreads all round your lovely eyes, so that the keen crystal eyes look like jewels set in a ring.

This is a new adornment you have got, whatever land it came from – no ring set on your hand, but a hundred rings round your throat.

The soft yellow tresses go curling round the straight neck; there is many a circlet round that throat – it is a haltered thrall indeed![2]

Irish; author unknown; fifteenth–sixteenth century?[2]

46. *Reconciliation*

Do not torment me, woman, let us set our minds at one; you to be my mate in Ireland, and let us put our arms around each other.

1. See Notes.   2. See Notes.

Set your strawberry-coloured mouth against my mouth,
O skin like foam; stretch your lime-white rounded arm
about me, in spite of all our discord.

Slender graceful girl, be no longer inconstant to me; admit
me, soft slender one, to your bed, let us stretch our bodies
side by side.

As I have given up, O smooth side, every woman in Ireland
for your sake, do you give up every man for me, if it is
possible to do so.

As I have given to your white teeth passion which is
beyond reckoning, so you should give to me your love in the
like measure.

Irish; author unknown; fifteenth–sixteenth century?

47. *The Lover's Doubts*

SHE: 'How does my only love now, of all the men in the
world? It causes me keen anguish to hear that it goes hard
with you.'

HE: 'Till now I had thought that you loved me, fresh youthful girl, until I heard a different tale.'

SHE: 'Do not be too grieved with me, for the tale you have
heard is not true; I had no share in devising anything that
you have heard.'

HE: 'Fair and exquisite queen, I recognize that you do not
love me; but in requital for my desire I have been killed
by you at last.'

SHE: 'The men of the world together, though I had killed
them all by now, it is you, noble gentle one, that I should
kill the last.'

HE: 'Though you assert your love loudly, woman with
your fine lady's looks, it was but love in payment for love
until you proved your want of love.'

SHE: 'I would rather be in your company, since it was to you I gave my first love, than that I should have the kingdom of this world without you.'

HE: 'If all you say is true, let us not be cast down. How small is the cure for my sickness! Now I shall be nothing but glad.'

Irish; author unknown; fifteenth–sixteenth century?

48. Do Not Torment Me, Woman

Do not torment me, woman, for your honour's sake do not pursue me; whether my life be long or short do not torment me through all eternity.

I entreat a boon of you, O bright face and fair hair, do not torment me any more wherever I may be.

I have not spent night nor day, whether I have been here long or no, but that you have been beside me – slow-pacing foot and flowing hair!

O cheek like embers, do not come in dreams to seek me in my sleep; and when I wake, stately and sweet one, come not to drive me to distraction.

Though it is hard for me to tell you, let me see you no more, do not destroy me; since I cannot escape from death, come not between me and the love of God.

You, my one love of all creation, mild sapling whom God has taught, woe to you who have so slain me, when I never slew any man.

Alas, you had no need, O gentle bough with crystal eye; if you were witless as I am I would not slay you like this ever.

I know not what to do, your mouth like red berries has consumed me; my blessing on you, but for God's sake do not torment me, get you aside!

Sweet-smelling mouth and skin like flowers, many a man comes courting you; O woman, love of my soul, do not pursue me of all men.

Irish; author unknown; fifteenth–sixteenth century?

49. The Hidden Love

There is no sickness so woeful as secret love; och, long have I thought it! I shall refrain from declaring it no longer, my secret love for my slender gentle girl.

I have fallen in love, and I cannot hide it, with her spreading hair, with her calm mind, with her narrow eyebrow, her blue-grey eye, her even teeth, her soft face.

I have given also, though I do not admit it, the love of my soul to her smooth throat, to her melodious voice, to her sweet-tasting lips, to her snowy bosom, to her pointed breast.

Och, my grief! I cannot forget my melancholy love for her white body, for her straight smooth foot, for her narrow sole, for her slow smile, for her soft hand.

Though there has not been known before devotion like mine to her beyond all, there is not, there will not be, and there has not been a woman who more cruelly stole my love.

Irish; author unknown; fifteenth–sixteenth century?

50. Take Those Lips Away

Keep your kiss to yourself, white-toothed young virgin! In your kiss I find no taste; keep your lips away from me.

A kiss far sweeter than honey I got from a married woman for love; I shall not find, till Doomsday, taste in another kiss after that.

Until I see that one herself, through the will of the One Son of God of grace, I shall love no woman, old nor young, since *her* kiss is as it is.

Irish; author unknown; fifteenth–sixteenth century?

51. Trust No Man

A false love is the love of men – woe to the woman who does their will! Though their fine talk is sweet, their hearts are hidden deep within.

Do not believe their secret whisper, do not believe the close squeeze of their hands, do not believe their sweet-tasting kiss; it is through their love that I am sick.

Do not believe, and I shall not, one man in the world after the fate of all of us; I heard a story yesterday – ah God, it torments me cruelly!

They would offer silver and gold, they would offer treasure too; they would offer lawful marriage to a woman – till morning comes.

Not me alone have they deceived, many a one has been tricked before by the inconstant love of men; och, woe to her who has gone my way!

Irish; author unknown; fifteenth–sixteenth century?

52. Happy for You, Blind Man!

Happy for you, blind man, who see nothing of women! Ah, if you saw what I see you would be sick even as I am.

Would God I had been blind before I saw her curling hair, her white-flanked splendid snowy body; ah, my life is distressful to me.

I pitied blind men until my peril grew beyond all sorrow, I have changed my pity, though pitiful, to envy; I am ensnared by the maid of the curling locks.

Alas for him who has seen her, and alas for him who does not see her every day; alas for those trapped in her love, and alas for those who are set free!

Alas for him who goes to meet her, and alas for him who does not meet her always, alas for him who was with her, and alas for him who is not with her!

Irish; Uilliam Ruadh; sixteenth–seventeenth century?

53. Hate Goes Just as Far as Love

Woman so full of hate for me, by St MacDuach,[1] do you not recall that night when we were together, side by side, woman, you and I?

If you remembered, woman, how, while the sun lessened its heat, you and I were once – but is this not to say enough?

Or do you remember, O tender palm, long foot, smooth side, red lips, and breast like flowers, how you laid your arm under my head?

Or do you remember, O sweet shape, when it was you said to me that God who made heaven had not formed a man dearer to you than me?

But I remember once I had your love, as now I have your hate – why more? O skin like flowers, for hate goes just as far as love.

If I could show to everyone a woman who loves a man under the sun (and never will this be so, till Doom), let him not himself believe it true.

Irish; author unknown; fifteenth–sixteenth century?

54. The Blackthorn Pin

This blackthorn pin should not be in the cloak on that white breast while there were still, sweet red-lipped Mór, but one golden brooch in Ireland.

1. See Index

It is not right to put in that cloak less than a brooch of fine white bronze, or a marvellous brooch of goldsmith's work, my sweet-spoken red-lipped Mór.

Soft amber-coloured hair, steadfast graceful girl who have deceived no man, it is not fitting to put a blackthorn pin in your chequered yellow cloak.

Peerless red cheek, nut of my heart, you should not put in your yellow tartan cloak but a brooch such as Gaibhneann[1] might have made.

Crimson cheek that I love, your green cloak has seldom been without a gold brooch for a single hour, but for this hour, O bright hand!

> Irish; Fearchar Ó Maoilchiaráin; fourteenth century.

55. The Indifferent Mistress

She is my love, she who most torments me, dearer for making me thus sick than she who would make me well.

She is my dear, she who has left no strength in me, she who would not sigh when I am dead, she who would not even lay a stone on my grave.

She is my treasure, she whose eye is green as grass, she who would not put her arm under my head, she who would not lie with me for gold.

She is my secret, she who will not speak to me, she who will not listen to anything under the sun, she who will not cast an eye upon me.

Sad is my plight, strange how long I take to die; she who would not come near me, on my oath, she is my love.

> Irish; author unknown; fifteenth–sixteenth century?
> 1. The Irish Vulcan.

56. Parted Lovers

There is a youth comes wooing me; oh King of Kings, may he succeed! would he were stretched upon my breast, with his body against my skin.

If every thing were as I wish it, never should we be far divided, though the hint is all too little, since he does not see how the case is.

It cannot be, till his ship comes home, a thing most pitiful for us both; he in the east and I in the west, so that our desires are not fulfilled again.

> Scottish–Irish; Isobel, Countess of Argyll; fifteenth century.

57. The Message of the Eyes

A long farewell to yesternight! soon or late though it passed away. Though I were doomed to be hanged for it, would that it were this coming night!

There are two in this house tonight from whom the eye does not hide its secret; though they are not lip to lip, keen, keen is the glancing of their eyes.

Silence gives meaning to the swift glancing of the eyes; what matters the silence of the mouth when the eye makes a story of its secret?

Och, the scandalmongers won't allow a word to cross my lips, O slow eye! Learn then what my eye declares, you in the corner over there: –

'Keep this night for us tonight; alas that we are not like this for ever! Do not let the morning in, get up and put the day outside.'

Ah, Mary, graceful foster-mother, Thou Who art chief over all poets, help me, take my hand – a long farewell to yesternight!

> Scottish–Irish; Niall Mór MacMhuirich; early seventeenth century.

58. She's the White Flower of the Blackberry

She's the white flower of the blackberry, she's the sweet flower of the raspberry, she's the best herb in excellence for the sight of the eyes.

She's my pulse, she's my secret, she's the scented flower of the apple, she's summer in the cold time between Christmas and Easter.

Irish; traditional folk song; before 1789.

59. How Glad Are the Small Birds

How glad are the small birds that rise up on high, and chirp to each other on one tree bough! Not so with me and my hundred thousand times dear one, we are far from each other when every day dawns.

She is whiter than the lily, she is fairer than beauty, she is sweeter than the fiddle, she is brighter than the sun, her dignity and grace are better than all those; and God in heaven, free me from my torment!

Irish; traditional folk song; before 1831.

60. Young Lad of the Braided Hair

Young lad of the braided hair, with whom I was a while together, you went this way last night and did not come to see me; I thought it would do you no harm if you came to seek me, and that a little kiss of yours would give me comfort if I were in the midst of a fever.

If I had wealth and money in my pocket I should have a short-cut made to the door of my love's house, hoping to God I should hear the sweet sound of his shoe; and for many a day I have not slept but in hopes for the taste of your kiss.

And I thought, my sweetheart, that you were the moon and

the sun, and I thought after that that you were the snow on the mountain, and I thought after that that you were lightning from God, or that you were the Pole Star going before and behind me.

You promised me silk and satin, hoods and shoes with high heels, and you promised after that that you would follow me swimming; I am not like that, but like a hawthorn in the gap[1] every evening and every morning watching my mother's house.

Irish; traditional folk song.

61. At the Fiddlers'

At the fiddlers', at Christmas, I first met my heart's love; lovingly we sat down together and we began courting.

From that time for seven years my love and I met often, and she promised me with her false tongue she would never desert me.

Sunday evening before Ash Wednesday I went to see my heart's love; she raised her hands over my hands that she would marry none but me.

I came home with a glad heart, and nothing to cause me grief; the first news I heard on Ash Wednesday morning was that my love was married to another.

My curse on the wench, and I courting her for so many days; when she found she had no love for me she could have refused me in time.

I will not give her my ill curse or malediction, I will not pray for bad luck to come her way, but may she bring happiness to her friends, though she has made nothing but a mock of me.

But for the walnut tree that never spoke no other witness had I; now my love has proved false and I am left alone.

1. A proverbial expression meaning a poor substitute.

I shall go to the St Patrick's Day festival,[1] I shall dress myself like any young lad, I shall pass by my love in the midst of the fair, I shall not let on that I see her.

I shall be standing before the fair, I shall get my choice of many a one; but she who has married her false deceiver cannot exchange or alter.

The great long road that I had to walk and the steep slope to make me tired, I could not sit down to take my rest but that I would think always of my heart's love.

O that the great wind would blow that I might hear from my love, and that she might come to me over the high mountains; we would meet each other beside the shore.

Gladly, gladly I would go to meet her if I knew that my love was there; O, gladly, gladly would I sit down beside her with my arm as a pillow to her under her head.

O that the great sea would dry up to make a way, that I might go through; the snow of Greenland shall grow red like roses before I can forget my love.

Manx; traditional folk song.

62. He Whose Hand and Eye Are Gentle

To tell you from the start, I have lost him whose hand and eye are gentle; I shall go to seek him of the slender eyebrows, wherever the most generous and fairest of men may be.

I shall go to the midst of Gwent without delaying, to the south I shall go to search, and charge the sun and the moon to seek for him whose hand and eye are gentle.

I shall search through all the lands, in the valley and on the mountain, in the church and in the market, where is he whose hand and eye are gentle.

1. 17 March.

Mark you well, my friends, where you see a company of gentlemen, who is the finest and most loving of them; that is he whose hand and eye are gentle.

As I was walking under the vine the nightingale bade me rest, and it would get information for me where was he whose hand and eye are gentle.

The cuckoo said most kindly that she herself was quite well informed, and would send her servant to inquire without ceasing where was he whose hand and eye are gentle.

The cock-thrush advised me to have faith and hope, and said he himself would take a message to him whose hand and eye are gentle.

The blackbird told me she would travel to Cambridge and to Oxford, and would not complete her nest till she found him whose hand and eye are gentle.

I know that he whose speech is pleasant can play the lute and play the organ; God gave the gift of every music to him whose hand and eye are gentle.

Hunting with hawks and hounds and horses, catching and calling and letting slip, none loves a slim dog or a hound like him whose hand and eye are gentle.

Welsh; popular song; sixteenth century.

63. The Black-haired Lad

I'll not climb the brae and I'll not walk the moor, my voice is gone, and I'll sing no song; I'll not sleep an hour from Monday to Sunday while the Black-haired Lad comes to my mind.

It is a pity I was not with the Black-haired Lad on the brow of the hill under the rainstorms, in a small hollow of the wilds or in some secret place; and I'll not take a grey-beard while you come to my mind.

I would drink the health of the Black-haired Lad from the black water of the bog as gladly as wine; though I am without fortune many come to woo me, and I'll not take a greybeard while you come to my mind.

I should love to have a claim on the Black-haired Lad, to get him in marriage if God should will it; I would go with you to Holland, ochone, it were my wish; and I'll not take a greybeard while you come to my mind.

Coaxing of mouth you are, the love of the girls you are, a drinker of wine you are, and a generous man ungrudging; you are manly and hard-striking, a hunter on the moors; and I'll not take a greybeard while you come to my mind.

Restless is my sleep since Wednesday morning, troubled is my heart unless You help me, God; last night I slept on an ill bed, soon I shall grow grey, while the Black-haired Lad comes to my mind.

My handsome black lad, though all think you reckless I would marry you without consent of my kindred; I would fare far with you through dells and wild places, while the Black-haired Lad comes to my mind.

My fine black lad, I will not leave you, if I saw you in company I'd choose you above all the rest; though I saw five thousand, sure, I'd think you the best of them, while the Black-haired Lad comes to my mind.

Scottish Gaelic; traditional folk song; before 1776.

64. The Laundress's Sweetheart

As I was washing under the end of Cardigan bridge with a battledore of gold in my hand and my sweetheart's shirt under it,

A man met me on a horse, broad-shouldered, swift and proud, and he asked me if I would sell the shirt of the lad I loved the best.

And I said I would not sell it for a hundred pounds nor a hundred loads, nor for the fill of two hillsides of wethers or white sheep, nor for the fill of two meadows of oxen with their yokes, and for the fill of St David's churchyard of herbs trodden out; that was the way I would keep the shirt of the lad I loved the best.

Welsh; popular poem; sixteenth century.

65. Mary, My Darling

Mary, my darling, my curly-haired sweetheart, do you remember how we walked in the dew on the green grass, flower of the fragrant apple-trees, of the yellow nuts and the berries? I have never abandoned your love, though I am sadly pleading with you.

Dear love, my secret, come to me some night when my family are in bed, and we may talk together, my arm round your little waist, affirming my tale to you; and it was your love, girl, which took the sight of the Kingdom of God from me.

If my brother knew my complaint and my trouble, if he knew, by the Pope, he would be very grieved that my dearest love should desert me and be betrothed to another; and she is my bright love, whom I'll never hate, beyond all the fair women of Ireland.

Fair precious girl, you are the desolation of my heart, with your curling yellow hair, sun of the women of Ireland; you have injured me, and alas, there's no cure for it, and why should I wish to seek you, my dear love, when I should not win you?

If I were a fisherman yonder by Howth, and Mary of the white throat were a salmon in Lough Erne, gladly and merrily should I go to seek her, and should catch in my net the sun of the women of Ireland.

If I were like a wild duck with the wide hills before me, and the sight of Heaven to save my soul, I should bring the girl home if I were able, and should let her father be seeking her a while.

If I were in London as chief of the Guard, and had leave from the French to sail my ship on the sea, though I were worth five thousand pounds every day I would give her my estate, my choice is Mary.

Get up, boy, and set off on your pony, and every way you go be asking for my dear love; she was betrothed to me while I was yet a child, and I thought her nine times sweeter than the cuckoo or the organ.

Irish; traditional folk song.

66. Kate of Garnavilla

Have you ever been in Garnavilla, or have you seen in Garnavilla the gay young girl of the golden locks, my sweetheart, Kate of Garnavilla?

She's whiter than the swan on the pool, or the snow on the crest of the bending bough; her kiss is sweeter than the dew on the rose, my sweetheart, Kate of Garnavilla.

Her song is more tuneful than the blackbird or thrush, or the nightingale on the willow bough; like a ship in sail on the mistless wave I see my sweet in Garnavilla . . .

Irish; Edward Lysaght; 1763–1810.

67. The Ballad of Marivonnik

The first day of November the English landed at Dourduff.

At Dourduff when they had landed they stole a young girl.

They stole a pretty girl to carry her with them to their ship.

Marivonnik was her name, she was born at Plougasnou.

Marivonnik said, as she passed by her father's door:

'Farewell my mother, farewell my father, my eyes will never see you again.

'Farewell my brother, farewell my sister, I shall never see you on earth.

'Farewell my relatives and friends, I shall never see you in the world.'

Marivonnik wept, and found no one to comfort her.

She found no one to comfort her, but the big Englishman, he did so.

'Marivonnik, do not weep, for you shall not lose your life;

'For you shall not lose your life, but as to your honour, I do not speak.'

'I value my honour more than all the ships on the sea.

'Sir Englishman, tell me, shall I be subjected to any but you?'

'To me myself, to my cabin boy, to my sailors whenever they wish.

'To my sailors whenever they wish; there are a hundred and one of them.'

'Sir Englishman, tell me, will you let me walk on the bridge?'

'Yes, walk on the ship's bridge, but beware of drowning.'

Marivonnik said, as she walked on the deck:

'Virgin Mary, tell me, shall I drown myself or not?

'For your sake, Virgin Mary, I would not wish to offend you.

'If I go in the sea, I shall be drowned, and if I stay I shall be killed.'

She obeyed the Virgin, she threw herself headlong in the sea.

A little fish from the bottom of the sea brought Marivonnik to the top of the water.

The English lord said then to his sailors there:

'Sailors, sailors, hasten, I will give you five hundred crowns!'

The English lord said to Marivonnik that day:

'Marivonnik, you have done wrong; if you had wished you should have been my wife.'

Breton; traditional ballad.

68. Fhir a' Bhàta

From the highest hill I look out often
to try if I can see the Boatman;
come you today, or come you tomorrow?
And sad am I if you come never.

Oh, the Boatman, *na hóro eile*,
oh, the Boatman, *na hóro eile*,
oh, the Boatman, *na hóro eile*,
my long farewell wherever you go to.

My heart within is bruised and broken
and from my eyes the tears are streaming;
come you tonight, shall I expect you,
or shut the door with heavy sighing?

Oh, the Boatman, *etc.*

Often then I ask the boatmen
if they have seen you, if you're in safety;
but every one of them is saying
that if I love you I am foolish.

Oh, the Boatman, *etc.*

Though they said that you are fickle
that did not lessen my fondness for you;
you are my dreaming in the night time,
and in the morning I'm seeking for you.

Oh, the Boatman, *etc.*

All my friends unceasing tell me
that I must forget your image,
but their advice is just as idle
as to dam the tide when it is flowing.

Oh, the Boatman, *etc.*

Scottish Gaelic; traditional folk song.

69. *The Slender Lad*

As I was walking in the fields last Tuesday of all days, in a hollow under the quiet wood I heard two talking together. I drew nearer to them until I was at the very place, and who should be there conversing but my sweetheart with her mother.

'My dear daughter, here you are by me with your hands free, your costume fair, handsomely set up – and I mean to marry you off. You shall mount your horse, my delicate maiden, with obsequious grooms to curry it, and you shall have worldly wealth of yellow gold and bright silver at your side.'

'Though I had a share in the lands of India, the silks of Persia, the gold of Peru, I prefer the lad I love, and shall stand true to him.' 'Oh, is it so? and that's your purpose? Then you shall make your bed among thorns; unless you mark my words, it will be a bitter play if you trust yourself to the Slender Lad.'

'To the Slender Lad I will trust myself, mother, to tell you true; I shall leave wealth to misers, and trust myself to him who is the flower of the shire, with his white face and his yellow hair, and in his cheeks are two roses – happy is the girl who sleeps the night in his arms.

If my love has gone far over the seas, if he has gone and left me on the shore, yet may St David[1] give him good fortune and 'guide him in every place. I shall not weep, no, nor fret, nor cry out after him; for if it is so fated for me, my dear love will come back yet.

With his own hand he wrote a letter, and on its back was a wax seal, and nothing broke my heart like reading it morning and evening. In it there are three letters which are taking away my looks and figure; and unless he comes back to spell them out they will bring me down to my grave.'

Welsh; folk poem; seventeenth century?

1. Patron saint of Wales.

EPIGRAM

NOTE

The word is used here in the sense which it has when we speak of the *epigrams* of the Greek Anthology; that is, short poems of a few lines in which some single idea or image is expressed in carefully picked and completely adequate words, to give the maximum of compression and force. Indeed, a number of the verses given here remind one strongly of the Greek Anthology; nos. 70 and 73 for instance recall the dedicatory epigrams written for wayside fountains.

It is these verses which show most of all the sense of style which was noted by Matthew Arnold as characteristic of Celtic literature. In the sixth of his lectures *On the Study of Celtic Literature* he said: 'Style, in my sense of the word, is a peculiar recasting and heightening, under a certain condition of spiritual excitement, of what a man has to say, in such a manner as to add dignity and distinction to it.' He quoted from the Old Irish verses on the death of Oenghus the Culdee, and added, 'a Greek epitaph could not show a finer perception of what constitutes propriety and felicity of style in compositions of this nature.' This heightened spiritual excitement, and this propriety and felicity, together with a striking power of compression and clarity, are regular features in certain kinds of Celtic poetry.

The examples translated here fall into three groups. One is Irish, mostly early, consisting in almost every case of single quatrains which are found scribbled in the margins of manuscripts, or are quoted as illustrative examples in medieval tracts on metre. They may well be taken from longer poems in some cases, for all we know; but if so, they still have the rounded self-completeness characteristic of the 'epigram'. A second group is Welsh, being traditional poems, usually single verses, sometimes more than one, preserved mostly in seventeenth-century manuscripts and belonging probably to the sixteenth and seventeenth centuries. These *penillion* are anonymous, and largely the work of folk or popular poets, expressing the universally felt human emotions; their metre is very simple. Third, there are a number of examples here of the Welsh *englyn*, a much more complicated metre (usually only one verse makes the poem, but not necessarily), which might be said to have been created for the purpose of epigram, so well does the metric arrangement favour compression and pointed contrast. The *englyn* in various forms goes back to the earliest times, but its use in single verses for the expression of epigram is specially characteristic of the period from the eighteenth century to the present; and all the examples here belong to that age. The *englynion* on the court of Ifor Hael, no. 126, might well have been included under Elegy; but the epigrammatic treatment is so marked that they are given in the present group, particularly as some of the epigrams in the Greek Anthology are quite as long.

EPIGRAM

70. *The Wayside Fountain*

Cenn Escrach of the orchards, a dwelling for the meadow bees, there is a shining thicket in its midst, with a drinking-cup of wooden laths.

Irish; author unknown; ninth–tenth century?

71. *The Blackbird's Song*

The little bird has given a whistle from the tip of its bright yellow beak; the blackbird from the yellow-tufted bough sends forth its call over Loch Loígh.

Irish; author unknown; eighth–ninth century?

72. *The Hermit Blackbird*

Ah, blackbird, it is well for you where your nest is in the bushes; a hermit that clangs no bell, sweet, soft, and peaceful is your call.

Irish; author unknown; eleventh–twelfth century?

73. *The Spring*

Spring of Tráigh Dhá Bhan, lovely is your pure-topped cress; since your crop has become neglected your brook-lime is not allowed to grow.

Your trout out from your banks, your wild swine in your wilderness; the stags of your fine hunting crag, your dappled red-breasted fawns.

Your nuts on the crest of your trees, your fish in the waters
of your stream; lovely is the colour of your sprigs of arum
lily, green brook in the wooded hollow! . . .

Irish; author unknown; twelfth century.

74. Heather Flowers

Gaily they grow, the quiet throng, fair gems of the realm of
sun and wind, the hanging bells of the high crags, flowers
of the rocks, like cups of honey.

Welsh englyn; Eifion Wyn; 1867–1926.

75. Mountain Lakes

The calm green lakes are sleeping in the mountain shadow,
and on the water's canvas bright sunshine paints the picture
of the day.

Welsh englyn; Gwilym Cowlyd; 1827–1905.

76. Sliabh gCua

Sliabh gCua, haunt of wolves, rugged and dark, the wind
wails about its glens, wolves howl around its chasms; the
fierce brown deer bells in autumn around it, the crane
screams over its crags.

Irish; author unknown; ninth century?

77. Merioneth

Living paradise of flowers, land of honey, land of violets
and blossoms, land rich in crops, land of nut-bushes, and
dear land of the hills.

Welsh englyn; Machreth; nineteenth century.

78. The Pole Star

A lamp are you, above all stars of night, to guide sailors in the dusk; lovely is your colour, sweet maid, standing in the doorway of the Pole.

Welsh *englyn*; Carnelian; 1834–1910.

79. Night

The dim night is silent, and its darkness covers all Snowdon; the sun in the bed of the sea, and the moon silvering the flood.

Welsh *englyn*; Gwallter Mechain; 1761–1849.

80. Night and Morning

One stormy night when I went out to walk on the shores of the Menai, silently pondering, the wind was high and the white waves were wild, and the sea was dashing over the walls of Carnarvon.

But next day in the morning when I went out to walk to the shores of the Menai, all there was at peace; the wind was quiet and the sea was gentle, and the sun was shining on the walls of Carnarvon.

Welsh; traditional verses; seventeenth century?

81. The Wind

It has broken us, it has crushed us, it has drowned us, O King of the star-bright Kingdom; the wind has consumed us as twigs are consumed by crimson fire from Heaven.

Irish; author unknown; eighth–ninth century

82. The Storm

Cold is the night in the Great Moor, the rain pours down, no trifle; a roar in which the clean wind rejoices howls over the sheltering wood.

Irish; author unknown; eighth–ninth century?

83. Thick Snow

A thick cloak as high as the houses in the glen, an aerial tallow freezing the valley, a crop of frost up the Berwyn, a covering like white salt.

Welsh *englyn*; Huw Morus; 1622–1709.

84. The Snowfall

White flour, earth-flesh, a cold fleece on the mountain, small snow of the chill black day; snow like a platter, bitter cold plumage, a softness sent to entrammel me.

White snow on the cold hill above has blinded me and soaked my clothes. By the blessed God! I had no hope I should ever get to my house.

Welsh *englynion*; Gwerfyl Mechain; fifteenth century.

85. Flood-tide

Look before you to the north-east at the glorious sea, home of creatures, dwelling of seals; wanton and splendid, it has taken on flood-tide.

Irish; attributed to 'Finan'; ninth century?

86. *Autumn*

The whole land, every dale and glen, weeps its long sorrow after the graceful summer; no tree-top can do more, nor weep leaves after that.

Welsh *englyn*; Thomas Nicholson; nineteenth century.

87. *Winter Has Come*

Winter has come with scarcity, lakes have flooded their sides, frost crumbles the leaves, the merry wave begins to mutter.

Irish; author unknown; ninth century?

88. *Women's Tongues*

I've read that in some way there came eight parts of speech into the world, and that the women (much good may it do them!) went off with seven of them between them.

Welsh; traditional verse; seventeenth century?

89. *Women's Hats*

Three things that are wondrous high – Cader Idris in the north there, Plinlimmon's crest, the far-seen mountain, and a girl whose hat's of the new fashion.

Welsh; traditional verse; seventeenth century?

90. *The Proud Lady*

Madam, you need not have reproached me that my horse is loaned to me; for they say all through the village that I could take a loan of *you*.

Welsh; traditional verse; seventeenth century?

91. The Twig and the Root

What need for you to be so angry that someone else should like me? Though the wind may shake the twig, one needs a pick to get the root up.

Welsh; traditional verse; seventeenth century?

92. Love Gives Wings

Long the road and wide the mountain from Cwm Maw-ddwy to Trawsfynydd, but where a lad's desires may lead him the hill seems a descent.

Welsh; traditional verse; seventeenth century?

93. Her Light Step

There's my darling merry star, flower of the parish of Llangeinwen; beneath her foot the grass no more bends than does a rock beneath a bird's foot.

Welsh; traditional verse; seventeenth century?

94. Like the Birch-tree

Slender and exquisite like the birch-tree, of shape as sweet as the fine clover, of colour as fair as a summer morning, she is the type of the glory of all lands.

Welsh; traditional verse; seventeenth century?

95. Lovelier than the Sun

Lovely is the sun's smile as it rises in its full brilliance, lovely are the moon's smiles at night, more lovely is my darling's cheek.

The moon is pretty on the waves, the stars are pretty on a bright night, but neither stars nor moon are half so pretty as my darling.

Welsh; traditional verse; seventeenth century?

96. *Red and White Roses*

There's my sweetheart on the hill, the red rose and the white; the red rose drops its petals, but the white rose is my sweetheart.

Welsh; traditional verse; seventeenth century?

97. *Promiscuity*

I do not know with whom Edan will sleep, but I do know that fair Edan will not sleep alone.

Irish; author unknown; ninth century?

98. *Dream and Reality*

I thought, if only I could marry I should have nothing but song and dancing; what did I have, though, after marriage, but to rock the cradle and hush the baby?

Welsh; traditional verse; seventeenth century?

99. *The End of the Day*

With the night the house grows dark, with the night comes candle light, with the night comes the end of play, and with the night comes Daddy home.

Welsh; traditional verse; seventeenth century?

100. *The Boorish Patron*

I have heard that he does not give horses for songs of praise; he gives what is natural to him – a cow.

Irish; author unknown; ninth century?

101. *Finn's Generosity*

If the brown leaves were gold that the wood lets fall, if the white wave were silver, Finn would have given it all away.

Irish; author unknown; twelfth century.

102. *Weariness of Body and Weariness of Spirit*

Weariness of the legs after some active deed is better than apathy and weariness of spirit; weariness of spirit lasts for ever, weariness of the legs lasts only for an hour.

Scottish Gaelic; author unknown; fifteenth–sixteenth century?

103. *How Happy Are the Wild Birds*

How happy are the wild birds, they can go where they will, now to the sea, now to the mountain, and come home without rebuke.

Welsh; traditional verse; seventeenth century?

104. *Quando Ver Venit Meum?*

The sun rises when morning comes, the mist rises from the meadows, the dew rises from the clover; but oh, when will my heart arise?

Welsh; traditional verse; seventeenth century?

105. Sorrow

My heart is as heavy as a horse that climbs the hill; in seeking to be merry, I cannot for my life. My poor shoe pinches in a place you do not know, and many an anxious thought is breaking my heart.

Welsh; traditional verse; seventeenth century?

106. Woe Is Me that I Ever Was Born

Woe is me that I ever was born and my father and mother reared me, that I did not die with the milk of the breast before reaching the age for love!

Welsh; traditional verse; seventeenth century?

107. Old Age Comes not Alone

'Old age comes not alone' – it comes with sighs and lamentation, and with long waking now, and with a long sleep after.

Welsh *englyn*; John Morris Jones; 1864–1929.

108. Old Age and Death

I must travel through feebleness on the same road as my fathers – the weary tedious hours draw near me, and the long night.

Welsh *englyn*; Robert ap Gwilym Ddu; 1767–1850.

109. Life's Uncertainty

Whether morning, whether evening, whether by land or by sea, though I know I shall die, alas, I know not when.

Irish; author unknown; ninth century?

110. Thoughts of Death

When a man is past forty, though he flourishes like the trees in leaf, the sound of a vault being opened makes his face change.

Welsh; traditional verse; seventeenth century?

111. Stealthy Death

Death comes unannounced, abruptly he may thwart you; no one knows his features, nor the sound of his tread approaching.

Welsh *englyn*; Glasfryn; nineteenth century.

112. Not Divided in Death

Oh, my heart has no peace from my endless yearning; Lord God, at my death grant that we may lie in one grave!

Welsh *englyn*; author unknown; nineteenth century.

113. On the Tomb

I shall not go to my bed tonight, my love is not in it; I shall lie on the gravestone – break, if you must, my poor heart.

There is nothing between him and me tonight but earth and coffin and shroud; I have been further many a time, but never with a heavier heart.

Welsh; traditional verses; seventeenth century?

114. The Lover's Grave

I walked in the churchyard where a hundred bodies lie; I set my foot on my sweetheart's grave, I felt my poor heart leap.

Welsh; traditional verse; seventeenth century?

115. For a Grave at Trawsfynydd

I'm helpless now, and if they call me home I cannot answer; for the black cold bare dank earth of Trawsfynydd covers my face.

Welsh *englyn*; David Jones of Llangwyfen; eighteenth century.

116. Epitaph on a Little Girl

The sorrows and sins of life I did not see; do not weep for me. I am cured of all sicknesses, and in my grave – happy am I!

Welsh *englyn*; Dafydd Ionawr; 1751–1827.

117. Everyman's Epitaph

Into his grave, and he is gone, no more talk about him; earth's crop, which generation by generation slips away into oblivion.

Welsh *englyn*; Ioan Arfon; 1828–81.

118. On Two Shipwrecked Sailors

They were driven on our shores, in a sad plight, on the bier of the waves; the Lord Himself knows their names, He will come one day to raise them both.

Welsh *englyn*; Gwilym Berw; 1854–1926.

119. The Praises of God

It is folly for any man in the world to cease from praising Him, when the bird does not cease and it without a soul but wind.

Irish; author unknown; eleventh century.

120. Christ before Pilate

How strange to see Him, on a false charge, in Roman hands, questioned by a vile worm; and judgement passed before Man on God.

Welsh *englyn*; Robert ap Gwilym Ddu; 1767–1850.

121. A Vain Pilgrimage

Coming to Rome, much labour and little profit! The King whom you seek here, unless you bring Him with you you will not find Him.

Irish; author unknown; ninth century.

122. The Monk's Mistress

The sweet little bell that is rung on a windy night, I would rather go to meet it than to meet a wanton woman.

Irish; author unknown; ninth century?

123. On Mael Mhuru the Poet

The choice earth has not covered, there will not come to the towers of Tara, Ireland of the many fields has not enfolded a man like the pure gentle Mael Mhuru.

There has not drunk bravely of death, there has not reached the fellowship of the dead, the cultivated earth has not closed over a sage more wonderful than he.

Irish; author unknown; 887.

124. Dinas Bran

Englyn and harp and harp-string and the lordly feasts, all these have passed away; and where the nobility of Gwynedd used to be the birds of night now reign.

Welsh *englyn*; Taliesin o Eifion; 1820–76.

125. Imperial Caesar Dead and Turned to Clay

The world has laid low, and the wind blows away like ashes Alexander, Caesar, and all who were in their trust; grass-grown is Tara, and see Troy now how it is – and the English themselves, perhaps they too will pass!

Irish; author unknown; seventeenth–eighteenth century.

126. The Court of Ifor Hael

The court of Ifor Hael,[1] how mean the sight, where it lies in ruins among the alders! The thorns and blighted thistles own it all, and brambles now, where was magnificence.

There are no poets there, nor bards, nor cheerful banquet-tables, nor gold, among its walls; nor largesse and the generous lord to give it.

For Dafydd, that skilled singer, what cold grief to lay Ifor in the clay! The pathways where once song was heard are the haunts of the owl.

1. See Notes.

For all their glory, short is the fame of lords, both their grandeur and their ramparts pass away; it is a strange place for pride to make its home – in the dust!

Welsh *englynion*; Evan Evans; 1731–88.

'CELTIC MAGIC'

NOTE

The phrase 'Celtic magic' arises from a misconception and has led to further misconceptions. It derives from the Romantic response to Macpherson's *Ossian* (though the actual term was coined by Matthew Arnold); and it is owing mainly to Yeats, AE, and the other writers of the 'Celtic Revival', one of the final forms of expression of the Romantic Movement, that the idea is still so commonly accepted in our own day. This question has already been discussed in negative terms, p. 19. Positively, though it is true that Celtic literature is unquestionably much occupied with tales of magic and the supernatural, the spirit and treatment are quite different from what is generally understood by 'Celtic magic'. The translations given here are a fair selection, and the unprejudiced reader can see for himself that there is nothing in them of the mystic, esoteric quality regularly attributed to the Celtic literatures by those who do not know them. The magic which we do find is the magic of the folk-tale; the world of these stories is an ordinary human one, with this difference – that in this world any supernatural event may occur without incongruity because, just as in the folk-tale, that distinction between natural and supernatural which is the consequence of civilized thought has not yet been clearly drawn. So the extraordinary experiences of Mael Dúin and his companions (no. 132) are told in the most straightforward way conceivable, as though they were as normal as Cinderella's pumpkin. Of course it all creates a sense of wonder and delight, and was intended to do so, but so does the tale of Cinderella – and the *Odyssey* and the travel tales of Sir John Mandeville, some of which might easily have come out of Mael Dúin's story. Yet no one has thought of seeing 'Celtic magic' in Cinderella and the *Odyssey* and Mandeville. The only real difference between the Celtic tales and those of Cinderella and Mandeville in respect of the super-natural is that often the Celtic story-tellers had a vastly greater power of inventiveness and imagination and descrip-tion, and a much more subtle sense of the uncanny.

There is one genre which may seem to give some colour to the Yeatsian concept of Celtic literature, namely the stories of the fairy people and the Earthly Paradise, involv-ing the belief in the existence of a race of fortunate beings who are immortal, ever beautiful, ever happy, and ever young, to whom men are nothing but 'the Dead', whereas they themselves are 'the Living' (cf. nos. 127, 144). But again, there is nothing of the characteristics of Yeats's 'Celtic Twilight' about these people; they are not the pale, languishing creatures of the pre-Raphaelite imagination, living in a half-lit world of inexpressible mysteries, any more than are the inhabitants of the Greek Elysium or For-tunate Isles; on the contrary, they behave like ordinary humans, who it happens are lucky enough to possess certain supernatural blessings which mortal men lack, and are surrounded with all kinds of wonders, clearly described in the high sunlight of the Celtic vision.

The last three passages, nos. 138–40 (and parts of no. 135), belong really to the sphere of the medieval Latin marvel, but the treatment is irrepressibly Celtic all the same.

127. The Adventure of Conle

Conle the Redhaired, a son of Conn of the Hundred Battles, was with his father one day on the heights of Uisnech, when he saw a woman[1] in a strange dress. Conle said, 'Where have you come from, woman?' The woman replied, 'I have come from the Lands of the Living, where there is neither death nor sin nor transgression. We enjoy everlasting feasts without their needing to be served. We have goodwill without strife. We live in a great fairy hill, whence we are called the People of the Fairy Hills.' 'Who are you speaking to?' said Conn to his son, for no one saw the woman except Conle alone. The woman replied, 'He speaks to a young beautiful woman of noble race, who expects neither death nor old age. I have fallen in love with Conle the Redhaired, and I summon him to the Plain of Delights, where Boadhagh is king everlasting, a king without weeping and without woe in his land since he became ruler. Come with me, Conle the Redhaired, with your bejewelled neck and eyes like a candle flame! A golden crown upon you over your ruddy face shall be the patent of your royalty. If you come with me your form shall not wither from its youth or beauty till apocalyptic Doomsday.' Conn said to his druid, Corann by name, when they had heard all that the woman whom they could not see had said:

'I beseech you, Corann, great in song, great in skill; I am overpowered by a force which is greater than my counsel, which is greater than my strength, a struggle such as has not come to me since I took kingship, a deceitful combat with invisible shapes which overwhelm me to steal away my handsome son by magic spells; he is carried off from my royal side through the spells of women.'

1. See Notes.

143

Then the druid sang a charm against the woman's voice, so that no one heard the voice of the woman and Conle did not see the woman at that time. As the woman went away before the overpowering song of the druid, she threw an apple to Conle. For a month after that Conle was without food or drink, and did not care to eat any victuals but his apple. However much he ate, the apple grew no less, but was still whole.

Then longing seized Conle for the woman he had seen. On the day when the month was up, Conle was beside his father in the plain of Archommin. He saw the same woman coming, and she said to him:

'On a high throne sits Conle among the ephemeral Dead, waiting for fearful death. The immortal Living invite you; they will summon you to Tethra's[1] folk, who see you every day in the gatherings of your native land among your dear familiars.'

When Conn heard the woman's voice he said to his followers, 'Call the druid to me! I see that her tongue has been loosened for her today.' Then the woman said:

'Conn of the Hundred Battles, do not love druidry, for in a short while there will come a righteous man[2] with many companies, many and wonderful, to give judgement on our wide shores; soon his Law will reach you. He will scatter the spells of druids, with their wicked learning, in the sight of the Devil, the Black Magician.'

Conn marvelled then that Conle spoke to no one when the woman came. 'Does it pierce your heart, what the woman says, Conle?' said Conn. Conle said, 'It is not easy for me, for I love my people; yet longing for the woman has seized me.' The woman said:

'You are struggling (most difficult of desires) against the wave of your longing which tears you from them; in my crystal boat we might come to the fairy hill of Boadhagh, if we could reach it.

1. See Notes.   2. St Patrick.

There is another land which it would be no worse to seek;
the sun sets, I see it – though it is far we shall reach it before
night.

That is a land which rejoices the heart of everyone who
explores it; there is no other sort there but women and girls.'

Then Conle sprang away from them into the crystal boat.
They saw them in the distance; scarcely could their eyes
follow how they rowed away over the sea. They were not
seen from then till now.

Irish; author unknown; eighth century.

128. *The Story of Lludd and Llefelys*

Beli the Great, son of Manogan, had three sons – Lludd[1] and
Caswallawn and Nynniaw; and according to the story a
fourth son of his was Llefelys. And after Beli died, the
kingdom of the island of Britain fell into the hands of
Lludd, his eldest son, and it was ruled by Lludd prosper-
ously. He restored the walls of London, and surrounded it
with countless towers. And then he ordered the citizens to
build houses in it, so that there should be no houses in the
kingdoms so grand as those that were there. And besides
that, he was a good fighter, and gave food and drink
generously and freely to all that asked for them. And
though he had many cities and forts, he loved this one more
than any; and he lived in it the greater part of the year; and
for that reason it was called *Caer Ludd*,[2] and in the end *Caer
Lundein*. And when a foreign people came there, it was
called *Lunden*, or *Londres*.

Lludd loved Llefelys most of all his brothers, since he
was a wise and careful man. And when he heard that the
king of France had died without leaving any heir to himself
except one daughter, and had left the kingdom in her
hands, he came to his brother Lludd to ask advice and help
of him; and not so much to further himself, as rather to

1. See Notes.   2. 'The City of Lludd'; see Notes.

seek to add honour and dignity and rank to their family, if he could go to the kingdom of France to ask for that girl as his wife. And his brother agreed with him at once, and thought well of his plan in this matter; and ships were got ready straight away, and filled with armed knights, and they set out for France. And as soon as they disembarked they sent messengers to tell the nobles of France the purpose of the errand which they had come to ask about; and by joint agreement of the nobles of France and its princes, the maid was given to Llefelys and the crown of the kingdom with her. And after that he ruled the domain carefully and wisely and with good fortune, as long as his life lasted.

And after a space of time had slipped by, three plagues fell on the island of Britain, the like of which no one in the islands had seen before. The first of them was a certain people which came which was called the Corannieid; and so great was their science that there was no talk all over the face of the island, however low it was spoken, which they would not know, if only the wind met it; and for that reason no harm could be done them. The second plague was a scream which was given every May-Day eve over every hearth in the island of Britain; and this would go through the hearts of the people and terrify them so, that the men lost their colour and their strength and the women miscarried, and the boys and girls lost their minds, and all the animals and the trees and the earth and the waters were left barren. The third plague was, that however great were the provisions and stocks that were got ready in the courts of the king, though it might be stocks of food and drink for a year, nothing of it was ever found except what was used up on the first night alone.

As for the two other plagues, there was no one who knew the cause of them; and so there was more hope of getting rid of the first than there was of the second or the third. And so King Lludd fell into great care and trouble, because he did not know how he should get rid of those plagues. And he called to him all the nobles of his domain, and asked their advice, what they should do in the face of those plagues; and by the common agreement of his nobles, Lludd son of Beli went to his brother Llefelys, king of France, since he was a wise man and of good counsel, to ask advice of him. And then they got ready a fleet, and that secretly and silently, for fear that that people should come to know the purpose of the expedition, or anyone except the king and his councillors. And when they were ready, they went into their fleet, Lludd and those he had chosen with him, and began to plough the seas towards France.

And when news of that came to Llefelys, since he did not know the reason for his brother's fleet, he himself came from the other side to meet him, and with him a fleet of very great size. And when Lludd saw that, he left all his ships out on the high sea except one ship, and in that one he came to meet his brother. He for his part came to meet his brother in another single ship. And when they came together either of them embraced the other, and each welcomed the other with brotherly love. And when Lludd told his brother the cause of his mission, Llefelys said that he himself knew the cause of his coming to those lands; and after that they took counsel together how to talk of their affairs in some other way than that, so that the wind might not come upon their speech, for fear the Coranieid should learn what they said. And then Llefelys ordered a long horn of copper to be made, and through that they talked together. But whatever words either of them would say to the other through the horn, nothing reached either of them but hateful hostile words. And when Llefelys saw that, and that there was a devil thwarting them and making mischief through the horn, he had wine put in the horn to wash it, and through the virtue of the wine the devil was driven out of the horn.

And once their talk was unhindered, Llefelys said to his brother that he would give him certain insects, and that he should keep some of them alive to breed, for fear a plague of that sort might happen to come a second time; and that he should take others of the insects and grind them up in water; and he assured him that that was good for destroying the people of the Corannieid. That is to say, when he had come home to his kingdom, he should summon all the folk together to one meeting, his people and the people of the Corannieid, as if he meant to make peace between them; and when every one of them was together, he should take that magic water and throw it on all alike. And he assured him that that water would poison the people of the Corannieid, but would not kill and would not hurt anyone of his own people.

'The second plague,' he said, 'which is in your kingdom, it is a dragon; and a dragon of another, foreign, race is fighting with it and trying to overcome it. And for that reason,' he said, 'your dragon gives a terrible scream. And in this way you may come to know the truth of that. After you go home, have the island measured, both in its length and in its breadth, and where you find the very middle point to be, have a pit dug there; and then have a tub set in that pit, full of the best mead that can be made, with a cloth of brocaded silk over the face of the tub. And then keep watch, you yourself; and then you will see the dragons fighting in the shape of terrible creatures. And in the end they will go up into the air in the shape of dragons; and last of all, when they have grown tired with the fierce and dreadful struggle, they will drop down in the shape of two porkers on to the cloth, and will make the cloth sink with them and will drag it to the bottom of the tub, and will drink up all the mead, and will fall asleep after that. Then you fold the cloth around them at once, and bury them in a stone chest and cover them up in the earth, in whatever place you may find to be the most secure in your kingdom. And so long as they are in that secure place, no plague will come to the island of Britain from any other place.'

'The cause of the third plague,' he said, 'is a mighty magical man who carries off your food and drink and your provisions; and through his enchantment and his magic he makes everyone fall asleep. Therefore you must watch your feasts and your stocks, you yourself; and for fear his sleep should overcome you, let there be a tub full of cold water at your hand, and when sleep is overwhelming you, get into the tub.'

And then Lludd turned back to his own land. And without delay he summoned to him everyone of his people and of the Corannieid all together, and, as Llefelys had instructed him, he ground up the insects in water, and threw that on everyone alike; and in this way he destroyed the whole nation of the Corannieid at once, without hurting any of the Britons.

And some time after that, Lludd had the island measured, both in its length and in its breadth, and found the middle point to be at Oxford. And there he had the earth dug up, and in that pit he set a tub, full of the best mead that could be made, and a cloth of brocaded silk over its face; and he himself kept watch that night. And while he was like this, he saw the dragons fighting, and when they grew weary and began to tire, they sank down on top of the cloth and dragged it with them to the bottom of the tub. And when they had finished drinking the mead they fell asleep, and in their sleep Lludd folded the cloth around them and hid them in a stone chest in the safest place he found in Snowdonia. This is the way that place was called after that – Dinas Emreis, but before that, Dinas Ffaraon Danndde. That was one of the three governors who broke their hearts from vexation.[1] And so ceased the tempestuous scream which was in his kingdom.

And when that was finished, King Lludd had a feast provided, of very great size; and when it was ready, he had a tub full of cold water set at his side, and he himself kept watch over it in person. And as he was so, dressed in armour, see, about the third watch of the night he heard many matchless entertainments and songs of every kind, and drowsiness was forcing him to sleep. And at that, this is what he did, for fear that his purpose should be thwarted and he should be overcome with his sleep – he went several times into the water. And at last, see, a man of enormous size, dressed in strong heavy armour, came inside with a

1. See Notes.

hamper; and as his custom had been, he put all the provisions and stocks of food and drink into the hamper and set off with them. And Lludd thought nothing so strange as that there should be room in that hamper for so much. And then King Lludd started up after him, and spoke to him as follows: 'Stop, stop!' he said, 'though you have caused many injuries and losses before now, you shall do so no more, unless your warrior skill proves you to be stronger and braver than I am.' And at once the other set the hamper on the floor and waited his coming. There was a violent struggle between them, until the fiery sparks flew from their weapons; and in the end Lludd grappled him, and Fate willed that the victory should fall to Lludd, by throwing the oppressor down from himself to the ground; and once he was overcome by force and violence he begged him for quarter. 'How,' said the king, 'could I give you quarter, after all the losses and injuries you have caused me?' 'All the losses that I have ever caused you,' said the other, 'I will restore the same to you as good as what I took; and I will not do the like from this time on; and I will be a faithful man to you henceforwards.' And the king accepted this from him.

And so Lludd rid the island of Britain of the three plagues; and from then to the end of his life Lludd son of Beli ruled the island of Britain in peace and prosperity. And this tale is called the Adventure of Lludd and Llefelys; and so it ends.

Welsh; author unknown; twelfth century?

129. Ruadh in the Land Under the Wave

. . . There was a famous king here in Ireland, Ruadh son of Ríghdhonn of Munster. He had a meeting arranged with the Norwegians. He went to his meeting with the Norwegians round Scotland from the south, with three ships; there were thirty men in each ship of them. His fleet became stuck fast from below in the midst of the ocean, and there was no wealth nor treasure thrown into the sea[1] which would set it free. They consulted the lottery, to find out to which of them it would fall to go down under the ocean and discover what had stopped them. The lot fell to the king himself. So the king, Ruadh son of Ríghdhonn, leaped into the sea and was covered by the sea immediately. He arrived in a great plain, and there he came upon nine lovely women. They confessed to him that it was they who had held up the ships, so that he should come to them; and they offered him nine golden vessels in return for sleeping nine nights with them, a night with each one of them. He did so. Meanwhile his men were unable to leave because of the magic power of the women. One of the women said that she had conceived, and that she would bear a son; and that he should visit them as he came back to them from the east, to fetch the boy. Thereupon he went to his men, and they went their way. They remained with their friends for seven years, and they came back by a different way, and did not go to the same place; so that they landed at Inbher Ailbhine. There the women overtook them. As they were drawing up their fleet on land, the men heard a wailing coming from a copper ship; then the women came to land, and thereupon threw the boy from them. The shore was stony and rocky, and the boy struck one of the stones, so that he died of it . . .

Irish; author unknown; eighth–ninth century original.

130. The Creation of Blodeuwedd[2]

. . . They came to Math son of Mathonwy and complained most urgently about Arianrhod, and told how she had provided him[3] with all the weapons. 'Come,' said Math, 'let us try, you and I, with our magic and enchantment, to conjure up a wife for him out of flowers.' Now by that time he was a grown man, and was the most shapely lad that

1. i.e. as a propitiation of whatever magic power was holding it back.
2. See Notes. 3. Lleu.

man had ever seen. And then they took the flowers of the oak-trees and the flowers of the broom and the flowers of the meadow-sweet, and out of these they created the fairest and most perfect girl that man had ever seen. And they baptized her by the baptism they used in those days, and called her Blodeuwedd[1] . . .

Welsh; author unknown; eleventh-century original?

131. The Magic Gaming-board

. . . And Peredur came to the castle, and the castle gate was open. And when he reached the hall, the door was open; and when he went inside he saw a gaming-board in the hall, and either of the two sets of pieces was playing against the other, and the one to which he gave his help began to lose the game. And the other side gave a shout, just as if they had been men. Then he grew angry, and took the set of pieces on his lap and threw the board in the lake. And when he had done so, see, a black girl came in, and said to Peredur, 'May God not welcome you! You do harm more often than you do good.' 'What have you against me, black girl?' said Peredur. 'You have caused the Empress to lose her board, and she would not wish that for all her empire.' 'Is there any way of getting the board?' 'There is, if you go to the Castle of Ysbidinongl. There is a black man there, laying waste much of the Empress's domain. By killing him you would get the board; but if you go there you will not come back alive.' . . .

Welsh; author unknown; twelfth century.

132. From The Voyage of Mael Dúin

. . . After that they were three days and nights on the sea. On the morning of the fourth day afterwards they discovered another large island; its soil was sandy. As they

1. i.e. 'Flower-Face'.

approached the beach of the island they saw a creature in the island like a horse. It had feet like a hound, with short rough claws, and great was its joy to see them, and it was prancing before their eyes; for it longed to eat both them and their boat. 'It is not sorry to see us,' said Mael Dúin; 'let us withdraw from the island.' They did so; and when the creature saw that they were fleeing, it came down to the shore and began to dig up the beach with its short claws, and to pelt them, and they thought they would not escape it . . .

After they came away from that island, they were rowing for a long time, hungrily, without food; until they came upon an island with a great cliff round it on every side, and a long narrow wood in it, and great was its length and its narrowness. As he came up to it Mael Dúin took a branch of that wood in his hand, going past it. For three days and three nights the branch was in his hand, as the boat sailed along the cliff, and on the third day he found a cluster of three apples at the tip of the branch. Each apple fed them for forty nights.

After that they came upon another island, with a palisade of flagstones around it. When they came near, a great beast arose in the island and ran all round the island. It seemed to Mael Dúin to be swifter than the wind. And then it went up to the top of the island and stretched its body upright there, with its head down and its feet up. And this is how it was, turning round inside its skin; that is, the flesh and bones were turning and the skin outside was unmoved. But sometimes the skin outside turned round like a mill, and the bones and flesh remained still. When it had been like this a long time, it got up again and ran all round the island as it had done at first. Then it went again to the same place, and this time the half of its skin which was below was unmoved, and the other half which was above raced round like a millstone. That was its behaviour while it was circling the island. Mael Dúin and his men fled with all their warriors' strength; and the beast noticed that they were fleeing, and came to the beach to get at them, and began to strike and pelt and flail them with stones from the rocks after them. One of the stones went into their boat, so that it passed through Mael Dúin's shield and into the keel of the boat . . .

When those apples had been used up, and there was great thirst and hunger upon them, and they were almost destroyed, and when their mouths and noses were filled with the stench of the sea, they saw a small island with a fortress on it and a high white rampart round it, as if the rampart were made of lime and as if it were all one stone of chalk. Great was its height from the sea, and it almost reached the clouds of heaven. The fortress was open. There were bright snowy white houses in it, like the rampart. They came into the biggest house of them, and there was no one there but a small cat which was in the middle, playing on four stone pillars. It was leaping from one pillar to the other. It looked at the men for a little, and did not interrupt its play. They saw then three rows all round the wall of the house from one doorpost to the other; first, there was a row of gold and silver brooches, with their pins in the wall; a second row of big collars of gold and silver, like the hoops of a barrel; and the third row of big swords with hilts of gold and silver. The cubicles of the house were filled with white feather beds and bright bedclothes. They saw then a broiled ox and a salt pig in the midst, and a big vessel of good intoxicating ale. 'Has this been left for us?' said Mael Dúin to the cat. It looked at them for an instant, and began to play again. Then Mael Dúin realized that it was for them that the meal which they saw had been left. They drank and dined and fell asleep; and they put the dregs of the ale in their bottles and kept the remains of the food, and then considered leaving. One of Mael Dúin's three foster-brothers said, 'Shall I take one of these collars with me?' 'No,' said Mael Dúin, 'the house is not without a guard.' He took it with him all the same, as far as the middle of the courtyard. The cat came after him, and jumped through him like a fiery arrow, and burned him to ashes. It went again and sat on its pillar. Mael Dúin soothed the cat with his words, and set the collar in the same place, and cleaned the ashes from the middle of the courtyard and threw them over the sea cliff. And they went into their boat then, and praised and implored the Lord, and gave thanks to Him . . .

When they went from that island of the mill, they came upon another island, with a great crowd of men with black bodies and black clothes in it. They had hoods on their heads, and did not cease from wailing. The lot fell to one of Mael Dúin's two foster-brothers to go on the island to the people who were wailing; and at once he became their companion and began to wail with them. Then Mael Dúin said, 'Let four of you go with your weapons and bring the man away with you by force; and do not look at the ground nor the air, but put your clothes round your noses and round your mouths, so that you may not breathe in the air of the land; and do not take your eyes from your own man.' The four went and did as Mael Dúin said, and brought the man of their company with them by force. And Mael Dúin asked him what he saw in the island. 'I do not know,' he said, 'but what I saw I did, after the manner of the people among whom I was.' Then they left that island . . .

A little while after that they saw an island with a fortress in it, and a bridge of glass at its door. As often as they tried to go up on the bridge they would fall down back again. They saw a woman come out of the fortress with a bucket in her hand. She lifted up a plank of glass from the floor of the bridge and filled her bucket from the well which was beneath the plank. Then she went into the fortress. 'Let the steward come to receive Mael Dúin,' said Germán. 'Mael Dúin, indeed!' said the woman, as she shut the door behind her; and she made the brazen pillars and the brazen net[1] which was on them shake at that, and the noise these made was soft sweet-stringed music, and it put them to sleep until the next morning. When they woke up in the morning, they saw the same woman come out of the fortress with her bucket in her hand, and she filled it from the same

1. The door appears to have had jambs and a kind of portcullis of bronze.

well which was beneath the plank. 'But let the steward come to receive Mael Dúin,' said Germán. 'Much I care for Mael Dúin!' said she, as she closed the door. The same music prostrated them and put them to sleep again until the next day. For three days and three nights they continued like this. Then on the fourth day the woman came to them, and in a lovely guise she came. A white cloak round her, and a circlet of gold round her hair. Her hair was golden. Two silver shoes on her pink and white feet. A silver brooch with golden filigree in her cloak, and a filmy robe of silk next to her white body. 'Welcome, Mael Dúin,' she said, and she called every man in turn by his own proper name. 'For a long time your coming here has been known and accepted,' she said. Then she took them with her into a great house which was close to the sea, and had their boat pulled up on land. They saw then in the house ready for them a bed for Mael Dúin and a bed for every three of his followers. She brought them food in a hamper, like cheese or sour buttermilk, and she gave out helpings for three at a time. Each man found in it whatever taste he desired. Then she served Mael Dúin by himself. She filled a bucket beneath the same plank, and poured drink for them. She made a trip for every three men in turn. She saw when they had had enough, and ceased pouring for them. 'A woman fit for Mael Dúin is this woman,' said every man of his followers. After that she left them, with her hamper and her bucket. His men said to Mael Dúin, 'Shall we speak to her to ask whether she would sleep with you?' 'What harm would it do you,' said he, 'if you speak to her?' She came the next day at the same time to serve them, as she did before. They said to the girl, 'Will you make a match with Mael Dúin, and sleep with him? Why not stay here tonight?' She said that she had not learned and did not know what sin was. Then she went away to her house, and came the next day at the same time with her service for them. When they were surfeited and drunk, they said the same words to her. 'Tomorrow then,' said she, 'you shall be given an answer about this.' She went after that to her house, and they fell asleep on their beds. When they awoke, they were in their boat on a rock, and they did not see the island nor the fortress nor the woman nor the place where they were before . . .

Afterwards, when they had been travelling far over the waves, they saw an island before them. As they went near to it, they heard the sound of smiths striking a mass of red-hot metal on an anvil with hammers, as if three or four men were striking it. When they came close, they heard one man ask another, 'Are they near?' said he. 'Yes,' said another. 'Who is that,' said another man, 'that you say is coming here?' 'They look like little boys in a little trough out there,' said he. When Mael Dúin heard this that the smiths said, 'Let us go back,' said he, 'and do not turn the boat, but keep it stern foremost, so that they may not realize that we are fleeing.' They rowed then with the stern of the boat foremost. The same man who was in the forge asked again, 'Are they nearer to the shore now?' said he. 'They are not moving,' said the watchman, 'although they are not coming hither they are not going away.' Not long after that he asked again, 'What are they doing now?' said he. 'I think,' said the watchman, 'that they are fleeing; it seems to me they are further now from the shore than they were a while ago.' The blacksmith came out of the forge at that, with a great mass of red-hot iron in the tongs in his hand, and threw that mass after the boat into the sea, so that the whole sea boiled. But it did not reach them, for they fled with all their battle-strength quickly and hastily out to the ocean.

After that they rowed till they came to a sea which was like green glass. It was so clear that the pebbles and sand at the bottom of it were visible, and they saw no beasts nor creatures in it at all, nor any rocks, but only the clean pebbles and the green sand. They were a large part of the day rowing across that sea, and great was its splendour . . .

After that they came upon another island, round which the sea was risen up so that it made vast cliffs all round about it. When the people of that land observed them, they fell to screaming at them and saying, 'It is They, it is They yonder!' at the top of their voices. They saw many people then, and great herds of cattle and horses, and flocks of sheep. There was a big woman pelting them from below with great nuts, so that they landed beside them on the waves up above. They collected many of those nuts, and took them with them. They came away back from the island, and the screams stopped. 'Where are They now?' said one of the men who came up at the screaming after them. 'They have gone away,' said another of the kerns. 'It is not They at all, then,' said another kern . . .

They rowed after that until they came upon a great silver pillar with four sides, each side being two oar-strokes of the boat in length, so that its whole circumference was eight oar-strokes of the boat; and there was not a single sod of land round it, but only the boundless ocean, and they did not see the nature of its base below, nor of its apex to the top. There was a silver net reaching far out from its top, and the boat came under sail through the mesh of that net; and Díurán gave a blow with the edge of his spear across the mesh of that net. 'Do not spoil the net,' said Mael Dúin, 'for what we see is the work of mighty men.' 'For the glory of the name of God,' said Díurán, 'I do this, so that my tale may be the better believed, and I shall lay it on the altar at Armagh, if I reach Ireland.' Two and a half ounces were in it, when it was weighed at Armagh. After that they heard a great bright clear voice from the top of that pillar, but they did not know what language it spoke nor what it said.

Then they saw another island, on one leg, that is, a single leg held it up; and they rowed round it, looking for a way into it, but they did not find any way into it. But below at the bottom of the leg they saw a locked door. They realized that this was the way by which one went into the island; and they saw a plough on top of the island, but they did not speak to anyone and no one spoke to them. They retreated . . .

For a very long time after that they were travelling over the waves, until they came upon an island with trees in it like the willow or hazel. There were marvellous fruits on

them, with great berries. Then they stripped a small one of
the fruit-trees, and cast lots next to see who should taste the
fruit of the tree. The lot fell to Mael Dúin. He squeezed part
of them into a vessel and drank, and it sent him to sleep
from that time until the same time the next day; and it was
not known whether he was alive or dead, with the red
foam round his lips, until he woke up the next day. He said
to them, 'Gather this fruit,' he said, 'for its worth is great.'
They gathered it then, and mixed water with it to moderate
its power to intoxicate and send to sleep. They gathered a
great quantity of it then and pressed it, and filled a great
many vessels with it; and they rowed away from that
island.

They landed after that on another large island. One half
of it was a wood, with yews and large oaks in it. The other
half of it was a field, with a small lake in it. There were great
flocks of sheep there. They saw a little church there, covered
with ivy. They went to the church. There was an old grey
priest in the church, and his hair completely covered him.
Mael Dúin asked him, 'Where are you from?' said he. 'I
am one of the fifteen men of the company of Brénainn of
Birr who came on their pilgrimage in the ocean until they
arrived at this island. They all died except myself alone.'
And after that he showed them Brénainn's writing-tablet,
which they had brought with them on their pilgrimage.
They crossed themselves with the writing-tablet then, and
Mael Dúin kissed it . . .

Irish; author unknown; eighth–ninth century original.

133. The Magic Pigs of Cruachu

. . . Out of it[1] also came these pigs. Neither corn nor grass
nor leaf would grow for seven years in any place that they
frequented. Wherever they would be counted, they would
not stay, but if anyone tried to count them they would go
to another land.[2] They were never completely counted; but

1. The magic cave of Cruachu.   2. See Notes.

'There are three,' said one; 'More, seven,' said another; 'There are nine,' said another; 'Eleven pigs'; 'Thirteen pigs.' In that way it was impossible to count them. Moreover, they could not be killed, for if they were shot at they would disappear. Once upon a time Medhbh of Cruachu and Ailill went to count them, in Magh Mucraimhe. They were counted by them then. Medhbh was in her chariot; one of the pigs leaped over the chariot. 'That pig is one too many, Medhbh,' said everyone. 'Not this one,' said Medhbh, seizing the pig's leg, so that its hide split on its forehead and it left the hide in her hand with the leg; and it is not known where they went after that. Hence it is called Magh Mucraimhe[1] . . .

Irish; author unknown; ninth–tenth century.

134. The Black and White Sheep and the Blazing Tree

. . . And then Peredur travelled on until he came to a beautiful valley, and there was a river in the valley, and the sides of the valley were wooded with fair smooth trees of equal height, and there was many a fine meadow in the valley. And on one side of the river there was a flock of white sheep, and on the other side a flock of black sheep; and when one of the black sheep bleated, one of the white sheep would come to them, and would become pure black; and when one of the white sheep bleated one of the black sheep would come to them, and would become pure white. And he saw a tree on the river bank, and one half of the tree was blazing up to its very top, and the other half in leaf with its bark growing beautifully . . .

Welsh; author unknown; twelfth century.

135. From The Voyage of the Uí Chorra[2]

. . . They rowed the boat across the sea, until there appeared to them great flocks of birds of many colours, and their

1. 'Plain of Pig-Counting.'   2. See Index.

number was very large. One of the birds alighted on the gunwale of the boat. 'It would be welcome,' said they, 'if this were a messenger from the Lord to bring us news.' The elder raised his face at that. 'God could bring that to pass,' said the elder. 'Indeed, it is to talk with you that I have come,' said the bird. The colour of that bird was blood-red, with three lovely resplendent rays as brilliant as the sun on its breast. 'I am of the land of Ireland,' said the bird, 'and I am the soul of a woman; I am one of your nuns,' said she to the elder. 'Tell me this,' said the elder, 'are we going to Hell?' 'You will not go,' said the bird. 'Thank God,' said the elder, 'for we have deserved to go to Hell in the flesh.' 'Come then to another place,' said the bird, 'to listen to the birds there. The birds that you see are the souls which go out of Hell on Sunday.' 'Let us go away from here,' said the elder. 'We will go the way you go,' said his companions. As they were going they saw three wonderful streams out of which the birds were coming; a stream of otters, and a stream of eels, and a stream of black swans. And the bird said, 'Do not let these phantasms that you see make you low-spirited, for the birds which you see are the souls of people in torment for the sins they have committed, and the phantasms yonder following and persecuting them are devils; so that the souls raise great heavy cries as they go fleeing from their torments at the hands of the devils. Here I shall leave you,' said the bird; 'the foreknowledge of your adventures has not been entrusted very far to me, and someone else will tell it to you.' 'Say,' said the elder, 'what are those three very beautiful rays on your breast?' 'I will tell you,' said the bird; 'I had a husband when I was alive, and I did not do his will and did not keep the lawful marriage bond. He was sick, and I was not with him; but I went three times to visit him – once to see him, the second time with food for him, and the third time to serve and tend him; and those are these three very beautiful rays which are on my breast. And that would be my colour all over, if I had not deserted the lawful marriage bond.' The bird left them after that and said farewell to them.

Another beautiful shining island appeared to them. Bright grass was there, with spangling of purple-headed flowers; many birds and ever-lovely bees singing a song from the heads of those flowers. A grave grey-haired man was playing a harp in the island. He was singing a wonderful song, the sweetest of the songs of the world. They greeted each other, and the old man told them to go away.

They rowed thence for a long time, until they saw a single man digging with a fiery spade in his hand. A vast red wave would come over him, red and blazing. But when he raised his head he was shrieking and wailing pitifully, as he endured that torment. 'What are you, man?' they said. 'I am one who used to dig on Sunday,' said he, 'and this is my punishment; and for God's sake, pray with me that my torment may be lightened.' So they prayed with him, and went away after that . . .

There appeared to them after that another beautiful shining island; a smooth wood was in it, and it was full of honey; a heath of green grass in its midst, very soft. A bright sweet-tasting lake was there. They stayed there a week, putting their weariness from them. As they were leaving it then a monster rose out of the lake, and each one of them thought it would attack him, so that they trembled exceedingly before it; until it sank down afterwards into the same place again . . .

Irish; author unknown; eleventh-century original.

136. The Three Werewolves from the Cave of Cruacha[1]

. . . Then the same man said, 'Well, Caílte my soul, do you know the other persecution which troubles me in this land?' 'What persecution is that, my soul?' said Caílte. 'Three she-wolves come out of the Cave of Cruacha every year and destroy all the wethers and sheep that we have, and we get no chance at them before they go back again into the Cave of Cruacha; and we should welcome a friend who

1. Cf. no. 133.

should succeed in ridding us of them.' 'Well, Cas Corach my soul,' said Caílte, 'do you know what the three wolves are which rob the warrior?' 'Indeed I know,' said Cas Corach, 'they are the three daughters of Airitech, of the last of the Grievous Company from the Cave of Cruacha, and they prefer to rob in the shape of wolves rather than in human shape.' 'And do they trust anyone?' said Caílte. 'They do not, except one sort of people only,' said he. 'What sort of people is that?' said Caílte. 'If they saw men of this world with harps and lutes, they would trust them.' 'They will trust Cas Corach if so,' said Caílte, 'and where do they use to come?' 'To the Cairn of Bricre here,' said the warrior. 'And how would it be for me,' said Cas Corach, 'to go tomorrow and take my lute with me to the top of the cairn?'

He got up early next day and went to the top of the cairn, and was playing and continually thrumming his lute till the clouds of evening came down. And as he was there, he saw the three wolves coming towards him, and they lay down before him and listened to the music; but Cas Corach found no means of making any attempt on them, and they went away from him northwards to the Cave at the end of the day. And Cas Corach came back to Caílte and told him this story. 'Go there again tomorrow,' said Caílte, 'and tell them it would be better for them to be in human shape when listening to music and melody, rather than to be in the shape of wolves.' And Cas Corach came next day to the same cairn, and posted his followers round the cairn; and the wolves arrived at the cairn, and lay down on their forelegs listening to the music. And Cas Corach kept saying to them, 'If you were humans by nature,' said he, 'it would be better for you to listen to the music in human shape rather than in the shape of wolves.' And they heard that, and they took off the long dark skins which were on them, because they liked the plaintive fairy music. And as they were side by side and elbow to elbow, Caílte saw them, and set his warrior forefinger in the thong of the spear, so that the spear fetched up in its deadly flight in the upper part of the breast of the woman who was furthest from him, after passing through all three of them; so that they were like a tight-wound ball of thread on the spear in that way ... And Cas Corach went to them and cut off their three heads. So the Glen of the Werewolves is the name of the glen on the north side of the Cairn of Bricre from then till the present day ...

Irish; author unknown; twelfth century.

137. How the Fenians Found the Fairy Hill

... 'We roused a beautiful skittish wild fawn,' said Caílte, 'at Tory in the north of Ireland, and six warriors of us followed it from Tory to this mountain, the mountain of Aighe son of Iughaine, and the skittish wild fawn went head-first underground there, and we did not know where it went after that. And a great and heavy snow fell then, so that it made the crest of the wood into twisted wickerwork; and the weight of the rain and the storm that came on took from us our speed and our skill in handling our weapons. And Finn said to me, "Caílte, will you find shelter for us tonight from the storm which is here?" And I cast about over the shoulder of the hill to the south, and as I gazed around me I saw a fairy hill, brightly lit, with many drinking-horns and bowls and cups of glass and of pale gold in it, and I was staring at it for a long time at the doorway of the fairy hill. And I considered what I should do, whether I should go into the fairy hill to discover all about it, or whether to seek Finn where I had left him when I had gone away from him over the shoulder of the hill southwards, looking for a lodging. And this is the plan I settled on, I went across into the fairy hill and sat down,' said Caílte, 'in a crystal chair on the floor of the fairy hill, and gazed at the house all around me, and I saw twenty-eight warriors on one side of the house with a lovely fair-headed woman beside every man of them, and six gentle youthful yellow-haired girls on the other side of the house, with shaggy cloaks round their shoulders; and a gentle yellow-haired girl in a chair on the floor of the house, with a harp in her hand which she was playing and continually thrumming. And every time she sang a song a horn was given her for her to drink out of it, and she would give the horn into the hand of the man who gave it to her; and they were sporting and amusing themselves all around her,' said Caílte. '"Let me wash your feet, Caílte my soul," said the girl. "I will not allow it at all," said Caílte, "for there is a company which is nobler than myself with me near at hand, that of Finn son of Cumhall, and he desires to get lodging and food for the night in the fairy hill tonight." Then one of the warriors said, "Go, Caílte my soul, to fetch Finn son of Cumhall, for no man was ever turned away in Finn's house, and he shall not be turned away by us." Then I went to fetch Finn' . . .

Irish; author unknown; twelfth century.

138. The Air Ship[1]

One day the monks of Clonmacnoise were holding a meeting on the floor of the church, and as they were at their deliberations there they saw a ship sailing over them in the air, going as if it were on the sea. When the crew of the ship saw the meeting and the inhabited place below them, they dropped anchor, and the anchor came right down on to the floor of the church, and the priests seized it. A man came down out of the ship after the anchor, and he was swimming as if he were in the water, till he reached the anchor; and they were dragging him down then. 'For God's sake let me go!' said he, 'for you are drowning me.' Then he left them, swimming in the air as before, taking his anchor with him.

Irish; author unknown; fourteenth–fifteenth century?

139. The Burial of the Priest's Concubine[2]

This is a tale about a priest's concubine when she died. Many people came to her to carry her away to bury her,

1. See Notes.   2. See Notes.

and they could not lift her because she was so heavy. And they all wondered greatly at this, and everyone said, 'O One God, Almighty Father, how shall she be taken to be buried?' And they consulted a cunning professor, and the professor said to them as follows: 'Bring two priests' concubines to us to carry her away to the church.' And they were brought, and they carried her away very lightly to the church; and the people wondered greatly at this, and the professor said to them, 'There is no cause for you to wonder at their actions, O people; that is, that two devils should carry off one devil with them.' *Finit*.

Irish; author unknown; fourteenth–fifteenth century?

140. Drowned Giantesses[1]

A woman, whose breasts had not grown, was cast up on a sea shore in Europe. She was fifty feet tall, that is from her shoulders to her feet, and her chest was seven feet across. There was a purple cloak on her. Her hands were tied behind her back, and her head had been cut off; and it was in this way that the wave cast her up on land. *Finit*.

Another woman was cast up from the sea in Scotland, and *she* was a hundred and ninety-two feet long; there were seventeen feet between her breasts, and sixteen was the length of her hair, and seven the length of the finger of her hand. Her nose was seven feet long, and there were two feet between her eyebrows. Every limb of her was as white as the swan or the foam of the wave.

Irish; author unknown; fourteenth–fifteenth century?
(Source of the second paragraph ninth century).

1. See Notes.

DESCRIPTION

NOTE

The imaginative power of the early Celtic mind has already been mentioned. It is not, of course, limited to nature or supernatural themes, and is to be found in descriptions of many kinds. It is linked with another feature which is characteristic of Celtic and distinguishes it from other ancient and medieval literatures, that is, a very clear sense of colour. Whereas elsewhere – in Homer and Greek lyric, or in *Beowulf* and Anglo-Saxon elegiac poetry – we have adjectives meaning 'bright, flashing, glittering, pale, white, dun, dark, gloomy, grey, black' (the adjectives of a colour-blind man), in the Celtic literatures there is a constant use of distinctive colour words, often minor varieties of a colour: 'red, rusty-red, blood-red, crimson, purple, sky-blue, blue-grey, green, bright yellow, greyish-brown, auburn,' and so on, are frequent. For a coloured picture in a few simple words, and for the emotional human reaction to it, it would be difficult to find a parallel in medieval literature to no. 141, Froech with the berry-branch in the dark pool. The response to sunshine indoors in nos. 146 and 147 is notable too; and its silver sheen on a ruffled lake is hit off in a single line in no. 149.

Nos. 160–65 are examples of a special development in medieval Irish. Early Irish prose is usually very simple syntactically, with short sentences and few subordinate clauses; but there was a convention in the hero-tales for including certain stereotyped descriptive passages, in which strings of alliterating nouns and adjectives were grouped in a more or less rhythmical fashion. As time went on the ordinary prose style became much more highly developed, with a very large number of coordinate and a considerable complication of subordinate clauses; a good example of this may be seen in no. 6. So too with the decorative passages; from a few lines they had grown sometimes to several pages, and their influence on the regular prose might be considerable, so much so that later it is not always possible to say where one begins and the other ends. However, the decorative paragraphs tend to be confined to certain fixed subjects, such as the description of the hero's chariot, of a battle, of a sea voyage, and so on. These still survive in unbroken tradition, though in a meagre and debased form, in the modern folk-tales of Ireland and Scotland. The tale-tellers recite them in a kind of hurried chant which betrays that they are felt to be poetry rather than prose; and no doubt they were so recited in the Middle Ages. Of the examples given below, no. 164 must be one of the longest in Irish.

DESCRIPTION

141. Froech in the Dark Pool

... He went to come out of the water then. 'Do not come out,' said Ailill, 'till you bring me a branch of that mountain-ash on the bank of the river. Beautiful I think its berries.' He went away then and broke a spray from the tree, and carried it on his back through the water. And this was what Findabhair used to say afterwards of any beautiful thing which she saw, that she thought it more beautiful to see Froech across the dark pool; the body so white and the hair so lovely, the face so shapely, the eye so blue, and he a tender youth without fault or blemish, with face narrow below and broad above, and he straight and spotless, and the branch with the red berries between the throat and the white face ...

Irish; author unknown; eighth-century original.

142. Froech and the Fairy Women

... They heard a sound of wailing throughout Cruachu; and three times fifty women were seen with purple tunics and green hoods, and silver bracelets round their arms. People went to meet them to find out why they were lamenting. 'For Froech son of Idhath,' said one of the women, 'the darling boy of the king of the fairy hills of Ireland.' Then Froech heard their wail. 'Take me out,' said he to his followers, 'that is the wail of my mother and of the women-folk of Boann.' He was taken out thereupon and brought to them. The women came round him, and took him away to the fairy hill of Cruachu. The next evening they saw him come back, with fifty women around him, whole and hale without blemish or wound. All the women were of like age

and like shape and like loveliness and like beauty and like
straightness and like figure, in the dress of the fairy women,
so that there was no telling one from the other. The people
were almost smothered in crowding round them. They
departed at the gateway of the courtyard. As they went
away, they gave forth their cry, so that the people who were
in the court were thrown prostrate. Hence it is that the
musicians of Ireland have got the tune 'The Wail of the
Fairy Women' . . .

Irish; author unknown; eighth-century original.

143. Midhir's[1] Invitation to the Earthly Paradise

'Fair woman, will you go with me to a wonderful land
where music is? The hair is like the primrose tip there,
and the whole body is the colour of snow.

There, there is neither 'mine' nor 'thine'; white are the
teeth there, black the eyebrows; a delight to the eye is the
full number of our hosts; every cheek there is of the colour
of the foxglove.

The ridge of every moor is purple, a delight to the eye are
the blackbird's eggs; though the plain of Ireland is fair to
see, it is like a desert once you know the Great Plain.

Fine though you think the ale of Ireland, the ale of the
Great Land is more heady; a wonderful land is the land I
tell of, the young do not die there before the old.[2]

Sweet mild streams flow through the land, choice mead
and wine; matchless people without blemish, conception
without sin, without guilt.

We see everyone on all sides, and no one sees us; it is the
darkness of Adam's trespass that screens us from being
counted.[2]

1. A lord of the fairy people.   2. See Notes.

Woman, if you come to my mighty people a crown of gold shall be on your head; honey, wine, ale, fresh milk, and beer you shall have there with me, fair woman.'

Irish; author unknown; ninth century.

144. The Islands of the Earthly Paradise

. . . When they were all gathered together in the palace, they saw a woman in a strange dress in the middle of the hall. Then she sang these fifty verses to Bran, while the company listened to them, and they all saw the woman:

'Here is a branch from the apple-tree of Emhain,[1] like those that are familiar; twigs of white silver on it, and crystal fringes with flowers.

There is an island far away, around which the sea-horses glisten, flowing on their white course against its shining shore; four pillars support it.

It is a delight to the eye, the plain which the hosts frequent in triumphant ranks; coracle races against chariot in the plain south of Findargad.[1]

Pillars of white bronze are under it, shining through aeons of beauty, a lovely land through the ages of the world, on which many flowers rain down.

There is a huge tree there with blossom, on which the birds call at the hours; it is their custom that they all call together in concert every hour.

Colours of every hue gleam throughout the soft familiar fields; ranged round the music, they are ever joyful in the plain south of Argadnél.[1]

Weeping and treachery are unknown in the pleasant familiar land; there is no fierce harsh sound there, but sweet music striking the ear.

1. See Notes.

Without sorrow, without grief, without death, without any sickness, without weakness, that is the character of Emhain;[1] such a marvel is rare.

Loveliness of a wondrous land, whose aspects are beautiful, whose view is fair, excellent, without a trace of mist.

Then if one sees Airgthech,[1] on which dragon-stones and crystals rain down, the sea makes the wave wash against the land, with crystal tresses from its mane.

Riches, treasures of every colour are in Cíuin,[1] have they not been found? Listening to sweet music, drinking choicest wine.

Golden chariots across the plain of the sea rising with the tide to the sun; chariots of silver in Magh Mon,[1] and of bronze without blemish.

Horses of golden yellow there on the meadow, other horses of purple colour; other noble horses beyond them, of the colour of the all-blue sky.

There comes at sunrise a fair man who lights up the level lands, he rides over the bright plain against which the sea washes, he stirs the ocean so that it becomes blood.

There comes a host across the clear sea, to the land they display their rowing; then they row to the bright stone from which a hundred songs arise.

Through the long ages it sings to the host a melody which is not sad; the music swells up in choruses of hundreds, they do not expect decay nor death.

Emhnae[1] of many shapes, beside the sea, whether it is near or whether it is far, where there are many thousands of motley-dressed women; the pure sea surrounds it.

If one has heard the sound of the music, the song of the little birds from Imchíuin,[1] a troop of women comes from the hill to the playing-field where it is.

1. See Notes.

Freedom and health come to the land around which laughter echoes; in Imchíuin with its purity come immortality and joy.

Through the perpetual good weather silver rains on the lands; a very white cliff under the glare of the sea, over which its heat spreads from the sun.

The host rides across Magh Mon,[1] a lovely sport which is not weakly; in the many-coloured land with great splendour they do not expect decay nor death.

Listening to music in the night, and going to Ildathach[1] the many-coloured land, a brilliance with clear splendour from which the white cloud glistens.

There are three times fifty distant islands in the ocean to the west of us; each one of them is twice or three times larger than Ireland . . .

My words are not for all of you, though their great wonders have been told; from among the throng of the world let Bran listen to the wisdom expounded to him.

Do not sink upon a bed of sloth, do not let your bewilderment overwhelm you; begin a voyage across the clear sea, to find if you may reach the Land of Women.'

Then the woman went from them, and they did not know where she went, and she took her branch with her . . .

Irish; author unknown; seventh–eighth century original.

145. The Arrival at the Earthly Paradise

. . . A fair wind came on the warriors after that, and they raised their sail, and the boat shipped less water on them; and a smoothness fell upon the ocean, and the sea went down, so that there was a bright fair calm; and there came a warbling of unknown birds of many kinds around them in

1. See Notes.

every direction. And then they saw before them the shape of a pleasing land with lovely shores, and they rejoiced and were glad at the sight of this land; and they reached the land, and found a beautiful green-bosomed river-mouth there, with pure-welling pebbles shining all one silver, and spotted ever-handsome salmon with splendid colours of dark purple on them; and lovely purple-crested woods round the pleasing streams of the land to which they had come. 'Beautiful is this land, my warriors,' said Tadhg, 'and happy the man whose natural lot it might be to live in it . . . Lovely and fruitful is this land to which we have come,' said Tadhg; 'and let us go on shore,' said he, 'and haul up your boat and dry it out.' They went forward then, twenty strong warriors of them, and left another twenty guarding their boat; and though they had undergone great cold and fasting and storm and tempest, the champions had no wish for food or fire after reaching the land they had come to, for the smell of the scented bright-purple trees of that country was enough food and repletion for them. They went forward after that all through the wood nearest to them, and found an orchard with lovely purple-crested apple-trees and leafy oaks of beautiful colour and hazels with clustering yellow nuts. 'It is wonderful to me, my men,' said Tadhg, 'what I have noticed – it is winter with us in our land now, and it is summer here in this land,' said Tadhg.

The loveliness of the place to which they had come was unbounded. And they left it, and came upon a beautiful bright wood after that, and great was the virtue of its smell and its scent, with round purple berries on it, every berry as big as a man's head. There was a beautiful brilliant flock of birds feeding on these grapes, and it was a strange flock of birds that was there, for they were white birds with purple heads and beaks of gold. They sang music and minstrelsy as they fed on the berries, and that music was plaintive and matchless, for even the sick and the wounded would have fallen asleep to it . . .

Irish; author unknown; fourteenth-fifteenth century?

146. Morning Sun

. . . One summer morning they were in their bed, and he[1] at the outer side; and Enid was awake in the glass-win-dowed room, and the sun was shining on the bed, and the clothes had slipped down from his breast and arms as he slept. She gazed at the marvellous beauty of the sight of him, and said, 'Alas,' she said, 'that it is through me that these arms and breast are losing all the fame and valour that was theirs.' And with that she wept a flood of tears, so that they fell on his breast . . .

Welsh; author unknown; twelfth century.

147. Sunshine through the Window

Pleasant to me is the glittering of the sun today upon these margins, because it flickers so.

Irish; marginal note by an unknown scribe; ninth century.

148. The Mowers

. . . After a space of the day they left the wood, and came to an open plain, and there were meadows on one side of them, and mowers mowing the meadows. And they came to a river before them, and the horses bent their heads and drank the water; and they went up out of the river on to a steep bank. And there they met a slender young lad with a cloth round his neck, and they saw a bundle in the cloth, but they did not know what it was; and there was a small blue pitcher in his hand and a cup at the mouth of the pitcher. And the lad greeted Gereint. 'God prosper you,' said Gereint, 'and whence do you come?' 'I come,' said he, 'from the city there before you. Lord,' said he, 'is it displeasing to you to ask where you come from too?' 'Not

1. Gereint; see Index.

so,' said he, 'I came through the wood yonder.' 'You did not come through the wood today.' 'No,' he said, 'I spent last night in the wood.' 'I suppose,' said he, 'that your state there last night was not good, and that you got neither food nor drink.' 'No, before God,' said he. 'Will you do as I advise,' said the lad, 'and take your meal. from me?' 'What sort of meal?' he said. 'The breakfast I was bringing to the mowers yonder, bread and meat and wine; and if you wish, sir, they shall get nothing.' 'I do wish it,' he said, 'and God reward you' . . .

Welsh; author unknown; twelfth century.

149. The White Lake of Carra

. . . When Patrick, glorious in grace, was suffering on goodly Cruach[1] – an anxious toilsome time for him, the protector of lay men and women –

God sent to comfort him a flock of spotless angelic birds; over the clear lake without fail they would sing in chorus their gentle proclamation.

And thus they called, auspiciously: 'Patrick, arise and come! Shield of the Gael, in pure glory, illustrious golden spark of fire.'

The whole host struck the lake with their smooth and shadowy wings, so that its chilly waters became like a silver sheen.

Hence comes the bright name *The White Lake of Carra* of the contests; I tell you this triumphant meaning as I have heard it in every church.

Irish; author unknown; eleventh century.

1. Croaghpatrick mountain, see Index.

150. Iubhdhán's Fairy House

I have a house in the land to the north, one half of it of red gold, the lower half of silver.

Its porch is of white bronze and its threshold of copper, and of the wings of white-yellow birds is its thatch, I think.

Its candlesticks are golden, with a candle of great purity, with a gem of precious stone in the very middle of the house.

But for myself and the high-queen, none of us are sad; a household there without old age, with yellow curly-crested hair.

Every man is a chess-player, there are good companies there without exclusion; the house is not closed against man or woman going to it.

> Irish; author unknown; twelfth–thirteenth century.

151. Uncomfortable Lodgings

. . . When they came towards the house what they saw was an old black grange with a flat gable-end, and a great deal of smoke coming from it. When they came inside they saw an uneven pavement full of holes, and wherever there was a hummock on it, a man could hardly stand on it because the ground was so slippery with the dung and stalings of cattle; and wherever there was a hole, a man would go in above his ankle, what with the mixture of water and cattle-stalings. There were holly twigs spread thickly on the ground, with their tips eaten away by the cattle. And when they came to the upper end of the hall of the house, they saw dusty bare alcoves, and an old hag tending a fire in one of the alcoves; and when she felt a fit of cold, she would throw a lapful of husks over the fire, so that it was not easy for anyone in the world to put up with the smoke from it going into his nostrils. In the other alcove they saw the yellow hide of a steer on the raised floor; and whoever of them should come to lie on that hide would find himself lucky.

When they had sat down they asked the hag where the people of the house were, and the hag would say nothing to them but surly words. And at that, the people arrived; a red-headed partly-bald wrinkled man, with a load of twigs on his back, and a little pale thin woman with a bundle under her arm. They greeted the men coldly, and the woman lit a fire of twigs for them and went to cook; and she brought them their food, barley bread and cheese and watered milk.

And at that, the wind and rain got up, so that it was not easy for anyone to go out for a necessary purpose;[1] and because their journey had been so unpleasant, they lost heart, and went to bed. When they looked at the bedstead, there was nothing on it but dusty chopped straw full of fleas, with the stumps of twigs sticking through it in plenty, and such straw as there was on it above their heads and below their feet had been eaten away by the steers. A stiff threadbare faded-red blanket, full of holes, was spread over it, and a sheet with gaping holes and rents on top of the blanket; and a half-empty pillow with a filthy pillowcase upon the sheet. They went to bed, and a heavy sleep fell on Rhonabwy's two companions, after first being tormented by the fleas and the discomfort; but Rhonabwy, since he could neither sleep nor rest, thought that it would be less of a torture for him if he went on the yellow steer's hide in the alcove to sleep. And there he slept . . .

Welsh; author unknown; early thirteenth century.

152. *The Cliff of Alternan*

. . . One day, as Suibhne ranged swiftly and restlessly over the land of Connaught, he came at last to Alternan in Tireragh. That was a lovely glen, with a lovely green-gushing stream flowing precipitously down over the cliff;

1. See Notes.

and there was a holy site there, where there was an assembly of very many saints and righteous people. Many too, there, were the fair and lovely trees with heavy luxuriant fruit, on that cliff; many there also were the sheltering ivy bowers, and the heavy-headed apple-trees bending to the ground with the weight of their fruit; and there were likewise on that cliff wild deer and hares and great heavy swine; and moreover, many were the fat seals which used to sleep there on that cliff, after coming out of the great sea beyond . . .

Irish; author unknown; twelfth century.

153. Édaín the Fairy

. . . He saw a woman at the edge of the spring, with a bright silver comb ornamented with gold, washing her hair in a silver bowl with four golden birds on it, and little flashing jewels of purple carbuncle on the rims of the bowl. She had a shaggy purple cloak made of fine fleece, and silver brooches of filigree work decorated with handsome gold, in the cloak; a long-hooded tunic on her, stiff and smooth, of green silk with embroidery of red gold. Wonderful ornaments of gold and silver with twining animal designs, in the tunic on her breast and her shoulders and her shoulder-blades on both sides. The sun was shining on her, so that the men could plainly see the glistening of the gold in the sunlight amid the green silk. There were two golden-yellow tresses on her head; each one was braided of four plaits, with a bead at the end of each plait. The colour of her hair seemed to them like the flower of the water-flag in summer, or like red gold that has been polished.

She was loosening her hair to wash it, and her arms were out through the opening at the neck of her dress. Her upper arms were as white as the snow of a single night, and they were soft and straight; and her clear and lovely cheeks were as red as the foxglove of the moor. Her eyebrows were as black as a beetle's wing; her teeth were like a shower of pearls in her head; her eyes were as blue as the bugloss; her lips were as red as vermilion; her shoulders were high and smooth and soft and white; her fingers were pure white and long; her arms were long; her slender long yielding smooth side, soft as wool, was as white as the foam of the wave. Her thighs were warm and glossy, sleek and white. Round and small, firm and white, were her knees. Her shins were short, white and straight. Her heels were even and straight and lovely from behind. If a ruler were laid against her feet, it would be hard to find any fault in them, unless it should make the flesh or skin swell out on them. The bright blush of the moon was in her noble face; the lifting of pride in her smooth brows; the ray of love-making in both her royal eyes; a dimple of sport in both her cheeks, in which there came and went flushes of fast purple as red as the blood of a calf, and others of the bright whiteness of snow. A gentle womanly dignity in her voice; a steady stately walk, a queenly pace. She was the fairest and loveliest and most perfect of the women of the world that the eyes of men had ever seen; they thought she must be of the fairies . . .

Irish; author unknown; ninth-century original.

154. Olwen

. . . And she came, wearing a flame-red silken tunic, and a massive collar of red gold round the girl's neck, with precious pearls and rubies in it. Her head was yellower than the flowers of the broom; her flesh was whiter than the foam of the wave; her palms and fingers were whiter than the flowers of the melilot among the small pebbles of a gushing spring. No eye was fairer than hers, not even the eye of the mewed hawk nor the eye of the thrice-mewed falcon. Whiter than the breast of a white swan were her two breasts; redder than the foxglove were her cheeks. All who saw her became filled with love for her. Four white clover flowers would grow up in her footprints wherever she went; and hence she was called *Olwen*[1] . . .

Welsh; author unknown; tenth-century original.

1. i.e. 'White Footprint.'

155. Gruffudd ap Cynan's Wife

... He took a wife, Angharad by name, daughter of Owein son of Edwin, who the wise men of the kingdom say was of noble birth, well-grown, with fair hair, large-eyed, of fine shape, with queenly figure and strong limbs and well-made legs and the best of feet, and long fingers and thin nails; kindly and eloquent, and good at food and drink; wise and prudent, a woman of good counsel, merciful towards her kingdom, charitable to the needy, and just in all things ...

Welsh; author unknown; twelfth century.

156. The Reign of Gruffudd ap Cynan

... He was renowned and famous both in lands far away and in those near to him. And then, he multiplied every kind of good thing in Gwynedd,[1] and the inhabitants began to build churches in all directions there, and to set woods and plant them, and to make orchards and gardens and encircle them with fences and ditches, and to make walled buildings, and to support themselves from the produce of the earth in the manner of the Romans. And Gruffudd, too, made great churches for himself at the chief courts, and built courts and honourably gave continual feasts. Indeed, he made Gwynedd glitter then with whitewashed churches as the heavens with stars ...

Welsh; author unknown; twelfth century.

157. From The Misty Corrie

... Your kindly slope, with bilberries and blaeberries, studded with cloudberries that are round-headed and red; wild-garlic clusters in the corners of rock terraces, and abounding tufted crags; the dandelion and pennyroyal, and

1. North Wales.

the soft white bog-cotton and sweet-grass there on every part of it, from the lowest level to where the peaks are at the topmost edge.

Fine is the clothing of Craig Mhór – there is no coarse grass for you there, but moss saxifrage of the juiciest covering it on this side and on that; the level hollows at the foot of the jutting rocks, where primroses and delicate daisies grow, are leafy, grassy, sweet and hairy, bristly, shaggy – every kind of growth there is.

There is a shady fringe of green water-cresses around every spring that is in its lands, a sorrel thicket at the base of the rough rocks, and sandy gravel crushed small and white; gurgling and plunging, coldly boiling, in swirls of water from the foot of the smooth falls, the splendid streams with their blue-braided tresses come dashing and spirting in a swerving gush . . .

Scottish Gaelic; Duncan Bàn MacIntyre; 1724–1812

158. *From* The Song of Summer

When I arose early while the dew was in the wood, on a bright morning in the small dark dell, I heard a piping melodiously playing, and the echo from the rocks giving sweet answer . . .

Every thick lonely copse has a green dress growing over it; sap is flowing upwards from all the lowest roots, through the twisting veins to bring forth the flowers; and cuckoo and thrush at evening chant their litany in the tree-tops.

The month of speckled eggs, of showers, of wild garlic, of delicate roses, of prosperity, which puts adornment unblemished on even the dreariest places; which banishes snow and cold to the rim of the high peaks, and in great dread of the sun they fade into the sky in a mist . . .

Even the weakest of creatures goes to the wood rejoicing;

the wren, brisk and valiant, hardy and neat, welcomes the morning without ceasing with its fine soft sweet reed-pipe, and the robin sings bass to it on the bough overhead.

Pure is the thrush's flute playing its elegant piping, on the flowery tree-tops and in the tall bare oak thicket in the dells of the wilderness, that are sweeter-smelling than wine; and trilling its rapid melody with quick accurate fingering . . .

The swift slender salmon in the water is lively, leaping upside-down, brisk, in the scaly white-bellied shoals, finny, red-spotted, big-tailed, silvery lights clothing it, with small freckles, glittering in colours; and with its crooked jaws all ready it catches flies by stealth . . .

It is most lovely to hear from the fold the faint low of the calf, vigorous, piebald, handsome, white-backed, short-haired, gentle, white-headed, keen-eyed, red-eared, white-bellied, lively, young, shaggy, soft-hoofed, well-grown, as it leaps to the lowing of the cows.

Light yellow primrose on the banks, delicate and bright and comely is your face, as you grow entwined in clusters, soft and shining, neat, spreading; you are the hardiest rose which comes from the earth, and you are decked out in the spring while the others still hide their eyes.

Fragrant is the smell of your sprig, meadow-sweet of the cairns, handsome and graceful in round bunches, tall-stemmed and bonny, in tufty, smooth-faced clumps, yellow-topped, curly and tall, round the lonely knolls where the wood-sorrel grows.

There are the shining hedgerows which cast a bountiful glow on every patch of daisies and fine heads of shamrock; so too with the enclosures bright with the wood-sorrel of the hollows, by the pleasant marshes where the hinds often come . . .

Scottish Gaelic; Alexander Macdonald; published 1751.

159. You Are Whiter than the Swan

. . . You are whiter than the swan on the swampy lake, you are whiter than the white sea-gull of the stream, you are whiter than the snow on the lofty peaks, you are whiter than the love of the angels of Heaven.

You are the lovely red rowan that calms the wrath and anger of all men, like a wave of the sea from flood to ebb, like a wave of the sea from ebb to flood . . .

Scottish Gaelic; from a traditional folk charm.

160. At the Battle of Magh Mucraimhe

. . . Moreover, the air above them was black meanwhile with devils waiting for the wretched souls, to drag them to Hell. There were no angels there, except only two, and they were above the head of Art wherever he went in the army, because of the just character of that rightful prince. Then either of the two armies made for the other. Fierce was the onslaught they made on either side. Bitter sights were seen there – the white fog of chalk and lime going up to the clouds from the shields and targes[1] as they were struck with the edges of swords and the points of spears and arrows, which were skilfully parried by the heroes; the beating and shattering of the bosses, as they were belaboured with swords and stones; the noise of the pelting weapons; the gushing and shedding of blood and gore from the limbs of the champions and the sides of the warriors . . .

Irish; author unknown; ninth–tenth century.

161. The Battle of Ventry

. . . After that however either of those two armies, equally fervent and equally eager, burst forth against the other like

1. The early Irish shields were whitewashed.

thick woods with crushing, clattering strokes, like the black gushes of a flood, quickly and roughly and dangerously, violently and fatally and destructively, boldly and swiftly and hastily; and many then were the gratings of swords against bones and the noises of bone being hacked; and the bodies being gashed and eyes being blinded and arms being cut off short, and mothers without sons and fair wives without husbands. Moreover the upper elements echoed the meeting of the battle, telling of the evils and the sufferings which were fated to take place that day, and the sea muttered, telling of the losses, and the waves raised a vast and pitiful heavy cry in long lamentation for them, and the sea beasts bellowed, telling of them in their bestial way, and the wild hills shouted at the danger of that attack, and the woods trembled in bewailing the heroes, and the grey rocks cried out before the deeds of the sharp spear-points, and the winds sobbed in telling of the great deeds, and the earth trembled in foreboding the heavy slaughter, and the sun veiled itself in darkness before the shouting of the grey hosts, and the clouds became lustrous black for the space of that time; and the hounds and the wolf-packs and the ravens and the wild women of the glen and the spectres of the air and the wolves of the forest shrieked together from every direction and from every side around them, and a demoniac devilish array of tempters to evil and wrong were urging them on against each other . . .

Irish; author unknown; fourteenth century.

162. The Monster of Scattery Island

. . . When the monster heard them, it shook its head, and its bristles and its rough hair stood up on it, and it looked at them unlovingly and furiously. Not calm, friendly, or gentle was the look it gave them, for it was astonished that anyone should come to it in its island. It marched towards them, then, firmly and impetuously, so that the ground shook under its feet. Repulsive, outlandish, fierce, and very terrifying

was the beast that arose there. Its front end was like a horse,
with a glowing blazing eye in its head, sharp, savage,
furious, angry, keen, crimson, bloody, very harsh, rapidly
rolling. Anyone would think that its eye would go through
him, as it looked at him. It had two hideous thick legs under
it in front. Iron claws on it, which struck showers of fire
from the stony rocks where they trod across them. It had a
fiery breath which burned like embers. It had a belly like
a pair of bellows. The tail fins of a whale on it behind, with
iron nails on them, pointing backwards; they laid bare the
surface of the ground wherever they went, behind the monster. It would travel over sea and land alike, when it wished.
Now the sea would boil with the extent of its heat and its
venomousness, when it rushed into it. Boats could not catch
it; no one escaped it to tell the tale of it, from then till now . . .

> Irish; author unknown; tenth-century original?

163. St Brendan's Vision of Hell

. . . However the Devil revealed the gate of Hell to Brénainn
then. And Brénainn beheld that rough murky prison, full of
stench, full of flame, full of filth, full of encampments of
venomous demons, full of the weeping and shrieking and
injury and pitiful cries and great wailings and lamentation
and beating together of hands, of the tribes of sinners; and
a dismal sorrowful life in kernels of torture, in prisons of
fire, in streams of waves of everlasting fire, in a cup of
eternal sorrow, in black dark sloughs, in chairs of mighty
flame, in profusion of sorrow and death and torment and
bonds and irresistible heavy combat, with the terrible
yelling of the venomous demons; in the eternally dark,
eternally cold, eternally stinking, eternally foul, eternally
gloomy, eternally rough, eternally long, eternally melancholy, deadly, baneful, severe, fiery-haired dwelling place
of the most hideous depths of Hell, on the slopes of mountains of everlasting fire, without stay, without rest; but
troops of demons are dragging them into pitiful, grievous,

rigid, fiery, dark, deep, hidden, empty, base, black, idle, filthy, antiquated, old and stinking, everlastingly quarrelsome, everlastingly pugnacious, everlastingly wearisome, everlastingly deadly, everlastingly tearful prisons; sharp, fierce, windy, full of wailing, screaming, complaining, and bitter crying; horrible.

There are curly, cruel, bold, big-headed maggots; and yellow, white, great-jawed monsters; fierce ravening lions; red, black, brown, devilish dragons; mighty treacherous tigers; inky bristly scorpions; red high-soaring hawks; rough sharp-beaked griffins; black hump-backed beetles; sharp snouted flies; bent bony-beaked wasps; heavy iron mallets; ancient old rough flails; sharp swords; red spears; black demons; stinking fires; streams of poison; cats scratching; dogs rending; hounds hunting; demons calling; fetid lakes; great sloughs; dark pits; deep gullies; high mountains; hard crags; a mustering of demons; a filthy camp; torture without cease; a ravenous swarm; frequent conflict; endless fighting; demons torturing; torment in abundance; a sorrowful life.

A place in which there are frosty, bitter, everlastingly fetid, widespread, wide-stretched, agitated, grievous, putrid, deliquescent, burning, bare, rapid, full-fiery streams; hard, rocky, sharp-headed, long, cold, deep, swampy little straits of the sea; bare burning plains; peaked rugged hills; hard verminous ravines; rough thorny moors; black fiery forests; filthy monster-infested roads; congealed stinking-billowed seas; huge iron spikes; black bitter waters; many extraordinary places; a dirty everlastingly-gloomy assembly; bitter wintry winds; frosty everlastingly-falling snow; red fiery blades; base dark faces; swift ravening demons; vast unheard-of tortures.

Then his followers asked Brénainn, 'Who are you talking to?' said they. Brénainn told them that it was the Devil who was talking to him; and told them a little of the tortures he had seen, as we have said, according as it has been found in the ancient writings of the Old Testament . . .

Irish; author unknown; twelfth century.

164. The Homeward Voyage

. . . Then that deadly hostile army arose and went to the havens and the quays where their boats were ready for them; and they set afloat their terrible wonderful very dreadful sea-monsters, and their swift long firm barques, and their dark many-coloured sombre ships, and their slippery straight-thwarted strong steady cutters, and their very trim stitched sloops, from their wide and very smooth stocks, to make their way from the land of Spain to Ireland. Into every swift-sailing ship of them were put very neat even rows of very smooth long handy oars; and they began a precise, steady, proper, unified, vigorous, nimble-handed, swift, ardent-coursing, very dexterous, unhesitating rowing in the face of the waves and the currents and the eddying storms; so that wild and high, arrogant and haughty-hearted were the stout rude-fronted hateful-billowing retorts of the waves as they talked with the cutters and the shapely prows. The fierce proud watery pools were white-streaked wild-streaming levels, scattering and tossing the bright-sided thick and slippery fishes from off the red oars, among the very-dense foamy-coursing ocean waves, till they were swept from the shelter of the coasts and the protection of the lands and the gentle calm of the shores; so that that company saw nothing of the whole world but the high haughty stormy waves of the deep and the rough roaring sea, tossing under the wild-rushing courses of the gale as it fell upon them, and the great frenzied throngs of the thick squalls as they struggled with them over the wide hollows of the wave-troughs, and the uncouth perilous showery-crested sea feeding its strength against the swift sailing of the ships; until the sea grew choppy, wearisomely shuddering, and dripping with mist, under the contention of the winds and the wild waves, in spite of the labouring arms of the mighty crews as they made their ships leap across the ocean.

Then there came upon them a truce between the elements and the high constellations, and they got a favourable wind straight behind them; and the manly crews arose to their tasks, and fastened the stiff thick firm sheets to the red gunwales neatly and in unison, without stretching or excessive straining; and the fierce very-ready crews busied themselves expertly and cunningly with the long ropes, handling them without negligence or error from clew-lines to braces. And under the labour of their hands the ships went forward boldly on their journey, over the deep wet depths of the sea, and over the swaying ridges of the hilly ocean, and over the mountainous rollers of the main, and over the heavy sullen ramparts of the waves, and over the dark shower-dripping hollows of the shores, and over the haughty close-sided billows of the currents, and over the turbulent furious fierce horizons of the deep; until the sea became clamorous, wild and arrogant as it swelled and rose under the wrath of the cold wind whelming it, so that the high constellations understood readily the anger and the malice of the ocean as it grew and increased, when the ghastly howlings of the wind came to excite it.

Woe indeed to him who chanced to be all unprotected between those two mighty elements, the sea and the gale, athwart the sides of the strong ships and the firm galleys and the fine cutters! until its sand and its pebbly seaweed cast up from bottom to surface became a hideous howling expanse over the skerries and the depths of the ocean; so that the wind did not leave them a plank not started, nor a bolt not fused, nor a rib not crushed, nor a cord not snapped, nor a berth not rapidly bailed, nor a mast not shaken, nor a yard not twisted, nor a sail not tangled, nor a hero not injured, nor a warrior not dismayed, nor a soldier not discouraged; but the nobles and the great chiefs, the braves and the leaders of the army, were gathering and collecting their ropes and their tackle, as long as the sea should be spending its spirits and its uproar on the gale.

However, when the wind had blown out its fury, and got neither welcome nor homage from the ocean, it went away, reckless and light-headed, to the upper abode of its dwelling. Moreover the sea was tired of its clamour, and the contrary waves abandoned their course, so that the waters calmed down and became a steady level; and the spirit returned to their nobles, and the strength to their army, and the skill to their heroes, and the senses to their warriors; and they sailed on under that course to the Island of Beare of the shingly shores . . .

Irish; author unknown; thirteenth–fourteenth century.

165. The Troublesome Gillie

. . . He had not been there long when he saw coming straight towards him from the east a bold and very ugly giant, a devilish mis-shapen creature, a surly ill-favoured slave; and this is how he was, with a stout black ugly-coloured dismal-looking shield on the humped slope of his back, and a broad-grooved clean-cutting sword at his black twisted left thigh, and two accursed broad-bladed spears, which for a long while before that had not been taken up in time of fight or encounter, sticking out over his shoulder. He had a ragged threadbare cloak over his clothes and his garments; and every limb of him was blacker than a blacksmith's coal quenched in cold icy water. He had a bad-tempered mis-shapen bare-ribbed horse, with meagre grey shambling feeble-legged hindquarters and a rough iron halter, and he was dragging it after him; and it was a great wonder that he did not wrench its head off its handsome body or off its neck, with every tug that he gave the rough iron halter, trying to knock some travel and progress out of it; and even greater than that was the wonder that the horse did not tear the long thick lengthy arms of the big man out of the trunk of his chest with every baulk and every stop that it made, trying to go backwards. And like the roaring of a great and mighty wave was every stout vigorous strong penetrating thwack that the big man struck on the horse with his iron club, trying to knock some travel and progress out of it . . .

Irish; author unknown; fifteenth–sixteenth century?

HUMOUR AND SATIRE

NOTE

One would not expect the land of Swift, Shaw and Joyce to be devoid of a power of satire and sense of humour in its native literature. In fact, from the earliest times satire was one of the main functions of the Celtic poet. A chief who did not reward a bard for his song of praise with gifts thought adequate to the occasion would be punished through a satire; and in a warrior aristocracy, where a reputation for the princely virtues of generosity and courage was of the highest social importance, this might be a disaster. Hence satire was always greatly dreaded; in some parts of Ireland people still hesitate to offend a poet for fear of being satirized. The most typical example in this book has been included in the next group (no. 192), because it is a bardic poem and is partly a eulogy. It will show how savage and how personally damaging such an attack could be. Others, less strictly of the bardic kind or later than that period, are given here.

The humour of Celtic literature in its early period is mostly of a rather elementary kind, as one might expect; a Homeric sort of humour, or that of the folk-tale. Bricriu's trick on the intoxicated women (no. 167), the misfortunes of Ysbaddaden (no. 166), the marvellous men in the entourage of the Celtic king Arthur (no. 169), and the surely intentionally humorous passages in the early Welsh laws (no. 173), illustrate this. A more sophisticated treatment is not usual till later, notably with Dafydd ap Gwilym (nos. 174–8), who had a well-developed faculty for laughing at himself. The two passages from the *Midnight Court* (nos. 184, 185) show that blend of humour, satire and pure gusto which is so marked in this extraordinary poem, and is so characteristically Irish. Readers of James Joyce will be at home here; and those who wish to know more of this, one of the most remarkable products of the Celtic genius, should read Frank O'Connor's verse translation (London, Fridberg, 1945).

No. 171 includes a piece of parody, since the similes applied to the fleas in the blanket are a skit on the same similes used in the hero-tales of the numbers of the enemy killed in the victorious charge of a warrior. Parody is a definite genre in Celtic literature, and is common in the *Vision of Mac Conglinne*, from which this piece is taken.

HUMOUR AND SATIRE

166. A Cursed Undutiful Son-in-law

. . . They went up after her into the fort; and they killed
nine porters that were at the nine gates without a man of
them screaming, and nine mastiffs without one of them
giving a squeal; and they went on to the hall. Said they,
'The greetings of God and men to you, Ysbaddaden, Chief
Giant!' 'And you, where are you journeying?' 'We journey
to seek Olwen your daughter, for Culhwch son of Cilydd.'
'Where are my naughty servants and my rascals?' said he;
'push the forks up under my eyelids, so that I may see my
future son-in-law.' That was done. 'Come here tomorrow,
and I will give you some answer.' They arose; and Ysbaddaden, Chief Giant, grasped one of the three poisoned darts
which were at his hand, and threw it after them; and Bedwyr
caught it and threw it back, and pierced Ysbaddaden,
Chief Giant, neatly through the kneecap. Said he, 'A
cursed undutiful son-in-law! I shall walk up a slope the
worse for this. The poisoned iron has stung me like the bite
of a horse-fly. Cursed be the smith who made it, and the
anvil on which it was made – so sharp it is!'

They lodged that night in the house of Custennin; and
the next day, having set fine combs in their hair, they came
in state to the hall. Said they, 'Ysbaddaden, Chief Giant,
give us your daughter in return for her bride-price and her
maiden-fee to be paid to you and to her two kinswomen;
and if you will not give her you shall get your death for
her.' 'Her four great-grandmothers and her four great-
grandfathers are still alive; I must consult with them.' 'You
shall have that,' they said; 'let us go to our meal.' As they
arose, he seized the second dart that was at his hand and
threw it after them; and Menw son of Teirgwaedd caught

it and threw it back, and pierced him through the midst of his breast, so that it sprang out at the small of his back. 'A cursed undutiful son-in-law! The hard iron has stung me like the bite of a horse-leech. Cursed be the furnace in which it was smelted! When I go up a hillside I shall have griping, and colic and frequent queasiness.'

They went to their meal; and the third day they came to the court. They said, 'Ysbaddaden, Chief Giant, do not shoot at us any more, do not bring upon yourself wounding and mortal injury and your death.' 'Where are my servants? Raise up the forks, for my eyelids have fallen over my eyeballs, so that I can look at my future son-in-law.' They arose, and as they arose he seized the third poisoned dart and threw it after them; and Culhwch caught it and threw it just as he wanted, and pierced him through the eyeball, so that it came out through the back of his neck. 'A cursed undutiful son-in-law! As long as I am left alive, the sight of my eyes will be the worse for this; when I go against the wind they will water; I shall have headache and giddiness every new moon. Cursed be the furnace in which it was smelted! I feel it like the bite of a mad dog, how the poisoned iron has pierced me.' They went to their meal . . .

Welsh; author unknown; tenth-century original.

167. Bricriu's Practical Joke

. . . Now Bricriu and his queen were in their gallery, and from his couch he could see the arrangements in the palace and what was going on there. He searched his wits, how he should contrive to set the women against each other, as he had set the men. And when Bricriu had done searching his wits as to how he should contrive it, at that very moment Fedhelm of the Youthful Form came out of the palace with fifty women, heavy with drink. Bricriu saw them go by. 'It is well tonight, wife of Loeghaire the Victorious! Fedhelm of the Youthful Form is no misnomer for you, because of the perfection of your form and of your mind and of your lineage. Conchobhar, king of a province of Ireland, is your father, and Loeghaire the Victorious is your husband; only, I should not think it too much that none of the women of Ulster should come before you into the Banquet Hall, and that all the women of Ulster should be at your heels. If it is you who come first into the house tonight, you shall enjoy for ever the prime of queenship above all the women of Ulster.' Fedhelm went away then, across three fields from the house.

After that Lennabhair came out, the daughter of Éoghan son of Durthacht, wife of Conall the Triumphant. Bricriu called her, and said, 'It is well, Lennabhair,' he said, 'Lennabhair is no misnomer for you, you are the sweetheart[1] and darling of all the men of the world for your brilliance and your fame. As much as your husband surpasses the warriors of the world in valour and form, by so much do you surpass the women of Ulster.' Though the wiles which he used on Fedhelm were great, he used twice as much on Lennabhair in the same way.

Then Eimher came out, with fifty women. 'Greetings, Eimher, daughter of Forghall the Dexterous,' said Bricriu, 'wife of the best man in Ireland! Eimher of the Lovely Hair is no misnomer for you, the kings and princes of Ireland are ever thinking of you. As much as the sun surpasses the stars of heaven, by so much do you surpass all the women of the world in form and figure and lineage, in youthfulness and brilliance and fame, in glory and understanding and utterance.' Though the wiles which he used on the other women were great, he used three times as much on Eimher.

The three companies went away after that until they were all in the same place, three fields distant from the house; and none of them knew of the others that they had been set against each other by Bricriu. They came towards their house then. A steady fine dignified pace in the first field, scarcely did any of them put one foot past the other.

1. See Index sv. Lennabhair.

In the second field their steps were shorter and quicker there. In the field nearest to the house, however, each woman kept up with difficulty with the others, and they picked up their smocks to their buttocks in contending to get into the house first; because what Bricriu had said to each of them, unknown to the others, was that she should be queen of the whole province who went into the house the first of them. The commotion as they struggled to go first, each in front of the other, was as great as the noise of fifty chariots coming there, so that the whole palace shook, and the warriors sprang to their weapons and all sought to massacre one another in the house. 'Stop!' said Senchae, 'they are not enemies who have come, but it is Bricriu who has set a quarrel between the women who have gone out. I swear by the oath of my tribe,' said he, 'unless the house is closed against them our dead will be more than our living.' The porters shut the door then. Eimher, daughter of Forghall the Dexterous, wife of Cú Chulainn, arrived first before the other women at top speed and set her back against the door, and called to the porters before the other women; and the men inside arose at that, each man to open for his wife, so that it might be his wife who should come into the house first . . . At that, this is what the men who were inside did, namely Loeghaire and Conall the Triumphant, as their warrior's glow burst from them on hearing the talk of the women, they broke one of the pillars of the palace outwards, opposite themselves, and that was the way their wives came in to them. But Cú Chulainn heaved up the house beside his couch, so that the stars of heaven outside were visible beneath, under the wall; and that was the way his wife came in, with the fifty women belonging to each of the other two wives and the fifty women belonging to his own wife, so that there might be no comparison between her and the other wives, for there was no comparison between him and anyone else. Cú Chulainn let the palace down afterwards, so that seven cubits of the wattling of the house sank into the earth, so that the whole stronghold shook; and Bricriu's gallery was thrown to the very ground, and Bricriu himself and his queen fell into the dunghill in the middle of the courtyard among the dogs . . .

Irish; author unknown; eighth-century original.

168. Culhwch's Arrival at the Court of King Arthur

. . . The lad said, 'Is there a porter?' 'There is.[1] And you (may you lose your head!), why do you ask? Every New Year's Day I act as Arthur's porter, but my deputies however for the rest of the year; namely Huandaw and Gogigwr and Llaesgenym and Penpingion, who travels on his head to spare his feet, not pointing towards the sky nor pointing towards the earth, but like a stone rolling on the floor of a courtyard.' 'Open the gate!' 'I will not open it.' 'Why will you not open it?' 'The knife has gone into the food and the drink into the horn, and they are bustling about in Arthur's hall. Except the son of a rightful king of a country, or a craftsman who brings his craft, no one may be allowed inside. You shall have food for your hounds and corn for your horse, and hot peppered steaks for yourself, and brimming wine, and songs as entertainment. Food for fifty men shall be brought you to the guest house, where foreigners and sons of other lands eat, those who do not make good their right to enter Arthur's court. You will be no worse off there than Arthur in his court. You shall have a woman to sleep with you, and songs as entertainment at your side. Tomorrow at the hour of tierce, when the gate is opened for all those who have come here today, for you first of all shall the gate be opened; and you may sit wherever you choose in Arthur's hall, from its upper end to its lower.'

The lad said, 'I will do none of these things. If you will open the gate, it is well. If you will not open it, I will bring dishonour to your lord and ill fame to you; and I will give three screams before this gate so that they shall be heard equally at the headland of Penwith in Cornwall and in the lowland of Din Sol in the North and in Esgeir Oerfel in

1. Glewlwyd Gafaelfawr speaks; see below.

Ireland, and all the pregnant women in this court shall miscarry, and as for those that are not pregnant their entrails shall turn over disastrously within them, so that they shall never be pregnant from today on.' Said Glewlwyd Gafaelfawr, 'However you may scream at the regulations of Arthur's court, you shall not be let in until I go first to speak to Arthur' . . .

Welsh; author unknown; tenth-century original.

169. Some of King Arthur's Wonderful Men

. . . Morfran son of Tegid – no man set his weapon in him in the battle of Camlan because he was so ugly; everyone thought he was an assistant devil. There was hair on him like the hair of a stag. And Sandde Angel-Face – no one set his spear in him in the battle of Camlan because he was so beautiful; everyone thought he was an assistant angel . . . And Henwas the Winged, son of Erim, and Henbeddestr son of Erim, and Scilti the Lightfooted, son of Erim. Those three men had three magic qualities. Henbeddestr never found any man who could run as fast as he, either on horse or on foot. Henwas the Winged, no four-footed creature could ever keep up with him for the length of one acre, much less any further than that. Scilti the Lightfooted, when the urge to travel on his lord's business was on him, he never looked for a road if he knew which way he should go; but when there was a wood, he would go along the tops of the trees, and when there was a mountain he would go along the tips of the rushes; and throughout his life not a rush bent under his feet, much less broke, because of his lightness. Teithi the Old, son of Gwynhan, whose domains the sea overwhelmed, and he himself barely escaped, and came to Arthur. And there was a magic quality on his knife, since he came here, that no haft would ever stay on it; and for that reason a sickness grew in him and a languishing, as long as he lived, and he died of that . . .

Drem the son of Dremidydd, who could see, from Celli

Wig in Cornwall as far as Penn Blathaon in Scotland, when
the gnat rose up with the sun in the morning . . . Cynyr of
the Beautiful Beard – Cei was said to be his son. He said to
his wife, 'If I have any share in your child, girl, his heart
will be cold always, and there will be no warmth in his
hands. He will have another magic quality, if he is a son of
mine; he will be obstinate. He will have another magic
quality; when he carries a burden, whether it be great or
small, it will never be seen, neither when face to face nor
from behind his back. He will have another magic quality;
no one will endure water or fire so well as he. He will have
another magic quality; there will never be a servitor or
official like him.' . . . Gwallgoig was another one; whatever
township he came to, though there were three hundred
homesteads in it, if he needed anything he would never
allow sleep on the eyes of anyone as long as he was
there . . .

Osla of the Big Knife, who carried a short broad side-
arm; whenever Arthur and his armies came before a
torrent, a narrow place was looked for across the water and
his knife in its sheath was laid over the torrent; it would be
bridge enough for the army of the three lands of Britain
and its three adjacent islands,[1] with their booty . . . And
Gilla Stag-Leg; he would jump three hundred acres at a
single jump – the champion jumper of Ireland. Sol and
Gwaddn Osol and Gwaddn of the Bonfire. Sol could stand
a whole day on one foot. Gwaddn Osol, if he stood on top
of the biggest mountain in the world it would become a
level plain under his foot. Gwaddn of the Bonfire, the flashing sparks from his soles when anything hard came in
contact with him were as great as a hot mass of iron when it
is drawn out of the forge. He would clear the way for Arthur
on the march. Hir Erwm and Hir Atrwm, the day when they
came to a feast they would raid three hundred townships
to supply them; they feasted till noon and caroused till
night; when they went to bed they ate the heads of the
vermin for hunger, as if they had never eaten food. When

1. See Notes.

they went to a feast they left neither fat nor lean, neither hot nor cold, neither sour nor sweet, neither fresh nor salt. Huarwar the son of Halwn, who demanded his fill from Arthur as a gift. It was one of the three excessive plagues of Cornwall and Devon when his fill was got for him. He was never found to smile except when he was full . . .

Sugn the son of Sugnedudd, who would suck up a sea on which there were three hundred ships, until it was nothing but a dry strand; he had red-hot heartburn. Cachamwri, Arthur's servant; when a barn was shown him, though there were the crop of thirty ploughs in it, he would thresh it with an iron flail until the posts and the rafters and the cross-beams were no better than the small oats on the floor of the barn . . . Gwefl son of Gwastad; on a day when he was sad, he would let one of his lips hang down to his navel and the other would become a cap over his head. Uchdryd Cross-Beard, who would throw the bristly red beard which he had across the fifty rafters that were in Arthur's hall . . . Clust son of Clustfeinad; though he were buried seven fathoms in the earth, he would hear the ant fifty miles away when it set out in the morning from its lair. Medr son of Medredydd, who from Celli Wig could shoot a wren at Esgeir Oerfel in Ireland right through its two legs. Gwiawn Cat's-Eye, who could cut off the haw from the eye of a gnat without hurting the eye . . .

Cei had a peculiar gift; for nine nights and nine days would his breath last under water; for nine nights and nine days could he be without sleep. No doctor could cure a sword-cut of Cei's. Skilful was Cei; he could be as tall as the highest tree in the wood when he chose. Another magic quality he had; when the rain was heaviest, whatever was in his hand would be dry for a handsbreadth above his hand and another beneath his hand, because of the extent of his heat. And when his companions felt the cold most, that would be a means of kindling for them to light a fire . . .

Welsh; author unknown; tenth-century original.

170. 'Eating a Mouse Includes its Tail'

... 'That is true,' said the king, 'this is Lughaidh, and it is through fear of me that they do not name themselves'[1] ... 'Well now,' said the king, 'kill me a batch of mice.' Then he put a mouse in the food served to each man, raw and bloody, with the hair on, and this was set before them; and they were told they would be killed unless they ate the mice. They grew very pale at that. Never had a more distressing vexation been put upon them. 'How are they?' said the king. 'They are miserable, with their plates before them.' ... 'Tell them they shall be killed unless they eat.' 'Bad luck to him who decreed it,' said Lughaidh, putting the mouse in his mouth, while the king watched him. At that all the men put them in. There was one poor wretch of them who gagged as he put the tail of the mouse to his mouth. 'A sword across your throat,' said Lughaidh, 'eating a mouse includes its tail.' Then he swallowed the mouse's tail. 'They do as you tell them,' said the king from the door. 'I do as they tell me, too,' said Lughaidh. 'Are you Lughaidh?' said the king. 'That is my name,' said Lughaidh ...

Irish; author unknown; ninth–tenth century.

171. The Guest House at the Monastery of Cork

... The guest house was open when he arrived. That day was a day of three things – wind, and snow, and rain in its doorway; so that the wind left not a straw from the thatch nor a speck of ash that it did not sweep through the opposite door, under the beds and couches and partitions of the royal house. The blanket of the guest house was rolled up in a bundle on its bed, and it was full of lice and fleas. That was natural, because it was never aired by day nor turned by night, since it was rarely unoccupied when it might be turned. The guest house bath had last night's water in it,

1. See Notes.

and with its heating-stones was beside the doorpost. The scholar found no one to wash his feet, so he himself took off his shoes and washed his hands and feet in that dirty washing-water, and soaked his shoes in it afterwards. He hung his book-satchel on the peg in the wall, put up his shoes, and tucked his arms together into the blanket and wrapped it round his legs. But as multitudinous as the sands of the sea or as sparks of fire or as dew-drops on a May-day morning or as the stars of heaven were the lice and the fleas biting his feet, so that he grew sick at them. And no one came to visit him nor to wait on him . . .

Irish; author unknown; twelfth century.

172. *The Elders of the End of the World*

More bitter to me than Death coming between my teeth are the folk that will come after me, who will be all of one kind.

Wicked is the time which will come then; envy, murder, oppression of the weak, every harm coming swiftly, and neither layman righteous nor righteous priest.

No king who concedes right or justice, no virgin bishop over the altar, no landowner who will raise tithes from his herds and his fine cattle.

The elders who did God's will at the beginning of time were bare-haunched, scurvy, muddy; *they* were not stout and fat.

The men of keen learning, who served the King of the Sun, did not molest boys or women; their natures were pure.

Scanty shirts, clumsy cloaks, hearts weary and piteous, short rough shocks of hair – and very rough monastic rules.

There will come here after that the elders of the latter-day world, with plunder, with cattle, with mitres, with rings, with chessboards,

With silk and sarsenet and satin, with delightful feather-beds after drinking, with contempt for the wisdom of beloved God – they shall be in the safe-keeping of the Devil.

I tell the seed of Adam, the hypocrites will come, they will assume the shapes of God – the slippery ones, the robbers.

They shall fade away with the same speed as grass and young corn in the green earth; they shall pass away together like the flower of the fields.

The imposters of the latter-day world shall all go on one path, into the grasp of the Devil, by God's will, into dark bitter torments.

Irish; author unknown; twelfth century?

173. From the Early Welsh Laws

. . . A hundred cows for every *cantref*[1] in his kingdom are to be paid as the fine for an insult to the king; and a rod of silver long enough to reach from the ground to the top of his head when he is sitting on his throne, as thick as his third finger, with three knobs at the top and three at the bottom, as thick as the rod; and a bowl of gold big enough to contain in it a full drink for the king, as thick as the finger-nail of a ploughman who has ploughed for seven years, with a golden cover on it as thick as the bowl and as broad as the king's face . . .

. . . Whoever kills the cat that guards the king's barn, or steals it, its head is to be set down on a clean level floor, and its tail is to be held up, and then wheaten grains are to be poured around it until they cover the tip of its tail. Any other cat is worth four legal pence . . . In law, essential qualifica-tions of a cat are that it should be perfect of ear and eye and tail and teeth and claws, not singed by the fire; and that it should kill mice and not eat its kittens, and should not be caterwauling every full moon . . .

1. See Index.

... A freeman's wife may give away her tunic and her mantle and her kerchief and her shoes, and her flour and cheese and butter and milk, without her husband's permission, and may lend all the household utensils. The wife of a villein may not give away anything without her husband's permission except her headdress; and she cannot lend anything except her sieve and riddle, and that only as far as her cry may be heard when her foot is on her threshold ...

... An adult woman who elopes with a man and is taken by him to a wood or a thicket or a house, and is violated and let go again, if she complains to her family and in the courts, as proof of her chastity a bull of three winters is to be taken and its tail is to be shaved and smeared with fat, and then the tail is to be thrust through a hurdle; and then the woman shall go into the house and put her foot on the threshold and take the tail in her hands; and a man shall come on either side of the bull with a goad in the hand of each, to stir up the bull; and if she can hold the bull she may take it for her insult-fine and as recompense for her chastity; and if she cannot she may take as much of the fat as sticks to her hands. A woman who gives herself up to a man in wood or thicket, and is abandoned by the man to woo another, and comes to complain to her family and to the courts, if the man denies it let him swear an oath on a bell without a clapper; but if he offers to make compensation, let him pay her with a penny as broad as her behind ...

Welsh; authors unknown; twelfth century (see Notes).

174. The Vanity of Women

SOME of the girls of these lands put pearls and pure bright rubies splendidly set in gold upon their brows, for the merry fair-day; and wear red (a very effective colour for a girl) and green — and bad luck to her who has no lover! Not an arm is seen, nor the neck of any maid of slender eyebrows, without its load of beads around it; bold hawks of the sunlight they, the marvel of one's life. Does the sun on his wearying travels need to leave the place where he is and seek more colour? No more is there need for my lovely mistress to put a frontlet on her fair brow, nor to gaze over into the mirror – the white girl's looks are well enough without. A yew bow unsound for battle, and reckoned as being almost in two bits (truly a durable piece of gear!) has its back gilded, and this bow is sold for a great price; I know it for a fact. Men don't suspect, though the thought is true, that there can be flaw or deceit in a pretty thing. Marry, is the white wall any the worse for being under a serviceable covering of lime-wash, than if a pound had been paid (a bogus price for a man!) to a painter to come to paint the bare space handsomely, all speckled and gaudy, with colour of shining gold and other handsome tints as well, and with fine figures of armorial bearings? Truly, O brighter than the stars, my body aches wherever I go – you, your lover's ruin, white-toothed maiden who deserve praise, you are better in your fine pale grey robe than a countess in cloth of gold.

Welsh; Dafydd ap Gwilym, *c.* 1325–*c.* 1380.

175. The Girls of Llanbadarn

I AM twisted with passion – plague on all the girls of the parish! since I suffered from trysts which went amiss, and could never win a single one of them, neither gentle hopeful maid, nor little lass, nor hag, nor wife. What fright is this, what mischief, what failure, that they'll have none of me? What harm could it be for a fine-browed maiden to meet me in the thick dark wood? It would be no shame to her to see me in my leafy lair. There has never been a time when I did not fall in love with one or two in a single day; there was never a spell so persistent as this, not even on those as passionate as Garwy.[1] Yet for all that I was no nearer to winning one of them, than if she were my enemy. There

1. A legendary lover.

was never a Sunday at Llanbadarn but that I was there, while the others found fault with it, with my face turned to some dainty girl and the nape of my neck to holy God.[1] But after all my long staring past my hat's feather across the congregation, one fine sprightly maid would say to another one, fortunate and discreet, 'That pale boy with the wanton face and long hair like his sister's on his head, how lascivious is the sidelong glance of his looks! He knows sin well.' 'Is that how it is with him?' says the other at her side, 'he shall get no response while the world lasts – to the Devil with him, the silly thing.' The bright girl's curse bewildered me, a poor return for my giddy love! I must succeed in giving up these ways, these awful fantasies; I must be a man and turn hermit (O villainous trade!). I have learned a sharp lesson; after much staring behind me, the image of frustration, I, the lover of mighty song, have cricked my neck and won no mate.

Welsh; Dafydd ap Gwilym, c. 1325–c. 1380.

176. A Night at an Inn

I CAME to a choice city with my handsome squire in my train, a place of liberal banqueting, a fine gay way of spending money, to find a public inn worthy enough, and I would have wine – I have been vain since childhood. I discovered a fair lissome maiden in the house, my sweet soul! and I set my heart wholly upon the slender, blessed girl like the sun in the east. I paid for a roast and expensive wine, not merely out of boastfulness, for myself and the fair girl yonder; and invited the modest maiden to my bench, a sport which young men love. I was bold and persistent, and whispered to her two words of magic, this is certain; and, no laggard lover, I made a pact to come to the sprightly girl, the black-browed maid, when the company should have gone to bed. When all were asleep but I and the lass I sought most skilfully to find my way to the girl's bed – it

1. i.e. with his back to the altar.

was a miserable journey, and came to grief. I got a vexatious fall there, and made a clatter – not a good exploit; in such reckless mischief it is easier to get up awkwardly than very nimbly. I did not spring up unhurt; I struck my shin (oh, my shank!) above the ankle against the side of a silly squeaking stool, left there by the ostler. In rising where I was placed, unable to step freely but continually led astray in my frenzied struggles – my Welsh friends, it was a deplorable affair, too much eagerness is not lucky – I knocked my forehead against the end of a table, where a basin rolled freely for a while, and an echoing copper pan. The table, a bulky object, fell, and its two trestles and all the utensils with it. The pan gave a clang behind me which was heard far away, and the basin yelled, and the dogs began to bark at me – I was a wretched man! Beside the big walls there lay three Englishmen in a stinking bed, fussing about their three packs, Hickin and Jenkin and Jack. One of these varlets muttered angry words to the other two, with his slobbering mouth: 'There's a Welshman prowling sneakily here, and some busy fraud is afoot. He's a thief, if we allow it; look out, and be on your guard against him.' The groom roused all the company together, and an ignominious affair began, they hunting about furiously to find me, and I, haggard and ghastly in my anguish, keeping mum in the darkness. I prayed, not fearlessly but hiding away like one terrified; and by dint of praying hard and from the heart, and by the grace of the true Jesus, I regained my former lodging in the grip of sleeplessness, and without the reward I had looked for. I escaped, for the saints stood by me; and I implore God for forgiveness.

Welsh; Dafydd ap Gwilym, *c.* 1325–*c.* 1380.

177. *The Magpie's Advice*

ONCE I was in the grove, sick for the sake of my bright girl, composing a love-charm, a brilliant snatch of song, on a day of sweet sky at the beginning of April. The nightingale was on the green boughs, and in his turret among the leaves the handsome blackbird, the bard of the wood who lives in his woodland dwelling; and the thrush in the verdant tapestry of the green tree-tops loudly singing his golden-voiced notes before the rain; and the lark with his soft tune, the beloved grey-cowled bird of cunning voice, soaring up from the bare field into the airy heights in utter ecstasy of singing, like a gentle prince, climbing on his backward course.[1] I, the poet of a tall slender maid, though my heart was broken with musing on memories and my soul raw within me, was very glad in the green grove with the joy and high spirits of seeing the trees wearing their fresh array, and the shoots of vine and wheat after the dew and the sun-bright rain, and the green leaves on the brow of the glen, and the thorn-brake green under its tips of white flowers. By Heaven, the Magpie too, the most crafty bird in the world, that handsome humbug, was building in the bristly crest of the midst of the thicket a fine gatehouse of leaves and chalky clay, and her mate was helping her. Haughty and sharp-beaked, from the thorn thicket the Magpie muttered a querulous grumble: 'You fret yourself much with your worthless, bitter song, all to yourself, you aged man! Better for you, by Mary of eloquent words, to be by the fire, you old grey man, than here among the dew and rain in the green grove and the cold shower.' 'Hold your noise and let me be for a short while, until it is time for my tryst. This fretting of mine is caused me by my great love for a good chaste girl.' 'It is idle for you, and only serves vice, you grey, undignified, half-mad, decrepit man, to drivel about the bright girl; it is nothing but a silly simulation of the office of love.' 'You too, Magpie, with your black beak, hellish and most bad-tempered bird, you too, for all your false parade, have tedious work and greater toil. Yours is a nest like a furze-bush, a close-packed creel of withered, broken branches. With your black pied feathers and your raven's head, you're a shock to look at, my faithful friend; in motley dress of gay colours, your voice is hoarse,

[1] See Notes.

from your ugly mansion; winged in black stripes, you could learn to mimic any tongue, however hard and remote the language. You, black-headed Magpie, help me if you have skill, and give me the best advice you know for me in my pining all away.' 'I know fine good advice for you – follow it, if you will, before May arrives. Poet, you have no claim on the fair girl, and there is no counsel for you but one: skilled in hard metres, become a hermit and love no more, you silly man!' I give my oath, may the Lord take note of it, if ever I see a magpie's nest, sure, from this time on she shall not get either egg or chick.

Welsh; Dafydd ap Gwilym, c. 1325–c. 1380.

178. The Poet and the Grey Friar

ALAS that my glorious girl, who holds her court in the woods, does not know the talk of the mouse-coloured Friar about her today! I had gone to the Friar to confess my sins. To him I had admitted that I was indeed a sort of poet, and that I was always in love with a white-faced black-browed girl, and that from her who slew me I had neither profit nor reward from my lady; only that I loved her long and lastingly and languished greatly for her love, and that I spread her fame throughout Wales, and failed to win her for all that; and that I longed to have her in my bed between me and the wall. Then said the Friar to me, 'I will give you good advice, since you have loved this foam-white girl, paper-coloured, for so long before this. Make less the punishment on the Day that will come; it would profit your soul to desist, and to be silent from your poems and busy yourself with your beads. Not for poems and verses did God redeem Man's soul. You minstrels, your art is nothing but jabber and vain noises, and incitement of men and women to sin and wickedness; not good is the fleshly praise that leads the soul to the Devil.' As for me, I answered the Friar for every word that he said: 'God is not so cruel as the old folk say, God will not damn the soul of a gallant gentleman for loving woman nor maid. Three things are loved throughout the world – woman, fair weather, and good health; a woman is the fairest flower in Heaven beside God Himself; every man of all the nations was born of woman, except three.[1] Therefore it is not strange that one loves girls and women. From Heaven comes good cheer and from Hell every grief; song gladdens old and young, sick and whole. I must needs compose poems just as you must preach, and it is as proper for me to go wandering as a minstrel as it is for you to beg alms. Are not hymns and church sequences only verses and odes? and the psalms of the prophet David are but poems to blessed God. God does not nourish Man on food and seasoning alone; a time has been ordained for food and a time for prayer, a time for preaching – and a time to make merry. Song is sung at every feast to entertain the girls, and paternosters in the church to win the land of Paradise. It is true what Ystudfach said, carousing with his bards, "A glad face means a full house, a sad face comes to no good." Though some love piety others love good cheer; few know the art of sweet poetry, but everyone knows his paternoster. Therefore, scrupulous Friar, it is not song that is the greatest sin. When everyone is as ready to listen to prayers with the harp as the girls of North Wales are to hear ·wanton poems, *then*, by my hand, I shall sing my paternoster without cease. Till then, shame on Dafydd if he sings any prayers but love-songs!'

Welsh; Dafydd ap Gwilym, *c.* 1325–*c.* 1380.

179. *My Purse, Gramercy to You for This!*

My velvet purse, my priest, my coffer of gold, my lord of remedy, my prophet, my dear preserver, you are my mate of the same speech as mine. No better guardian is there under the sky, giver of grace, nest of gold, than you; none better to pay the bills that strangers bring – my purse, gramercy to you for this!

1. Adam, Eve, and Melchisedek.

Horses I owned, and honour, jewels and arms, medallions on my shirt, bright gems, a load of rings, chains and brooches ninefold, matchless raiment fit for a well-dressed man, and purposed so to continue, in my land; in Emlyn my would-be kin was numerous – my purse, gramercy to you for this!

I learned somewhat in the book of Solomon, and the seven arts with their fame; I learned the guides to win to Paradise, a peaceful lore, led by the churchly lamp; I learned, folk said, with earnest care and victorious struggle, to wield the *awdl*, single *cywydd*, and *englyn*[1] – my purse, gramercy to you for this!

A numerous flourishing family, nine times more than mine is really, claims kinship with me; a shock to my good spirits – it is sharp practice! I can have sworn brothers every day of my life, in eight degrees of affinity, well I know; every vagabond, every pauper, every wandering minstrel, every worn-out seaman, every lick-spittle, comes to beg of me – my purse, gramercy to you for this!

Good is the profit, as Gwenddydd said in verse, good are the things which I have every day, drinks, modish foods, and all provision in commendable guise. I get welcome, am politely called by name, men speak me fair in public, as though bewitched; I get great respect in every market-place, a throne at every banquet in my land, great and long-lasting honour done before me – my purse, gramercy to you for this!

If I am taken in manifest theft, red-handed, and haled to court, I know I shall win acquittal when inquest and judgement come upon my case; for forty will swear by perjury, meek enough, on my behalf, three Sundays in succession, and the liberal officers of interrogation all together will be on my side. You are my herald, and my golden coin – my purse, gramercy to you for this!

1. See Index.

I have had great love from women, and would have got whatever favours I might ask; all the pandars in Is Conwy I would have, a million of them, if I wished for more. I need not leave the tavern, while I live and choose so, for men compete to take me by the arm and escort me to the mead. I know myself much honoured, protector of petitioners – my purse, gramercy to you for this!

My gold will buy (I know the cost) the whole world, delightful and bounteous, for me; I'll win all Wales, nothing lost of it, with its houses and its castles and its land; I'll win love in Paradise, I'll win God in my whole body (a grave thought), power to my name, and Heaven for my soul; indulgences from the Popes would be attained, and appeasing every enemy in war – my purse, gramercy to you for this!

Welsh; attributed to Sion Cent, fl. *c.* 1400–1430.

180. Welsh Harper and English Bagpiper

LAST Sunday I came – a man whom the Lord God made – to the town of Flint, with its great double walls and rounded bastions; may I see it all aflame! An obscure English wedding was there, with but little mead – an English feast! and I meant to earn a shining solid reward for my harper's art. So I began, with ready speed, to sing an ode to the kinsmen; but all I got was mockery, spurning of my song, and grief. It was easy for hucksters of barley and corn to dismiss all my skill, and they laughed at my artistry, my well-prepared panegyric which they did not value; John of the Long Smock began to jabber of peas, and another about dung for his land. They all called for William the Piper to come to the table, a low fellow he must be. He came forward as though claiming his usual rights, though he did not look like a privileged man, with a groaning bag, a paunch of heavy guts, at the end of a stick between chest and arm. He rasped away, making startling grimaces, a horrid noise, from the swollen belly, bulging his eyes; he twisted his

body here and there, and puffed his two cheeks out, playing
with his fingers on a bell of hide – unsavoury conduct, fit
for the unsavoury banqueters. He hunched his shoulders,
amid the rout, under his cloak, like a worthless ballad-
monger; he snorted away, and bowed his head until it was
on his breast, the very image of a kite with skilful zeal
preening its feathers. The pigmy puffed, making an outlandish cry, blowing out the bag with a loud howl; it sang
like the buzzing of a hornet, that devilish bag with the stick
in its head, like a nightmare howl, fit to kill a mangy goose,
like a sad bitch's hoarse howl in its hollow kennel; a harsh
paunch with monotonous cry, throat-muscles squeezing out
a song, with a neck like a crane's where he plays, like a
stabbed goose screeching aloud. There are voices in that
hollow bag like the ravings of a thousand cats; a monotonous, wounded, ailing, pregnant goat – no pay for its hire.
After it ended its wheezing note, that cold songstress whom
love would shun, Will got his fee, namely bean-soup and
pennies (if they paid) and sometimes small halfpennies, not
the largesse of a princely hand; while *I* was sent away in
high vexation from the silly feast all empty-handed. I
solemnly vow, I do forswear wretched Flint and all its
children, and its wide, hellish furnace, and its English
people and its piper! That they should be slaughtered is
all my prayer, my curse in their midst and on their
children; sure, if I go there again, may I never return alive!

Welsh; authorship uncertain (see Notes); fifteenth century.

181. The Letter of O'Neill to Sir John McCoughleyn

Our greetings to you, McCoughleyn. We have received
your letter, and what we make out from it is that you offer
nothing but sweet words and procrastination. For our part
in the matter, whatever man would not be on our side and
would not spend his efforts for the right, we take it that that
man is a man against us. For this reason, wherever you
yourself are doing well, hurt us as much as you are able,

and we shall hurt you to the best of our ability, with God's will.

At Knockduffmaine, 6th February, 1600.
O'NEILL.

Irish; Hugh O'Neill, Earl of Tyrone; 1600.

182. 'Civil Irish' and 'Wild Irish'

You who follow English ways, who cut short your curling hair, O slender hand of my choice, you are unlike the good son of Donnchadh!

If you were he, you would not give up your long hair (the best adornment in all the land of Ireland) for an affected English fashion, and your head would not be tonsured.

You think a shock of yellow hair unfashionable; *he* hates both the wearing of love-locks and being shaven-headed in the English manner – how unlike are your ways!

Eóghan *Bán*, the darling of noble women, is a man who never loved English customs; he has not set his heart on English ways, he has chosen the wild life rather.

Your ideas are nothing to Eóghan *Bán*; he would give breeches away for a trifle, a man who asked no cloak but a rag, who had no desire for doublet and hose.

He would hate to have at his ankle a jewelled spur on a boot, or stockings in the English manner; he will allow no love-locks on him.

A blunt rapier which could not kill a fly, the son of Donn-chadh does not think it handsome; nor the weight of an awl sticking out behind his rear as he goes to the hill of the assembly.

Little he cares for gold-embroidered cloaks, or for a high well-furnished ruff, or for a gold ring which would only be vexatious, or for a satin scarf down to his heels.

He does not set his heart on a feather bed, he would prefer to lie upon rushes; to the good son of Donnchadh a house of rough wattles is more comfortable than the battlements of a castle.

A troop of horse at the mouth of a pass, a wild fight, a ding-dong fray of footsoldiers, these are some of the delights of Donnchadh's son – and seeking contest with the foreigners.

You are unlike Eóghan *Bán*; men laugh at *you* as you put your foot on the mounting-block; it is a pity that you yourself don't see your errors, O you who follow English ways.

Irish; Laoiseach Mac an Bhaird; sixteenth century.

183. *The Student's Life*

The student's life is pleasant, carrying on his studies; it is plain to you, my friends, his is the most pleasant in Ireland.

No king nor great prince nor landlord, however strong, coerces him; no taxes to the Chapter, no fines, no early-rising.

Early-rising or sheep-herding, he never undertakes them, nor yet does he pay heed to the watchman in the night.

He spends a while at backgammon, and at the tuneful harp, or again another while at wooing, and at courting a fair woman.

He gets good profit from his plough-team when early spring comes round – the frame of *his* plough is a handful of pens!

Irish; author unknown; seventeenth century.

184. *A Smart Young Woman*

. . . I'm no miserable wench nor ungainly woman,
but a handsome beauty, charming and bonny;
I'm no slovenly slut or untidy slattern
or lumpish lout without joy or contentment,
no stinking sluggard or feckless hussy,
but a neat young woman as choice as they make them.

219

If I were useless like most of my neighbours,
clottish and dull, without sense or experience,
without vision or smartness in wielding my rights,
alas then, how could I help despairing?
But I never was seen yet among the people
at a vigil or wake for young or old,
at the playing-field, the race-track or dance-floor
along with the mob on the crowded meadows,
but I was got up demurely without one flaw
in a well-fitting dress from top to toe.
There'd be powder enough strewn in my hair,
my coif would be starched and cocked behind,
a white hood without lack of ribbons,
and a spotted gown with ruffs all proper.
It's rare that I lack the jaunty facings,
pleasing and fine, on my crimson cloak,
and many a plant and tree and bird
on my striped and splendid cambric apron;
heels well-shaped, narrow and even,
high and smooth, screwed into my shoes;
buckles and rings and gloves of silk,
hoops and bracelets and costly laces. . . .

Irish; Brian Merriman; 1780.

185. The Midwives and the Father

. . . What a terrible turmoil, fretful and bothered –
the baby swaddled and the housewife feeble,
their posset laid on the glowing embers,
and they thumping a churnful of milk with energy;
claw-fingered Muirinn O'Bent-Grey the midwife
with a heaped-up dishful of milksop and sugar.
A committee was gathered by some of my neighbours
beside the fire, muttering about me;
they fired off their whispers close to my eardrums:
'A thousand praises to the Light of all Lights!
Although his body's not quite full term

I can see his father in his posture and looks.
Do you see, Sadhbh dear, the lie of his limbs,
his form without stiffness, his members and fingers,
the strength of the hands with their fighting fists,
the make of the bones and the growth of the flesh?'
They pretended my stock had sprung up in him,
the charm of my features, the form of my visage,
the twist of my nose and the cut of my forehead,
the grace of my mould, my aspect and looks,
the set of my eyes, and even my smile;
and they went on thence from head to heels.
Look nor sight could I get of the wretch
from the household gang who tried to hookwink me –
'The wind would destroy him quite, without cure;
one little puff would dissolve the creature!'
But I spoke out harshly, and called on Jesus,
and fiercely and roughly I threatened a flare-up,
I declared my wrath in reckless terms,
and the hags in the house, why, they trembled before me.
Unwilling to wrangle, they let me have him –
'Carry him carefully, mind not to crush him,
it's easy to mangle him, rock him gently!
Some fall she got brought him on untimely.
Take care not to squeeze him, but let him lie;
for death's so near him, he'll go off any minute!
If only he lives till day undamaged,
and the priest is got, it's the best we can hope for.' . . .

Irish; Brian Merriman; 1780.

186. Where Are You Going to, my Pretty Maid?

'Where were you going, fair maid,' said he,
'with your pale face and your yellow hair?'
'Going to the well, sweet sir,' she said,
'for strawberry leaves make maidens fair.'[1]

1. Supposed to refer to washing the face with water in which strawberry leaves had been soaked.

'Shall I go with you, fair maid,' said he,
'with your pale face and your yellow hair?'
'Do if you wish, sweet sir,' she said,
'for strawberry leaves make maidens fair.'

'How if I lay you on the ground,
with your pale face and your yellow hair?'
'I'll get up again, sweet sir,' she said,
'for strawberry leaves make maidens fair.'

'How if I get you with child,
with your pale face and your yellow hair?'
'Then I will bear him, sweet sir,' she said,
'for strawberry leaves make maidens fair.'

'Whom will you find to father your child,
with your pale face and your yellow hair?'
'You'll be his father, fair sir,' she said,
'for strawberry leaves make maidens fair.'

'What will you get for clothes for your child,
with your pale face and your yellow hair?'
'His father shall be tailor, fair sir,' she said,
'for strawberry leaves make maidens fair.'

Cornish; popular poem[1]; seventeenth century.

187. Egan O'Rahilly and the Minister

There was a splendid green-boughed tree of great value
growing for many years close by a church which the wicked
Cromwell had plundered, above a spring overflowing with
bright cold water, in a field of green turf which a thieving
minister had extorted from an Irish gentleman; one who
had been exiled across the wild seas through treachery, and
not through the edge of the sword. This stinking lout of a
damned minister wanted to cut a long green bough of the
tree to make household gear of it. None of the carpenters or
workmen would touch the beautiful bough, for its shade was

1. See Notes.

most lovely, sheltering them as they lamented brokenly and bitterly for the bright champions who were stretched beneath the sod. 'I will cut it,' said a bandy meagre-shanked gallows-bird of a son of this portly minister, 'and get me an axe at once.' The dull-witted oaf went up into the tree like a scared cat fleeing a pack of hounds, until he came upon two branches growing one across the other. He tried to put them apart by the strength of his wrists, but they sprang from his hands in the twinkling of an eye across each other again, and gripped his gullet, hanging him high between air and Hell. It was then the accursed Sassenach was wriggling his legs in the hangman's dance, and he standing on nothing, and his black tongue out the length of a yard, mocking at his father. The minister screamed and bawled like a pig in a sack or a goose caught under a gate, and no wonder, while the workmen were getting a ladder to cut him down.

Egan O'Rahilly[1] from Sliabh Luachra of the Heroes was there, watching the gallows-bird of the noose, and he recited this verse:–

'Good is your fruit, tree;
may the bounty of this your fruit be on every branch!
Alas, that the trees of Ireland
are not covered with your fruit every day!'

'What is the poor wild Irish devil saying?'[2] said the minister. *'He is lamenting your darling son,'*[2] said an idler who was beside him. *'Here is twopence for you to buy tobacco with,'*[2] said the fat badger of a minister. *'Thankee,*[2] minister of the son of curses,' i.e. the Devil, said Egan; and he recited a verse:–

'Hurroo, minister who gave me your twopence
for lamenting your child!
May the fate of that child befall the rest of them
down to the last of them.'

Irish; author unknown; eighteenth century.

1. See Index.   2. In English.

188. On the Murder of David Gleeson, Bailiff

There is cause now for poets to laugh and rejoice with glee, since the loutish severe damned bailiff is dead; I forgive all the plunderings that Death has ever done, since he has laid low David, that clod, the devilish old bum-bailiff.

I swear, Brian's[1] Ireland is the better off for ever, now that skinflint has gone to the place he was fated to reach – to brimming Acheron, swimming in flames of torment; there is David along with his Master, in the name of the Devil.

His trade was cursed in the village from long ago, the scum who left a trail of villainy wherever he went, jailing and persecuting hordes of folk every year; now David is bound as a captive in the toils of the Devil.

David was brazen and spiteful and crooked, his nature and trade did not please the schools of the poets; the hand that plunged the dagger in his breast, may it never grow less! and my curse go after him to his assured dwelling with the Devil.

It is pleasant to hear, in Cork and the midst of the region, of this rending and gashing of yellow Gleeson's carcass, which is hanging on high from the end of a gallows-tree, and with unwearied fire Vulcan[2] is burning him below.

Irish; Seán na Ráithíneach; 1737.

1. See Index.　　2. Used in Irish as a name for the Devil.

BARDIC POETRY

NOTE

The word *bard* is a Celtic one, and has a technical sense which it lacks in English. Celtic society was organized as an aristocracy; the kings and chiefs supported client poets, poets laureate, whose primary business it was to sing the praises of their patrons, memorize their genealogies, celebrate their victories, and lament their deaths; they were not composers of personal lyric, but functionaries with a duty to society. These men were trained in their art at special 'bardic schools', or learned it individually from some poet of established reputation. The poetry is complicated and highly conventional, with fixed traditions about what is proper in a bardic poem, how and in what words it should be said; and above all a most elaborate and subtle system of metres. Translating an Irish bardic poem is like unravelling a stanza of Horace's Odes, because of the inversions of normal order; the Welsh poems are even more complicated because they are not usually limited to the quatrain form, and also because they are couched in a rushing, torrential, allusive style like that of a Pindaric ode (e.g. no. 189), unlike the clear-cut jewel-work of Irish and Scottish bardic composition. Poet-laureate verse is usually dull, and the exaggeratedly conventional nature of Celtic bardic poetry often makes it even more so; but the brilliant Celtic imagination did not desert even this unpromising field. In fact, there are a number of bardic poems, or parts of poems, which do seem worthy of Celtic literature at its best. It is unfortunate that the technical skill of the bards cannot be reproduced in translation; a stanza of an Irish or Scottish bardic poem is a marvel of compression and elegance.

The bardic poetry of Ireland and Scotland reached its height in the later Middle Ages, between the thirteenth and seventeenth centuries. In Ireland the entire craft disappeared, together with its craftsmen, in the break-up of the old aristocratic order under Elizabeth and in the Cromwellian and Williamite wars of the seventeenth century; the bards no longer had patrons to support them. No. 199 is the complaint of a bard whose poems have no place in the new order, where they are neither appreciated nor understood. In Scotland the system lasted a little longer, but was quite dead by the first half of the eighteenth century. Even so, during the eighteenth century the poets of the new schools of popular poetry in both countries sometimes wrote works that were basically a continuation of the old bardic pattern, though in the new popular metres and composed now for more lowly (in Ireland sometimes even English) patrons. Examples are nos. 200 and 201; the latter should be compared with no. 198, which is a true bardic poem.

In Wales also the system of client bards goes back to ancient times, but it reached its peak in the so-called 'period of the princes,' from the coming of the Normans in the eleventh century to the extinction of Welsh independence at the end of the thirteenth. As in Ireland and Scotland, poems whose content and purpose were fundamentally bardic continued to be composed for less noble patrons after the downfall of the independent Welsh princes, and indeed the practice lingered on in a vestigial form well into the eighteenth century.

If there was ever any bardic poetry in Manx, which is improbable, we know nothing about it. The Isle of Man was in the hands of Norwegian rulers until 1266, and later of the Stanleys, so that it had no Gaelic aristocracy. There was none in Cornish unless before the ninth century, because from that time the overlords were English; nor in Brittany, where, though the aristocracy was native, Breton was looked down upon in the later Middle Ages and French was largely the language of polite society. It is significant that in an Old Cornish vocabulary composed about 1100 the word *barth* is glossed *mimus vel scurra*, 'a mime or buffoon'.

BARDIC POETRY

189. Elegy on Llywelyn ap Gruffudd[1]

COLD is the heart in my breast for dread and sorrow after the king, the oaken gate of Aberffraw! Bright gold was paid out by his hand, a golden crown was his desert. The golden drinking-horns of my golden prince no more will come to me, Llywelyn's gladness; no more will he freely give me bountiful clothing. Woe to me for my lord, the blameless hawk, woe to me for the disaster of his fall! Woe to me for the loss, woe to me for the fate, woe to me that I heard of the wound upon him! Whose camp was like Cadwaladr's,[2] who was a pledge of the sword-blade, the youth of the red spear, the golden-handed leader, scatterer of wealth, who clothed me with his clothes every winter; the lord rich in cattle, no more will he profit our hands, but eternal life is in store for him. It is for me to be angry with the English for doing me this violence, for me to complain bitterly against Death, for me with good reason to blaspheme God who left me without him; it is for me to praise him without cease, without silence, for me henceforward long to remember him, for me to grieve for him all my lifetime, and since sorrow is mine, it is for me to weep. I have lost a lord (I may long tremble), a lord of a princely palace, who was killed out of hand; true, just Lord God, hear me, how loudly I lament, alas for the lamentation! – a thriving lord, before his eighteen comrades[3] were killed in the fight, a generous lord, the grave is now all his estate. A lord as bold as a lion, ruling the earth, a lord whose destruction is cause of distress, a lord whose enterprises prospered, before he left Emreis the English would not have dared to provoke him;

1. On the names and events in this poem see Notes.
2. The traditional Welsh hero; cf. *Henry V*, act v, scene i.
3. See Notes.

229

a lord, a prince of the Welsh like a stone roof, of the line that held Aberffraw by right. Lord Christ, how sad I am for him, my true lord from whom salvation came; for the heavy swordstroke through which he fell, for the long swords which overwhelmed him, for the fever for my chieftain which makes me shiver, for the news of the prostration of the ruler of Bod Faeaw! In his full manhood he was slain at the hands of his enemies, but the full rights of his ancestors were his; the candle of princes, the strong lion of Gwynedd, enthroned in honour, there was need of him. Since the death of all Britain, the preserver of Cynlleith, since the slaying of the lion of Nancoel, the breastplate of Nancaw, many a flowing tear courses down the cheeks, there is many a flank all red with a gash upon it, much blood that has dripped down underfoot, many a widow who wails for it, many a heavy heart all wandering, many a son left without father, many a homestead smudged by the blaze passing through it, many a desert created by yonder pillage, many a pitiful wail as at the battle of Camlan, many a tear rolling over the cheek; since the slaying of the buttress, the golden-handed leader, since the death of Llywelyn, my human reason fails me, chill is the heart in my breast for dread, and sportiveness withers like the dry brush-wood. Do you not see the course of the wind and the rain? Do you not see the oak-trees crashing together? Do you not see the ocean devouring the land? Do you not see that Judgement is being made ready? Do you not see the sun hurtling through the sky? Do you not see that the stars have fallen? Do you not believe in God, besotted mortals? Do you not see that the world is in peril? Ah God, that the sea might surge up to You, covering the land! – why are we left to linger? There is no refuge from the terrible Prison, there is nowhere to tarry, woe for the tarrying! There is neither precaution, nor lock, nor key, nor any way to deliverance from the dread sentence of terror! Every household troop was worthy of him, every warrior held himself under him, every champion swore by his hand, every prince, every land was his; every province, every village is invaded; every family, every tribe, all are in ruins; every weak man, every strong man maintained at his hands, every child in the cradle, all are bewailing. It is small gain to me, only deception, that my head is left me when he has lost his; when that head was cut off men welcomed terror, when that head was cut off it was better to submit. The head of a warrior, the head ever to be praised, the head of a champion, of a hero, was his; the head of Llywelyn the fair, it is dire terror to the world that an iron stake has pierced it; the head of my lord, the torment of his grievous fall is upon me; the head of my life without a name; the head which owned the homage of nine hundred lands, and which had nine hundred feasts; the head of a prince who showered iron javelins, the head of a proud hawk-prince who breached the battleline, the head of a princely wolf who was impetuous, may the princely Head of Heaven be his protection! The blessed prince, the over-lord, the maintainer of a happy host whose ambitions reached even to Brittany, the true rightful king of Aberffraw; may the holy Kingdom of Heaven be his dwelling.

Welsh; Gruffudd ab yr Ynad Coch; 1282.

190. The Battle of Tal Moelfre[1]

I PRAISE the generous man of the race of Rhodri, the defender of the frontiers, the lawful chief, the rightful one of Britain, Owein, spirited in adversity, the prince who does not grovel, who does not hoard plunder. There came three hosts in vessels of the flood, three great armadas to make sharp trial of him; one from Ireland, another of armed men of the Norwegians armed with long spears, from the ocean, and a third over the sea from Normandy – immense labour, from which it got no good. The Dragon of Anglesey, how reckless in battle is his nature! A desperate turmoil was their demand, expressed through slaughter; before him a mob in close-packed confusion, and ruin and struggle and dismal death. Battle on bloody battle, panic on horrifying

1. See Notes.

panic, and around Tal Moelfre a thousand war-cries; slaughter on flashing slaughter, spears upon spear, terror on raging terror, drowning upon drowning, and the Menei's ebb blocked by the flooding streams of gore and dyed with the blood of men in the sea; grey-armoured warriors in the swoon of calamity, and dying men in heaps before the red-speared king. Through the army of the English and the encounter with it, and their overthrow in confusion, the fame of him of the stern sword shall rise up in seven-score tongues for his lasting praise.

Welsh; Gwalchmei; 1157.

191. The Killing of Hywel ab Owein[1]

While we were seven, thrice seven dared not attack us, nor made us retreat while we lived; alas, there are now but three of the seven, men unflinching in fight.

Seven men were we who were faultless, undaunted, irresistible in attack, seven mighty men from whom flight gave no protection, seven who would brook no wrong till now.

Since Hywel is gone, who bore battle gladly, by whom we used to stand, we are all avowedly lost, and the host of Heaven is the fairer.

The sons of Cedifor, an ample band of offspring, in the dale above Pentraeth they were fierce and full of bold purpose, and they were cut down alongside their foster-brother.

Because of the treason hatched by Cristin and her sons – un-Christian Britons! – may no man of the bald freckled descendants of Brochfael be left alive in Anglesey.

Come what may of wealth from land domain, yet this world is a deceptive dwelling-place; with a spear (woe to false Dafydd!) Hywel the Tall, the hawk of war, was pierced.

Welsh; Peryf ap Cedifor; 1170.

1. See Notes.

192. Maguire and MacDermot[1]

There are two chiefs in the land of Ireland, the one mere dregs, the other a choice man of slender fingers; an old outlandish starveling cripple and a bountiful man of noble lineage.

It is not wrong to compare them, a rod of alder and a rod of yew, a stick of twisted alder wood and my manly very generous timber.

The beggarly tainted chief of Ulster and the brave king of Connaught, the bright liberal merry lad and the stingy grudging man.

MacDermot of Moylurg and Maguire the refractory; it is justice gone askew to compare them, meagre rye beside wheat.

Tomaltach deals in pure feats of valour, Tomás in vice and arrogance; his paws are always in the scales, so that half my poems have rotted away.[1]

It is not right to set side by side the warrior and the refuse of the hosting; the stinking-gummed half-blind oaf, ah me! and the warrior of the strong sword-blade and the many retainers . . .

The lord Tomaltach is a second Niall Frosach, generous son of Ferghal, or a Guaire son of Colmán of the bright cheeks, full of pride and spirit.

A lame big-bellied hack carries Maguire when he goes out; he puts his pillion of rotten sticks on its mangy patchy hump.

A lovely-eyed spirited colt carries MacDermot when he goes out; the hero's slender horse, as it flies, makes a breach for the clean wind.

1. See Notes.

Maguire, without vigour or brilliance on the stinking yellow hack, the greater clown is he when he comes, and the more refined is the source of derision.

A long bright coat of chain-mail is on the bright-hued MacDermot, when battle is declared against him he wears a shoulder-piece and a well-wrought helmet.

Like a thicket of fine herbs growing is Tomaltach, who wins bright grace; bulge-bottomed Tomás from the glen is like a holly bough.

A rusty coat of mail of most wretched appearance and a dirty shapeless shoulder-piece are on Maguire, the withered leper, who did not abide the payment due to barbarians.

The king of populous Moylurg has a golden shield on his breast like crystal; he sets by his brilliant side a thin sword and pointed spear.

Tomás draws from his black sheath an old dull bilbo, blunt and ancient; Maguire with his palsied hand has a weapon which will not stand combat.

The one like crazy Suibhne who wins no victory and the other like Ioruath of the red weapons, a cowardly unhandy boor and a noble who would not cry out at the volley.

The one like wicked sinful Cain and the other like Abel son of Adam; the king of Loch Cé is a man above men, he is the delight of the Gael.

The one a strong famous accomplished king, the other a weak incompetent boor; a noble who is open-handed to poets is better than a boor who is tight-fisted and grudging.

It is my duty to compose difficult verses to him whose face is as ruddy as dark wine, MacDermot of the furrowed locks, the young noble long-haired sapling.

Tomaltach, whose oath is no trifle, gave me his food and his bragget, and a harp for my sake; that hand is the best I have found.

Maguire, the greater his disgrace, the shameless misshapen monster – how unlike are the sack of straw and the tall noble granary!

Maguire the weak scoundrel, the wicked incompetent feeble boor, evil grows great in him, Tomás who is without body or flesh.

Maguire the mean-spirited is a stick from the rotten alder brake; he of the proud hand, theme of lengthy songs, is the brown curly-haired MacDermot.

> Scottish–Irish; Giolla Críost Brúilingeach; mid-fifteenth century.

193. The Fertile Lands of Cathal Ó Conchobhair[1]

... When on a summer morning early the curly-haired chief arises for the deer-hunt, there is dew on the grass, the blackbird warbling, and the life has gone out of the frost.

Swift horses beside the Shannon in the blue meadows white with flowers, a graceful herd on the water-meads of Moy; green-headed ducks on every ford.

The arms of the apple-trees bend to the ground in the land of Cathal of Cruachan Aeí; every young hazel bush there perforce bows itself down on bended knee.

Every plump nut puts forth its shell at the tip of its branch, beside the field; the yellow grain puts out its husk already at the tops of the thicket of fresh young corn.

A ruddy cluster among dusky leaves in the green woods with their smooth turf; nuts in their brown shells rain down from them in heavy showers ...

> Irish; Giolla Brighde MacConmidhe; thirteenth century.

1. See Notes.

194. Prosperity in the Time of Tadhg Ó Conchobhair[1]

. . . The nobleman for whom from wide-plained Codhal in the south the fruit and nuts of soft Munster have grown bright; owing to our chieftain every bright-branched hazel has become red, and the fruits of the pleasant bending sloe-bushes have grown jet black.

In his time the cattle are like part of the Cattle-Tribute;[1] nuts are the hue of coppery gold for the descendant of gentle Mugh; the fruit-flowers in their fresh white tresses have sweetened the cool streams of the tree-blessed shore; green corn grows from the earth close up to the mighty woods, and the bright hazel branches are filled with sap.

At evening, the flowers of the fair-plaited hazel have cooled the sunny earth, the home of stranger birds; drops of honey and of dew, like dark tears, will keep the fringe of the thin-grassed wood bent down; the saplings around the Boyle are bowed with nuts because the slow soft eye of the descendant of Bron looks down on them.

Nuts dropping into the white-foamed murmuring Boyle will fall down beside the great trees with twisted boles; the flower of every tree of them, like dark purple, is empurpled for the race of great Muirchertach.

A shower of honey upon slim-formed saplings in the fresh bowed forks of the golden graceful wood – this is but another boon from his holding of the peace – and the slow cows with their full udders from the lands of the plain of great Tuam . . .

Irish; Seaán Mór Ó Clumháin; fourteenth century.

195. The Praise of Fermanagh

The paradise of Ireland is Fermanagh, the peaceful fruitful plain, the land of bright dry smooth fields, in form like the shores of Heaven.

1. See Notes.

The cry of her waves is heavenly music, golden flowers on her land, a honeyed vision is the sweetness of her streams, and the tresses of her wood bowed down.

Smooth glens above tilled plains, blue brooks above the glens; a wood of yellow nuts beyond the flowers, a golden plumage of leaves enfolding it.

It is enough to take all fever from a man – the brownness of her branches, the blue of her waters, the redness of her leafage, the brightness of her clouds; heavenly is her soil and her sky.

Like the songs of Paradise through the plaintive sweet blue-welled land is the sound of her pure sandy streams mingled with the angelic voice of her birds.

Indeed no tongue can tell half her beauty, the land of tender curly crops, of shallow brooks; what is it but the true paradise of Ireland? . . .

Irish; Tadhg Dall Ó hUiginn; 1550–91.

196. The Harp of Cnoc Í Chosgair

Harp of Cnoc Í Chosgair, you who bring sleep to eyes long sleepless; sweet, subtle, plangent, glad, cooling, grave.

Excellent instrument with the smooth gentle curve, trilling under red fingers, musician that has charmed us, red, lion-like, of full melody.

You who lure the bird from the flock, you who refresh the mind, brown spotted one of sweet words, ardent, wondrous, passionate.

You who heal every wounded warrior, joy and allurement to women, familiar guide over the dark-blue water, mystic sweet-sounding music.

You who silence every instrument of music, yourself a pleasing plaintive instrument, dweller among the Race of Conn, instrument yellow-brown and firm.

The one darling of sages, restless, smooth, of sweet tune, crimson star above the fairy hills, breast-jewel of High Kings.

Sweet tender flowers, brown harp of Diarmaid, shape not unloved by hosts, voice of the cuckoos in May!

I have not heard of music ever such as your frame makes since the time of the fairy people, fair brown many-coloured bough, gentle, powerful, glorious.

Sound of the calm wave on the beach, pure shadowing tree of true music, carousals are drunk in your company, voice of the swan over shining streams.

Cry of the fairy women from the Fairy Hill of Ler, no melody can match you, every house is sweet-stringed through your guidance, you the pinnacle of harp-music . . .

Irish; Gofraidh Fionn Ó Dálaigh; c. 1385.

197. From the Lament for the Four Macdonalds[1]

. . . The heroes of the Race of Conn are dead, how bitter to our hearts is the grief for them! We shall not live long after them, perilous we think it to be bereaved of the brotherhood.

They did not stint their gifts of clothing to poets, their horses nor their golden cups; now that they have gone under the clay and are hidden, to be left after them is a shock of sorrow.

Since the earth has covered them, there is no hope of increase among herds, the woods are barren-crested so, and fruits do not bend down the branching boughs.

Through their death no strand bears jetsam, the noise of the storm has a bitter sound; little profit is there in all the drinking at the feast of sorrow that has befallen our land.

1. See Notes.

There is a note of lament in the mountain streams, cries of wailing in the voices of the birds, no catch in the net from the lake, the storm has destroyed the young corn and the hay.

Dry weather is unknown in our land; grief is driving me from my senses; the lament of the bardic schools has become manifest, now that the poets have put on their mourning dress.

Our rivers are without abundance of fishing, there is no hunting in the devious glens, there is little crop in every tilth, the wave has gnawed to the very base of the peaks.

For their sake the fury of the ocean never ceases, every sea lacks jetsam on its shore; drinking wine at the time of carousal, the warriors grieve more than the women.

The chill of the full rivers is destroying us; the pied bird has no chance of getting food; every river, full of ice-floes, can be forded; the trout does not dare to swim for the frost.

There is gloom and wrath in the words of men; the song of the cuckoos is not heard, the wind has taken on a senseless violence, the stream washes away its banks over the heather.

Because the men of Clanranald have gone from us we poets cannot pursue our studies; it is time for the chief bard to depart after them, now that presents to poets will be abolished . . .

Scottish–Irish; Cathal MacMhuirich; 1636.

198. To the Earl of Argyll before the Battle of Flodden[1]

. . . It is fitting to rise up against the English, we expect no hesitant uprising; the edges of swords, the points of spears, it is right to ply them gladly.

Let us make harsh and mighty warfare against the English, I tell you, before they have taken our native land; let us

1. See Notes.

not give up our country, but anxiously watch over our patrimony just like the Gael of Ireland.

I have heard that Ireland was once upon a time under the rule of the Fomorian race (a cause of wrath to the prince of the Cattle-Tribute),

Until Lugh came over the water with many warrior bands whose host was good, by whom Balar grandson of Néd was killed; may its comparison be an example to us.

Just so for a while to the English we were paying tribute from our native land, because everyone was afraid; mistrust is great upon us.

Who now, like that man, will rescue the Gael from the English in our time, as Lugh did when he sided with his people against reproach?

I know someone who could do the same if he chose, like Lugh throughout Ireland – it is proper to compare him to you.

Archibald, who have refused no man, you are the latter-day Lugh; Earl of Argyll, be an exultant hero.

Send out your summons from east and west to the Gael who came from Ireland, drive the English back over the high seas, let Scotland not be divided again . . .

The roots from which they grow, destroy them, their increase is too great, and leave no Englishman alive after you nor Englishwoman there to tell the tale.

Burn their bad coarse women, burn their uncouth offspring, and burn their sooty houses, and rid us of the reproach of them.

Let their ashes float down-stream after burning their remains, show no mercy to a living Englishman, O chief, deadly slayer of the wounded.

Remember, O cheek like the strawberry, that we have had from the English tyranny and spite in your time, by which the English rule has spread.

Remember Colin, your own father, remember Archibald too, remember Duncan before them, the kindly man who loved hounds.

Remember the other Colin, remember Archibald of Arran, and Colin of the Heads, whose frame was great, by whom the stake was won.

Remember that these men did no homage to the English for fear; why should you any the more do homage at this time?

Since there remain none but survivors of slaughter among the Gael from the field of danger, gather the men together and put fear of yourself on the enemy.

Push against the English in their own home, awake, MacCailéin! Too much sleep is not good for a man of war, you of the golden hair.

Scottish–Irish; author unknown; 1513.

199. Who Will Buy a Poem?[1]

I ask, who will buy a poem? Its meaning is the true learning of sages. Would anyone take, does anyone want, a noble poem which would make him immortal?

Though this is a poem of close-knit lore, I have walked all Munster with it, every market-place from cross to cross — and it has brought me no profit from last year to the present.

Though a groat would be small payment, no man nor any woman offered it; not a man spoke of the reason, but neither Irish nor English heeded me.

1. See Notes.

An art like this is no profit to me, though it is hard that it should die out; it would be more dignified to go and make combs – why should anyone take up poetry?

Corc of Cashel lives no more, nor Cian, who did not hoard up cattle nor the price of them, men who were generous in rewarding poets – alas, it is good-bye to the race of Éibhear.

The prize for generosity was never taken from them, until Cobhthach died, and Tál; I spare to mention the many kindreds for whom I might have continued to make poetry.

I am like a trading ship that has lost its freight, after the FitzGeralds who deserved renown. I hear no offers – how that torments me! It is a vain quest about which I ask.

Irish; Mahon O'Heffernan; early seventeenth century.

200. On the Death of William Gould

What is this mist on the fields of Ireland? what is this haze on the land of Éibhear?[1] what is this grief on the cries of the birds? what is this wrath which vexes the heavens?

What has silenced the schools of poets? what makes the Feale and Shannon tremble? what sets the mighty ocean roaring? what is this spoliation on the slopes of Slemish?

What has caused the poets to be in chains and helpless, and the nobles in bonds, long to be kept there? Friars in straits, and clergy and priests, warriors, prophets, and bards unfed?

The cause of their tears – a vexatious tale – is that fair William Gould, of the blood of the nobles, the golden candlestick and torch of heroes, has died at Nantes[2] – what grief to the Gael!

The giver of horses and cloaks and clothing, giver of gold in plenty, without effort, giver of silks and wines and trinkets, giver of silver and weapons to warriors.

Irish; Egan O'Rahilly; c. 1670–1726.

1. See Note on No. 199.   2. In Brittany.

201. *To Arouse the Gael in Support of Prince Charles*[1]

Oh let us set off over the water and over the wave, oh let us go over to Charles! Let none stay daunted where he stands, oh let us sail gladly to Charles!

Unless you come soon to our aid with force, with wealth, and with arms, we shall faint under the cruel oppression of George,[1] and your fine people will be no better than slaves.

Though they have robbed us of all we had, both money, cattle, and goods, not yet have they taken our courage and vigour, and we are as loyal as always.

Let us make ready, all you King's Men, to strike a blow with Charles; and if he does not come we'll go over to him, but we would rather he came, and gladly.

My curse on the coward who skulks in fright, with looks dejected and faint, or deserts his Faith, his Land, or his King, and does not show himself true to Charles!

You have heard my summons, make use of it, and put on your armour bravely; Charles is coming with a fierce strong fleet, which will advance against those monsters.

Though you have no weapons, no clothes, no cattle, from himself you will get every kind that your bodies and souls may need to use, until you banish that monster.[2]

Scottish Gaelic; Alexander Macdonald; 1745.

1. Charles Stuart, the Young Pretender.   2. George II.

ELEGY

NOTE

The term *elegy* is used here not only of laments for the dead, but also in the wider sense of pathetic or reflective poetry in general. The elegy for the dead is characteristic in Celtic literature. The practice of 'keening' still survives in parts of Ireland, where at a funeral the chief mourners may break into a rhythmic chant expressive of their grief, describing the dead man and his virtues, his death, and so on; and the attendant mourners come in between as a chorus. A fine example of such a keen raised to a high power of literary expression is the lament for Art O'Leary, no. 221; compare also nos. 204 and 218. Others are of a more purely literary turn. Still others, which belong to the bardic tradition, have been included above under Bardic Poetry.

A favourite theme in the Celtic literatures, as elsewhere, is the lament on a ruined building and on the power and glory which the poet remembers, or has heard, to have flourished there. Tom Moore's *The Harp that Once through Tara's Halls* is traditional in this respect, though its romanticism makes it otherwise quite un-Celtic. Nos. 203, 209, and 217 are examples, and 126 might have been given here; 203, bewailing the destruction by the Mercians of the British power in the middle Severn valley, takes us back to the seventh century, and has been known by English readers for many years for its tragic intensity and vividness. No. 217 on the other hand, composed in 1814, shows the touch of contemporary English literature. No. 212 belongs to the group of Jacobite vision-poems composed in Ireland in the eighteenth century, foretelling the return of the Stuarts; Mr Frank O'Connor's fine verse translation in *The Fountain of Magic* (London, 1939) is well known.

Still a third type of elegiac poetry much in evidence in Celtic literature is the lament of the individual for his own wretched plight, naturally often linked with the preceding group. Nos. 205–7 are from the story of Suibhne, the Wild Man of the Woods who, driven mad in battle, fled to the wilderness and became a crazy forest-dweller. No. 210 comes from the legend of Llywarch Hen, supposedly a sixth-century Briton from southern Scotland whose lands were overwhelmed and his twenty-four sons killed by the conquering English, and he himself became a wretched exile in Wales in his old age. One might look far to discover a finer expression of the miseries of senility in early literature.

ELEGY

202. From the Gododdin[1]

... WEARING a brooch, in the front rank, bearing weapons in battle, a mighty man in the fight before his death-day, a champion in the charge in the van of the armies; there fell five times fifty before his blades, of the men of Deira and Bernicia a hundred score fell and were destroyed in a single hour. He would sooner the wolves had his flesh than go to his own wedding, he would rather be prey for ravens than go to the altar; he would sooner his blood flowed to the ground than get due burial, making return for his mead with the hosts in the hall. Hyfeidd the Tall shall be honoured as long as there is a minstrel ...

The men went to Catraeth, swift was their army, the pale mead was their feast, and it was their poison; three hundred men battling according to plan, and after the glad war-cry there was silence. Though they went to the churches to do penance, the inescapable meeting with death overtook them ...

The men went to Catraeth with the dawn, their high courage shortened their lives. They drank the sweet yellow ensnaring mead, for a year many a bard made merry. Red were their swords (may the blades never be cleansed), and white shields and square-pointed spear-heads before the retinue of Mynyddawg the Luxurious ...

The men went to Catraeth, they were renowned, wine and mead from gold cups was their drink for a year, in accordance with the honoured custom. Three men and three score and three hundred, wearing gold necklets, of all that hastened out after the choice drink none escaped but three,

1. See Notes.

249

through feats of sword-play – the two war-dogs of Aeron, and stubborn Cynon; and I too, streaming with blood, by grace of my brilliant poetry . . .

The men hastened out, they galloped together; short-lived were they, drunk over the clarified mead, the retinue of Mynyddawg, famous in stress of battle; their lives were payment for their feast of mead. Caradawg and Madawg, Pyll and Ieuan, Gwgawn and Gwiawn, Gwynn and Cynfan, Peredur of the steel weapons, Gwawrddur and Aeddan, charging forward in battle among broken shields; and though they were slain they slew, none returned to his lands.

The men hastened out; they were feasted together for a year over the mead – great were their vaunts. How pitiful to tell of them, what insatiable longing! Cruel their resting-place, not a mother's son succoured them. How long the grief for them and the yearning, after the fiery men from the wine-fed domain. For the spirited men, Gwlyged of Gododdin contrived the famous feast of Mynyddawg – and the costly, when paid for by the fight at Catraeth.

The men went to Catraeth in column, raising the war-cry, a force with steeds and blue armour and shields, javelins aloft and keen lances, and bright mail-coats and swords. He led, he burst through the armies, and there fell five times fifty before his blades – Rhufawn the Tall, who gave gold to the altar and gifts and fine presents to the minstrel . . .

The warriors arose together, together they met, together they attacked, with single purpose; short were their lives, long the mourning left to their kinsmen. Seven times as many English they slew; in fight they made women widows, and many a mother with tears at her eyelids . . .

After wine-feast and mead-feast they hastened out, men famous in battle-stress, reckless of their lives; they fed together round the wine-bowl in shining array, to wine and mead and malt they set their hands. For the retinue of

Mynyddawg I am bitterly sad, I have lost too many of my
true kinsmen; of three hundred champions who set out for
Catraeth, alas, but for one man none came back . . .

It is grief to me that after the toil of battle they suffered the
agony of death in torment, and a second heavy grief it is
to me to have seen our men falling headlong; and continual moaning it is, and anguish, after the fiery men lying
in the clodded earth – Rhufawn and Gwgawn, Gwiawn
and Gwlyged, men of most manly station, strong in strife;
after the battle, may their souls get welcome in the land of
Heaven, the dwelling-place of plenty . . .

Welsh; attributed to Aneirin; original about 600.

203 From the Elegy on Cynddylan[1]

Stand out, maids, and look on the land of Cynddylan; the
court of Penngwern is ablaze; alas for the young who long
for their brothers! . . .

Cynddylan the bright buttress of the borderland, wearing
a chain, stubborn in battle, he defended Trenn, his father's
town.

Cynddylan of the bright heart, the stately, wearing a chain,
stubborn in the army, he defended Trenn while he lived . . .

How sad it is to my heart to lay the white flesh in the black
coffin, Cynddylan the leader of a hundred hosts.

The hall of Cynddylan is dark tonight, without fire, without
bed; I shall weep a while, I shall be silent after.

The hall of Cynddylan is dark tonight, without fire, without
candle; but for God, who will give me sanity?

The hall of Cynddylan is dark tonight, without fire, without
light; longing for you comes over me.

1. See Notes; and for the names, the Index.

The hall of Cynddylan, its vault is dark after the bright company; alas for him who does not do the good which falls to him!

Hall of Cynddylan, you have become shapeless, your shield is in the grave; while he lived you were not mended with hurdles.

The hall of Cynddylan is loveless tonight, after him who owned it; ah, Death, why does it spare me? . . .

The hall of Cynddylan, it pierces me to see it, without roof, without fire; my lord dead, myself alive . . .

The hall of Cynddylan is still tonight, after losing its chief; great merciful God, what shall I do? . . .

The eagle of Eli, loud is his scream tonight; he swallowed gory drink, the heart's blood of Cynddylan the fair.

The eagle of Eli was shrieking tonight, he wallowed in the blood of men; he in the wood, a heavy grief to me.

The eagle of Eli I hear tonight; he is bloodstained, I dare not go near him; he in the wood, a heavy grief upon me . . .

The eagle of Penngwern, grey-crested, uplifted is his cry, greedy for the flesh of Cynddylan.

The eagle of Penngwern, grey-crested, uplifted is his claw, greedy for the flesh I love . . .

The chapels of Bassa are his resting-place tonight, his last welcome, the pillar of battle, the heart of the men of Argoed . . .

The chapels of Bassa are a fallow field tonight, the clover has made it; they are red; my heart is full.

The chapels of Bassa have lost their rank after the destruction by the English of Cynddylan and Elfan of Powys . . .

The white town in the breast of the wood, this is its symbol ever – blood on the surface of its grass.

The white town in the land, its symbol is green graves, and blood under the feet of its men.

The white town in the valley, glad is the kite at the bloodshed of battle; its people have perished . . .

After my brothers from the lands of the Severn round the banks of the Dwyryw, woe is me, God! that I am alive . . .

I have looked out on a lovely land from the gravemound of Gorwynnion; long is the sun's course – longer are my memories . . .

I had brothers who were not vicious, who grew up like hazel saplings; one by one they have all passed away.

I had brothers whom God has taken from me, it was my ill-luck that caused it; they did not earn fame by fraud . . .

Welsh; author unknown; ninth century.

204. Eimher's Keen over Cú Chulainn

. . . Then Cenn Berraide arose and brought the head to Dún Delgan, and gave it into Eimher's hand; and she had it washed and put on its own body, and Eimher[1] took it to her, and she clutched it to her breast and her bosom after that, and began to bewail and lament over him, and began to kiss his lips and drink his blood,[2] and she put a silken shroud about him.

'Och, och,' said the girl, 'good was the beauty and the shape of this head, though it be as it is today; and many daughters of the kings and princes of the world would be lamenting you today if they knew you were like this. And those too who beg for gold and money and boons in Ireland and Scotland, you were their one choice and their one love among the men of the world; and it is pitiful that I am left after you today, for there was not a woman in Ireland or Scotland or the whole world, married or single, who did not

1. Cú Chulainn's wife.   2. Cf. Note on no. 221, verse 8.

envy me until today; for many were the treasures and riches and taxes and tributes from the ends of the earth that would come to me through the strength and valour of Cú Chulainn.' And she took his hand in her hand, and began to tell forth his fame and his renown, and she said: 'Sad is this,' said Eimher, 'many of the kings and princes and champions of the world were sent to death and dreadful doom by the swift blows of this hand, and many of the birds and witless creatures of the earth fell by you, and much of the riches and wealth of the earth was scattered and given away by this hand to the poets and sages of the world.' . . .

Irish; author unknown; fifteenth century.

205. The Wild Man of the Woods[1]

Dismal is this life, to be without a soft bed; a cold frosty dwelling, harshness of snowy wind.

Cold icy wind, faint shadow of a feeble sun, the shelter of a single tree on the top of the level moor.

Enduring the shower, stepping along deer-paths, traversing greenswards on a morning of raw frost . . .

Irish; author unknown; twelfth century.

206. The Wild Man's Life

. . . A dismal life, to be without a house, it is a sad life, dear Christ! food of green-topped perennial water-cress, drink of cold water from the clear brook.

Falling out of the tops of withered boughs, roaming through the gorse, in very truth; shunning humans, befriending wolves, running with the brown stag over the plain.

Sleeping at night in the wood, without a quilt, in the crest of a thick bushy tree, without listening to human voice or speech; O Son of God, it is a great grief!

1. i.e. Suibhne, see Note to no. 22.

I run a course giddily to the peak – few have surpassed me
in vigour! I have lost my looks, which were unexcelled;
O Son of God, it is a great grief!

Irish; author unknown; twelfth century.

207. The Wild Man Comes to the Monastery

. . . There was a time when I thought sweeter than the
quiet converse of monks, the cooing of the ringdove flitting
about the pool.

There was a time when I thought sweeter than the sound of
a little bell beside me, the warbling of the blackbird from
the gable and the belling of the stag in the storm.

There was a time when I thought sweeter than the voice of
a lovely woman beside me, to hear at matins the cry of the
heath-hen of the moor.

There was a time when I thought sweeter the howling of
wolves, than the voice of a priest indoors, baa-ing and bleating.

Though you like your ale with ceremony in the drinking-
halls, I like better to snatch a drink of water in my palm
from a spring.

Though you think sweet, yonder in your church, the gentle
talk of your students, sweeter I think the splendid talking
the wolves make in Glenn mBolcáin.

Though you like the fat and meat which are eaten in the
drinking-halls, I like better to eat a head of clean water-cress
in a place without sorrow . . .

Irish; author unknown; twelfth century.

208. Deirdre's Farewell to Scotland[1]

A beloved land is that land in the east, Scotland with its
wonders; I should not have come hither out of it if I had
not come with Noíse.

1. On the place-names see Notes.

Beloved are Dún Fidhgha and Dún Finn, beloved is the stronghold above them, beloved is Inis Draighen, and beloved is Dún Suibhne.

The wood of Cuan, to which Ainnle used to go, alas! Short we thought the time, I and Noíse on the shores of Scotland.

Glenn Laígh, I used to sleep beneath the shapely rock; fish and venison and badger's fat, that was my food in Glenn Laígh.

Glen Massan, tall was its wild garlic, bright its grasses; we used to have a broken sleep above the wooded river-mouth of Massan.

Glen Etive, there I raised my first house; lovely is its wood, and when it rises a cattle-fold of the sun is Glen Etive.

Glenn Urchaín, that was a straight glen of fair ridges; no man of his age was prouder than Noíse in Glenn Urchaín.

Glen Daruel, happy is any man who is its native; sweet is the voice of the cuckoo on the bending bough on the peak above Glen Daruel.

Beloved is Draighen with its firm beach, beloved is its water in the pure sand; I should not have come out of it from the east if I had not come with my beloved.

Irish; author unknown; fifteenth century.

209. Elegy on Druim nDen

How bare is your stronghold, Druim nDen! Very bare is your rampart and your site. I see, of the flowers once lavish on you from now for ever you shall be bare.

Lovely were your borders and your verge, sweet the call of cuckoos that dwelt around you; shining was your wall, spacious and splendid, and your fortress encircled with green-leaved oaks.

You were a protection against need and sorrow, you were a fence and a forest clearing; it is my longing to set my back to your wall and my face towards your wide demesne.

But I am in the west of Ireland, and you in the east are all on fire; the grazing herd crops the meadow, the meal is ground without the miller.

Rarely comes any that would be better; every fame shall be brought low; you shall be a hall for tearful austere nuns, though now you are grass-grown and bare.

Irish; author unknown; eleventh century.

210. Senility

Before I was bent-backed, I was eloquent of speech, my wonderful deeds were admired; the men of Argoed always supported me.

Before I was bent-backed, I was bold; I was welcomed in the drinking-hall of Powys, the paradise of Wales.

Before I was bent-backed, I was handsome, my spear was in the van, it drew first blood – I am crooked, I am sad, I am wretched.

Wooden staff, it is Autumn, the bracken is red, the stubble is yellow; I have given up what I love.

Wooden staff, it is Winter, men are talkative over the drink; no one visits my bedside.

Wooden staff, it is Spring, the cuckoos are brown,[1] there is light at the evening meal; no girl loves me.

Wooden staff, it is early Summer, the furrow is red, the young corn is curly; it grieves me to look at your crook.

1. See Notes.

Wooden staff, knotty stick, support the yearning old man, Llywarch, the perpetual babbler . . .

Boisterous is the wind, white is the hue of the edge of the wood; the stag is emboldened, the hill is bleak; feeble is the old man, slowly he moves.

This leaf, the wind drives it, alas for its fate! It is old – this year it was born.

What I have loved from boyhood I now hate – a girl, a stranger, and a grey horse; indeed I am not fit for them.

The four things I have most hated ever have met together in one place; coughing and old age, sickness and sorrow.

I am old, I am lonely, I am shapeless and cold after my honoured couch; I am wretched, I am bent in three.

I am bent in three and old, I am peevish and giddy, I am silly, I am cantankerous; those who loved me love me not.

Girls do not love me, no one visits me, I cannot move about; ah, Death, why does it not come for me!

Neither sleep nor joy come to me after the slaying of Llawr and Gwen; I am an irritable carcass, I am old.

A wretched fate was fated for Llywarch ever since the night he was born – long toil without relief from weariness.

Welsh; attributed to 'Llywarch Hen'; ninth century.

211. Elegy on Gruffydd ab Addaf ap Dafydd

What matchless joy, when the nightingale calls night and day under the apple boughs by the whitewashed wall of the orchard with its splendid throng of trees! – the ceaseless songster with its pure bright voice, from its hollow nest, like a bird of Heaven, bell-like and clear in its call of golden poetry from its pleasant perch on the green bough. But when the fierce archer comes, wildly leaping – oh bitter

song! – by deep treachery to bring destruction with his
four-square bolt of birchen wood, though the trees are full
with the blissful gift of the fair burden of sweet fruit, poetry
will have lost, in overwhelming grief, the bright gem of the
flowering trees. Powys, that eloquent, fair, and fruitful land
possessed of fine taverns and sweet drinking-horns, was the
pleasant orchard, till the wise youth was slain with the grey
sword. Now that land of hawks has its singing nightingale
no more – alas for its widowed state! Now it is beggared of
poets, their odes without honour, hated by its enemies. If
we must grieve these three months, would that it were a
lesser grief than this for the falling of the sword-blade with
a great angry cry on the place where it was so loathed.
Gruffydd, sweet bird of song, son of Addaf, most guiltless
one, every honourable man called him the lord of the lovely
boughs of May, the most pleasant far-heard organ, the
golden beloved nightingale, the ever-active bee of song, the
learned springtime of Gwenwynwyn's land.[1] It was madness
for his kinsman so to strike him, with steel in his hand, in
reckless anger. The coward at heart, he laid his weapon
upon my brother, making a deep gash through the fine
hair of the hawk of proud lineage; ah me, the keenness of
its edge! With a blow like a saw-cut the triple-edged sword
went through the brave pure man's yellow hair, oh pitiful!
an ugly rent in a most lovely head, like splitting a goose's
skull in two – my wrath, was it not a barbarous deed? His
cheeks were of the colour of a pale angel, and he himself
like a golden tower – and now the man is dead.

Welsh; Dafydd ap Gwilym, *c.* 1325–*c.* 1380.

212. *The Vision*

One morning before Titan[2] thought of moving his feet I
went to the top of a high and lovely hill; I met a band of
merry, delightful girls, a host from the bright halls of Síodh
Seanaibh in the north.

1. Powys.   2. The sun.

A magic mist showered down, not dark in hue, from Galway of the bright-coloured stones to Cork of the bays; every tree-top bore fruit and nuts unceasing, acorns on every wood, and honey still on the stones.

They lit three candles, with a glow I cannot describe, on the top of high Cnoc Fírinne in red Conello; I followed the band of hooded women to Thomond, and I asked them whence the zeal of their office upon their rounds.

The girl Aoibheall,[1] not swarthy of colour, replied, 'The cause for lighting three candles in every harbour is for the sake of the resolute king[2] who will be with us soon, ruling the Three Kingdoms, and maintaining them lastingly.'

From my dream I leaped up softly, without delay, and I thought that Aoibheall spoke truth in the good news she told; but oh, I became weak and trembling, gloomy and sad, one morning before Titan thought of moving his feet.

Irish; Egan O'Rahilly, *c.* 1670–1726.

213. *The Unquiet Grave*

I am stretched on your grave, and you'll find me there always; if I had the bounty of your arms I should never leave you. Little apple, my beloved, it is time for me to lie with you; there is the cold smell of the clay on me, the tan of the sun and the wind.

There's a lock on my heart, which is filled with love for you, and melancholy beneath it as black as the sloes. If anything happens to me, and death overthrows me, I shall become a fairy wind-gust down on the meadows before you.

When my family thinks that I am in my bed, it is on your grave I am stretched from night till morning, telling my distress and lamenting bitterly for my quiet lovely girl who was betrothed to me as a child.

1. A queen of the Fairies of Munster.
2. James Stuart, the Old Pretender.

Do you remember the night when you and I were under the blackthorn tree, and the night freezing? A hundred praises to Jesus that we did nothing harmful, and that your crown of maidenhood is a tree of light before you!

The priests and the monks every day are angry with me for being in love with you, young girl, when you are dead. I would be a shelter from the wind for you and protection from the rain for you; and oh, keen sorrow to my heart that you are under the earth!

Irish: traditional folk-song.

214. Ty'n y Coed

I was in service for a while near Ty'n y Coed, and that was the most delightful place that ever I was in. The little birds were warbling, and the trees murmuring together – but my poor heart broke in spite of all those.

Welsh; traditional folk verse; seventeenth century?

215. Longing

Tell me, men of learning, what is Longing made from? What cloth was put in it, that it does not wear out with use?

Gold wears out, silver wears out, velvet wears out, silk wears out, every ample garment wears out – yet Longing does not wear out.

Great Longing, cruel Longing is breaking my heart every day; when I sleep most sound at night Longing comes and wakes me.

Longing, Longing, back, back! do not weigh on me so heavily; move over a little to the bedside and let me sleep a while.

On the sea-shore is a smooth rock, where I talked with my love; around it grows the lily and a few sprigs of rosemary.

May the mountain which covers Merioneth be under the sea! Would that I had never seen it before my gentle heart broke.

Longing has seized on me, between my two breasts and my two brows; it weighs on my breast as if I were its nurse.

Welsh; traditional folk verses; seventeenth century?

216. The Braes of Glen Broom

Take my true greeting to the girl of thick tresses with whom I often played on the braes of Glen Broom.

Mournful am I, so far from you this year; sorrow has wasted me, lamenting your lost love.

I cannot be cheerful, it is my wont to be sad, I shall not climb the brae, my agility has faded.

My speed has become slow when I see my sweetheart no more; I used to be with you in the little glen of the willows.

In the wood where the ringdove sang its sweet song to us, and cuckoo and thrush awoke us, pouring forth their joyful strain.

Often you and I sported, while the others searched for us, till we chose to return to the meadow where the calves were.

We on the hill crest, my arm round your neck, listening to the chorus in the tops of the branches.

I declare it, and I cannot deny it, that many a hardship comes to the worthy man who does not expect it.

I am vexed now and in subjection in a French prison, oppressed by all,

In locked cells without music or sport, without the order from England to send me home free.

How unlike my custom, to be walking the wilds and climbing the high hills, stalking the deer;

Roaming the craggy peaks with my gun which never misses,
and my powder flasks on my knee in the heather.

Scottish Gaelic; attributed to William Ross, 1762–90.

217. Elegy on the Ruins of Timoleague Abbey

One night I was, depressed and sad, beside the mighty-
surging sea, reflecting earnestly and reciting the cruel
vicissitudes of this world.

The moon was up, and the stars, no noise of wave or ebb
was heard; there was not any gust of wind to shake the
tree-tops or the flowers.

I went in mute reverie, not noticing what way I walked,
until I saw a church door on the level path before me.

I halted in the old doorway, where alms and guidance used
to be given to the sick and weak, when the people of the
house were alive.

There was a crooked bench beside it, it was fashioned long
ago, where sages and clergy used to sit and travellers who
walk the road.

I sat down there, full of thought; I laid my hand under my
cheek, and showers of tears fell fast from my eyes down on
the grass.

I spoke then from my sense of loss, as I sadly wept: 'There
was a time when this house was cheerful and glad.

Here there were priests and bells, hymns, and theology
being read, choral song and music, praising the majesty of
God.

Useless and empty ruin, dwelling-place with your ancient
towers, many a storm and wind has lashed the bare tops
of your walls.

Many a rain-shower and chill and storm from the sea you

have endured since you were first dedicated as a dwelling for the King of Creation.

Sacred wall with your grey gables, once an adornment to this land, your ruin is a keen distress to me, and the dispersal of your saints.

Deserted you are now, there is no choir nor music in you, only the harsh screaming of the owls in place of cheerful psalms.

The ivy spreads over your arch, and wild nettles on your dank floor; the sharp yelp of the cunning foxes and the murmur of the rapids at your corner.

Where the lark would call early to the clergy as they sang their Hours, there is not a tongue stirring now except the croaking tongues of the jackdaws.

No food in your refectory, your dormitory has no soft bed, your sanctuary lacks sacrifice by priests and Mass being said to God.

Your Abbot and your Rule are gone, and your ever-pious Brothers; and in your precinct I find nothing now but a little heap of mouldy bones.

Alas! Oppression and arrogance, cruel tyranny and injustice, hostile ill-use and harsh plundering have left you deserted as you are.'

I too was happy for a time, but ah, my figure is worn away! This world's persecutions have come against me, there is no strength in me but sorrow.

My vigour and activeness are gone, my eyesight and my energy; my kinsfolk and my children lie low and mouldering in this church.

There is a grimness in my face, my heart is all one husk of gore; if Death should deliver me, it is certain I should welcome him.

Irish; Seán Ó Coileáin; 1814.

218. Lament for Reilly[1]

One lovely evening as I walked by the strand, whom should I find but fair-haired Reilly? His cheeks were flushed and his hair was curling; and oh my great grief, that you got your death through me!

A maid and a widow God made of me in my first youth, when I heard them repeating that my eager darling was drowned; if I had been out that night with nets ready for you, on my word, Reilly, I should have saved you your sorrow.

Do you remember that day when this street was full of people? There were priests and monks there and were talking of our names. There was music of trumpets there, and the harp being plucked, and twelve gentle women to bring my love to my bed.

No wonder that your father and mother are broken-hearted, and your white-breasted nurse who suckled you as a baby! Shall I count also your wedded wife, who never lay in bed with you, and when I thought to be kissing you it was your wake that was the wedding?

My grief, Reilly, that you were not the king's son-in-law, with bright white curtains around you as you lay, a quiet stately lady combing your hair; and since we were plighted, oh my grief that you died in my lifetime!

The wright that made the boat, may his hands perish! — yet it was not the wright who was guilty, but the fault that was in the plank there; for if they had gone to Kinsale to fetch the ship that was made there, my love would not have been drowned on this shore at Clontealan.

But the sea-beasts have your eyes and the crabs have your mouth, and your long soft white hands that would be fishing for salmon. If I had been out that night with my

1. See Notes.

nets all ready, by my word, Reilly, I should have saved you your sorrow.

My grief that you were among the three men who went to Duhallow, escorting Father Peter who was aged four-score years! I was awaiting you a month, but alas, you did not return; and is it not great pity a woman alone and her man afloat on the waves?

Fine and fairly your sword became you as you rode your slender horse, blowing your horn, with your hounds all around you. You would lift the grief from my heart, abroad on the hill-top; and my great sorrow and my woe that you died in my lifetime!

Irish; traditional folk-song.

219. Elegy for His Daughter Ellen

Too sad is the grief in my heart! down my cheeks run salt streams. I have lost my Ellen of the hue of fair weather, my bright-braided merry daughter.

My darling, bright-shaped, beautiful, my warm-smiling angel; a golden speech was the infant talk of her lips, the girl of the colour of the stars (what profit now to speak?), whose form was delicate, whose voice was soft, with a happy cry to welcome her father, that orphaned man. Orphaned is her father, with a crushing wound in his pierced and broken heart, in inconsolable distress – how well I know, bound down with my yearning for her!

Since I lost my neat slender girl, all the time I mourn her sadly and ponder on her ways. When I think of her, anguish springs up and wretched affliction in my breast, my heart is faint for her and broken because of her; it is a pang to speak of her, my trim daughter, of the dear gentle words she uttered, and of her delicate pale white hands.

Farewell, my soul, my joyful gay princess, farewell again, my

Nelly, pure of heart, farewell my pretty little merry daughter, my angel, resting in the midst of the graveyard at Walton, until the far assembly of the white Saints and the cry of the clamour of the unfailing Messengers.[1] When the earth shall give up its meek and innocent, when the throngs shall be summoned from the mighty oceans, you shall get, my soul, you too, a fine gold crown and a place in the light of the host of angels.

Welsh; Goronwy Owen; 1755.

220. The Death of Màiri

She died, like the ruddy clouds in the east at the break of day, which are envied by the sun for their beauty as it rises in its glory to darken them.

She died, like a glimpse of sunlight when the shadow races in pursuit; she died, like a rainbow when the shower has fallen and its glory is past.

She died, like snow which lies on the shore by the sea, when the pitiless tide flows over it – oh whiteness! – and it did not enjoy it for long.

She died, like the voice of the harp when it is sweetest and most solemn; she died, like a lovely tale when the telling has barely begun.

She died, like the gleam of the moon when the sailor is afraid in the dark; she died, like a sweet dream when the sleeper is sad that it has gone.

She died, at the beginning of her beauty; Heaven could not dispense with her; she died, oh Màiri died, like the sun quenched at its rising.

Scottish Gaelic; Evan Maccoll; 1808–98.

1. i.e. the Judgement Day.

221. *The Lament for Art O'Leary*[1]

HIS WIFE:

My steadfastly beloved, on the day that I saw you beside the market-hall, my eye gave heed to you, my heart gave love to you; I stole away from my family with you, far from home with you.

Nor did I repent it. You gave me a parlour brightened for me, rooms decorated for me, the oven heated for me, loaves made for me, roast meat on spits for me, beeves butchered for me, sleep on ducks' feathers for me until high morning, or later if I chose.

My steadfastly beloved, in my heart I remember that fine spring day, how well your hat became you with a gold band stretched round it, and a silver-hilted sword in your bold right hand; dashing and menacing, a very terror to your wily enemies, as you got ready to trot on your graceful white-faced steed. The English would bow down to the ground to you, and not from good-will to you but from sheer terror; though at their hands you fell, darling of my soul.

White-handed horseman, well your pin became you, fastened in the cambric, and your hat with its lace. When you returned from overseas the street would be cleared for you, and not out of love for you but in exceeding dread of you.

My steadfastly beloved, when they come home to me, little Conor my darling and Fear O'Leary the baby, they will ask me straightway where I left their father. I shall tell them woefully that I left him at Kilnamartery; they will cry for their father, but he will not be there to answer them.

My dear and my sweetheart, kin of the Earl of Antrim and of the Barrys of Youghal, well your blade became you, your hat with its band, your slim foreign shoe, and your suit of the yarn spun beyond for you.

1. On the incidents, people, and places in this poem, see Notes.

My steadfastly loved one, I never thought you could be dead, till your horse came to me with its reins trailing to the ground, and your heart's blood on its face and thence to your polished saddle, where you would rise and fall in your stirrups. I gave one leap to the threshold, another leap to the gate, and a third leap upon your horse.

Quickly I clapped my hands and set off at a gallop as well as I could, till I found you dead before me by a little low furze-bush; without Pope, without bishop, without cleric, without priest to read the psalm over you, but an ancient worn old woman who had spread the end of her cloak on you; your blood was streaming from you, and I did not stop to wipe it, but drank it up from my palms.[1]

My steadfastly beloved, rise up and come home beside me, to have beeves butchered, to order a lavish banquet. Let us have music playing, and let me make a bed for you, with white sheets and fine patchwork quilts which will make you sweat, in place of the chill you have taken.

HIS SISTER:

My dear and my darling, I had a dream last night in my drowsiness, alone in my bed and late, at Cork: that our whitewashed court was fallen, that Gearagh had withered, and no voice was left to your slim hounds nor song to the birds; when you were found spent, out on the hillside, without priest, without cleric, but an aged old woman who had spread the end of her kerchief on you, when you were stretched on the earth, Art O'Leary, and your blood gushing out in the bosom of your shirt.

My dear and my treasure, many a comely handsome maid from Cork of the sails to Toon Bridge, who would bring as her dowry a great herd of cattle to you and a fistful of yellow gold to you, would not go to sleep in her room the night of your wake.

HIS WIFE:

My dear and my sweetheart, do not believe the whisper you

1. See Notes.

have heard from them, nor the tale of those who hate me, that I went to sleep; it was not slumber upon me, but that your children were restless, and wanted to have me to settle them to sleep.

Dear people, is there a woman in Ireland who had lain beside him by night and borne him three young ones, who would not run mad after Art O'Leary, who has lain spent here beside me since yesterday morning?

Wretched Morris, sorrow on you! May your heart's blood, and your liver's, be upon you! May your eyes be blinded and your knees be smashed! You who had my darling killed, and there was not a man in Ireland who would shoot you.

My dear and my beloved, och, rise up, Art! Leap up on your horse, go off into Macroom and back to Inchigeelagh, a bottle of wine in your grasp, as there used to be in your father's room.

My long grief and bitter sorrow that I was not beside you when the bullet was fired at you! that I might have taken it in my right side, or in the lap of my shift, and let you take to the hills, horseman of the gentle hands!

My bitter grief that I was not behind you when the powder was fired! that I might have taken it in my right flank or in the lap of my dress, and let you go free, grey-eyed horseman, since you were best be let get at them.

My dear and precious beloved, how abhorrent to set out these preparations for a hero! A coffin and a shroud for the high-hearted horseman, who would be fishing in the streams and drinking in the halls among white-breasted women. Och, my thousand frenzies that I have lost your companionship!

Burning and destruction on you, loathly treacherous Morris! who have robbed me of my husband, the father of my young children, two of them already walking in the house, and the third one in my womb, and it is likely I shall not bear it.

My love and my delight, when you went out of the gate you turned back quickly and kissed your two babies, and kissed the tip of my hand. You said, 'Eileen, get up and put your business in order quickly and swiftly; I am leaving home, and perhaps shall never come back.' But I only mocked at your words, you would often say that to me before.

My dear and my own, horseman of the bright sword, rise up now and put on your fine clean clothes, put on your black beaver hat, draw on your gloves. There is your whip up there, here is your mare outside, strike the narrow road eastwards yonder, where the very bushes shall lie flat for you, where the stream shall shrink for you, where men and women shall bow to you if they still know their manners, but I fear that now they do not.

My love and dear companion, it is not those of my kindred who have died, nor if my three children should die, nor Donall *Mór* O'Connell, nor Conall whom the flood-tide drowned, nor the woman of twenty-six years who went across over the water to make kinship with kings – it is not all these that I am calling on with the sighs of my breast, but generous Art O'Leary, Art of the fair hair, Art the victorious and courageous, the rider of the brown mare, laid low last night on the Inch of Carriganimmy – may it perish, both name and style!

My love and my darling, Art O'Leary, son of Conor son of Keady son of Louis O'Leary! From the west from Gearagh and from the east from Greenan (where the berries grow, and yellow nuts on the branches, and apples in masses at their proper time), no one would wonder if Iveleary should catch fire, and Ballingeary and holy Gouganebarra, after the horseman of the gentle hands, who would wear down the quarry, riding hard from Grenagh when the slim hounds gave up. O horseman of the glancing eyes, what came over you last night? For I thought myself, when I bought you your clothing, that the whole world could not kill you.

HIS SISTER:

My love and my dear, kinsman of the nobles of the country, if you had had eighteen nurses at one time they would all have got their pay – a milch cow and a mare, a sow and her litter, a mill on the ford, yellow gold and white silver, silk and fine velvet, and a piece of land for estate – that they might suckle you, calf of the stately women.

My love, my secret treasure, my love, my white pigeon, though I did not come to you and did not bring my men with me, I thought that no shame, for they were all cramped in closed-up vaults in narrow coffins, in a sleep without waking.

But for the smallpox and the black death and the spotted fever, that fierce troop of riders, shaking their bridles, would have been making a clatter as they came to your burial, white-breasted Art.

My love and my delight, kinsman of that wild troop of riders who used to hunt in the glen! You would make them turn back and bring them into the hall, where knives were being sharpened, pork being carved on the table, and ribs of mutton innumerable and bright-brown filled-out oats which would make the steeds whinny; and their graceful long-maned horses with their grooms beside them – they would not be charged for their beds nor for grazing for their horses, though they stayed for a week, O my brother, heart of our family.

My love, my secret treasure, how well these things became you – your five-ply hose, your boots to the knee, your three-cornered Caroline hat, and your active whip, as you sat your lively gelding; and many a modest well-bred maid would be gazing after you.

HIS WIFE:

My steadfastly beloved, when you went to grim fortified cities the wives of merchants would curtsey to the ground to you, for they knew in their hearts that you were a fine bedfellow, or to ride pillion behind, or father of children.

Jesus Christ knows, there shall be no coif on my head, nor shift on my body, nor shoe under my sole, nor goods throughout my house, nor bridle on the brown mare, but that I will spend them all at the law, and I will go across over the wave to talk with the King; and if he'll pay me no heed, I shall come back again to the black-blooded oaf who stole my treasure from me.

My love and my darling, if my cry could reach to great Derrynane down yonder and to Carhen of the yellow apples, many a light-foot spirited horseman and many a stainless white-coifed woman would be here without delay, weeping over your body, merry Art O'Leary.

My heart's affection for the little dark women of the mill because they weep so well for the rider of the brown mare.

Cruel burning of heart upon you, John son of Ooney! If it was the reward that you wanted you should have come to see me, and I would have given you much – a long-maned horse which would have carried you away over the hills on the day of your danger, or a fine herd of cows for you, or sheep bearing lambs for you, or a gentleman's suit with spurs and boots – though I should think it great pity to see that upon you, for I hear it said that you are a filthy little lout.

White-handed horseman, since your strong arm was laid low, go to Baldwin, the odious little scum, the spindle-shanked fellow, and get compensation from him in place of your mare and for the way he treated your fair love; may his six children never thrive! – Not wishing harm to Mary, and not with love to her either, only that it was my mother gave a bed in her body to her throughout nine months.

My love, my secret treasure, your ricks are on their staddles, your tawny cows are milking; and on my heart there is grief for you such as the whole province of Munster could not cure, nor all the craftsmen of Ireland. Until Art O'Leary comes back to me my grief will not be scattered, where it is crushed down deep in my heart and closed in fast, as by a lock on a chest when the key has gone astray.

You women weeping out there, stay on your feet till Art son of Conor calls for a drink, and others for the poor, before he goes in to join the school – not to study learning or song, but to bear the weight of clay and stones.

Irish; attributed to Eileen *Dubh* O'Connell; 1773.

RELIGION

NOTE

The people of Ireland were among the first outside the furthest extent of the Roman world to be converted to Christianity by missionaries from within the Empire. The disasters of the fifth century, which ruined the Roman organization and cut Ireland off from easy contact with it, meant that the Irish were left alone for some centuries to develop their own type of Christianity. Then when contact was re-established, it was found that Ireland had clung, and now continued obstinately to cling, to certain archaic dogmas and practices which had become superseded on the Continent; and a long battle was waged before the Celtic church finally gave in. In fact the Irish church was not fully assimilated to the Roman until the coming of the Normans with their Continental customs in the twelfth century. Even then the process was not complete, for religious traditions still survived, going back to the very early days of the church, which had died out entirely elsewhere. The Irish have always loved a good tale, and in the Middle Ages a good religious tale was irresistible to them, never mind whether it was considered un-canonical by the far-away church of Rome. Hence medieval Irish literature is full of all sorts of fascinating stories, amounting sometimes to sheer folklore, which students of religious history on the Continent know only in very early Apocryphal sources or in the oldest practices of the primitive Church. Some examples of these tales will be found here. The best as a work of art is the Vision of Adhamhnán, from which a large selection is given in no. 231; this eleventh-century text is based partly upon much older Latin sources, but the extraordinary imaginative treatment is typically Celtic.

A characteristic of early Celtic Christianity is the fervour of asceticism practised by the monks and 'saints'. Those interested may consult Dom Louis Gougaud's *Christianity in*

Celtic Lands (London, 1932). The Celtic hermits went to the most desolate wilds and ocean rocks to win salvation in their own way; three of the poems translated here (nos. 222–4) are put in the mouths of these hermits, and are evidently the work of men who knew at first hand what they were writing about. It is a marked feature of this body of Irish literature that the writers had an intimate affection for wild life and wild nature, such as we may find elsewhere in Christian sources perhaps only in the story of St Francis. This is seen for instance in no. 234 and in no. 223; no. 18 has been included with the Nature group because it is almost entirely a nature poem, but still it is a description by a hermit of his peaceful woodland retreat, and stems from the more purely religious type of poem seen in nos. 223 and 224. Together with this love of wild nature, another remarkable feature of Celtic Christianity is the very strong personal relationship which the religious seem to have felt with God. They speak of God as 'my darling' (no. 22), and other terms of human love are often used. This sense of intimacy could hardly be pushed further than in no. 226, the wish of St Íde to be allowed to nurse the infant Jesus in her cell; we see it also in no. 227, where the poet would like to entertain the people of Heaven at a religious banquet.

The two Cornish extracts (nos. 240, 241) are taken from miracle plays, which were particularly popular in Cornwall and Brittany in the Middle Ages and even later. These are of course of Continental origin and inspiration, but they have an unconventionality and vividness which betrays their Celtic handling.

RELIGION

222. St Columba's Island Hermitage

Delightful I think it to be in the bosom of an isle, on the peak of a rock, that I might often see there the calm of the sea.

That I might see its heavy waves over the glittering ocean, as they chant a melody to their Father on their eternal course.

That I might see its smooth strand of clear headlands, no gloomy thing; that I might hear the voice of the wondrous birds, a joyful tune.

That I might hear the sound of the shallow waves against the rocks; that I might hear the cry by the graveyard, the noise of the sea.

That I might see its splendid flocks of birds over the full-watered ocean; that I might see its mighty whales, greatest of wonders.

That I might see its ebb and its flood-tide in their flow; that this might be my name, a secret I tell, 'He who turned his back on Ireland.'

That contrition of heart should come upon me as I watch it; that I might bewail my many sins, difficult to declare.

That I might bless the Lord who has power over all, Heaven with its pure host of angels, earth, ebb, flood-tide.

That I might pore on one of my books, good for my soul; a while kneeling for beloved Heaven, a while at psalms.

A while gathering dulse from the rock, a while fishing, a while giving food to the poor, a while in my cell.

A while meditating upon the Kingdom of Heaven, holy is the redemption; a while at labour not too heavy; it would be delightful!

Irish; author unknown; twelfth century.

223. *The Wish of Manchán of Liath*

I wish, O son of the Living God, ancient eternal King, for a secret hut in the wilderness that it may be my dwelling.

A very blue shallow well to be beside it, a clear pool for washing away sins through the grace of the Holy Ghost.

A beautiful wood close by around it on every side, for the nurture of many-voiced birds, to shelter and hide it.

Facing the south for warmth, a little stream across its enclosure, a choice ground with abundant bounties which would be good for every plant.

A few sage disciples, I will tell their number, humble and obedient, to pray to the King.

Four threes, three fours, fit for every need, two sixes in the church, both south and north.

Six couples in addition to me myself, praying through the long ages to the King who moves the sun.

A lovely church decked with linen, a dwelling for God of Heaven; then, bright candles over the holy white Scriptures.

One room to go to for the care of the body, without wantonness, without voluptuousness, without meditation of evil.

This is the housekeeping I would undertake, I would choose it without concealing; fragrant fresh leeks, hens, speckled salmon, bees.

My fill of clothing and of food from the King of good fame, and for me to be sitting for a while praying to God in every place.

Irish; author unknown; tenth century.

224. *The Hermit*

Alone in my little hut without a human being in my company, dear has been the pilgrimage before going to meet death.

A remote hidden little cabin, for forgiveness of my sins; a conscience upright and spotless before holy Heaven.

Making holy the body with good habits, treading it boldly down; weak tearful eyes for forgiveness of my desires.

Desires feeble and withered, renunciation of this poor world, clean live thoughts; this is how I would seek God's forgiveness.

Eager wailings to cloudy Heaven, sincere and truly devout confession, fervent showers of tears.

A cold anxious bed, like the lying-down of the doomed, a brief apprehensive sleep, invocations frequent and early.

My food, my staple diet – it is a dear bondage – my meal would not make me full-blooded, without doubt.

Dry bread weighed out, well we bow the head; water of the fair-coloured hillside, that is the draught you should drink.

A bitter meagre meal, diligently feeding the sick, suppression of quarrelling and visiting, a calm serene conscience.

It would be desirable, a pure, holy blemish, cheeks dry and sunken, skin leathery and lean.

Treading the paths of the Gospel, singing psalms every Hour; an end of talking and long stories; constant bending of the knees.

My Creator to visit me, my Lord, my King, my spirit to seek Him in the eternal kingdom where He is.

Let this be the end of vice in the precincts of churches, a lovely little cell among many graves, and I alone there.

Alone in my little hut, all alone so, alone I came into the world, alone I shall go from it.

If being alone I have done wrong at all, through the pride of this world, hear my wail as I lament all alone, O God!

Irish; author unknown; eighth–ninth century.

225. St Brendan and the Harper

Once when Brénainn of the race of Altae was at Clonfert, on Easter Day seven years before his death, he celebrated Mass in the church, and preached and made the offering. But when midday came the monks went to their refectory; there was a student inside with a harp in his hand, and he began to play for them, and they gave him their blessing. 'I should be delighted, now,' said the clerk, 'if Brénainn were in, so that I might play him three tunes.' 'He would not allow you to come to him,' said the monks, 'for Brénainn has been for seven years without smiling and without hearing any of the music of the world; but he has two balls of wax with a thread joining them, on the book before him, and when he hears music he puts the balls in his ears.' 'I shall go, nevertheless, to play to him,' said the student.

He went away, with his harp tuned. 'Open,' said the clerk. 'Who is this?' said Brénainn. 'A student come to play the harp for you.' 'Play outside,' said Brénainn. 'If you would not think it troublesome,' said the clerk, 'I should be glad to be allowed inside the church to play a while.' 'Very well,' said Brénainn. 'Open the door for me,' said the student. Brénainn opened for him. The clerk took his harp from his back; Brénainn put his two balls of wax in his ears. 'I do not like playing to you unless you take the wax out of your ears,' said the student. 'It shall be done, then,' said Brénainn; he put them on the book. He played him three tunes. 'A blessing upon you, student,' said he, 'with your music, and may you get Heaven for it!'

Brénainn put the balls in his ears afterwards, for he did

not wish to listen to it any more. 'Why do you not listen to the music?' said the student, 'is it because you think it bad?' 'Not for that,' said Brénainn, 'but like this. One day when I was in this church, seven years ago to this very day, after preaching here and after Mass, the priests went to the refectory; I was left here alone, and a great longing for my Lord seized me, when I had gone up to the Body of Christ. As I was there, trembling and terror came upon me; I saw a shining bird at the window, and it sat on the altar. I was unable to look at it because of the rays which surrounded it, like those of the sun. "A blessing upon you, and do you bless me, priest," it said. "May God bless you," said Brénainn;[1] "who are you?" said Brénainn. "The angel Michael," it said, "come to speak with you." "I give thanks to God for speaking with you," said Brénainn, "and why have you come?" "To bless you and to make music for you from your Lord," said the bird. "You are welcome to me," said Brénainn. The bird set its beak on the side of its wing, and I was listening to it from that hour to the same hour the next day; and then it bade me farewell.'

Brénainn scraped his stylus across the neck of the harp. 'Do you think this sweet, student?' he said; 'I give my word before God,' said Brénainn, 'that after *that* music, no music of the world seems any sweeter to me than does this stylus across the neck, and to hear it I take to be but little profit. Take a blessing, student, and you shall have Heaven for that playing,' said Brénainn.

Irish; author unknown; tenth century.

226. St Íde's Wish

'I will take nothing from my Lord,' said she, 'unless He gives me His Son from Heaven in the form of a baby to be nursed by me' . . . So that Christ came to her in the form of a baby, and she said then:—

---

1. Here Brendan's story drops temporarily into the third person.

'Little Jesus, Who is nursed by me in my little hermitage – even a priest with store of wealth, all is false but little Jesus.

The nursing which I nurse in my house is not the nursing of any base churl, Jesus with the folk of Heaven at my heart every single night.

Little young Jesus, my everlasting good, gives and is not remiss; the King Who has power over all, not to pray to Him will be repented.

It is Jesus, noble and angelic, not a paltry priest, Who is nursed by me in my little hermitage; Jesus the son of the Jewess.

Sons of princes, sons of kings, though they come to my land, not from them do I expect any good, I prefer little Jesus.

Sing a chorus, girls, to the One Who has a right to your little tribute; He is in His place on high, though as little Jesus He is on my breast.'

Irish; author unknown; ninth century?

227. I Should Like to Have a Great Ale-Feast[1]

I should like to have a great ale-feast for the King of Kings; I should like the Heavenly Host to be drinking it for all eternity.

I should like to have the fruits of Faith, of pure devotion; I should like to have the seats of Repentance in my house.

I should like to have the men of Heaven in my own dwelling; I should like the tubs of Long-Suffering to be at their service.

I should like to have the vessels of Charity to dispense; I should like to have the pitchers of Mercy for their company.

1. See Notes.

I should like there to be Hospitality for their sake; I should like Jesus to be here always.

I should like to have the Three Marys of glorious renown; I should like to have the Heavenly Host from every side.

I should like to be rent-payer to the Lord; he to whom He gives a good blessing has done well in suffering distress.

Irish; author unknown; tenth–eleventh century.

228. The Little Boys Who Went to Heaven

. . . Donnán son of Liath, one of Senán's disciples, went to gather dulse on the shore, with two little boys who were studying along with him. The sea carried off his boat from him, so that he had no boat to fetch the boys, and there was no other boat on the island to rescue the boys. So the boys were drowned on a rock; but on the next day their bodies were carried so that they lay on the beach of the island. Their parents came then and stood on the beach, and asked that their sons should be given them alive. Senán said to Donnán, 'Tell the boys to arise and speak with me.' Donnán said to the boys, 'You may arise to talk with your parents, for Senán tells you to do so.' They arose at once at Senán's command, and said to their parents, 'You have done wrong to us, bringing us away from the land to which we came.' 'How could you prefer,' said their mother to them, 'to stay in that land rather than to come to us?' 'Mother,' they said, 'though you should give us power over the whole world, and all its enjoyment and delight, we should think it no different from being in prison, compared with being in the life and in the world to which we came. Do not delay us, for it is time for us to go back again to the land from which we have come; and God shall bring it about for our sake that you shall not mourn after us.' So their parents gave them their consent, and they went together with Senán to his oratory; and the sacrament was given them, and they went to Heaven, and their bodies were buried in front of the oratory where Senán lived. And these were the first dead who were buried in Scattery Island ...

Irish; author unknown; tenth-century original?

229. *A Ghost Story*

There were two students who were studying together, so that they were foster-brothers since they were small children. This was their talk, in their little hut: 'It is a sad journey on which our dear ones and our friends go from us, that they never come back again with news for us of the land to which they go. Let us make a plan, that whoever of us dies first should come with news to the other.' 'Let it be done, truly.' They undertook that whoever of them should die first should come before the end of a month with news to the other.

Not long after this, then, one of the two died. He was buried by the other, and he sang his requiem. He was expecting him until the end of a month, but the other did not come; and he was abusing him and abusing the Trinity, so that the soul begged the Trinity to let it go to talk with him. Now, the latter was making prostrations in his hut, and there was a little lintel above his head; his head struck against the lintel so that he fell lifeless. His soul saw the body lying before it, but it thought it was still in its body. It was looking at it. 'But this is bad,' it said, 'to bring me a dead body. It is the brotherhood of the church, truly,' it said, 'who have brought it.' At that it bounded out of the house. One of the clergy was ringing the bell. 'It is not right, priest,' it said, 'to bring the dead body to me.' The priest did not answer. It betook itself to everyone. They did not hear. It was greatly distressed. It betook itself out of the church to the reapers. 'Here I am,' it said. They did not hear. Fury seized it. It went to its church again. They had gone to take tithes to him, and his body was seen in the house, and it was brought to the graveyard.

When the soul went into the church, it saw its friend before it. 'Well now,' it said, 'you have been a long time coming; yours was a bad promise.' 'Do not reproach me,' said the other, 'I have come many a time, and would be beside your pillow pleading with you, and you did not hear; for the dense heavy body does not hear the light ethereal tenuous soul.' 'I hear you now,' it said. 'No,' said the other, 'it is your soul only that is here. It is from your own body that you are escaping. For you have begged me to meet you, and that has come about, then. Woe is him who does wrong! Happy is he who does right! Go to find your body before it is put into the grave.' 'I will never go into it again, for horror and fear of it!' 'You shall go; you shall be alive for a year. Recite the *Beati* every day for my soul, for the *Beati* is the strongest ladder and chain and collar to bring a man's soul out of Hell.'

It said farewell to the other, and went to its body, and as it went into it it gave a shriek, and came back to life; and went to Heaven at the end of a year. So the *Beati* is the best prayer there is.

Irish; author unknown; ninth century.

230. *The Resurrection of Bresal Son of Diarmaid*

A great feast was made for Diarmaid son of Cerbhall by his son Bresal son of Diarmaid; and nothing was lacking at that feast except a cow with fat livers. Bresal heard that a nun at Cell Elgraighe in the glebe lands of Kells, Luchair by name, had such a one; and Bresal went to buy it, offering seven cows and a bull for it. The nun did not yield it, and Bresal took the cow by force, and gave the feast to his father at Kells. While they were enjoying themselves drinking, the nun came screaming to the king to complain of Bresal. 'You have done unjustly,' said the king, 'to commit an outrage against the nun in the matter of the cow, when she was in her church, and to fly in the face of my kingship and my control, for it is not an ancestral custom for you to do so; and I will have you put to death for the deed that you have done.' So Bresal was put to death.

Then Diarmaid said to Colum Cille, 'Is there any help for me in this deed that I have done?' 'There is,' said Colum Cille; 'go to the old monk who is on the island, Begán of Ulster.' 'I dare not go,' said the king. 'I will go with you,' said Colum Cille. Now when they arrived, what they found was Begán making a stone wall, with a damp cloak on him, praying at the same time. When Begán looked at Diarmaid, he said to him, 'Under the ground, murderer of kinsmen!' said he, so that he sank down into the ground as far as his knees. 'The protection is without stay, Begán,' said Colum Cille, 'for the reason why the king has come to you is to beg forgiveness, and for you to resurrect his son.' Begán raised his right hand, and prayed three times to resurrect Bresal son of Diarmaid, so that he brought fifty Bresals out of Hell with each prayer; and Bresal son of Diarmaid came with the last prayer with the last batch of them.

Irish; author unknown; twelfth century?

231. From The Vision of Adhamhnán

. . . Finally, it was revealed to Adhamhnán Ó Tinne, the great sage of the Western World, who is told of here, when his soul went out of his body on the festival of John the Baptist, and was taken up to Heaven with the angels of Heaven, and to Hell with its rabble-rout. When the soul left the body, then, there appeared straightway to it the angel who had been its guardian while it was in the flesh, and took it with him first to see the Kingdom of Heaven.

The first land to which they came was the Land of the Saints. A fertile and shining land is that land. There are wonderful assemblies there of many kinds, with chasubles of white linen about them and bright hoods on their heads. The Saints of the Eastern World are in a separate assembly in the east of the Land of the Saints; then, the Saints of the Western World are in the west of that same land; the Saints of the Northern World again and those of the Southern are in two vast assemblies south and north. Hence everyone in the Land of the Saints is equally near to hear the songs and to contemplate the vessel in which are the Nine Orders of Heaven in accordance with their ranks and their station.

Part of the time the Saints sing a marvellous song in praise of God, and the rest of the time they listen to the song of the Heavenly Host, for the Saints have need of nothing but to be listening to the music to which they listen and to behold the light which they look at, and to be filled with the fragrance which is in the land. There is a wonderful kingdom facing them to the south-east, with a veil of crystal between them, and a golden antechamber to the south of it, and through this they see the forms and the shadows of the Heavenly Host; but there is no veil nor obscurity between the Heavenly Host and the Saints, for they are clearly visible and present to them on the side towards them for ever. There is a fiery circle about that land all around, and all pass in and out and it does not harm them.

Then, the Twelve Apostles and the Virgin maiden Mary are in a separate assembly around the mighty Lord. The Patriarchs and Prophets and Disciples of Jesus are close beside the Apostles. There are certain virgin saints on Mary's right hand, with a short space between them. There are infants and children about them on every side, and the song of the birds of the Heavenly Host makes music for them. Glorious bands of the guardian angels are continually doing obeisance and service among these assemblies in the presence of the King. No one in this world below can describe or tell of these assemblies, in what manner they truly are. Now the hosts and the assemblies which are in the Land of the Saints, as we have described, shall remain in this great and glorious state until the mighty meeting of Doomsday, when the righteous Judge will range them on the Day of Judgement in the stations and in the places in which they are to be, looking at the face of God without veil and without shadow between them through all eternity.

Yet though the splendour and the brightness which is in the Land of the Saints is great and immense, as we have said, a thousand times more immense is the brilliance which is in the Plain of the Heavenly Host round the throne of the Lord Himself. And this is how that throne is, an ornamented chair with four legs of precious stone under it; and though a man had no other music than the harmonious chorus of those four legs, he would have sufficiency of glory and delight. There are three matchless birds on the chair before the King, and their minds are set on their Creator through the ages; that is their art. They celebrate the eight canonical hours by praising and by acclaiming the Lord, with the choral song of the Archangels coming in in harmony. The birds and the Archangels lead the song, and all the Heavenly Host, both saints and holy virgins, answer them in antiphony.

Then, there is a great arch above the head of the Supreme Being on His royal throne, like an ornamented helmet or the crown of a king. If human eyes should see it, they would instantly be melted. There are three circles around Him between Him and the people, and their nature cannot be understood by description. There are six thousand thousands with the figures of horses and birds round the fiery chair, as it blazes without limit or end.

No one can describe the mighty Lord who is on that throne, unless He were to undertake it Himself, or unless He were to order the ranks of Heaven to do so. For none shall tell of His ardour and His power, His blazing and His brilliance, His splendour and His bliss, His constancy and His steadfastness, the multitude of His angels and His archangels singing songs to Him; His numerous messengers coming and going with very short answers to every company in turn; His gentleness and great lenience to some, and His ungentleness and great harshness to others of them.

If anyone should gaze long at Him, around Him from east and west, from south and north, he will find on every side of Him a peerless face, seven times as bright as the sun; but he will not see the shape of man on Him, with head or foot, but a fiery mass blazing throughout the world, and everyone trembling in terror before Him. Heaven and earth are filled with His brilliance, and there is a glow like that of a royal star all about Him. Three thousand different songs are being sung in chorus around Him by every choir. As sweet as the many songs of this world is each single several song of them itself.

Then, the City in which that throne is, this is how it is, seven crystal walls of diverse colours about it, each wall higher than the next. The floor and the foundation of the City is of bright crystal with the hue of the sun on it, variegated with blue and crimson and green and every other colour besides.

Now, a mild, very gentle, very kindly people, without lack of any good thing among them, are they who dwell in that City; for none reach it ever, nor dwell in it, but holy virgins and pilgrims desirous of God. For their order and their array, however, it is hard to understand how it came about, for none of them has his back or his side towards another, but the ineffable power of the Lord has arrayed and kept them face to face in ranks and in circles of equal height round about the throne, in splendour and in delight, with all their faces towards God.

There is a chancel-screen of crystal between every two choirs, with conspicuous ornament of red gold and silver on it, with surpassing rows of precious stone and with chequer-work of rare gems; and with stalls and canopies of carbuncle on those chancel-screens. Then, there are three precious stones making soft sounds and sweet music between every two principal assemblies, and their upper parts are blazing torches. Seven thousand angels in the shape of great candles give light to and illuminate the City round about, and seven other thousand in its centre blazing through the long ages throughout the royal City. All the men of the world in one place, though they are many, the fragrance of the tip of one of those candles would suffice them for food . . .

After the guardian angel had shown Adhamhnán's spirit these visions of the Kingdom of Heaven and of the first adventures of every soul after leaving its body, it took him with it after that to the depths of Hell with its many torments and tortures and its sufferings. The first land they came to was a black scorched land, empty and burned up, without any torments there at all. On the other side of it was a glen full of fire. There was a huge blaze in it, so that it came out over its sides on either hand. Black were its depths, red its midst and its upper parts. Eight monsters were in it, their eyes like fiery lumps of molten metal.

A huge bridge is across the glen; it reaches from one side to the other, high in the middle but low at each end. Three parties are attempting to go over it, and not all get across. One party, for them the bridge is wide from beginning to end, so that they cross it unhurt, without fear and without terror, over the fiery glen. Another party, however, as they approach it, it is narrow for them at first but wide at last, so that they cross in this way over that same glen after great peril. But the last party, for them the bridge is wide at first but narrow and strait at last, so that they fall from its midst into that same perilous glen, into the gullets of those eight fiery monsters which make their dwelling in the glen.

The people for whom that road was easy, they are the virgins, the zealous penitents, the bloody martyrs desirous of God. The group for which the road was narrow at first and wide at last after that are the people who are forced to do the will of God, and convert their constraint afterwards into the willing service of God. But those for whom the bridge was wide at first and was narrow at last are the sinners who listen to the teaching of the word of God, and do not perform it when they have heard it.

Again, there are great hosts in distress on the shore of everlasting torment on the other side of the murky land. Every other hour their torment ebbs, and the alternate hours it comes over them. Those who are in this state are those whose good and evil are equal; and on the Judgement Day it will be judged between them, and their good will cancel their evil on that day, and they will be taken after that to the place of life in the presence of God through all eternity.

Then there is another great host there beside that company, and their torment is very great. This is how they are, bound to fiery pillars with a sea of fire around them up to their chins, and fiery chains in the form of snakes round their waists. Their faces blaze with the torment. Those who are in this torment are sinners and murderers of kinsmen and those who destroy the church of God; and pitiless stewards of monasteries who, before the relics of the saints, and being in charge of the gifts and tithes of the church, embezzle those treasures instead of devoting them to the guests and the needy ones of the Lord.

Moreover there are great crowds standing there for ever in black puddles up to their belts, with short icy cloaks around them. They have neither pause nor stay through all eternity, but the belts burning them with both cold and heat. Hosts of demons around them, with fiery clubs in their hands, striking them on their heads, while they argue endlessly with them. The faces of all these wretches are towards the north, with a rough bitter wind on their very brows, along with every other ill. Red fiery showers rain on them every night and every day, and they cannot escape them, but must endure them through all eternity, wailing and lamenting.

Some of them have streams of fire in the holes of their faces; others, nails of fire through their tongues, and others through their heads from outside. Now those who are in this torment are thieves and perjurers and traitors and slanderers and robbers and reavers and unjust judges and litigious people, witches and satirists, renegade brigands and professors who preach heresy. There is another large company on islands in the midst of the fiery sea, with a silver wall around them of their clothes and their almsgivings.[1] These are the people who do acts of compassion without failing, and yet are in the frailty and wantonness of their

1. Which they gave away in charity during their life.

flesh up to the term of their death; and their almsgiving helps them in the midst of the fiery sea till Doomsday, and they are sent to the place of life after Doomsday.

Then there is another great band there, with red fiery cloaks about them to the ground. Their trembling and their cries are heard up to the firmament. An innumerable host of demons chokes them, and they hold stinking mangy dogs with their hands, which they egg on against them to eat and devour them. Red fiery collars are blazing unceasingly round their necks. They are carried up to the firmament every other while, and are cast down into the depths of Hell the alternate whiles. Infants and children are continually mangling and tearing them on all sides. Those who are in this torment are men ordained who have transgressed their orders, and apostates and imposters who deceive and pervert the people, and lay claim to prodigies and miracles which they cannot do for them. These are the infants who are mangling the men in orders, namely, those people who were entrusted to them to be improved, and they did not improve them and did not correct them for their faults.

There is moreover another huge throng there; back and forth they go without rest, across the fiery flags, struggling with the hosts of demons. Too many to be counted are the showers of arrows, blazing redly, from the demons upon them. They go running without stay or rest, till they reach black lakes and black rivers to quench those arrows in them. Miserable and pitiful are the cries and the weeping that the sinners make in those waters, for it is an increase of torment that they get. Those who are in this torment are dishonest smiths and fullers and merchants, unjust judges of the Jews and of others in general, and impious kings, crooked stewards who are lustful, adulterous women and the pandars who ruin them by their wicked deeds. There is a wall of fire on the other side of the land of torments; seven times harsher and more terrible is it than the land of torments itself. But the souls do not dwell there until Doomsday, for the demons alone keep it until Doomsday.

Woe to him who is in those torments, living together with

the people of the Devil! Woe to him who does not shun those people! Woe to him whose master is the fierce unworshipful demon! Woe to him who listens to the wails and weeping of the souls as they beseech mercy and pity from the Lord, that Doomsday may come to them speedily, to discover whether they may get some alleviation of their sentence, for they get no respite ever except three hours every Sunday. Woe to him who will be wont to belong to that land for ever! For this is how it is – broken thorny mountains there, bare plains burning, and stinking lakes full of monsters. Rough sandy earth, very rugged and icy. Broad fiery slabs on its floor. Great seas with terrible storms, where the home and dwelling-place of the Devil is always. Four huge streams across its midst; a stream of fire, a stream of snow, a stream of poison, and a stream of dark black water. In these the fierce hosts of demons bathe themselves, after their carnival and their sport in tormenting the souls.

Now while the saintly companies of the Heavenly Host sing joyfully and gladly the harmonious chorus of the eight canonical hours, praising the Lord, the souls give forth pitiful and grievous howls as they are beaten without respite by the throngs of demons. These are the torments and the sufferings which the guardian angel showed to Adhamhnán's spirit after visiting the Kingdom of Heaven . . .

Irish; author unknown; eleventh century.

232. The Tree of Life

. . . King of the Tree of Life with its flowers, the space around which noble hosts were ranged, its crest and its showers on every side spread over the fields and plains of Heaven.

On it sits a glorious flock of birds and sings perfect songs of purest grace; without withering (with choice bounty rather) of fruit and of leaves.

Lovely is the flock of birds which keeps it, on every bright

and goodly bird a hundred feathers; and without sin, with
pure brilliance, they sing a hundred tunes for every feather ...

Irish; author unknown; 988.

233. How St Scoithín Got His Name

Once upon a time he met Barra of Cork, he walking on the
sea and Barra in a ship. 'How is it that you are walking on
the sea?' said Barra. 'It is not the sea at all, but a flowery
blossomy field,' said Scoithín, and he took up in his hand a
crimson flower and threw it from him to Barra in the ship.
And Scoithín said, 'How is it that a ship is floating on the
field?' At those words, Barra stretched his hand down into
the sea and took a salmon out of it, and threw it to Scoithín.
And it is from that flower [*scoth*] that he is called Scoithín.

Irish; author unknown; tenth–eleventh century.

234. St Mael Anfaidh and the Bird's Lament for St Mo Lua

This was the Mael Anfaidh who saw a certain little bird
wailing and sorrowing. 'O God,' said he, 'what has happened there? I will not eat food until it is explained to me.'
While he was there he saw an angel coming towards him.
'Well now, priest,' said the angel, 'let it not trouble you
any more. Mo Lua son of Ocha has died, and that is why
the living things bewail him, for he never killed a living
thing, great nor small; not more do men bewail him than
the other living things do, and among them the little bird
that you see.'

Irish; author unknown; ninth–tenth century.

235. St Columba's Nettle Broth

Once when he was going round the graveyard in Iona, he
saw an old woman cutting nettles for broth for herself.

'What is the cause of this, poor woman?' said Colum Cille. 'Dear Father,' said she, 'I have one cow, and it has not yet borne a calf; I am waiting for it, and this is what has served me for a long time.' Colum Cille made up his mind then that nettle broth should be what should serve him mostly from then on for ever; saying, 'Since they suffer this great hunger in expectation of the one uncertain cow, it would be right for us that the hunger which we suffer should be great, waiting for God; because what we are expecting, the everlasting Kingdom, is better, and is certain.' And he said to his servant, 'Give me nettle broth every night,' said he, 'without butter or milk with it.' 'It shall be done,' said the cook. He hollowed the stick for stirring the broth and made it into a tube, so that he used to pour the milk into that tube and stir it into the broth. Then the people of the church noticed that the priest looked well, and talked of it among themselves. This was told to Colum Cille, and then he said, 'May your successors grumble for ever! Now,' said he to the servant, 'what do you give me in the broth every day?' 'You yourself are witness,' said the menial, 'unless it comes out of the stick with which the broth is mixed, I know of nothing in it except broth alone.' Then the explanation was revealed to the priest, and he said, 'Prosperity and good deeds to your successor for ever!' And this has come true.

Irish; author unknown; eleventh century.

236. Mo Chua's Riches

. . . Mo Chua and Colum Cille were contemporaries. And when Mo Chua (that is, Mac Duach) was in a hermitage of the wilderness, he had no worldly wealth but a cock and a mouse and a fly. The work the cock used to do for him was to keep matins at midnight. Now the mouse, it would not allow him to sleep more than five hours in a day and a night; and when he wished to sleep longer, being tired from much

cross-vigil[1] and prostration, the mouse would begin nib-
bling his ear, and so awoke him. Then the fly, the work it
did was to walk along every line he read in his psalter, and
when he rested from singing his psalms the fly would stay
on the line he had left until he returned again to read his
psalms. It happened soon after this that these three treasures
died; and Mo Chua wrote a letter afterwards to Colum
Cille when he was in Iona in Scotland, and complained of
the death of this flock. Colum Cille wrote to him, and this
is what he said: 'Brother,' said he, 'you must not wonder at
the death of the flock that has gone from you, for mis-
fortune never comes but where there are riches.' . . .

Irish; Geoffrey Keating; c. 1634.

237. *Repentance before Death*

THE praise of God at the beginning and in the end, He
does not reject, He does not refuse him who attempts it –
the only Son of Mary, the lord of princes; He will come like
the sun, from the east to the north. Mary Mother of Christ,
glory of maidens, intercede in Thy great mercy with Thy
Son to cast out our sins. God be above us, God before us,
God who rules, the Lord of Heaven, may he give us a share
of mercy. O Lordly-hearted One, may there be peace
between us without rejection, and may I make amends for
all the sins I have committed. Before going to my tomb, to
my green grave, in the darkness without candle to my gravemound, to my recess, to my hiding-place, to my repose, after
horses and trolling the pale mead, and carousal, and con-
sort with women, I shall not sleep, I will take thought for
my end. We are in a world of grievous wantonness, like
leaves from the treetops it will pass away. Woe to the miser
who amasses great wealth, and unless he devotes it to God,
though he be suffered in the course of this world, there will
be peril at his end. The fool knows not in his heart how to

1. Praying with the arms extended in a cross.

tremble, he does not rise early, he does not pray, he does not keep vigil, he does not chant prayers, he does not crave mercy; pride and arrogance and pomp, bitterly will they be paid for in the end. He plumps his body but for toads and snakes and lions, and practises iniquity; but Death will come in through the door and ravenously it will gather him up and carry him off. Old age and infirmity of mind draw nigh, your hearing, your sight, your teeth are failing, the skin of your fingers becomes wrinkled, old age and grey hairs do this to you. May Michael intercede for us with the Lord of Heaven for a share of mercy.

May-time, fairest season, noisy are the birds, green the woods, the ploughs are in the furrow, the ox in the yoke, green is the sea, the lands grow many-coloured. When the cuckoos sing on the tops of the splendid trees my wretchedness grows greater; the smoke is painful, my distress is manifest since my kinsmen have passed away. On hill, in dale, in the islands of the sea, in every way one goes, there is no seclusion from the blessed Christ. My Friend, my Intercessor, it was my desire to attain to the Land far away to which Thou wentest. Seven and seven score and seven hundred saints have gone to the one Tribunal, and in the presence of the Blessed Christ they have not endured terror. The gift I ask, may it not be denied me, peace between me and God; may I find the road to the Gate of Glory, Christ, may I not be sad before Thy throne.

Welsh; author unknown; twelfth century.

238. Damnation

. . . As in the season of ice there are caught in the snares birds seeking their food, and fish in nets, and none so much as dreamed till now of dying, yet now they are prepared for supper over the charcoal fire; so is your life, from beginning to end, which you pass in the world, always among sins, and if you do not amend them before the end of your days after all your pleasures, you will stay in the snares . . .

Breton; Mestre Jehan an Archer Coz; 1519.

239. Christ's Bounties

. . . O Son of God, do a miracle for me, and change my heart; Thy having taken flesh to redeem me was more difficult than to transform my wickedness.

It is Thou who, to help me, didst go to be scourged by the Jews; Thou, dear child of Mary, art the refined molten metal of our forge.

It is Thou who makest the sun bright, together with the ice; it is Thou who createdst the rivers and the salmon all along the river.

That the nut-tree should be flowering, O Christ, it is a rare craft; through Thy skill too comes the kernel, Thou fair ear of our wheat.

Though the children of Eve ill deserve the bird-flocks and the salmon, it was the Immortal One on the cross who made both salmon and birds.

It is He who makes the flower of the sloes grow through the surface of the blackthorn, and the nut-flower on other trees; beside this, what miracle is greater?

Irish; Tadhg Óg Ó hUiginn, died 1448.

240. The Murder of Abel

ADAM:

. . . 'There are two sons born to me, and they are grown to be men; you all see them.

Cain is my eldest son and Abel is my youngest son, humble and gentle children.

(*He speaks to Cain*):
I will assign to you to bear service, and to you to control corn and cattle. Cain, your charge shall be over oats, barley, and wheat, to make the faithful tithe.

(*He turns to Abel*):
And Abel the sacrifice of the beasts and the oxen and all the sheep of the field,

and when there is need to pay tithe take them to Mount Tabor and there burn them, for fear God be angry with you if we do not make faithful sacrifice.'

CAIN:
'Adam, my dear father, I will do your command firmly, without fail.

It is needful, very needful, to work and to till the ground here, to get us sustenance.'

ABEL (*a lamb ready with fire and incense*):
'I will go to the mountain and make the tithe now, and burn all these very clean;

and all the tithe of every thing, I will send it all forth with fire, surely making a sacrifice of it.'

CAIN:
'I will not burn it, the corn nor the fruits indeed; be silent for me, Abel, you empty-head!

I shall gather prickles and thorns and dried cow-dung to burn, without compunction, and shall make a great cloud of smoke.'

ABEL:
'Cain, that is not well done; to the glory of God the Father let us make our faithful sacrifice.

God appoints Him to be worshipped with the best fruits at all times; I will do it, beyond marvelling.

Cain, my brother, look and consider – that is a sweet smoke.'

CAIN:

'Be quiet, hang you! *This* is better, surely, you pot-bellied fool!'

ABEL:

'It cannot be, since you make your sacrifice with dried cow-dung.'

CAIN:

'By God who made us, I could wish you to be hanged up on high!

Truly, for striving against me I shall strike you, stubborn villain, so that you roll on the back of your neck.

(*A jawbone ready*)

Take that, you filthy knave, on the jaw with the jawbone!'
(*Abel is struck with the jawbone and dies*)

ABEL:

'Woe, alas! you have killed me, Cain, my brother. For your deed in this world you shall surely suffer punishment, do not think otherwise.'

CAIN:

'See, a whoreson churl is dead. I will not be controlled; the world is now rid of him. I could wish he were hidden in some hole in the hedge.

The fellow would have burned our corn, indeed; I could not bear that.

God has no need ever to get our goods, I know for certain.
(*Casts Abel into a ditch*)

Though my father should be angry when he hears the news that he is killed, I am the heir; I shall not care one bit.

See where he is thrown into a ditch to rot; I do not repent at all though he is killed by my hand, as I am a sharp dealer.'

THE FATHER (*when the Father speaks to Cain let him look down*):
'Cain, tell me, where is Abel? Answer me quickly.'

302

CAIN:

'I do not know, Lord, truly; you know well I am not his keeper; perhaps a wolf, so help me, killed him a while since, the filthy villain!

He is sharp and astute – why could he not take care of himself? I won't be his servant.'

THE FATHER:

'See, the voice of the death of Abel your brother is always calling on you from the earth everywhere.

Be you accursed for ever, and all the land that is yours is accursed for your deed.

May it never bear good fruit nor goodness of apple at any time. I give you My curse; take to yourself the curse of My Son and My Spirit' . . .

Cornish; William Jordan; 1611.

241. St Meriasek Arrives in Cornwall

MERIASEK:

. . . 'Jesus be thanked, to a foreign country here have I come; I will go on shore – Lord Jesus, kind heart, guide me to a good place that I may worship my dear Christ and Mary the virgin flower. I have come to land and am weary with travelling. Mary, mother and maid, if you have house or mansion near here, guide me to it, for indeed I should greatly wish to make me an oratory beside Mary's house. Good man, joy be with you, what chapel is this?'

SERVANT:

'I will tell you straightway, Mary's chapel of Camborne that same house is called. Whence are you that you ask it? Tell me that for your part, my good friend.'

MERIASEK:

'From Brittany to this land have I come, in truth, across the sea, as God would instruct me; and I wish here, beside the chapel of the blessed Mary, to make me an oratory. Is there water here nearby? For truly no other drink ever crosses my lips.'

SERVANT:
'Water is very scarce here, indeed one must go a good way hence to fetch it; *I* would take beer or wine, sure, I would not drink water, it would do me no good.'

MERIASEK (*let him go over to the meadow*):
'North east of this chapel I will go to wander, truly, to seek out water for myself; Jesus, Lord,

(*He kneels*)
I pray Thee, Jesus, grant me water speedily, through Thy grace, as Thou didst once for Moses from the hard rock.'
(*Here the well springs up with water.*)

SERVANT:
'Good man, blessing be on you, there is water here for us so sweet, for our comfort; surely, you are beloved of God, it is proven here clearly before us in this place.' . . .

Cornish; author unknown; fifteenth century.

242. The Best and Worst Nail in the Ark

The shipwright who made the Ark left empty a place for a nail in it, because he was sure that he himself would not be taken into it. When Noah went into the Ark with his children, as the angel had told him, Noah shut the windows of the Ark and raised his hand to bless it. Now the Devil had come into the Ark along with him as he went into it, and when Noah blessed the Ark the Devil found no other way but the empty hole which the shipwright had left unclosed, and he went into it in the form of a snake; and because of the tightness of the hole he could not go out nor come back, and he was like this until the Flood ebbed; and that is the best and worst nail that was in the Ark.

Irish; author unknown; sixteenth century?

243. *A Prayer to the Virgin*

The Virgin was seen coming, the young Christ at Her breast, angels bowing in submission before Them, and the King of the Universe saying it was fitting.

The Virgin of ringlets most excellent, Jesus more surpassing white than snow, melodious Seraphs singing Their praise, and the King of the Universe saying it was fitting.

Mary Mother of miracles, help us, help us with Thy strength; bless the food, bless the board, bless the ear, the corn, and the victuals.

The Virgin most excellent of face, Jesus more surpassing white than snow, She like the moon rising over the hills, He like the sun on the peaks of the mountains.

Scottish Gaelic; traditional folk prayer.

244. *A Charm with Yarrow*

I will pick the smooth yarrow that my figure may be more elegant, that my lips may be warmer, that my voice may be more cheerful; may my voice be like a sunbeam, may my lips be like the juice of the strawberries.

May I be an island in the sea, may I be a hill on the land, may I be a star when the moon wanes, may I be a staff to the weak one: I shall wound every man, no man shall wound me.

Scottish Gaelic; traditional folk charm.

NOTES

The references are to the editions of each text used in making the transla-
tions; this does not necessarily mean that there are no other editions in
existence.

1. C. O'Rahilly, *Táin Bó Cúalnge* (Dublin, 1967), pp. 23–5.
Note that smiths held a high rank in early Irish society.
2. J. Strachan and J. G. O'Keeffe, *The Táin Bó Cúailgne* (Dublin,
1912), pp. 30–31.
3. J. Strachan and O. Bergin, *Stories from the Táin* (3rd ed.;
Dublin, 1944), pp. 29–33. The conversation at the end involves a
pun on the name Cú Chulainn, 'The Hound of Culann'; compare
no. 1.
4. J. Strachan and J. G. O'Keeffe, op. cit., pp. 52–3.
5. C. O'Rahilly, op. cit., pp. 100–101, 104–5.
6. A. G. Van Hamel, *Compert Con Culainn* (Dublin, 1933), pp.
84–92. 'The Ulster warriors are in the sickness of labour' refers to
the story of how a curse was laid upon the grown men of Ulster
that at certain times they should all become as weak and sick as
women in child-bed. Cú Chulainn was unaffected by this. The
enemies of Ulster naturally chose these occasions to attack the
province. The *tabus* referred to are the supernatural injunctions
and prohibitions which might be laid upon the warriors in the
early hero-tales; to break them was a sure presage of disaster and
death.
7. V. Hull, *Longes Mac nUislenn* (New York, 1949).
8. K. Meyer, *The Death-Tales of the Ulster Heroes* (Royal Irish
Academy Todd Lecture Series, XIV; Dublin, 1906), pp. 4–10.
The text is corrupt in places, and I have adopted one or two
readings from the Edinburgh MS. XL, as given by Meyer.
9. K. Meyer, op. cit., p. 28.
10. W. Stokes, *Zeitschrift für Celtische Philologie*, III, 2–3.
11. R. T. Meyer, *Merugud Uilix maic Leirtis* (Dublin, 1958), p. 8.
12. K. Meyer, *Four Old Irish Songs of Summer and Winter* (London,
1903), pp. 8 ff. and G. Murphy, *Early Irish Lyrics* (Oxford, 1956),
no. 52. There are several obscurities in this difficult poem, and
some words whose meaning is unknown; these are simply omitted

in the translation given here, but will be found discussed by the editors mentioned; and by myself in *Studies in Early Celtic Nature Poetry* (Cambridge, 1935), p. 42, where a more conservative translation is given, pp. 23–4, and in the reprint of that work (see the Preface above).

13. W. Stokes, *Revue Celtique*, XX, 258; K. Meyer, op. cit., p. 14; and D. Greene and F. O'Connor, *A Golden Treasury of Irish Verse* (London, 1967), no. 21.

14. K. Meyer, *Revue Celtique*, XI, pp. 130-31, and op. cit.,p. 16; and Greene and O'Connor, op. cit., no. 31.

15. K. Jackson, *Early Welsh Gnomic Poems* (Cardiff, 1961), p. 18.

16. K. Meyer, *Ériu*, VII, 2–4, and Greene and O'Connor, op. cit., no. 33. See the reprint of my *Studies in Early Celtic Nature Poetry*, pp. 45–6, and the Preface above.

17. K. Meyer, *Otia Merseiana*, II, 76–83; for some notes, and differences from Meyer's readings and interpretation, see my *Studies in Early Celtic Nature Poetry*, pp. 47–8 and its reprint; M. O'Brien in *Études Celtiques*, III, 367; and Greene and O'Connor, op. cit., no. 29; and the Preface above. The poem is attributed to Rumann mac Colmáin (eighth century), but so early a date is impossible linguistically.

18. K. Meyer, *King and Hermit* (London, 1901); G. Murphy, op. cit., no. 8; and my *Studies in Early Celtic Nature Poetry*, pp. 5–8, 36–8, and its reprint; and the Preface above. There are a number of obscurities in the poem which are left out in the translation given here.

19. W. Stokes, in W. Stokes and E. Windisch, *Irische Texte*, IV, pt. i (Leipzig, 1900), pp. 10–11; and T. F. O'Rahilly, *Measgra Dánta* (Cork, 1927), I, 59–60. One or two of the readings given by O'Rahilly have been adopted where they differ from Stokes's; but the metrically more perfect text offered by the MSS. used by O'Rahilly need not necessarily have been original – the poem may have been improved on. I have mostly preferred the older version. In a couple of places the translation given here differs therefore significantly from that in my *Studies in Early Celtic Nature Poetry*, pp. 15–16; see the reprint of it.

20. T. F. O'Rahilly, op. cit., II, p. 119. The second verse refers to the tale of the elopement of Diarmaid ('Ó Duinn'), a member of the Fianna, with Finn's bride Gráinne.

21. T. F. O'Rahilly, op. cit., II, pp. 122–3.

22. R. Thurneysen, *Old Irish Reader* (Dublin, 1949), p. 39; Murphy, op. cit., no. 43; and Greene and O'Connor, op. cit., no. 22.

In the MS. the poem is attributed to Suibhne the Wild Man; cf. nos. 23, 24, 152, 205, 206, 207.

23. J. G. O'Keeffe, *Buile Shuibhne* (London, 1913), § 40; Murphy, op. cit., no. 46.

24. W. Stokes, in O. J. Bergin, R. I. Best, K. Meyer, and J. G. O'Keeffe, *Anecdota from Irish Manuscripts*, II (Halle, 1908), pp. 23–4; Murphy, op. cit., no. 44. One of the poems attributed to Suibhne the Wild Man, cf. nos. 23, 152, 205, 206, 207. See my article in *Essays and Studies Presented to Eóin MacNeill* (ed. J. Ryan; Dublin, 1940), pp. 536 ff.

25. T. Parry, *Gwaith Dafydd ap Gwilym* (Cardiff, 1952), no. 69.

26. I. Williams and T. Roberts, *Cywyddau Dafydd ap Gwilym a'i Gyfoeswyr* (Cardiff, 1935), no. 43. The authenticity is doubted by Parry, op. cit., p. clxxxix.

27. ibid., no. 41. The authenticity is doubted by Parry, op. cit., p. clxxxi; it may be the work of Ieuan ap Rhys, 15th cent.

28. ibid., no. 39. The authenticity is doubted by Parry, op. cit., p. c.

29. ibid., no. 40. The authenticity is doubted by Parry, op. cit., p. ciii.

30. ibid., no. 19. The authenticity is doubted by Parry, op. cit., p. clxxxviii.

31. T. Williams, *Iolo Manuscripts* (Llandovery, 1848), p. 228. This is one of the forged poems composed by Edward Williams ('Iolo Morgannwg'), the Welsh Macpherson, and attributed by him to his invented twelfth-century poet 'Rhys Goch ap Rhiccert'.

32. I. Williams and T. Roberts, op. cit., no. 65. 'Though the gift . . . make grimaces'; I owe the interpretation of this passage to Prof. Parry (*enir = gen + hir*).

33. T. H. Parry-Williams, *Canu Rhydd Cynnar* (Cardiff, 1932), pp. 396–9; D. Lloyd-Jenkins, *Cerddi Rhydd Cynnar* (Llandysul, n.d.), pp. 169–70; and T. Parry, *The Oxford Book of Welsh Verse* (Oxford, 1962), no. 121. This poem, though written in the new 'free metres', is compacted with the old complicated alliterative system of *cynghanedd*; here and there in the translation some small effort has been made to render something of the effect in English.

34. A. Carmichael, *Carmina Gadelica*, III (Edinburgh, 1940), p. 310.

35. ibid., p. 284.

36. ibid., p. 300.

37. T. Gwynn Jones, *Ceiriog* (Wrexham, 1933), p. 116.

38. W. J. Gruffydd, *Y Flodeugerdd Gymraeg* (Cardiff, 1931), p. 13.

39. F. Shaw, *The Dream of Oengus* (Dublin, 1934), pp. 43 ff. Except for Ailill and Medhbh, the actors in this story are all of the fairy people. 'It is fated for you to make a match with her'; reading *ro tocad*, with Vendryes, *Études Celtiques*, I, 162.

40. I. Williams, *Bulletin of the Board of Celtic Studies*, V, 116–21. The date is uncertain, but the language of the prose parts appears to be early Modern Welsh. The verse parts (omitted here as of no literary merit) are no doubt considerably older; and the prose is very likely a more modern version of a lost ancient tale. The oldest MS. was written about 1550. The story of Tristan and Isolde is of course of early Celtic origin.

41. T. Parry, *Gwaith Dafydd ap Gwilym* (Cardiff, 1952), no. 74.

42. I. Williams and T. Roberts, op. cit., no. 4. The authenticity is doubted by Parry, op. cit., p. clxxii. The Jealous Husband hates all things associated for Dafydd and his mistress with love-making in the woods.

43. T. Parry, op. cit., no. 118. 'She is a Venus'; cf. A. Conran, *The Penguin Book of Welsh Verse* (London, 1967), p. 279.

44. T. F. O'Rahilly, *Dánta Grádha* (Cork, 1926), p. 4.

45. ibid., p. 17. The puns in the second verse between *cuach* 'cuckoo' and *cuach* 'lock of hair'; and in the last verse on *idh* 'halter, collar, ring, ringlet' and between *brágha* 'throat' and *brágha* 'captive', are difficult to render. In this and the following poems by unknown authors from *Dánta Grádha* which are dated here *fifteenth-sixteenth century?*, the query means that this is a likely date for any of them; but they may range from the fourteenth to the seventeenth century. No. 57 is exceptionally late, because this type of poetry lasted later in Scotland than in Ireland.

46. T. F. O'Rahilly, *Dánta Grádha* (Cork, 1926), pp. 24–5.

47. ibid., pp. 19–20.

48. ibid., pp. 60–61.

49. ibid., p. 32.

50. ibid., p. 104.

51. ibid., pp. 106–7.

52. ibid., pp. 37–8. There is a double pun in v. 3, l. 4, which it is impossible to render in English. O'Rahilly suggests (p. 148) that 'Uilliam Ruadh' is Liam Ruadh Mac Coitir, who died in 1738; but though the poem appears comparatively late, such a date seems rather improbable.

53. ibid., p. 112.

54. ibid., p. 18.

55. ibid., pp. 25–6.

56. W. J. Watson, *Scottish Verse from the Book of the Dean of Lismore* (Edinburgh, 1937), pp. 307–8.

57. T. F. O'Rahilly, op. cit., pp. 51–2.

58. Charlotte Brooke, *Reliques of Irish Poetry* (Dublin, 1789), p. 232.

59. Róis ní Ógáin, *Duanaire Gaedhilge*, I (Dublin, 1921), p. 27.

60. ibid., p. 33.

61. J. Strachan. *Zeitschrift für Celtische Philologie*, I, 55–7.

62. T. H. Parry-Williams, *Canu Rhydd Cynnar* (Cardiff, 1932), pp. 72–3.

63. W. J. Watson, *Bardachd Ghàidhlig* (3rd ed., Stirling, 1959), pp. 50–52.

64. T. H. Parry-Williams, op. cit., p. 85. In v. 1 the word *olffan* seems obscure, as *oliffant*, 'ivory', appears to give no sense. The context implies one of the instruments still used by rural washerwomen in France to beat the washing, a 'battledore', and the word is so taken here.

65. J. O'Daly, *The Poets and Poetry of Munster* (3rd ed., revised by W. M. Hennessey, Dublin, n.d.), pp. 272–6.

66. Róis ní Ógáin, op. cit., II (Dublin, n.d.), p. 1.

67. Collected and edited by F. M. Luzel, *Chants Populaires de la Basse Bretagne* (Lorient, 1868), I, 350–52. Sung by Janet ar Gall, Kerarborn, 1849.

68. M. Maclean, *The Literature of the Highlands* (2nd ed., London, 1925), pp. 235–6.

69. W. J. Gruffydd, *Y Flodeugerdd Gymraeg* (Cardiff, 1931), pp. 52–4.

70. R. Thurneysen, in W. Stokes and E. Windisch, *Irische Texte*, III, pt. i (Leipzig, 1891), p. 146.

71. K. Meyer, *Bruchstücke der Älteren Lyrik Irlands* (Abhandl. Preuss. Akad. Wiss., Phil.-Hist., 1919; Berlin), p. 66.

72. ibid., p. 66.

73. W. Stokes, in W. Stokes and E. Windisch, *Irische Texte*, IV, pt. i (Leipzig, 1900), pp. 3–4.

74. W. J. Gruffydd, *Blodeuglwm o Englynion* (Swansea, n.d.), p. 23.

75. ibid., p. 6.

76. K. Meyer, op. cit., p. 66.

77. W. J. Gruffydd, op. cit., p. 5.

78. ibid., p. 32.

79. ibid., p. 31.

80. W. J. Gruffydd, *Y Flodeugerdd Gymraeg* (Cardiff, 1931), p. 75.

81. K. Meyer, op. cit., p. 67.

82. ibid., p. 67.

83. W. Davies, *Eos Ceiriog* (Wrexham, 1823), p. 392.

84. T. Gwynn Jones, *Y Gelfyddyd Gwta* (Aberystwyth, 1929), p. 25.

85. K. Meyer, op. cit., p. 65.

86. W. J. Gruffydd, *Blodeuglwm o Englynion* (Swansea, n.d.), p. 36.

87. K. Meyer, op. cit., p. 67.

88. J. T. Jones, *Penillion Telyn* (Wrexham, n.d.), p. 21.

89. ibid., p. 23.

90. ibid., p. 22

91. ibid., p. 9.

92. ibid., p. 14.

93. ibid., p. 6.

94. T. Parry, *Baledi'r Ddeunawfed Ganrif* (Cardiff, 1935), p. 61.

95. J. T. Jones, op. cit., p. 7.

96. ibid., p. 8.

97. K. Meyer, *A Primer of Irish Metrics* (Dublin, 1909), p. 17.

98. J. T. Jones, op. cit., p. 24.

99. ibid., p. 11.

100. J. Pokorny, *A Historical Reader of Old Irish* (Halle, 1923), p. 20.

101. S. H. O'Grady, *Silva Gadelica* (London, 1892), I, 96.

102. W. J. Watson, *Scottish Verse from the Book of the Dean of Lismore* (Edinburgh, 1937), p. 250.

103. J. T. Jones, op. cit., p. 17.

104. ibid., p. 28.

105. ibid., p. 29.

106. ibid., p. 6.

107. W. J. Gruffydd, *Blodeuglwm o Englynion* (Swansea, n.d.), p. 50.

108. T. Parry, *Hanes Llenyddiaeth Gymraeg Hyd 1900* (Cardiff, 1944), p. 249.

109. K. Meyer, *A Primer of Irish Metrics* (Dublin, 1909), p. 9.

110. J. T. Jones, op. cit., p. 31.

111. W. J. Gruffydd, op. cit., p. 53.

112. ibid., p. 56.

113. J. T. Jones, op. cit., p. 30.

114. T. Parry, *Baledi'r Ddeunawfed Ganrif* (Cardiff, 1935), p. 61.

115. W. J. Gruffydd, op. cit., p. 60.

116. ibid, p. 63.

117. ibid., p. 57.

118. ibid., p. 61.

119. K. Meyer, *The Gaelic Journal*, IV, 115.

120. W. J. Gruffydd, op. cit., p. 47.

121. W. Stokes and J. Strachan, *Thesaurus Palaeohibernicus* (Cambridge, 1901–3), II, 296. 'Coming'; normally means 'going', but the other is possible, and the context demands it.

122. K. Meyer, *A Primer of Irish Metrics* (Dublin, 1909), p. 21.

123. K. Meyer, *Bruchstücke* (*see* no. 71), p. 51. Mael Mhuru died in 887.

124. W. J. Gruffydd, op. cit., p. 20.

125. T. F. O'Rahilly, *Búrdún Bheaga* (Dublin, 1925), p. 9.

126. W. J. Gruffydd, op. cit., p. 20. Ifor was Dafydd ap Gwilym's patron.

127. J. Pokorny, *Zeitschrift für Celtische Philologie*, XVII, 195–201. 'The woman' is one of the people of the Happy Otherworld, the Earthly Paradise ('The Plain of Delights'); the Immortals, the Ever-Living, to whom mortals were no better than the dead. 'Tethra' was probably originally a god of this land.

128. I. Williams, *Cyfranc Lludd a Llevelys* (Bangor, 1922). *Lunden;* the text has the Welsh *Lundein* here, but the Anglo-Saxon form is obviously meant; *Londres* is the Norman form (*Llwndrys* in the Welsh). The derivation of *London* from *Lludd* is of course erroneous, though it gained currency in England early; whence *Ludgate*, etc. *Dinas Emreis*, 'The Fort of Ambrosius'; *Dinas Ffaraon Dandde*, 'The Fort of Pharaoh the Fiery'; on this passage see Williams, op. cit., pp. 28–9; 'the three governors' refers to a tradition independent of the present tale.

129. A. G. Van Hamel, *Compert Con Culainn* (Dublin, 1933), pp. 39–41.

130. I. Williams *Pedeir Keinc y Mabinogi* (Cardiff, 1930), p. 83. Lleu is the reflex of the Celtic god Lugus, the same as the Irish Lugh in no. 198. Here in early Welsh mythological legend he appears as son of Arianrhod, who has sworn he shall never marry a human woman; hence the wife made from flowers. Math is another of these 'mythological' characters.

131. J. Rhys and J. G. Evans, *The Text of the Mabinogion* (Oxford, 1887), I, 240.

132. A. G. Van Hamel, *Immrama* (Dublin, 1941), *Immram Maíle Dúin*, §§ 4, 7, 8, 11, 15, 17, 21, 22, 24, 26, 27, 29, 30.

133. W. Stokes, *Revue Celtique*, XIII, 448–50. The point of counting the pigs is that this was the way to exorcize them; cf. Note to no. 143.

134. J. G. Evans, *The White Book Mabinogion* (Pwllheli, 1907), pp. 308–9.

135. A. G. Van Hamel, op. cit., pp. 104–6, 108.

136. W. Stokes, in W. Stokes and E. Windisch, *Irische Texte*, IV, pt. i (Leipzig, 1900), pp. 214–16.

137. W. Stokes, op. cit., pp. 136–7.

138. K. Meyer, *Anecdota from Irish Manuscripts*, III (see no. 24), pp. 8–9. In the thirteenth century Norse *Speculum Regale* the same tale is told, likewise as having happened at Clonmacnoise. Cf. *Ériu*, IV, 12 f.

139. ibid., p. 9. This is a learned popular tale in medieval and Renaissance sources such as Gervase of Tilbury, the *Speculum Laicorum*, and Johannes Pauli; see Stith Thompson, *Motif-Index of Folk-Literature* (Helsinki, 1932–34), no. X. 521.

140. ibid., p. 10. The MS. says the second woman was *nine* hundred and twelve feet long, but this is ridiculously disproportionate. What is evidently the source of the second paragraph occurs in the Annals (Annals of Ulster AD 891; cf. W. Stokes, *Lives of Saints from the Book of Lismore*, p. xlii); from which it appears that for nine *hundred* we should read nine *score*, with the Annals of Innisfallen. The last sentence is a quotation from the stock descriptions found in the traditional early tales.

141. W. Meid, *Táin Bó Fraích* (Dublin, 1967), p. 8.

142. ibid., p. 9 f.

143. O. J. Bergin and R. I. Best, *Ériu*, XII, 180–82; see also R. Thurneysen, *Zeitschrift für Celtische Philologie*, XXII, 20–21, and G. Murphy, *Early Irish Lyrics*, no. 41. 'The young do not die before the old': the people of the Earthly Paradise were normally immortal, but what Midhir means is 'Not only does *no* one die there, but still less would the young die before the old, as often happens in your miserable mortal world'. 'Screens us from being counted': probably a reference to the idea that supernatural beings could be exorcised by being counted. Cf. no. 133 above, and (for the fairies), *Proceedings of the Scottish Anthropological and Folklore Society*, IV, 133.

144. K. Meyer, *The Voyage of Bran* (London, 1895), I, 5–17; and A. G. Van Hamel, *Immrama* (Dublin, 1941), pp. 9–13. There is still no completely satisfactory text, and some obscurities remain. I have followed chiefly Van Hamel's edition, with one or two of Meyer's interpretations preferred; see also the note by Vernam Hull in *Language*, XVII, 152–5. Emhain, Findargad, Argadnél, Airgthech, Cíuin, Magh Mon, Emhnae, and Imchíuin are

names descriptive of the various islands of the Earthly Paradise.

145. S. H. O'Grady, *Silva Gadelica* (London, 1892), I, 346–7.

146. J. G. Evans, *The White Book Mabinogion* (Pwllheli, 1907), cols. 416–17.

147. K. Meyer, *Zeitschrift für Celtische Philologie*, VIII, 175.

148. J. G. Evans, op. cit., cols. 424–5.

149. E. J. Gwynn, *The Metrical Dindshenchas*, pt. iii (Dublin, 1913), p. 378.

150. S. H. O'Grady, op. cit., pp. 244–5.

151. J. Rhys and J. G. Evans, *The Text of the Mabinogion* (Oxford, 1887), pp. 145–6; and M. Richards, *Breudwyt Ronabwy* (Cardiff, 1948), pp. 2–3. The word *parth*, translated here 'alcove', seems to mean actually a compartment between the pillars holding up the roof of the hall, apparently with a floor level higher than that of the main floor (corresponding therefore to the early Irish *imdae*); hence the Welsh has '*on* the *parth*' where I have translated '*in* the alcove' for lack of any English word corresponding exactly to the Welsh (except in the place where *ar y parth arall ... ar y parth* is translated 'in the other alcove ... on the raised floor', combining both ideas in this way). 'Dais' or 'raised floor' misses the idea of the separate compartments, of which there were evidently at least two, presumably more. 'For a necessary purpose': this traditional discreet phrase is exactly what the Welsh says.

152. J. G. O'Keeffe, *Buile Shuibhne* (London, 1913), § 72.

153. E. Knott, *Togail Bruidne Da Derga* (Dublin, 1936), pp. 1–2.

154. J. G. Evans, *The White Book Mabinogion* (Pwllheli, 1907), cols. 475–6.

155. A. Jones, *The History of Gruffydd ap Cynan* (Manchester, 1910), pp. 138–40.

156. ibid., p. 154.

157. A. Macleod, *The Songs of Duncan Ban Macintyre* (Edinburgh, 1952), pp. 166–8.

158. A. Macdonald, *The Poems of Alexander Macdonald* (Inverness, 1924), pp. 20 ff.

159. A. Carmichael, *Carmina Gadelica*, III (Edinburgh, 1940), pp. 186–8.

160. W. Stokes, *Revue Celtique*, XIII, 456.

161. C. O'Rahilly, *Cath Finntrágha* (Dublin, 1962), ll. 1041–66.

162. W. Stokes, *Lives of Saints from the Book of Lismore* (Oxford, 1890), pp. 66–7.

163. ibid., pp. 108–9.

164. K. Jackson, *Cath Maighe Léna* (Dublin, 1938), pp. 26–9.

165. S. H. O'Grady, *Silva Gadelica* (London, 1892), I, 259–60.

166. J. G. Evans, *The White Book Mabinogion* (Pwllheli, 1907), cols. 476–9. 'Undutiful': see *Celtica*, III, 228 ff. In this old tale and special context the original legal sense of *anwar* is probable. 'Porters', reading *porthawr* with the Red Book of Hergest. The 'javelins' are called *llechwayw*, which means literally 'flagstone spear', and suggests spearheads of flint; but the context shows they had iron heads, and in spite of the fact that the word occurs three times, we should probably read *lluchwayw*, 'javelin, dart'. The 'bride-price' was normally paid by the father, and the 'maiden-fee' to the overlord; however Culhwch and his companions offer to pay both to the girl's father and kindred. 'Her four great-grand-mothers . . .'; the White Book text reads . . . *ymdanei. Hi ay ffedeir gorhenuam* . . ., i.e. '. . . for her. She and her four great-grand-mothers . . .,' but in spite of the (no doubt secondary) reading of the Red Book, the sense seems to demand . . . *ymdanei hi. Y ffedeir gorhenuam* . . ., which is what is translated here.

167. G. Henderson, *Fled Bricrend* (London, 1899), pp. 16–22, 30.

168. J. G. Evans, op. cit., cols. 456–7. *Ny bo teu dy benn*, translated here 'May you lose your head' (*teu* 'thine'), is sometimes taken as 'let not your mouth be silent' (*teu* 'silent'?); but the interpretation adopted here seems preferable. 'Din Sol', unidentified; the emend-ation *Din Sel* (in Cornwall) is without foundation; the north of Britain is meant, as the third point, in Ireland, clearly shows. 'The three lands of Britain', etc., probably England, Wales, and Scotland and Anglesey, Man, and Wight; see *Bulletin of the Board of Celtic Studies*, XVII, 268.

169. J. G. Evans, op. cit., cols. 462–71; and J. Rhys and J. G. Evans, *The Text of the Mabinogion* (Oxford, 1887), I, 108–12, 113–14.

170. W. Stokes, *Revue Celtique*, XIII, 446. Lughaidh, a legendary prince of Munster, is in exile in Scotland. The purpose of the king's ruse was to discover which of the strangers was their captain, which they were unwilling to tell.

171. K. Meyer, *Aislinge Meic Conglinne* (London, 1892), pp. 11–13.

172. W. Stokes, *Lives of Saints from the Book of Lismore* (Oxford, 1890), pp. 135–6.

173. A. W. Wade-Evans, *Welsh Medieval Law* (Oxford, 1909), pp. 2–3, 82, 90, 96–7. The Welsh Laws as a body undoubtedly go back to early times, but the first codification about which we

know anything was that ordered by Hywel the Good (d. 950). This has not survived, except in the form of later recensions.

174. T. Parry, *Gwaith Dafydd ap Gwilym* (Cardiff, 1952), no. 49.

175. ibid., no. 48.

176. ibid., no. 124. Parry's edition is a vast improvement on the 1789 text used in the first edition of this book.

177. ibid., no. 63. 'On its backward course' refers to a characteristic of the skylark's flight whereby, fluttering into the wind, it lets itself drift backwards.

178. ibid., no. 137.

179. H. Lewis, T. Roberts, and I. Williams, *Cywyddau Iolo Goch ac Eraill* (Bangor, 1925), pp. 246–8. On the theme see B. Rees, *Dulliau'r Canu Rhydd* (Cardiff, 1952), p. 53, n. 1.

180. W. J. Gruffyd, *Y Flodeugerdd Newydd* (Cardiff, 1909), pp. 103–5; D. J. Bowen, *Barddoniaeth yr Uchelwyr* (Cardiff, 1957), no. 23; and a considerably different text in T. Roberts, *Gwaith Tudur Penllyn* (Cardiff, 1958), no. 30. The poem is variously attributed in MSS. to Lewis Glyn Cothi (*fl. c.* 1455–85) and Tudur Penllyn (*fl. c.* 1465–85). 'With a neck ... plays', following a suggestion of Prof. Parry's; 'Its wide furnace' probably refers to the iron-smelting which was a local industry.

181. S. H. O'Grady, *Catalogue of Irish MSS. in the British Museum* (London, 1926), I, 468.

182. O. J. Bergin, *The Irish Review*, II (1912), pp. 471–2.

183. T. F. O'Rahilly, *Measgra Dánta* (Cork, 1927), I, 16–17.

184. R. Ó Foghludha, *Cúirt an Mheadhon Oidhche* (Dublin, 1912), pp. 44–5.

185. ibid., pp. 55–7.

186. N. W. Lloyd, *Y Cymmrodor*, VI, 94. The poem is not of Cornish origin, but is an adaptation of an English folk-song; see *Scottish Studies*, VII, 37 ff., specially 45 f.

187. P. Dinneen and T. O'Donoghue, *The Poems of Egan O'Rahilly* (London, 1911), pp. 262–4.

188. D. Corkery, *The Hidden Ireland* (Dublin, 1925), pp. 113–14.

189. J. Vendryes, *Revue Celtique*, L, pp. 146–9 (and see ibid., p. 412 f.) and T. Parry, *Oxford Book of Welsh Verse* (Oxford, 1962), no. 36. Llywelyn ap Gruffudd of Gwynedd (North Wales) was the last independent prince of the Welsh, and leader in the wars with England. After uniting practically the whole of Wales, and taking the title of Prince of Wales in 1258, he was killed with only a few companions (cf. the mention of eighteen in the poem) in 1282, and his head was sent to London. This was the end of Welsh inde-

A CELTIC MISCELLANY

pendence. Aberffraw in Anglesey was one of the chief palaces of the princes of North Wales; Emreis is a poetical term for Snowdonia, in which mountain stronghold Llywelyn was safe until he sallied out on his last expedition. Bod Faeaw is on the coast of Carnarvonshire; Cynlleith is a small border region in Wales west of Oswestry, Shrops.; Nancoel and Nancaw are unknown. The battle of Camlan, King Arthur's last fight, was traditionally a bloody and disastrous one. Halfway through the poem the poet foresees the signs of the coming of the end of the world, the Judgement Day, and the prison of Hell, all ushered in by the first portent, the death of Llywelyn.

190. Parry, op. cit., no. 21; J. Morris Jones and T. H. Parry-Williams, *Llawysgrif Hendregadredd* (Cardiff, 1933), pp. 13–14. The victory of Tal Moelfre was won by Owein, king of North Wales, over the fleet of Henry I at Moelfre on the E. coast of Anglesey in 1157.

191. opp. citt., no. 25 and pp. 332–3 respectively. This elegy on Hywel, a prince of North Wales, was composed by his foster-brother Peryf, one of the seven sons of Cedifor, on the occasion of his killing by the army of his stepmother Cristin and her sons Dafydd and Rhodri, at the battle of Pentraeth in S.E. Anglesey in 1170.

192. W. J. Watson, *Scottish Verse from the Book of the Dean of Lismore* (Edinburgh, 1937), pp. 46–58; see pp. 263, 267. Tomás, Maguire, became king of Fermanagh in 1430. Tomaltach, MacDermot, lord of Moylurg (N. Co. Roscommon), died in 1458; hence the poem was composed between 1430 and 1458. The point in verse 5 is that he never gave the poet fair largesse for his poems of eulogy, which were therefore wasted. Verse 7, Niall Frosach and Guaire, early historical kings famous for their generosity. In verse 16 'Suibhne' is a reference to Suibhne the Wild Man; cf. nos. 23, 24, 152, 205, 206, 207. 'Ioruath' was a traditional hero. Loch Cé (see Index) is in the N. of MacDermot's country.

193. E. C. Quiggin, in the *Miscellany Presented to Kuno Meyer* (ed. O. J. Bergin and C. Marstrander; Halle, 1912), pp. 172–4. Cathal Ó Conchobhair, king of Connaught, died in 1224. The constant bardic convention seen in this and the next two poems, based on a wide-spread popular belief, was that the fertility and prosperity of the land, and the continuance of good weather, was a direct consequence of good and just rule on the part of its king. Compare the note on no. 197.

194. L. McKenna, *Aithdioghluim Dána* (Dublin, 1939), I, 10–11;

NOTES

part of a eulogy on Tadhg Ó Conchobhair (d. 1374). 'The Cattle-Tribute', an ancient tribute exacted from Leinster by the Uí Néill of Northern Ireland.

195. E. Knott, *The Bardic Poems of Tadhg Dall Ó hUiginn* (London, 1922), I, 84–5. From a poem in praise of Brian Maguire of Fermanagh (d. 1583).

196. O. J. Bergin, *Studies*, XII, 273–6. The poem is really in honour of Diarmaid Mageoghehan (d. 1392), lord of Cenél Fiachach (in parts of Cos. Westmeath and Offaley); cf. verse 7.

197. A. Cameron, *Reliquiae Celticae*, II (Inverness, 1894), pp. 238–40. These verses are from an elegy on four chiefs of Clanranald (whose country was S. Uist, the Small Isles, and a small part of W. coast Inverness-shire), namely Ronald, Ronald, Iain, and Donald Macdonald, who all died in 1636. In this poem we have the converse of the situation in nos. 193–5; when the chief died, of necessity the whole land became infertile and the weather became wild, through sympathy.

198. W. J. Watson, op. cit., pp. 158–64. The poem is an incitement to battle composed for Archibald Earl of Argyll, Chancellor of Scotland, on his way to the battle of Flodden (1513), where he was killed. Verses 3–4 refer to the legend of the prehistoric conquest of Ireland by the mysterious race of the Fomorians under their chief Balar, and their expulsion by Lugh the divine hero. 'The Cattle-Tribute', see note on no. 194. In verses 14–15 the poet recites Archibald's genealogy.

199. O. J. Bergin, *The Irish Review*, III (1913), 82. Corc, Cian, Cobhthach, and Tál were legendary Kings and heroes of Munster; 'the race of Éibhear' means the dominant native aristocracy of Southern Ireland. The Fitzgeralds were a famous Norman family settled in various parts of S. Ireland. Now that the Gaelic lords had passed away, the new Ireland cared no more for the old bardic poetry which depended on them.

200. P. Dinneen and T. O'Donoghue, *The Poems of Egan O'Rahilly* (London, 1911), p. 136. 'The land of Éibhear', cf. note on no. 199.

201. J. L. Campbell, *Highland Songs of the Forty-Five* (Edinburgh, 1933), pp. 124–6.

202. I. Williams, *Canu Aneirin* (Cardiff, 1938), pp. 2–3, 4, 10, 14–15, 27, 28, 40. See K. Jackson, *The Gododdin, the Oldest Scottish Poem* (Edinburgh, 1969). Gododdin was a kingdom comprising E. Scotland S. of the Forth, and part of NE. England; and the name is the title of the heroic elegy, attributed to Aneirin, N.

British poet of the later sixth century, from which these extracts come. Mynyddawg was evidently the king of Gododdin c. 600. Nothing is known of the other heroes named here except Cynon, son of an Edinburgh man, living in Aeron (probably Ayrshire), and Gwlyged, apparently Mynyddawg's steward. At this time Deira was Yorkshire E. of the Pennines and Bernicia was the coastal lands northwards thence to Berwickshire. Catraeth is probably Catterick in N. Yorks. The enemy were the Angles of these lands.

203. I. Williams, *Canu Llywarch Hen* (Cardiff, 1935), pp. 33 ff. The poem is put in the mouth of Heledd, sister of Cynddylan of Powys, a seventh-century prince of the Welsh border whose lands in what is now England were conquered by the Mercians; but Williams has shown that it was probably composed in the ninth century.

204. A. G. Van Hamel, *Compert Con Culainn* (Dublin, 1933), pp. 123–4.

205. J. G. O'Keeffe, *Buile Shuibhne* (London, 1913), § 45.

206. ibid., § 61.

207. ibid., § 83.

208. W. Stokes, in W. Stokes and E. Windisch, *Irische Texte*, II, pt. ii (Leipzig, 1887), pp. 127–9. For the story cf. no. 7. Of the place-names, only Glen Etive, Glen Massan, and Glen Daruel seem identified with certainty, perhaps also Dún Suibhne; see Index.

209. E. J. Gwynn, *The Metrical Dindshenchas*, III (Dublin, 1913), p. 96.

210. I. Williams, *Canu Llywarch Hen* (see no. 203), pp. 8–11. Tradition says that Llywarch the Aged lived in the sixth century, but Williams has shown that this poem belongs to the ninth. Llawr and Gwen were two of his twenty-four sons. 'The cuckoos are brown'; the adult female is a slightly reddish brown.

211. T. Parry, *Gwaith Dafydd ap Gwilym* (Cardiff, 1952), no. 18. The poet Gruffydd, a contemporary of Dafydd's, belonged to SE. Powys.

212. P. Dinneen and T. O'Donoghue, op. cit., p. 22.

213. Róis ní Ógáin, *Duanaire Gaedhilge*, I (Dublin, 1921), pp. 49–50.

214. W. J. Gruffydd, *Y Flodeugerdd Gymraeg* (Cardiff, 1931), p. 74.

215. J. T. Jones, *Penillion Telyn* (Wrexham, n.d.), pp. 25–6.

216. J. Mackenzie and G. Calder, *Gaelic Songs by William Ross* (Edinburgh, 1937), pp. 148–50.

217. T. F. O'Rahilly, *Measgra Dánta* (Cork, 1927), II, 158–61; and Róis ní Ógáin, *Duanaire Gaedhilge*, II (Dublin, n.d.), 2–4.

218. From a version collected by the translator in West Kerry in 1934, from the singing of Peig Sayers the folk-tale teller; see *Éigse*, VI, 112–15. For other versions see ibid., pp. 19–21 and VIII, 32–42, and references there. The characters are unidentified. 'Clontealán' is unknown, and the form is probably corrupt; other versions give other unidentified names.

219. R. Jones, *The Poetical Works of the Rev. Goronwy Owen* (London, 1876), I, 147–50.

220. M. Maclean, *The Literature of the Highlands* (2nd ed., London 1925), pp. 186–7.

221. This fine 'keen' exists only in relatively modern versions recorded from oral tradition, versions which naturally sometimes vary considerably in the wording and the order of the verses; it is not always clear who is speaking, or whether certain lines found in some versions but not in others should be included at all. Most recently edited by S. Ó Tuama, *Caoineadh Airt Uí Laoghaire* (Dublin, 1961); see also the review in *Éigse*, X, 245 ff. Earlier editions, O. J. Bergin in the *Gaelic Journal*, VII (1896), 18–23; and S. Ó Cuív, *Cuine Airt Í Laere* (Dublin, 1908). I have followed Ó Tuama, but with a few reservations about wording, verse-order, and attribution to speakers, where older editions seem preferable.

Art O'Leary of Raleigh near Macroom, some 12 miles W. of Cork, was married to Eileen *Dubh* ('Black-haired') O'Connell, aunt of Daniel O'Connell 'the Liberator', and daughter of Donall *Mór* ('Big') O'Connell of Derrynane, at the SW. tip of Co. Kerry (cf. verses 22 and 23). He had a quarrel with Abraham Morris, High-Sheriff of Cork, and this was finally brought to a head by a dispute over O'Leary's brown mare. He challenged Morris to a duel, and Morris had him outlawed. O'Leary went on the run (cf. verse 20), threatening to kill Morris. A reward was offered, and information of his whereabouts was laid by 'John son of Ooney' (verse 33), apparently an O'Riordan; and on 24 May 1773, Morris's guard of two soldiers shot him dead on the Inch ('meadow') of Carriganimmy, about 6 miles NW. of Macroom (verse 22). His wife, to whom the 'keen' is attributed, fetched the body home and sent for his sister from Cork, and the wake was held at Raleigh on the night of 5 May. The sister excused herself for not bringing more of her family with her on the grounds that some were dead (verses 25–6); and seems to have accused Eileen of going to her room to sleep during the wake, which she denied (verses 11–12). The body was buried just outside the family burial-ground of Kilnamartery near Raleigh, since Morris would not allow it to be laid in consecrated ground, but some months later it was moved to the monastery at Kilcrea, halfway between Macroom and Cork. His wife swore vengeance (cf. verse 30), and at the inquest a verdict was brought against Morris, but he was acquitted at his trial. He left the region and died shortly afterwards. For a fuller account see Ó Tuama, op. cit., and Mrs Bromwich in *Éigse*, V, 236 ff.

The first nine verses appear to be spoken by Eileen over the body at Carriganimmy, and most of the rest by herself and her husband's sister at the wake that night at Raleigh; except that the last verse of all, and evidently some of the others preceding it (according to Ó Tuama, verses 31 to the end) belong to the burial at Kilcrea that autumn.

Verse 6: The kinship to the Earl of Antrim (NE. corner of Ireland) and the Barrys, a Norman family settled at Youghal (see *Éigse*, X, 249) in the SE. corner of Co. Cork, is unclear.

Verse 8: For the practice of drinking the blood of a dead relative cf. no. 204; also *Éigse* V, 249, and Ó Tuama, op. cit., p. 22 n.

Verse 10: Gearagh, the Ballingeary district in the upper valley of the Lee, W. of Macroom.

Verse 11: Toon Bridge, about 4 miles W. of Macroom.

Verse 15: Inchigeelagh, about 9 miles W. of Macroom.

Verse 22: Conall, Eileen's brother, drowned in 1765; 'the woman of twenty-six years', her sister Gobnet, who married a Major O'Sullivan in the Austrian army, and became a friend of the Empress Maria Theresa (who was her child's godmother, hence 'kinship').

Verse 23: Greenan, between Macroom and Inchigeelagh; Iveleary, the O'Leary country in the W. of Co. Cork; Ballingeary, about 5 miles W. of Inchigeelagh; Gouganebarra, on the Kerry border about 4 miles W. of Ballingeary; Grenagh, near Blarney, about 5 miles NW. of Cork.

Verse 24: the sister is expressing the wealth of the O'Learys when Art was an infant.

Verse 31: Carhen, home of Eileen's brother, about 12 miles N. of her family home of Derrynane; opposite Valencia Is.

Verse 32: This varies considerably in the versions, but Eileen is apparently making amends for having reproached the women at the mill at Carriganimmy for not having wept for Art's murder.

Verse 34: James Baldwin, husband of Eileen's sister Mary, is said to have handed over the mare which was the subject of the quarrel, and to have refused to join Eileen in her attempts to bring the murderers to justice. The verse begins as if Art were still alive.

Verse 36: This refers to the burial at Kilcrea monastery; 'the school' is the assembly of learned clergy buried there. Art is thought of as having a farewell drink before going to join them. The drinks offered to the poor probably represent the custom of giving largesse to the poor at funerals.

222. T. F. O'Rahilly, op. cit., II, 120–21. 'The cry by the grave-yard' refers to the waves breaking on the rocks by the island cemetery. The characteristic Celtic monastic foundation on an island always had its cemetery, often not far from the sea.

223. K. Meyer, Ériu, I, 39–40; Murphy, Early Irish Lyrics, no. 12; and Greene and O'Connor, Golden Treasury, no. 35. For some significant differences here from Meyer's translation see the notes on this poem in my Studies in Early Celtic Nature Poetry (Cambridge, 1935), pp. 35–6, and the reprint of this (see Preface above).

224. K. Meyer, Ériu, II, 55–6, and Murphy, op. cit., no. 9.

225. W. Stokes, Lives of Saints from the Book of Lismore (Oxford, 1890), pp. xiii–xv.

226. W. Stokes, On the Calendar of Oengus (Dublin, 1880), p. xxxv; and The Martyrology of Oengus the Culdee (London, 1905), p. 44. Also Murphy, op. cit., no. 11 and Greene and O'Connor, op. cit., no. 23.

227. D. Greene, Celtica, II, 150–53. A religious poet imagines himself as a tributary tenant of God, rendering the Irish legal dues of lodging and entertainment to his overlord and his retinue. Verse 2, 'seats', reading sosta.

228. W. Stokes, Lives of Saints (see no. 225), p. 70.

229. From the Book of Leinster, ed. R. I. Best and M. A. O'Brien (Dublin, 1967), V, 1222. Another copy in the Book of Lismore is edited by W. Stokes, Lives of Saints, pp. xi–xii; partly followed here. On the tale, of international origin, see R. Christiansen, Irish and Scandinavian Folktales (Copenhagen, 1959), p. 191.

230. W. Stokes, op. cit., pp. xxvii–xxviii. There is an earlier but somewhat different version in the Book of Leinster, p. 358, and the Stowe MS. B. IV. 2, f. 144a (see Zeitschrift für Celtische Philologie, VII, 305).

231. E. Windisch, Irische Texte (Leipzig, 1880), pp. 171–9, 184–92.

232. W. Stokes, Saltair na Rann (Oxford, 1883), pp. 9–10.

233. W. Stokes, *On the Calendar of Oengus* (Dublin, 1880), p. xxxii.

234. W. Stokes, *The Martyrology of Oengus the Culdee* (London, 1905), p. 56.

235. W. Stokes, *On the Calendar of Oengus*, pp. c–ci.

236. O. J. Bergin, *Stories from Keating's History of Ireland* (Dublin, 1930), p. 35.

237. H. Lewis, *Hen Gerddi Crefyddol* (Cardiff, 1931), pp. 3–5. The second half is possibly a separate poem.

238. E. Ernault, *Le Mirouer de la Mort* (Paris, 1914), p. 62.

239. L. McKenna, *Dán Dé* (Dublin, 1922), pp. 12–13.

240. W. Stokes, *Gwreans an Bys* (London, 1863), pp. 84–93. From a miracle play.

241. H. Lewis, *Llawlyfr Cernyweg Canol* (1st ed., Wrexham, 1923), pp. 76–7. From the miracle play *Beunans Meriasek*.

242. O. J. Bergin, *Ériu*, V, 49. For the theme, see F. L. Utley in *Internationaler Kongress der Volkserzählungsforscher in Kiel und Kopenhagen, 19.8–29.8.1959* (Berlin, 1961), pp. 446 ff.

243. A. Carmichael, *Carmina Gadelica*, III (Edinburgh, 1940), p. 114.

244. ibid., II (Edinburgh, 1900), p. 94.

PRONOUNCING INDEX OF NAMES

The pronunciation of Welsh, Cornish, and Breton names can be rendered fairly closely with the help of a few easy phonetic symbols in addition to some of the English letters; but that of Irish, Scottish Gaelic and Manx is so complicated that a large number of such symbols would be needed to give an accurate representation, including the elaborate system of glides, which are ignored here. Consequently the pronunciations given below for names in this the Gaelic group of languages are only very approximate (and those for Welsh rather so); however, they should serve to give the reader a rough idea of how to say the names, which is their purpose.

So far as this is at all possible, the pronunciations are intended to be those of the period,[1] stratum of language, or dialect to which each document belongs (hence more than one are sometimes given for one name); for instance a name in an Old Irish source will be rendered roughly as it is assumed to have been said in Old Irish, and names in Bardic poetry will be more archaic than in contemporary prose. Those who know only the modern languages should bear this in mind when confronted with a pronunciation which seems strange to them. On the other hand, in spelling Old and Middle Irish names I have not followed the orthography of the originals, as this is sometimes so misleading as to puzzle the reader unnecessarily; but have normalized them, always indicating the 'aspirated' consonants with *h*, spelling internal *b d g* as such instead of with *p t c*, always marking long vowels, and so on. So a name like Old Irish *Etain* is spelled here *Édaín*. The result may look odd to those who know the language, but should help that majority of readers who do not. Some degree of normalization is also used with Middle Welsh.

The following points about the phonetic spellings should be noted. They are always printed in square brackets. Every letter has one sound only; every vowel is sounded. The vowels have their regular standard European, 'Italian' or 'Latin' values, not the English. Long vowels are shown with a colon after them, and the

1. Except with no. 202, the original of which is so archaic that it would be impossible; in this case the pronunciation of the period of the manuscript is used.

'half-long' vowels of Welsh, Cornish, and Breton with a full-stop after them. Two vowels standing together always form a diphthong; so [ai] = *i* in 'high'; if not thus run together in a diphthong, but pronounced as two separate vowels, they are divided by a hyphen. In words of more than one syllable, the stress accent is shown by ['] before the stressed syllable, which in the Gaelic group is normally the first in a word and in the British group the last but one. Apart from the five ordinary vowels, the following additional vowel-symbols occur:—[ü] = German *ü* or French *u*; [ö] = German *ö* or French *eu*; [ə] = the *e* in 'hammer' or German *e* in *Dame*.

For the consonants it is to be noted that the Gaelic group divides almost all consonants into 'slender' and 'broad'. 'Slender' consonants sound somewhat as if a weak English *y* immediately followed them; so 'slender' *l* is like Italian *gl*, or the *lli* in 'million', 'slender' *n* is like Italian or French *gn* or the *ni* in 'onion'. 'Slender' consonants are printed here in italics in the phonetics. 'Broad' consonants are not specially distinguished here in the phonetic renderings, as their peculiar quality may be ignored for present purposes, for the sake of simplicity; but it should be noted that they have a characteristic 'hollow' sound, appearing to resonate at the back of the mouth (so 'broad' [l] may be compared with the Scottish *ll* in 'Wullie'), and that consonants before *a*, *o*, or *u* in the Gaelic spelling are normally 'broad'. In the Gaelic languages *l*, *r*, *n* (and earlier also *m*) may have strong and weak values; in the former case, sounded longer and stronger, they are printed here double. [g] is always 'hard'.

The following special consonant-symbols are used: [ṽ] = a nasal *v*, with breath escaping through the nose; [w̃] = a similar *w*. [θ] = the *th* in 'bath'; [ð] = the *th* in 'bathe'. [x] = the *ch* in Scottish 'loch', German *doch*; and the 'slender' variety, [*x*], = the *ch* in German *ich* or the *h* in English 'hue'. [ʒ] = the same sound voiced, i.e. like the 'soft' *g* in dialect German *tage*. [j] = *y* in 'yes'. [*s*] = English *sh*. [λ] = the famous Welsh *ll*, the nearest sound in English to this being the *tl* in 'little' (if this *tl* is pronounced with a violent expulsion of breath it makes a fair approximation to the Welsh sound). [ṗ] = the Welsh *rh*, which is a 'voiceless' or 'breathed' *r*, standing in the same relation to English *r* as English *wh* does (or used to) to English *w*. [ŋ] = the *ng* in 'singer', not that in 'finger'. [dž] = the English *j*.

Names in their Celtic spellings are given in the head-words in small capitals; common-nouns or adjectives in italics; and names in Anglicized spellings in lower-case letters. Names are identified here (or in the Notes or footnotes) unless they are unknown or unless the context makes obvious all that it is necessary to know. Anglicized or English forms are used in the translations and index in two types of instance: where a name is so well-known that it would be pedantic to do otherwise, as Munster, Cork, the Shannon, the Boyne, Cardigan, Anglesey, etc.; and in late Irish texts belonging to the period when such Anglicization had become normal practice, as in no. 221. In these cases no pronunciations are given in the index, as they are pronounced like English (except that *gh* generally = [x], sometimes silent). The references are to the numbered selections, not pages.

ARGOED ['argoid], 203, 210; unidentified region in Powys.

ARIANRHOD [ar'janɟod], 130; see Notes.

Arran, 19; the Scottish island, Firth of Clyde.

ART [art], 160; legendary early king of Ireland, brother of the Conle of no. 27.

Art O' Leary, 221; see Notes.

Arthur, (King), 40, 168, 169.

Assaroe, 7; on the r. Erne near Ballyshannon, Donegal Bay, NW. Ireland.

ATHAIRNE ['aθirrnni], 16; legendary early Ulster poet.

awdl [audl], 179; long poem consisting of several shorter ones with the same rhyme throughout.

BADHBH [baʒv], or probably already [baːw] in Ulster dialect; 6.

BALAR ['palər], 198; see Notes.

Baldwin, 221; see Notes.

bán [paːn], 157; [baːn], 182; 'white(-haired)', 'fair (-haired)'.

ban-lennán ['baɴllennaːn], 167 footnote; 'female sweetheart'; see LENNABHAIR.

BARRA ['barrə], 233; St Findbarr, 6th cent. Irish saint, patron of Cork.

Barrys, 221; see Notes.

BASSA ['basa], 203; perhaps Baschurch, Shropshire.

Beare, 164; island in SW. Kerry.

BEDWYR ['bedwir], 166; the Sir Bedivere of Arthurian romance.

BEGÁN ['begaːn], 230.

BELI ['be.li], 128; legendary ancient British king.

BENN BÓ [benn 'boː], 14; hills in NW. Co. Leitrim, SE. of Sligo.

Bernicia, 202; see Notes.

BERWYN ['berwin], 83; mountain range in NE. Merioneth and SW. Denbighshire.

BLODEUWEDD [blo'dəüweð], 130.

BOADHAGH ['boaðaʒ], 127; mythical king of the Happy Otherworld.

BOANN ['bo-ann], 39, 142; nymph of the river Boyne, wife of the Daghdhae, mother of Oenghus, and aunt of Froech.

BOD FAEAW [bo.d 'vaiau], 189; see Notes.

BODHBH [boðv], 39.

Boyle, 194; river in the N. of Co. Roscommon.

BRAN [bran], 144; a legendary king of Ulster.

Bregia, 10; region between Dublin and the Boyne.

BRÉNAINN ['breːninn], 132, 163, 225; St Brendan, 6th cent. Irish saint.

BRESAL ['bresəl], 230.

Brian, 188; Brian Boru, King of Ireland 1002–1014.

CEITHERN ['keθərrnn], 5; one of the early Ulster heroes.

CELL ELGRAIGHE [kell 'elgriji], 230.

CELLI WIG ['keλi 'wiːg], 169; identification uncertain.

CELTCHAR ['keltxar], 9; ['keltxər], 6; one of the early Ulster heroes.

CELYDDON [ke'lə.ðon], 40; forest in Scotland, apparently thought of as in the Southern Uplands.

CENN BERRAIDE [kann 'barridi], 204; one of the early Ulster heroes.

CENN ESCRACH [kenn 'eskrax], 70; unidentified.

CERBHALL ['kervəll], 230.

CET [ket], 8; one of the early Connaught heroes.

CIAN [kiən], 199; see Notes.

CILYDD ['ki.lið], 166.

CÍUIN [kiːun], 144; 'The Quiet (Land)'; see Notes.

Clanranald, 197; see Notes.

Clonfert, 225; near the Shannon in Co. Galway, SE. of Ballinasloe.

Clontealan, 218; unidentified.

CLUST [klüst], 169; 'Ear'.

CLUSTFEINAD [klüst'vəinjad], 169; 'Listener'.

CNOC FÍRINNE [knuk 'fiːriɲi], 212; the hill of Knockfierna.

CNOC Í CHOSGAIR ['knok iː 'xoskir], 196; Knockycosker, in S. Co. Westmeath.

COBHTHACH (1) ['kovθax], 10; legendary early king of Bregia. (2) ['kofəx], 6; a harpist of the early Ulster heroes. (3) id., 199; see Notes.

CODHAL ['koʒəl], 194; in N. Munster.

COLMÁN ['kolmaːn], 192.

COLUM CILLE ['koləm 'killi], 222, 230, 235, 236; = St Columba, Irish saint and founder of monasteries, including that of Iona in Scotland; missionary to the Picts; d. 597.

CONALL ['konall], 8, 167; ['konəll], 6; one of the early Ulster heroes.

Conall O' Connell, 221; see Notes.

CONCHOBHAR ['konxovor], 7, 8, 9, 39, 167; ['konxəvər], 1; ['konxuwər] or ['konxuːr], 6; king of Ulster in the early heroic period.

Conello, 212; district in NW. Co. Limerick.

CONLE ['konnlle], 127.

CONN [konn], 127, 196, 197; legendary ancient king of Tara and ancestor of various lines of kings and chiefs in Ireland and Scotland.

Connaught, 8, 39, 152, 192; the western province of Ireland.

CORANN ['korann], 127.

CORANNIEID [ko'ranjaid], 128.

CORC [kork], 199; see Notes.

DIARMAID ['diərmid]; (1),
196, Diarmaid Mageoghehan
(see Note). (2), 230, King
of Tara 544–565; cf.
Note to no. 20.

DINAS BRAN ['di.nas 'braɪn],
124; castle near Llangollen
in SE. Denbighshire.

DINAS EMREIS ['di.nas
'emrais], 128; about 1 mile
E. of Beddgelert, S.
Carnarvonshire.

DINAS FFARAON DANDDE
['di.nas fa'ra.-on 'danðe],
128.

DIN SOL [diːn 'soɪl], 168;
unidentified place in the far
north, probably in Scotland,
see Notes.

DÍSERT LÓCHAID ['diːsert
'lloːxid], 2; unidentified.

DÍURÁN ['diːuraɪn], 132; one
of Mael Dúin's men.

Donall Mór O' Connell, 221;
'Big Donall O' Conell'; see
Notes (and mór below).

DONNÁN ['donnaɪn], 228.

DONNCHADH ['donnxəʒ],
182.

DOURDUFF [dur'dü.], 67;
in the estuary of the
Morlaix river, Finistère, N.
coast of Brittany.

DRAIGHEN ['drajən], 208;
unidentified.

DREM [drem], 169; 'Look'.

DREMIDYDD [dre'mi.dið],
169; 'Looker'.

DRUIM NDEN [drumm 'nnen],
209; apparently in Meath.

DRUIM ROLACH [drumm
'rroləx], 18; unidentified.

dubh [duv], 221; 'black'.
Eileen Dubh O' Connell =
'Black-haired Eileen O'
Connell'.

DUBH SAINGHLENN [duv
'saŋlənn], 6.

DUBHTHACH ['duvθax], 7;
one of the ancient Ulster
heroes.

Duhallow, 218; region in NW.
Co. Cork.

DÚN DÁ BHENN ['duɪn daɪ
'venn], 5; near Coleraine,
coast of Co. Derry.

DÚN DELGAN [duɪn 'dalgən],
6, 204; Dundalk, Co.
Louth, Cú Chulainn's
home.

DÚN FIDHGHA [duɪn 'fiɪʒə],
208; unidentified.

DÚN FINN [duɪn 'finn], 208;
unidentified.

DÚN SUIBHNE [duɪn 'suvni],
208; perhaps Castle Sween,
at the entrance to Loch
Sween, S. Argyll.

DURADH FAITHLENN
['durəð 'faθlənn], 24;
unidentified.

DURTHACHT ['durθaxt], 7,
167.

DWYRYW ['duiriu], 203; the
headwaters of the Rhiw, a
tributary of the Severn in
Montgomeryshire.

ÉDAÍN ['eɪdaiɪn], 153; a
fairy woman.

EDAN ['edan], 97;
unidentified.

MacCailéin [mahk 'kale:n], 198; the 'style' of the Chief of Clan Campbell, here the Archibald to whom the poem is addressed.

MacDermot, 192; see Notes.

Mac Duach [mak 'duəx], 53; St Colmán of Kilmacduagh, Co. Galway, same person as the Mo Chua of no. 236.

Macha ['maxa], 7; = Emhain Mhacha, q.v.

Machaire Conaill ['maxiri 'konill], 6; plain in Co. Louth.

Machreth ['maxreθ], 77.

Mac Óag [mak 'o:-ag], 39; 'Young Boy'.

Macroom, 221; see Notes.

Mac Roth [mak 'rroθ], 5; the messenger of the Connaught army in the early hero tales.

Madawg ['ma.daug], 202.

Madu ['madu], 8.

Mael Anfaidh [mai:l 'anfið], 234; early saint, of Dairinis, near Youghal.

Mael Dúin [mai:l 'du:n], 132; legendary captain of a crew of seafarers.

Mael Mhuru [mai:l 'ṽuru], 123; poet, d. 887.

Maenmhagh ['mai:nṽaʒ], 18; plain round Loughrea, S. Co. Galway.

Magh Mon [maʒ 'mon], 144; 'The Plain of Sports', name of one of the islands of the Earthly Paradise.

Magh Mucraimhe [maʒ 'mukriṽe], 133, 160; plain between Athenry and Galway, Co. Galway.

Magh Muirtheimhne [maʒ 'murhiṽni], 6; plain in Co. Louth, Cú Chulainn's home district.

Maguire, 192; king of Fermanagh.

Mahon O' Heffernan, 199.

Maine ['mane], 7.

Maine Andoe ['mani 'anndəi:], 5; 'M. the Not-Silent', son of Ailill and Medhbh.

Maine Athramhail ['mane 'aθraṽil], 4; 'M. Like-his-Father', son of Ailill and Medhbh.

Màiri ['ma:ri], 220; unidentified.

Manannán ['manənna:n], 17; the pagan Irish god of the sea; in 17 the sea is called his wife.

Manchán ['manxa:n], 223; 7th cent. Irish saint, of Lemanaghan (see Liath), d. 665.

Manogan [ma'no.gan], 128.

March ap Meirchion ['marx ap 'məirxjon], 40; the 'King Mark' of Arthurian Romance, husband of Iseult.

Marivonn [ma'ri.von], 67; 'Marie-Yvonne'.

Marivonnik [mari'vonik], 67; 'little Marie-Yvonne'.

Mary O' Connell (Baldwin), 221; see Notes.

MATH [maːθ], 130; see Notes.

MATHONWY [ma'θo.nui], 130.

MEDHBH ['meðv], 2, 3, 4, 5, 7, 39, 133; Queen of Connaught in the early hero tales, wife of Ailill.

MEDR [medr], 169; 'Hit-the-Mark'.

MEDREDYDD [med're.dið], 169; 'Mark-Hitter'.

MEIS-GEGHRA [mes'geʒra], 8; a Connaught warrior killed by Conall.

MÉITHE ['meːθe], 3; not certainly identified, perhaps in Co. Louth.

MENAI, 80; MENEI, 190; ['me.nai]; the Menai Strait, between Anglesey and Carnarvonshire.

MENW [menw], 166; King Arthur's magician.

MERIASEK [mer'ja.džek], 241; St Meriadoc, an early Breton monk who settled in Cornwall.

Merioneth, 215; Welsh county.

Mestre Jehan an Archer Coz, 238; French, except coz [ko.s] 'old'; 'Master Jean the Old Gendarme'.

MIDHIR ['miðir], 143; a lord of the fairy people.

MO CHUA [mə 'xuə], 236; see MAC DUACH.

MO LUA [mo 'lua], 234; saint, of Clonfertmulloe, Co. Leix; 554–609.

MÓR [moːr], 54; unidentified.

mór [moːr], 10, 57, 194; [muər], 221; 'big'.

MORANN ['morann], 8; a legendary early wise judge.

MORFRAN ['morvran], 169.

MORFUDD ['morvüð], 25, 26; one of Dafydd ap Gwilym's sweethearts.

Morris, 221; see Notes.

Moy, 193; river flowing into Killala Bay between Cos. Mayo and Sligo.

Moylurg, 14, 192; region in N. Co. Roscommon.

MUCRAIMHE, 18; = MAGH MUCRAIMHE.

MUGH [muʒ], 194; ancestor of Tadhg Ó Conchobhair.

MUIRCHERTACH ['murxərtəx], 194; ancestor of Tadhg Ó Conchobhair.

MUIRINN ['mwirin], 185; imaginary midwife.

MYNYDDAWG [mə'nə.ðaug], 202; see Notes.

na hóro eile [na 'hoːro 'elə], 68; a meaningless refrain.

NANCAW ['nankau], 189; see Notes..

NANCOEL ['nankoil], 189; see Notes.

NÉD [nneːd], 198.

NIALL FROSACH [nniəll 'frosəx], 192; 8th cent. king of northern Ireland, see Notes.

NIALL MÓR MACMHUIRICH [nniall 'moːr mahk'vurix], 57.

NIAMH [nniəv], 6.

READ MORE IN PENGUIN

In every corner of the world, on every subject under the sun, Penguin represents quality and variety – the very best in publishing today.

For complete information about books available from Penguin – including Puffins, Penguin Classics and Arkana – and how to order them, write to us at the appropriate address below. Please note that for copyright reasons the selection of books varies from country to country.

In the United Kingdom: Please write to *Dept. EP, Penguin Books Ltd, Bath Road, Harmondsworth, West Drayton, Middlesex UB7 0DA*

In the United States: Please write to *Consumer Sales, Penguin USA, P.O. Box 999, Dept. 17109, Bergenfield, New Jersey 07621-0120*. VISA and MasterCard holders call 1-800-253-6476 to order Penguin titles

In Canada: Please write to *Penguin Books Canada Ltd, 10 Alcorn Avenue, Suite 300, Toronto, Ontario M4V 3B2*

In Australia: Please write to *Penguin Books Australia Ltd, P.O. Box 257, Ringwood, Victoria 3134*

In New Zealand: Please write to *Penguin Books (NZ) Ltd, Private Bag 102902, North Shore Mail Centre, Auckland 10*

In India: Please write to *Penguin Books India Pvt Ltd, 706 Eros Apartments, 56 Nehru Place, New Delhi 110 019*

In the Netherlands: Please write to *Penguin Books Netherlands bv, Postbus 3507, NL-1001 AH Amsterdam*

In Germany: Please write to *Penguin Books Deutschland GmbH, Metzlerstrasse 26, 60594 Frankfurt am Main*

In Spain: Please write to *Penguin Books S. A., Bravo Murillo 19, 1° B, 28015 Madrid*

In Italy: Please write to *Penguin Italia s.r.l., Via Felice Casati 20, I-20124 Milano*

In France: Please write to *Penguin France S. A., 17 rue Lejeune, F-31000 Toulouse*

In Japan: Please write to *Penguin Books Japan, Ishikiribashi Building, 2-5-4, Suido, Bunkyo-ku, Tokyo 112*

In South Africa: Please write to *Longman Penguin Southern Africa (Pty) Ltd, Private Bag X08, Bertsham 2013*

PENGUIN AUDIOBOOKS

A Quality of Writing That Speaks for Itself

Penguin Books has always led the field in quality publishing. Now you can listen at leisure to your favourite books, read to you by familiar voices from radio, stage and screen. Penguin Audiobooks are produced to an excellent standard, and abridgements are always faithful to the original texts. From thrillers to classic literature, biography to humour, with a wealth of titles in between, Penguin Audiobooks offer you quality, entertainment and the chance to rediscover the pleasure of listening.

You can order Penguin Audiobooks through Penguin Direct by telephoning (0181) 899 4036. The lines are open 24 hours every day. Ask for Penguin Direct, quoting your credit card details.

A selection of Penguin Audiobooks, published or forthcoming:

Little Women by Louisa May Alcott, read by Kate Harper

Emma by Jane Austen, read by Fiona Shaw

Pride and Prejudice by Jane Austen, read by Geraldine McEwan

Beowulf translated by Michael Alexander, read by David Rintoul

Agnes Grey by Anne Brontë, read by Juliet Stevenson

Jane Eyre by Charlotte Brontë, read by Juliet Stevenson

The Professor by Charlotte Brontë, read by Juliet Stevenson

Wuthering Heights by Emily Brontë, read by Juliet Stevenson

The Woman in White by Wilkie Collins, read by Nigel Anthony and Susan Jameson

Nostromo by Joseph Conrad, read by Michael Pennington

Tales from the Thousand and One Nights, read by Souad Faress and Raad Rawi

Robinson Crusoe by Daniel Defoe, read by Tom Baker

David Copperfield by Charles Dickens, read by Nathaniel Parker

The Pickwick Papers by Charles Dickens, read by Dinsdale Landen

Bleak House by Charles Dickens, read by Beatie Edney and Ronald Pickup

Anna Karenina by Fyodor Dostoyevsky, read by Juliet Stevenson

PENGUIN AUDIOBOOKS

The Hound of the Baskervilles by Sir Arthur Conan Doyle, read by Freddie Jones

Middlemarch by George Eliot, read by Harriet Walter

Tom Jones by Henry Fielding, read by Robert Lindsay

The Great Gatsby by F. Scott Fitzgerald, read by Marcus D'Amico

Madame Bovary by Gustave Flaubert, read by Claire Bloom

Mary Barton by Elizabeth Gaskell, read by Clare Higgins

Jude the Obscure by Thomas Hardy, read by Samuel West

Far from the Madding Crowd by Thomas Hardy, read by Julie Christie

The Scarlet Letter by Nathaniel Hawthorne, read by Bob Sessions

Les Misérables by Victor Hugo, read by Nigel Anthony

A Passage to India by E. M. Forster, read by Tim Pigott-Smith

The Iliad by Homer, read by Derek Jacobi

The Dead and Other Stories by James Joyce, read by Gerard McSorley

On the Road by Jack Kerouac, read by David Carradine

Sons and Lovers by D. H. Lawrence, read by Paul Copley

The Prince by Niccolò Machiavelli, read by Fritz Weaver

Animal Farm by George Orwell, read by Timothy West

Rob Roy by Sir Walter Scott, read by Robbie Coltrane

Frankenstein by Mary Shelley, read by Richard Pasco

Of Mice and Men by John Steinbeck, read by Gary Sinise

Kidnapped by Robert Louis Stevenson, read by Robbie Coltrane

Dracula by Bram Stoker, read by Richard E. Grant

Gulliver's Travels by Jonathan Swift, read by Hugh Laurie

Vanity Fair by William Makepeace Thackeray, read by Robert Hardy

Lark Rise to Candleford by Flora Thompson, read by Judi Dench

The Invisible Man by H. G. Wells, read by Paul Shelley

Ethan Frome by Edith Wharton, read by Nathan Osgood

The Picture of Dorian Gray by Oscar Wilde, read by John Moffatt

Orlando by Virginia Woolf, read by Tilda Swinton

READ MORE IN PENGUIN

A CHOICE OF CLASSICS

Armadale   Wilkie Collins

Victorian critics were horrified by Lydia Gwilt, the bigamist, husband-poisoner and laudanum addict whose intrigues spur the plot of this most sensational of melodramas.

Aurora Leigh and Other Poems   Elizabeth Barrett Browning

Aurora Leigh (1856), Elizabeth Barrett Browning's epic novel in blank verse, tells the story of the making of a woman poet, exploring 'the woman question', art and its relation to politics and social oppression.

Personal Narrative of a Journey to the Equinoctial Regions of the New Continent   Alexander von Humboldt

Alexander von Humboldt became a wholly new kind of nineteenth-century hero – the scientist–explorer – and in *Personal Narrative* he invented a new literary genre: the travelogue.

The Pancatantra   Visnu Sarma

The Pancatantra is one of the earliest books of fables and its influence can be seen in the *Arabian Nights*, the *Decameron*, the *Canterbury Tales* and most notably in the *Fables* of La Fontaine.

A Laodicean   Thomas Hardy

The Laodicean of Hardy's title is Paula Power, a thoroughly modern young woman who, despite her wealth and independence, cannot make up her mind.

Brand   Henrik Ibsen

The unsparing vision of a priest driven by faith to risk and witness the deaths of his wife and child gives *Brand* its icy ferocity. It was Ibsen's first masterpiece, a poetic drama composed in 1865 and published to tremendous critical and popular acclaim.

READ MORE IN PENGUIN

A CHOICE OF CLASSICS

Sylvia's Lovers Elizabeth Gaskell

In an atmosphere of unease the rivalries of two men, the sober tradesman Philip Hepburn, who has been devoted to his cousin Sylvia since her childhood, and the gallant, charming whaleship harpooner Charley Kinraid, are played out.

The Republic Plato

The best-known of Plato's dialogues, *The Republic* is also one of the supreme masterpieces of Western philosophy, whose influence cannot be overestimated.

Ethics Benedict de Spinoza

'Spinoza (1632–77),' wrote Bertrand Russell, 'is the noblest and most lovable of the great philosophers. Intellectually, some others have surpassed him, but ethically he is supreme.'

Virgil in English

From Chaucer to Auden, Virgil is a defining presence in English poetry. Penguin Classics' new series, Poets in Translation, offers the best translations in English, through the centuries, of the major Classical and European poets.

What is Art? Leo Tolstoy

Tolstoy wrote prolifically in a series of essays and polemics on issues of morality, social justice and religion. These culminated in *What is Art?*, published in 1898, in which he rejects the idea that art reveals and reinvents through beauty.

An Autobiography Anthony Trollope

A fascinating insight into a writer's life, in which Trollope also recorded his unhappy youth and his progress to prosperity and social recognition.

READ MORE IN PENGUIN

A CHOICE OF CLASSICS

Basho	**The Narrow Road to the Deep North**
	On Love and Barley
Cao Xueqin	**The Story of the Stone** also known as **The Dream of The Red Chamber** (in five volumes)
Confucius	**The Analects**
Khayyam	**The Ruba'iyat of Omar Khayyam**
Lao Tzu	**Tao Te Ching**
Li Po/Tu Fu	**Li Po and Tu Fu**
Sei Shonagon	**The Pillow Book of Sei Shonagon**
Wang Wei	**Poems**
Yuan Qu and Others	**The Songs of the South**

ANTHOLOGIES AND ANONYMOUS WORKS

The Bhagavad Gita
Buddhist Scriptures
The Dhammapada
Hindu Myths
The Koran
The Laws of Manu
New Songs from a Jade Terrace
The Rig Veda
Speaking of Siva
Tales from the Thousand and One Nights
The Upanishads

READ MORE IN PENGUIN

A CHOICE OF CLASSICS

READ MORE IN PENGUIN

A CHOICE OF CLASSICS

ANTHOLOGIES AND ANONYMOUS WORKS

The Age of Bede
Alfred the Great
Beowulf
A Celtic Miscellany
The Cloud of Unknowing and Other Works
The Death of King Arthur
The Earliest English Poems
Early Irish Myths and Sagas
Egil's Saga
English Mystery Plays
Eyrbyggja Saga
Hrafnkel's Saga
The Letters of Abelard and Heloise
Medieval English Verse
Njal's Saga
Roman Poets of the Early Empire
Seven Viking Romances
Sir Gawain and the Green Knight